Quest
FOR THE
Faradawn

Richard Ford

Illustrated by
OWAIN BELL

DELACORTE PRESS / ELEANOR FRIEDE

Published by
Delacorte Press/Eleanor Friede
1 Dag Hammarskjold Plaza
New York, N.Y. 10017

This work was first published in Great Britain by Granada Publishing
Limited.

Manufactured in the United States of America

9 8 7 6 5 4 3 2 1

For Reena, Daniel and all the Animals
Spring 1982

QUEST
FOR THE
FARADAWN

CHAPTER I

It was still snowing in Silver Wood. All night large flakes had been falling relentlessly, covering everything until now every blade of grass had a thick round column down one side and every twig supported a white replica of itself. Brock looked up and was mesmerized by the myriad of white specks in the air. They seemed to come down directly into his eyes as if they were being pulled towards the earth by a magnet; and yet not hurrying, more a determined drifting. He shook himself and a flurry of flakes flew off, so he retreated further under the Old Beech until only his head was exposed from the hole amongst the great roots which formed a low wall at either side of the entrance to his sett. He was enjoying the night; there was that stillness and complete quiet that occurs when every sound is muffled immediately by a thick blanket of white, and despite the snow the sky was quite clear so that he could see almost to the pond in the field at the front of the wood.

Beech Sett had been in Brock's family for generations, some said since Before-Man, and had in those times, of course, been right in the centre of the vast primeval forests that covered all the land. Now, since nearly all those forests had been consumed by man for his cultivating or living space, the fields had encroached almost up to the sett so that it was on the very edge of the wood and Silver Wood itself was only a short walk in length and width. The sett thus formed a useful look-out post and Brock had taken on the role of guardian of the wood, spending most nights looking out over the fields or walking along the edge while he looked for food. The other animals were happy with this arrangement because Brock had learnt to distinguish between real danger, when he would bark loudly two or three times, and a mere need for caution, when he would very often not alarm the wood at all but simply watch and wait until the incident was finished.

Tonight he was relaxed. On nights like this the great enemy almost never came out or if they did it was only to scurry past in the distance in that curious upright fashion of theirs, balanced on two legs with their heads down, and were very often gone as soon as Brock had spotted them. In a way he felt sorry that the peace and beauty of these nights were so seldom seen by them and he wondered whether this was one of the causes of their nature or the result of it. It was because of their hostility towards everything that they had been called, in the language of the Old Ones, Urkku or the Great Enemy.

Lost in these thoughts he was suddenly jolted into the present by a scent coming to him through the snow; he crouched lower and put his ear to one of the great roots at the side. Urkku were approaching; he could hear the unmistakable two-legged footfall, but there were only two and they were walking slowly and evenly. Keeping low, he peered hard through the flakes, which were now a nuisance as they got in his eyes and blurred his vision. Then he could see them walking round the side of the pond and starting to cross the big field at the front of the wood. They rested for a moment, leaning against the old wooden gate that led into the field, and then came on straight across it heading towards the sett. He wondered whether or not he should give the alarm; he rarely did at night, even when Urkku approached, because the few who came after dark rarely, if ever, caused damage and it was only if they carried the long thin instruments that blasted out death or that were used to dig with that he would alert the wood.

Every muscle tensed, his black nose-tip twitching, he watched as they came slowly forward, apparently now making for the stile into the wood which was only some thirty paces from the Old Beech. It was obvious that they knew the wood well for they did not hesitate or look around as most Urkku did but instead climbed over the stile and made straight for the Great Oak in the centre. To watch them now, Brock had to come out of the sett and pad slowly towards the little stream which ran across the middle of Silver Wood, from where he could see them clearly. He crouched in close against the bank of rhododendron bushes that went down to the stream and studied the scene. It was most strange. The first thing that struck him was that he did not have that awful feeling of fear which he nearly always felt whenever Urkku were near; somehow, all his instincts told him that there was no danger here and that, even if he were seen, no harm would come to him. Secondly, he now noticed that the taller of the two, the one with the shorter hair, was carrying a bundle which he handled very carefully and which was making a strange noise. The other one, who had much longer hair which was now flecked with white, simply stood quietly whilst the first placed the bundle down, right up against the oak, at the very base of the enormous trunk. He then proceeded to dig away at the snow and cover the bundle with the leaves and peat moss which he found underneath until only a small portion at the top was left from which Brock could hear strange noises, almost like those made by the river in the shallow places where it runs over pebbles.

Just as the man stood up, a peal of bells suddenly filtered through the still air. It was the church in the village calling the people to Midnight Communion on Christmas Eve. To Brock it was a death knell. The Midnight Bells came once a year and two days later came the slaughter. The wood must be warned. He turned back to the strange picture under the oak and saw the two kneeling over the bundle. The one with long hair placed her head close to the un-covered space, lingered there a second or two and then moved away. Then they both got off their knees and for a moment held each other in a way Brock had not seen before in the Urkku. He felt a great sense of tenderness and sadness radiate from them and in his own blood he felt a tingling sense of excitement and anticipation as he watched them walk slowly away, arm in arm, leaving the bundle there, under the Great Oak.

3

He waited until he saw them go back through the stile and begin to
cross the field and then he began, very slowly and cautiously, to inch
his way across the log which was the only way of crossing the stream
other than going all the way round by the stile. The log was slippery
at the best of times, being covered with moss and constantly wet from
the water, but now, with a layer of snow on top, it was treacherous.
He should have gone the long way round but he had always been a
hasty badger and he was now so curious to examine the strange
bundle that it would have been impossible for him to delay a second
longer. His enormous front claws gripped tight either side of the log
as he inched his way very slowly over it. He could see the brackish
water beneath him, jet black against the white of the two banks, and
he could see the way the snowflakes dissolved and vanished almost as
soon as they hit the surface. He was nearly at the far bank now. The

flakes had almost stopped falling and a familiar silver light began to reflect back from the water. He clambered carefully off the log and felt the snow soft and yielding again beneath his paws. This part of the wood was full of bracken and the snow was thick, so he had to be careful not to walk on a mound and fall right through; it was no use following the rabbit tracks either as the rabbits were so light they could walk over the treacherous bumps. He made his way carefully towards the oak, sniffing the air as he went, and every few paces he would stop and listen. The wood was bathed in moonlight now and there wasn't a sound; nothing was abroad tonight and even Brock began to feel cold on his back where the snow had made him wet and where it was now beginning to freeze on his fur. Finally he arrived within a pace or two of the noisy bundle and was able to look at it closely. What he saw astonished him; from the only part that had not been covered over he could see a small round pink face which, when it spotted Brock, broke into a wide smile. Happiness shone from its two little eyes and, despite its strangeness, Brock felt an overwhelming, impulsive surge of sympathy which overcame his caution and astonishment. He moved closer and put his nose against the baby's cheek. The face grinned even more and began to emit the strange gurgling noises Brock had heard earlier. He had only once before seen a creature like this; two or three summers ago two Urkku had come into the wood carrying one and had sat down and eaten right next to the Old Beech. They had still been there when evening fell and he had watched them closely for some time from the shadows of the entrance to the sett. He had reasoned it out then that it had been a human baby, and this little creature lying under the oak was unmistakably the same.

'Well, well,' he muttered to himself. 'This is odd. What am I going to do with you?' He looked curiously at the little face. His first thought was that it had been left temporarily and that the two Urkku who had brought it would come back for it soon; he realized now that they must have been its parents. But it was too cold to leave a young thing out in the wood and there had been something strange in the way the two had parted from it; something very final and sad yet beautiful. Brock felt all this intuitively, for badgers are known throughout the animal kingdom as the most sensitive of creatures; it is this, coupled with their wisdom born of centuries of history, that gives them their special place.

Now all his senses combined to give him that feeling of excitement which had come to him when he first saw the little bundle. In the recesses of his mind he was certain there were legends and prophecies which began with just such an incident as he was now witnessing and a thrill ran through him, making the hackles on his back rise.

He was still thinking about this when suddenly the night was shattered by an unearthly noise. The only time he had ever heard such a cry before was when the hares who lived in the fields round Silver Wood were injured by the Urkku with their death sticks. He looked down quickly to see the little face that had previously been one big smile transformed into a bawling horror. Brock concluded quickly that it was the cold; even he, with all his fur, was beginning to shiver. There was no time for thought; he must quickly get the baby warm and that meant he would have to take it back with him to the sett, where it would have to stay, at least for the remainder of the night. He gave a little snuffle of laughter as he thought what Tara, his sow, would say when he brought home a human baby: he had done some strange things in his time but nothing to compare with this. The baby was still crying away at the top of its lungs and Brock was afraid that soon all the creatures of the wood would be aroused and flock round to see what was causing the noise. The hatred that some of them felt for the Urkku was so strong that they would kill the baby on the spot, so Brock must quieten it down. He leant over it and, with his two big front claws around it, began to walk backwards, pulling the little creature along under his front legs with its body nestled against his chest. The warmth that came from his fur seemed to do the trick and it was soon gurgling happily again. There was no chance now of taking the short cut back across the log, so he began to go the long way round, through the new part of the wood and round, by the stile. The journey took a long time; Brock had to be careful not to get too much snow on the baby and to try to hold it up off the ground to keep it from getting damp and cold. Despite these difficulties, however, he enjoyed it; the baby kept putting its hands out and pulling at his fur or stroking the front of his leg and sometimes he would stop for a second or two and rub his wet nose under the baby's chin or around its neck to which it would react by breaking into a wide smile and giggling. He met no other creatures on the way, for which he was extremely grateful, as it would not have been easy to explain exactly what he was doing walking backwards with a human baby tucked under his legs. Finally, just as the clear silver light of the moon began to give way to a pale yellow sun, he arrived back at the Old Beech, exhausted, and braced himself to face the barrage of questions which he knew would come from the rest of his family. Weary but satisfied he began to descend backwards down the hole with his little human friend gurgling and smiling, blissfully unaware of the part that destiny had chosen for it to play.

CHAPTER II

Brock's forecast of Tara's reaction to his 'find' turned out to be completely accurate. As he came into the main chamber bearing his little charge she simply got up on her hind legs, put her two front paws on her hips and rocked in silent astonishment from side to side. She had thought none of the antics of her boar could shock her any more, ever since the time he had gone off with their two cubs Zinddy and Sinkka to explore the streets of the nearby village and brought back with them a dog they had befriended. This dog, who was called Sam, still visited them at fairly frequent intervals with news about the village. His master was one of the men who waged war on the wood and Sam would bring them advance knowledge of when he and the others were coming. The friendship with Sam had therefore turned out to be very useful; but this!

'This time you've gone too far. An Urkku; a member of the race that has persecuted and tortured our ancestors for generations, and not only ours but the ancestors of every living creature in this wood. Have you forgotten the tales of your great-great grandfather who was chained to a barrel and then had fierce dogs set on him to pull him to bits? And when he beat one lot, they set another lot on to him, and another, and another, until finally he was torn apart. And have you so soon forgotten the story that reached us of the killing of the entire sett over in Tall Wood that happened some ten full moons ago. They pumped some kind of poisonous air down the sett which made them vomit and which scorched their lungs so that they died a most horrible death. And this little thing here when it grows up will be a member of the Great Enemy! What are we going to do with it? How will we protect it from the other creatures in the wood, who hate the Urkku, if anything, more than we do? What will it live on?'

But somehow, when she looked at the helpless little creature lying on the earthen floor of the sett, it seemed so remote from the race of which she had been speaking that it seemed a different animal and her heart went out to it. It met her eyes with its wide smile and happy gurgle, putting out its little hand to grab at the air. She looked back at Brock, who had said nothing in reply to this avalanche of questions because there was nothing he could say. He was not the kind of badger who could leave a creature to die in the cold, and the only thing he could do was to bring it home. Besides, and he hadn't explained this yet, partly because he didn't quite know how to and partly because he wasn't certain whether Tara would understand anyway, he had a feeling that the whole thing had somehow been meant to happen and that he was really only playing a part that had been chosen for him.

He went up to her and they rubbed noses; she closed her eyes with pleasure and Brock thought how much he loved her. He began to stroke her head with his front paw. 'Our cubs aren't due until the Awakening and I thought perhaps it could have some of your milk until then. We could have it in here with us until it grows too big and I am sure that berries and fruits and toadstools will be as tasty for it as they are for us. Don't worry; it will be all right.' He wanted to say more but he was so exhausted that his eyes had closed against his will and he began to drift off into the world of sleep. 'Wake me at Sun-High,' he managed to mutter and then he rolled over on to the heap of dead bracken that was piled into the corner and began to snore heartily.

Tara then took the baby over to the far side of their large round room, and laid it to rest on the cushion of meadowsweet she had collected and saved from last year for her own cubs. The smell of the meadowsweet tended to overpower any other smells and so was extremely useful for cubs and, she supposed, human babies as well. She then took off the various layers of clothing and material with which it had been wrapped and put them in a corner to take out and bury later on. There was one article, though, which she decided to keep; it was a beautiful multi-coloured silk shawl and Tara liked both the colour and the feel of it. In later years, she thought, the little male creature lying there so peacefully might be glad of some reminder of his past; some link with his heritage. This shawl she carried over to one of the walls of their room and, having dug a small hole in the wall, placed it in and then covered it with soil. By the time she had finished, the baby had begun to screw up his little face again and started to cry. 'He must be famished,' she thought and lay down next to him. She hoped that her teats were full enough with milk; if not, she would really be lost as to what to give him to eat. Still her own cubs were due not too far away, as Brock had said, so she should be all right. She pulled the baby up towards her and drew his face near her teats with a paw. For an agonizing minute or two nothing happened but then, to Tara's intense relief, he began to suck. Physically he could have been one of her own cubs suckling, but emotionally she felt very strange; here she was, giving food from her own body to a baby human. It would have been odd enough if she had been suckling another sow's cub but this was a different animal and an Urkku at that!

Yet despite this strangeness she also felt the warmth and tenderness that Brock had experienced earlier towards the baby, and she undeniably felt a sense of excitement and adventure as she sat cradling this strange head in her paw and feeling the baby suck.

He was soon satisfied and Tara laid him down carefully on the meadowsweet and covered him with strips of birchbark on top of which she laid dead bracken. He was very soon asleep and Tara set about cleaning the room; dragging out all the old and soiled bedding and putting new fresh stuff on the floor from the piles around the outside of the room. She occasionally ran her paws along the roof to clear it of cobwebs for the ceiling was latticed with the roots of the Great Beech and the spiders liked to build along and at the side of them. She finally went over to the entrance to the tunnel and ran her paws down the three large roots that framed the doorway; one at the top and two down either side. This had been done so often through the centuries that they were now a wonderfully rich dark brown colour and they shone and felt smooth to the touch. There were also little gashes down them where, on the darkest wettest nights, badgers had been unable to go to the scratching post outside the sett and so had sharpened their claws on the two old hard roots at the side. These scratch marks always reminded Tara of the past generations of badgers who had lived here. She wondered how they had died; how many had been killed by the Great Enemy and how many had simply gone peacefully in their sleep.

When she had finished her housecleaning she went through the door and up the short passage which led out to the wood. She put her nose out into the air and immediately had to screw up her eyes to protect them from the glare, for the sun was shining brightly from a clear blue sky and was reflecting up from the snow which lay in thick white smoothness all around. She could tell without looking that the sun was high in the sky, shining down through the branches of the Great Beech. It was time to rouse Brock. She backed down the passage (for there was no space to turn round) and had to wait awhile when she was back in the room to let her eyes adjust to the light. She went over to Brock and gently placed the tip of her nose against his. He awoke without a start, yawned, stretched and got up.

'Hello,' he said sleepily and then saw the baby. 'Oh my goodness,' he exclaimed as the events of the previous night began to come back and the full impact of what he had done dawned on him.

'You wanted me to wake you at Sun-High,' Tara said.

'Yes; there's a lot to do and not much time. I heard the Midnight Bells last night and you know what that means for tomorrow, so I must call a Council for tonight. And then there is this baby Urkku. Did you manage to feed him?' Tara nodded. 'Good. But some of them won't like it and they may even try to kill him. They will have to be told, of course; we could never keep him secret when he gets bigger and it's better to tell them now when he is so helpless and harmless than later when he begins to grow and look more like an Urkku. It's a bad time, though, with the deaths and injuries that the Enemy will

11

cause tomorrow. I must go and tell Warrigal to summon the Council and then we'd better have a talk with the rest of the sett.' He went towards the door. 'Everywhere looks very clean,' he said, and vanished up the passage.

He emerged into the day and, like Tara, was almost blinded by the glare from the snow. 'It's too bright,' he muttered, 'too bright.' But the warmth of the sun felt wonderful on his back and face. It seemed to spread through his body and fill him with new life. He barked quietly twice, looking up at the Old Beech. There was no reply. 'He'll be fast asleep,' he thought. He barked again. Suddenly he felt someone behind him and turned round. It was Warrigal the Wise, standing blinking at him. 'Don't do that,' Brock said. 'You frightened me.' You could never hear Warrigal; it was almost uncanny the way he could fly, even through branches and thick rhododendrons, without making a sound.

'You want me to summon the Council,' Warrigal said. 'I heard the bells last night as well.'

'Yes,' said Brock. 'Call them for tonight. And listen, Warrigal; there's another matter which I want to raise and which I should like to mention to you briefly now.' Brock felt it would be prudent to tell Warrigal about his strange guest and get him on his side before the others were told. Everyone admired Warrigal for his knowledge and what he advised was always regarded with respect by the rest of the wood, albeit somewhat grudgingly by some of the loners like Rufus the Red. He also felt that a private chat with him might clear his own mind on a few matters before the whole affair came out into the open. Badgers and Owls had been allies in the protection of the Wood as far back as the beginning of legend. The Badgers' knowledge of the ground and the Owls' command of the air made a good combination. They were both creatures of extremely ancient heritage and tradition, unlike some of the more recent additions like the pheasants and squirrels, and between them they could muster a great deal of knowledge and intuitive wisdom. Brock therefore felt that if anyone could understand his feelings of the previous night, it was this trusted friend. Besides, the fact that he had a baby Urkku down in the sett this very minute was quite a devastating piece of news and it was a nice change to be able to tell Warrigal, who always seemed to

12

hear all the news first, something which he did not already know.

Surprisingly, and to Brock's annoyance, the owl did not seem very shocked although he obviously had not known. He merely listened attentively, occasionally giving a long slow blink, while Brock told the whole story. When he had finished Warrigal looked down at the snow and shifted his feet slightly on the root where he was standing. He stood like that for a few seconds and then turned his head round, first to the right and then to the left, as if looking for anyone who might be listening. Then he stared hard at the badger. 'Well,' Brock said impatiently, 'what do you make of it?'

'If I am right in my belief,' he said, with the air of someone who knew he always was, 'then you, Old Friend, have been picked for a task which will go down in legend as the most significant event in the history of the animal kingdom. An Honoured Badger indeed; one whose name will live for ever along with the names of the great heroes of Before-Man and whose role in history may be seen perhaps as even greater than theirs.'

'Stop, stop, for goodness sake,' the badger said. He had begun to feel extremely alarmed; it was one thing being a Guardian of the Wood who shared responsibility with Warrigal and whose task it was to call the Council together for emergency meetings, but quite another to be told of all this stuff about legend and history and how he would become famous. The owl exaggerated, of course; he took everything seriously and tended to make the simplest of events take on significant proportions. Still he really did look grave.

'But all I've done is rescue a human baby from dying of cold,' he said, not really unaware of the enormity of that event but trying now to make it less important by talking about it as being less important. 'Oh dear,' he said, as Warrigal just stood there, looking at him.

'Legend tells of an Urkku Saviour who arrives in the way your young friend arrived last night. I know no more than that. Your grandfather, Bruin the Brave, probably also knows of it but it is not a tale that is told often; partly because it is too unbelievable and partly because the ending has become lost in the mists of time. No one knows it,' he added, remembering with a sigh that sometimes his poetic turns of phrase, of which he was extremely proud, were misunderstood. 'The Elflord must be told; he, of course, knows of the legend and he will tell us how to proceed. I will see to that. In the meantime we must simply get the Council to agree to his remaining here, unmolested. Don't breathe a word to anyone, except Tara, of the legend or of the Elflord. We must keep things as quiet and normal as possible, otherwise the Urkku might sense something different about the wood and begin poking around. Leave things to me tonight; I know how to handle the Council. Till Moon-High then,' he said, and flew silently away.

Brock sat stunned, staring out at the field and thinking. He didn't want to go back down the sett just yet; he needed time to collect himself. The mention of the Elflord had sent shivers of fear and apprehension down his back. He remembered his strange feelings of destiny and fate when he first saw the baby, but he had never dreamt that it would come to this. The animals all knew, of course, of the Kingdom of the Elves but very few of them had actually seen an elf, let alone spoken to one, and it was frightening to think that his name was to be made known to the Elflord. Warrigal had seemed very nonchalant about telling him, as if he ate with the Elflord every day but Brock didn't really believe that the owl was that familiar with him. This was in fact the first time that Warrigal had mentioned the elves although, from certain oblique references in conversation, Brock had guessed that there was some contact between them and his friend. Still, it was extremely daunting to actually know of it; like everyone else in the Wood he had an uneasy fear of the elves even though they had never done him any harm. It was said that they had strange powers and could perform magic and that, although they normally used these powers for helping, sometimes they would use them to cause harm to an animal who had displeased them by threatening the stability of the wood. Stories were told of animals who had suddenly disappeared for no reason or who were found dead with no apparent injury. Brock therefore liked to keep these things at the back of his mind, and now, here he was, being brought to the attention of the elves, by what he was beginning to believe was an extremely unfortunate chain of events.

The sun was beginning to move down from the high place it had occupied in the middle of the day and had started to turn pale and watery the way it does on winter afternoons. The clear blue sky had given way to one streaked with wisps of grey cloud, so that now Brock was able to look at the expanse of snow which spread out before him without being dazzled.

The only sound to be heard was the three, evenly spaced 'Toowitt-Toowoos' of Warrigal as he glided, silent as a shadow, between the trees. This was the summons to the Council Meeting that night at which the leaders of the woodland animals would discuss tactics for the Killing tomorrow. The trees stood out, stark and black against the pale sky, each branch taking on an identity and character of its own and the twigs looking like the long bony fingers of an old woman. There was a feeling of utter calm in the scene before him which gave him a strength and resolve he had never before experienced; perhaps because he had never needed it. He turned slowly and made his way back through the earthen passage into the familiar sett, with its comforting atmosphere of home.

CHAPTER III

When Brock went through the doorway and saw the baby curled up in a cradle formed by Tara's two front legs, the gravity of Warrigal's words seemed far away and the sense of impending adventure which the owl had conveyed to him remote indeed. Tara was fast asleep, lying with her back resting against the smooth dark brown earth of the far wall, and the sight of her sleeping so peacefully made Brock realize how tired he was. He decided to have a rest before breaking the news to the other members of the family who lived in the sett. Then there would be the daunting task of facing the Council, although he was pleased, and relieved, that Warrigal had so readily taken it upon himself to help with this tricky business and he had a rather comforting feeling that his friend would do all the talking. However, at the same time he did not really want the owl to steal any glory that might be going and he felt a little uneasy about the possibility that Warrigal might 'take over'.

But his deep and refreshing sleep was all too quickly shattered by a violent shaking and the sound of lots of little frantic yelps. He opened his eyes blearily to see Old Bruin standing over him and the two cubs Zinddy and Sinkka, who were now almost three seasons old, jumping around Tara and trying to get her to explain what this strange new animal was doing in the sett and what type of creature it was. So, there was no need to break the news to the other inhabitants, the news had broken by itself. Brock spoke as sternly as he could to the cubs. 'Come on, you two; settle down and come over here to me and Bruin and I'll explain everything to you as best I can.' They stopped for a second and then began wrestling with each other, rolling over and over on the floor with their bodies locked together in a fighting embrace.

'Here!' said Brock sharply and they quickly disengaged themselves and scampered over to where he and Bruin stood. The baby had of course been awoken by all the noise and had begun to cry, but Tara began to nurse him and he soon settled down with his eyes closed and a look of intense concentration on his face.

Bruin stood gravely at Brock's side as the badger began to tell the three of them about the events that had led up to their finding a baby human curled in Tara's arms as they were quietly making their way through the front chamber out to the winter evening.

Bruin was Brock's grandfather and his only living relative; his father, mother and sister had all been killed by the gas one bright autumn evening when Brock, six seasons old and alone, had been out foraging. He had come back to see a whole group of Urkku gathered around the entrance to the sett, talking and laughing loudly in that strange guttural manner of theirs as if they wanted the whole wood to hear what they were saying. He had seen them put a large snake-like thing down the hole and then after a short time Bruin had come charging out, coughing and choking horribly and with his eyes streaming with tears. He had watched from behind the shelter of the nearby hedge as Bruin had savagely attacked the man nearest the sett, tearing his legs with his teeth until the man fell; the old badger had then jumped, snarling, at the face of another Urkku and knocked him down before running off towards the hedge where Brock was standing. Brock had joined him and they had both scampered round the side of the wood and made their way down to the big stream, where they stayed in hiding, fearful and terrified, for the rest of the night. The next day, when they made their cautious way back to the sett, they found that the air inside still burned their eyes and lungs so they had waited a number of nights before being able to go down. They had found all the other badgers of the sett dead; their eyes bulged horribly and their blackened tongues stuck out from twisted lips and mouths, so that the memory of their faces had never ceased to haunt Brock and for many seasons afterwards he had woken in the middle of the night yelping in terror.

After this episode, which had also been seen by Warrigal and Sterndale the Fierce, King of the Pheasants, Bruin had been christened 'The Brave' in honour of his valiant attack on the Urkku and his amazing escape from them. His hatred of the Great Enemy was immense and his head was full of legends and stories, particularly those in which man was vanquished or made to look stupid, which he loved to relate. When Brock had finished telling his strange tale, the old badger simply grunted and shuffled over to where the baby was lying on the other side of the chamber. He put his head, on which the two bold black stripes had begun to turn grey with age, very close to the face of the baby and began to rub his wet nose under his chin. The baby, which had been asleep, awoke and began to giggle, putting his tiny hands up to try and grab Bruin's ears and moving his whole body from side to side in a gesture of pure merriment. Bruin continued playing with him like that for a short time while the others watched, amazed and entranced at this exhibition of affection between the old badger and the baby Urkku. After a while he came away and, with a curious expression of both sadness and contentment on his face, turned to them all and said slowly, in his deep gravelly voice, 'Look after him, youngsters; look after him,' before ambling out through the door and up the passage into the cold winter night.

The two cubs stood in silent wonder for a second and then ran after him chattering and fighting as they went. They always went foraging with Bruin now for he had more time and patience than their father to teach them the ways of the wood, what was good to eat and what was poisonous and where to find the berries and juicy roots that they so enjoyed. There was also the chance, when they got back to the sett, of a story about the time Before-Man when the land was one vast forest and the earth was full of strange creatures with magical powers; creatures which flew as high as the sun and which ran so fast that the eye could not see them. He might also tell them again, for they never tired of hearing them, stories about the time the Great Enemy first arrived in the world.

Now that the sett was quiet again Brock had time to think about how Bruin had seemed to accept the baby Urkku so easily. He was relieved but also puzzled: his grandfather liked all young creatures and they in turn loved him, but his acceptance of this baby was more than that; he had almost seemed to have been expecting it. Warrigal had said that Bruin might know the legend of the Urkku Saviour, and the old badger's strange request to them to 'look after him' could only mean that he, as well as Warrigal, believed that this little thing was he. He wondered how much Bruin knew of the rest of the legend. Brock went over to Tara and the baby; he was asleep again after his last feed and lay, looking blissful and secure, snuggled deep into Tara's soft hair. She was awake. 'It's all too much for me,' she said. 'Why was grandfather so strange and nice to him; I thought he'd go into a towering rage.' Brock told her of his conversation with Warrigal and at the mention of the Elflord she shook her head in disbelief. When he had finished she looked at him affectionately, as she always did when he related his grandiose schemes to her, and said sweetly, 'Well, you see to all that side of it and I'll feed him and wash him and keep him warm and teach him when it's safe to go outside and . . .'

'You can scoff,' interrupted Brock, 'but we'll see who is right when the time comes. This time I've got a feeling, and I'm not the only one, that something really important is in the wind and I'm not going to ignore it simply because you're too hardheaded to see it.' He began to move towards the passage. 'You've no imagination,' he added caustically. 'I'm off to the Council.'

When he'd gone Tara looked down at the little pink creature lying against her black fur. 'Well,' she said to him softly, 'whether you're what they say you are or not, one thing is certain, you're no different from any other cub; all that bothers you is eating, sleeping and playing.' But though she said it, she couldn't help feeling that perhaps, this time, Brock was right and that something legendary was happening to them all.

CHAPTER IV

When Brock emerged into the cold night, the moon was shining down in between the great belt of rhododendrons to his left and the trunk of the Great Beech; there was still time enough to walk to the Council before Moon-High, when the meeting would open. He gave a little bark from the foot of the tree to tell Warrigal he was on his way and the owl answered 'Toowitt-Toowoo' before flying off through the trees. Brock made his way along the front of the wood to the old wooden stile at the corner, where he turned right and followed the little stream back into the wood until he was almost at the fields which lay at the rear. He had decided tonight not to take the short cut over the little stream; it would not bear thinking about if he fell in and turned up at this meeting, of all meetings, looking like a large drowned rat. Besides there was no hurry and he wanted time to think before he arrived. The little stream, which was really a drainage ditch dug by the Urkku, formed a large T and so divided Silver Wood roughly into three different sections, each of which was very different in character. Above the horizontal stroke of the T the wood was full of fairly new birches, very close together so that they had grown tall and thin and straight as they competed for light. The wood was dark here as, even in winter when there were no leaves, the light found it hard to penetrate the thick web of branches and twigs. In autumn the floor of this part of the wood was full of all types of toadstools but very little grew at any other time of the year. The front of the wood, to the left of the perpendicular stroke of the T, was

21

where Brock lived. This part again had two different sections and the Great Beech was at the centre of the division. To the right of it there were few trees, mostly oaks and elms and ash and the floor here was made up of large tussocks of grass with the odd clump of heather. To the left of the beech there was a large bank of rhododendrons which went right back to the little stream, and where these petered out at the edge of the wood there were some more enormous beeches along with some splendid elms. The whole of this front part of the wood looked out on to a square flat field, then another field which rose sharply into a bank. To the left of that stood the pond surrounded by hawthorns, hazel trees and elders. The back of the wood contained a large number of tall silver birch trees and it was these that gave the wood its name. Many of them had died and their trunks lay slowly rotting year by year. Fungi grew out of them, and ants, beetles and woodlice made their homes there. The floor of this part of the wood was nearly all bracken which in the summer formed a lush green jungle and on frosty winter days a crackly brown matting which crunched with every step. This area eventually gave way to another of giant elms and ash where the ground was peaty and grew grasses, mosses and, in the spring, a carpet of bluebells which scented the whole back of the wood with their perfume. The fields at the back formed a steep bank which led down again into a sandy hollow and then, in the distance, to the stream where Tara went in the summer to collect meadowsweet and rushes for the sett. And beyond that was Tall Wood where none of the animals had been and where it was said that the Elflord lived with the other magical peoples.

The Council Meetings were always held in the back part of the wood in a fairly large open space bordered on one side by the little stream with the rhododendrons behind it on the far bank and, on the other three, by a semi-circular belt of smaller rhododendrons, old tree stumps and new young birch and ash saplings. As Brock walked along the bank at the back of the wood he could hear hundreds of little crunching and rustling noises as the inhabitants of the wood made their way over the frozen snow. Suddenly, from behind him, he heard an enormous splash and he turned round to see Sam, the dog from the village, swimming vigorously and noisily across the stream.

He had spotted Brock on the far bank and now he bounded up to greet him. 'What a creature!' muttered Brock under his breath as the dog stood shaking himself and sending a shower of little drops of water spinning out which almost hit the badger. Brock then watched in amusement as the big dog started to roll on his back, his legs flailing from side to side in an effort to get thoroughly dry. Standing up again he gave himself another shake, which seemed to start from the tip of his tail and work its way slowly along his body until his whole head rotated and the black tip of his nose span round. He stood still for a second and then said, 'Hello Brock, how are you?' in a loud voice, so that Brock had to move close to him and tell him to keep his voice down. In general dogs had little to fear from the Great Enemy provided they were kept in a good home, and they had lost the natural instinct of all wild animals to be as quiet as possible at all times and their desire to remain unnoticed and unknown which had developed over the ages of man's domination of the earth. Dogs occupied a strange place in the relationship between man and animals in that they were to all intents and purposes allies of man and even helped him when man was out killing with the death sticks, running to pick up the dead or injured animal and taking it back to their human to save him the effort of going to fetch it. Sometimes whole packs of dogs would be used to chase and kill a fox or a hare while the Great Enemy rode behind on another animal ally, the horse; or when a hare was being chased man would run behind, shouting and yelling. For these reasons dogs were, in general, feared, hated and despised by all wild animals and at first, when Brock had tried to introduce Sam to the Council, he met with great resistance. However, as time passed and Brock brought to the Council more and more extremely valuable information which Sam had given him about the details of future killing times, the Council had finally relented and allowed Sam to attend. Warrigal would fly over the house where Sam lived and give him the call and the dog would bark in reply to let the owl know he had received the message. Some of the animals still did not completely trust Sam, but he had earned from most of them a grudging respect and a few had begun to count him as a friend. Of course, when the Killing was taking place Sam would be with his human but the animals now recognized this and realized that

23

it was the only way the dog could keep bringing them the information they found so useful.

Brock and Sam now made their way towards the corner of this back part of the wood, and they could see clearly, in the moonlight, the other animals heading for a gap in a belt of trees; this was the only way in for the larger creatures although the smaller ones like the rabbits and hedgehogs could squeeze through anywhere. When they went through the narrow gap, knocking some snow down on to themselves as they brushed against the branches of a little ash tree on one side, they saw that many animals were already there, arranged against the outside of the semi-circle. Facing this semi-circle, sitting along the straight side of the amphitheatre with their backs to the stream, on the far side of which stood the huge solid bank of rhododendrons, were the Council. Here were the legendary figures of the wood whose names had been linked with so many heroic stories and deeds that even they themselves had forgotten which were true and which imagined. They had arranged themselves along the far side of a large fallen tree-trunk which ran parallel to the stream and were now fully engrossed in conversation amongst themselves. The members of the Council were not so much elected as elevated; there was never any dispute as to who was entitled to sit; if there had been then that animal would not go on to the Council for he could not have earned his proper place. Meetings were held once in every season so that the necessary arrangements for that particular season could be made, but they were also held when there was a special need.

These extra meetings were usually concerned with matters such as security when they knew there was a Killing due, or with other emergency items such as plague or upset of the wood when the Urkku were carrying out some new operation such as digging a new drainage ditch or putting up a new fence. The meeting tonight was one of these extra meetings, as the regular winter one had already taken place. Any animal from the wood could go to a meeting and sometimes when an animal had a particular contribution to make or where it was of special interest to him, he would be specially asked to attend.

Brock loved going to these meetings; he always got a great thrill from seeing the famous names whose stories had been told to him when he was a cub by old Bruin, himself a member of the Council for the last three seasons. As he settled down now with Sam, their backs against a large elm and next to them some young rabbits, Brock could see Bruin at one end of the log talking to Rufus, whose magnificent russet red coat shone in the moonlight so that it almost looked polished. Here was the fox who had outrun and outsmarted every pack of hounds in the area and who was a master in the arts of doubling back, water-running (to conceal his scent) and sheep-mingling, which consisted of hiding in the middle of a flock of sheep to confuse the hounds and annoy the farmer whose land was being used for hunting. On one memorable day in the autumn many seasons ago Rufus had actually been caught by the leading hounds in a particularly fast pack and had been brought to the ground by them: snarling, he had sunk his teeth into the necks of two of them and broken the leg of a third before running off again like the wind to vanish in the wood, leaving the furious and disappointed huntsmen nursing their wounded dogs and shaking their fists at him. Recently he had taken to going into the village at night and getting food from the bins of rubbish which the Urkku kept; while there he would look through the windows of the houses and had learnt a lot about the ways of the Urkku. But he was getting old and he was losing that edge of speed which had made him famous and kept him out of the clutches of the hunt for so long. Brock, looking at his fine noble head with its two sharp triangular ears and long pointed nose, pondered with great sadness that it could only be a matter of time before Rufus was caught by the hounds and torn to pieces by them.

Brock put this distressing picture out of his mind and looked at Perryfoot the Fleet, sitting some few paces from Rufus. Perryfoot was a brown hare; another near-legendary hero whose speed, as his name implied, had earned him his status. He sat on his own, lost in his secret thoughts, with his body hunched over into a great grey-brown furry ball and his two long ears tucked down so that they lay along his back. Apart from his speed he was also famous for his sense of humour which, particularly in March, led to his performing some strange antics. It was felt by the wood, although no one actually knew this, that he had some knowledge of and connection with the Magical

Peoples and for this reason he was regarded with some wonder and awe by the others. His home was in the field at the front of Silver Wood but he was known to wander far and wide and his knowledge of the area surrounding the wood was second to none. He went regularly to Tall Wood and was rumoured to have gone even beyond there to The Heath.

Next to Perryfoot sat Pictor the Proud, a large rabbit who, as the head of a large colony of rabbits in the wood, was a highly respected figure. He had brought a new structure and organization to the rabbits of Silver Wood so that now their defences and warning systems against the coming of Urkku had become famous. Other colonies from the other woods would come to look and to learn so that losses to the Urkku were decreasing season by season. Recently however there had been a number of setbacks since the Urkku had begun to use that nightmare of all tunnel creatures, gas, and Pictor was under some pressure to come up with a new scheme which would combat this horror.

Perryfoot was talking to Bibbington the Brash, a hedgehog who  had once been captured by a family of Urkku and had stayed with them for an entire season. While there he had actually gone into the house and walked into all the rooms, looking around and memorizing what he saw. While with the family, he had watched, listened and learnt all he could of the ways of the Great Enemy and this knowledge had since proved to be invaluable to the Council in their discussions on defence and other matters concerning the Urkku. Since the virtual disappearance of the wandering Urkku known as Gypsies who used to eat them, the hedgehogs' only real enemies were the enormous noisy creatures which the Great Enemy rode to get from place to place and against which there was no defence.

Perching on top of the log next to these two, Brock could see the long magnificently coloured tail feathers of Sterndale the Fierce, King of the Pheasants. He was lost in conversation with his great friend and ally, Thirkelow the Swift, a magnificent steel-blue wood-pigeon with a chest like a tree trunk. It was an achievement for either a pheasant or a pigeon to survive more than four seasons and these two had now lived for more than twelve each. Knowledgeable in the killing ways of the Urkku and with an instinctive inborn cunning, they were the natural leaders of their two species. Thirkelow's speed was almost magical; he would streak across the sky like lightning and be gone before you could blink. The great Sterndale had acquired his title from an incident when he had attacked an Urkku who had just wounded one of his hens. He had stalked his way up to the killer through the undergrowth and suddenly flown at his face beating with his wings and biting and scratching with his beak and claws. The Urkku had dropped his gun, which went off and alerted other Urkku who, hearing the gun and the cries for help, came running through the wood. Instead of flying off, in which case he would almost certainly have been killed in the air, Sterndale had scuttled off through the undergrowth and watched, hiding, while they carried the killer off. This incident had earned him great admiration from the wood and he had set about using the knowledge and experience he had gained from it to try and lessen the enormous losses which the pheasants, in particular, suffered every autumn. He had attempted to train them not to call out when they were alarmed or when they took off and, most important of all, to keep dead still when the Urkku were in the wood. If they really had to move then they should walk, slowly and quietly, rather than fly off, presenting a perfect target for the death sticks.

Brock could also make out the other members of the Council; Digit the Grey Squirrel, Cawdor the Crow and Remus the Rook. Remus, like Bibbington, had been taken in by a family of Urkku and looked after by them for some three seasons before but, with some regrets for the safety and security of life in this particular household of Urkku, he had flown off and settled in Silver Wood where his knowledge of the Urkku had rendered him an extremely valuable member of the Council.

Suddenly Brock's thoughts were broken into by the realization that all the shuffling and muttering around him had slowly quietened until there was now an expectant silence. The only sound he could hear was the rustling of a light wind which blew through the bare branches of the tall silver birch trees surrounding them. Perched in the middle of the old trunk was Wythen the Wise, Warrigal's father and the leader of the Council: an owl who had lived for as long as any member of the wood could remember and whose links with the elves of Tall Wood were well known. Indeed it was even rumoured that he himself had some magical powers and, looking into his enormous brown eyes which seemed to see everything both visible and invisible, it could well be believed. Now he turned slowly round from his conversation with Rufus to address the meeting.

'Welcome to you all on this cold night,' he said in his clear magical tones. 'We are here to discuss two matters; the first, the question of preparations and defences for a Killing that is due to take place tomorrow and the second a matter which I would rather not mention until we have disposed of the first. I will now call upon Sam to inform us as to what he knows of tomorrow's shoot.'

The owl turned towards Sam as the dog stood up and began to relate all that he had heard his human saying to the Mistress in their kitchen yesterday morning. The main target was to be pheasants and there would be a large number of Urkku from the village involved. There would also be beaters, men with sticks who would walk through the wood from the back, hitting the undergrowth and making strange shouting and whistling noises. This was intended to force the animals to fly up or run away towards the front of the wood where the Urkku with their death sticks would be waiting for them. It was a standard procedure for the big killings and was greatly feared by the animals as, unlike the situation where there were just two or three Urkku walking through the wood, there was nowhere for them to run and hide. Although the main victims were the pheasants, no animal was safe and, if seen, would almost certainly be shot at.

When Sam had finished he was thanked by Wythen and he lay down again next to Brock. He was shaking all over from nerves and panting heavily, little drops of saliva running down his chin. 'Well done,' whispered Brock, who himself hated public speaking and

28

knew how his friend felt; particularly as in Sam's case there were still a number of animals who mistrusted him and would seize any opportunity to criticize.

'The Killing tomorrow is then one of the most dangerous and none of us is safe,' said Wythen in a stern and angry voice, remembering the time five seasons ago when one of his sons had been shot. It was not common for owls to be killed but by no stretch of the imagination could they be called safe and it was only an extremely unwise owl who would let himself be seen by the Urkku. 'You must all organize yourselves as best you can; now we have foreknowledge we at least have a chance of diminishing our losses. Sterndale, you must once again attempt to impress upon your flock the importance of not moving and of staying on the ground as much as possible and explain to them the folly of calling out when frightened. Thirkelow, your pigeons have more chance in the air than the pheasants but the best plan is still to use ground cover. Pictor, you must tell your rabbits to go in their burrows and stay there, and your hares, Perryfoot, would do well to stay under cover where they are and only to risk a bolt for it if they are a good distance away from the Urkku and out of range of their death sticks. Rufus, you and the foxes must stay in your holes; if Sam's information is correct there will be no hounds, nor will they be using the gas on any of the animals; but still both you and Bruin's family would do best to remain well hidden. You know what the Urkku are like on these mass slaughters of theirs; anything moves and they'll try and kill it. This of course applies to all the rest of you animals. We'll have the usual signalling system; my son Warrigal will be roosting on one of the trees by the pond: as soon as he spots the Urkku he'll call out four or five times and that will be the signal for everyone to get out of sight and stay quiet.'

There was dead silence in the snowy glade; the moon, shining down bright and silvery, showed all the intent, anxious and fearful faces of the animals as they tried to absorb the instructions given by Wythen. Little clouds of breath froze in the cold air and Brock could hear the frightened panting of the rabbits next to him. 'Whose turn will it be?' they were wondering, and through their minds flashed pictures of those they had seen in the past shot and killed or, worse still, injured and left to die with their back legs in pieces. And over all their fear, the eternal question which none could answer, not even Wythen – Why?

'And now,' broke in the owl, realizing that he must bring the minds of the meeting back to the second item for discussion, 'there is another matter to which I would like to draw your attention. I already know something about it as my son Warrigal has had a talk to me, but I would like to hear the matter from the beginning, first hand.' Brock's heart missed a beat; he looked for Warrigal and saw him perched low down on an elder branch to his right. The owl looked back and shrugged his shoulders.

'Brock,' continued Wythen, 'would you please relate to us all, slowly and clearly, exactly what occurred last night.'

Very nervously and shakily Brock moved slightly forward into the clear space in front of the Council and began to tell them the events of the previous night. He stuck strictly to the facts, leaving out all his ideas of 'destiny' and 'fate', because he would not be able to find the right words to express them and in any case they were private feelings which he didn't really want to share with all the other animals. By the time he had got to the part about going up to the baby and touching it, Brock was dimly aware of hundreds of little whispers and mutterings and he could see the Council all leaning forward intently to catch every word he said. When he got to the end, about taking the Urkku down his sett and his being suckled by Tara, there was a positive hubbub of raised voices and angry interchanges as this extraordinary tale began to register itself, with all its implications, in the minds of the animals.

Wythen let the hubbub continue for some time as he knew it would be useless to try and stop it, for it gave them all a chance to express their opinions before the discussion went any further. When the noise began to subside, he called out for silence and eventually the last mutterings died away. Brock was not so afraid as he felt he ought to be; in fact he felt strangely confident, although this may have been partly due to the fact that he was almost certain Wythen was on his side.

'I shall now ask Warrigal to give you his opinions and views on the matter before us,' said the owl, 'and you may then ask questions. Before we go on, however, I would first like to ask Sam to tell us whether there has been any talk of this in the village.' Sam stood up again and said that no, there had been no mention of it at all and it was the first he had heard of it.

Warrigal then flew down and stood in the centre of the open space. As he talked he turned round and round slowly so as to address every part of the meeting in turn, and he opened his wings when he wished to gesticulate or emphasize a particular point. His speech was masterful; it was full of references to legend and the time Before-Man and he sprinkled it with many veiled allusions to the Magical Peoples and the Elflord. He recited the legend of the Urkku Saviour with its ending which had been lost with the passage of time and which no one, save perhaps the Elflord himself, knew. Warrigal knew that the animals loved legends and stories and that the thought that they might actually be about to observe a legend at first hand would be enough to at least partly persuade them to allow the Urkku to stay in the wood. Coupled with this, the fear and respect with which all animals treated the name of the Elflord and the implication that he both knew of the Urkku and wished it to remain, should convince the Council and the other animals that it was right for the Urkku to stay.

When he had finished, he remained where he was and Wythen thanked him (feeling secretly very proud of his son for this extremely clever speech) and asked if there were any questions. At first there was only an embarrassed silence as every animal tried to pluck up courage to move forward and speak what was on his mind. Eventually Rufus broke it with a slightly nervous cough; he thought to himself that he would rather face six hounds than speak in public like this.

'I,' he started, and gave another cough to clear his throat, 'I think I speak for most of us when I say that none of us likes the idea of having an Urkku in the wood.' Little murmurs of approval greeted this statement and gave him courage to carry on. His voice grew bolder and louder. 'The Urkku have never done anything but harm to us; they destroy our homes, they poison our food and they try and kill us by any one of a hundred ways, all of which are liable to cause us the most horrible pain and suffering. Why then should we help any Urkku, even if it is only a young one?' He stopped for he could think

31

of no more to say: the thought of the Urkku made him angry and when he was angry he found it hard to think clearly; a fox must always remain cool and unflustered.

Pictor then voiced another point which was on all their minds. 'How can we trust him?' he said. 'While he's a baby I agree he can do us no harm but as he grows he will learn all our secrets and our defences and, worse still, he will find out where our homes are. What if then he joins the Urkku; he could destroy us all in a single day with what he knows. I don't like it.'

Then Sterndale spoke. 'I agree with everything Rufus and Pictor have said but I feel that we must put our trust and our faith in the opinions of our two "elder statesmen" Wythen and Bruin. In any case the Urkku can do no harm for a number of seasons yet, and if things turn out for the worse we shall have to kill him before he goes over to the Urkku. But I, for one, would like to wait and see for a while: if the legends are true then we would be foolish to get rid of him now.'

The rest of the Council agreed that the decision should be left with Wythen and Bruin. Bruin spoke first and said that, like his noble friend Sterndale, he thought that 'wait and see' was the best policy, although secretly he believed that the little baby in the sett would prove in some way, although he didn't know how, to be the friend and ally of which legend had spoken ever since he could remember.

Wythen, of course, agreed. When Warrigal had told him the news he had known immediately that the time had come of which he had dreamt for so long. The baby should stay with Brock, he told the meeting, because it was obviously safe and happy there and they could all trust Bruin's grandson whom they knew to be a brave and imaginative badger with a practical partner who would look after and guard the baby in the best possible way. The baby's progress would be reported to the Council at the seasonal meetings and decisions as to his future would be taken then.

With that he wished them all good luck for tomorrow and, as the moon began to sink in the night sky, all the animals of the wood made their way thoughtfully back to their various holes and setts and roosts, where they pondered over the strange story they had heard.

Mystery was in the air and there was not one of them who, beneath his overriding fear of the Killing tomorrow, did not feel a little thrill of anticipation as he settled down for what remained of the night.

CHAPTER V

The next day dawned bright and clear and cold; the sun shone down from a blue sky, cloudless except for a few wisps of white that drifted purposefully across. Already drips of thawing snow could be heard all over the wood and the icy crust that had formed on the surface began to give way to a mushy layer of large wet crystals which sank as they were trodden on.

Brock was suddenly woken by the persistent hooting of an owl. He looked across at Tara and the baby; she had been fast asleep when he came in from the meeting last night and he had not told her the good news that the Council had agreed that they could keep the Urkku in the wood – at least until he began to grow into an adult. She was awake now and, when he told her, she was both pleased and relieved. 'It's odd,' she said softly so as not to waken the baby, 'in only one day and night I've grown really fond of him and I think he trusts me and feels comfortable with me. I was dreadfully worried that the Council might take him away.'

'Listen,' said Brock, 'do you hear it; Warrigal's warning? He's by the pond; we arranged that he would roost there and hoot loudly when he saw the Urkku coming. You must stay down here of course when they're in the wood and keep the baby quiet. Although there's very little chance of their hearing him crying from above we must not take the risk.'

'Where are you going?' asked Tara.

'I'm going up to the surface to see what happens. Don't worry; I'll stay in the passage and just poke my nose out as far as I need to be able to watch. I'm anxious to see what comes of the plans the Council arranged last night. Besides, Bruin is too old to be up during the day now – he needs his sleep – and he asked me to report to him.'

When Brock reached the top he cautiously put the black tip of his nose out and looked to left and right before proceeding, a pace at a time, until he could see almost the whole of the field at the front. All around him, in the wood, hundreds of rabbits were running in from their morning feed and vanishing into their holes. He could see Pictor in the field shouting at them to get a move on, hopping after them and herding them in like a sheepdog until he himself finally vanished down his hole in the centre of the rhododendron bush to the left of the Great Beech. He could also make out in the distance a number of hares running off over the fields, although he couldn't tell whether Perryfoot was among them. If only they could keep their ears down when they ran, Brock thought, they would be so much more difficult to spot. Still they were far enough away from the Urkku not to be fired at and there were no mishaps.

He could see the Urkku approaching over the field. It was a frightening sight. There seemed to be very many of them and they were stretched in a single straight line right across the field. Slowly they walked towards Silver Wood with their death sticks pointing outwards and downwards from their bodies. There was a hum of conversation from the line which broke the stillness of the morning and shattered the peace. Brock could smell the unmistakable pungent smell of Urkku and the other smell which often came from them: a cloying smoky smell which rasped in his nose and stuck in his throat so that he found it hard to breathe. These smells lingered in the wood where the Urkku had been, sometimes for a whole day and night, tainting the air and serving as an awful reminder of the death and suffering they had caused, for it was extremely rare that Urkku came into Silver Wood except to kill.

When the line got to the very edge of the wood it stopped and an Urkku at one end gave a great shout; suddenly the air was full of a cacophony of strange whistles, shouts, guttural calls and the sound of the undergrowth being thrashed. This noise came from behind Brock, at the back of the wood, and slowly began to come nearer. These were the beaters.

Brock waited, his heart pounding. He could see very close to him one of the Urkku standing with his legs apart and the death stick raised against his shoulder ready to kill anything that flew out; his body was round and fat so that Brock could see, where the overjacket was open, a great roll of flesh hanging over the belt in the middle of the man's stomach; the face was a purply-red colour and had loose jowls of skin hanging down around the neck.

Sterndale had gathered his pheasants together in the innermost part of the wood where the rhododendrons and undergrowth were so thick that the beaters were unable to get through. They had been there since before dawn and he had been talking to them in his low murmuring cackle, telling them to stay on the ground, keep their heads down and their tails low and above all not to move, no matter how close the beaters came. If they stayed where they were then they would be safe, but if they lost their nerve and flew up they would be as good as dead. Some of the pheasants were last year's brood and there were a number of veterans of two or even three seasons; these experienced ones knew the routine and were fairly easy to handle. It was the current year's brood that were always difficult; they had been born and reared by the Urkku and kept in cages until they were old enough; then they had been let out into the fields and woods around the Urkku dwelling and fed with corn twice a day by hand. They had therefore got used to trusting the Urkku and expecting only food and protection from them; they were far more likely to go towards the beaters than away from them and were totally unable to comprehend the fact that if they flew up and were seen they would be shot at and injured or killed. Sterndale had had to have many long and frightening talks with them but it was really only when one of the arrogant young cocks who had consistently accused Sterndale of being old-fashioned and out of touch had come limping back one day with half his chest blown away by the very same Urkku who had some short time previously been throwing down corn for him, that they had begun to comprehend. The difficulty was that Sterndale couldn't explain, because he himself couldn't understand, why the Urkku went to such enormous trouble to protect them from poison or shooting by any of their natural enemies and then later, when they were fully grown, would organize themselves into groups and purposely try to slaughter as many as they could. In one of his talks with Wythen, the owl had told him that the Urkku were a race of creatures which enjoyed killing and that they protected the pheasants only so that they themselves could have the pleasure of killing them later on, but for a long time Sterndale had been unable to believe that.

The beaters were now coming closer. The cacophony of hoots, whistles and shouts drew slowly nearer and the thrashing of the undergrowth sounded deafening. This was the most difficult part; trying to keep his flock from panicking. He could see some of them now shifting about nervously from foot to foot and in their eyes he recognized the unmistakable glazed look of fear.

'Don't move,' he cackled as loud as he dared, but his command was lost in the din as the Urkku came nearer until the noise seemed to blot out everything and the undergrowth all around seemed to come alive. Sterndale felt his heart pounding and the blood rushing in his ears as he closed his eyes and with an enormous effort forced himself to blot out the sound and concentrate on rooting his feet to the ground and conquering all the natural instincts which urged him to fly away.

The worst happened. One of the younger cocks, thinking that he saw a chance to defy Sterndale's leadership and prove himself, took off straight ahead towards the guns. The young hens, who were already terrified, suddenly panicked and, seeing their cock flying off, followed him. Only Sterndale and the other veterans and three or four of the less flighty new hens kept their nerve and stayed where they were. The old pheasant, feeling sick to his stomach, waited an agonizing few seconds and then suddenly the wood erupted into a hideous bedlam of explosions as the Urkku blasted away and the birds plummeted to earth, to land with a series of sickening thuds on the snow. The air was full of the squawks and cries of pain and fear as the injured birds struggled desperately to get away into the undergrowth, leaving vivid trails of crimson over the snow. The cracks of the guns had stopped now and the Urkku were shouting and laughing with joy at the size of their kill. Sterndale and the others, crouching fearfully in the rhododendrons, could hear the loud crashing of the dogs as they ran after the injured or collected the dead to take them back to their masters. Suddenly Sterndale saw a great golden shape bound past a few paces away with a grim look on his face. He stopped and turned and ran back the way he had come. 'Sam,' croaked Sterndale, as quietly as he could, and the dog halted, looked round and then, spotting the pheasant, walked quietly towards him. 'A slaughter,' growled the dog, 'a massacre. What went wrong?'

'Inexperience and panic, Sam, but you had better go back or your human will be leaving you without food tonight or, worse still, he might even get rid of you. You must keep in his favour; we need your information desperately. Look, there's a young hen, she's stone dead, pick her up and take her back quickly.'

The dog went off and picked up the dead pheasant. With a last sad look at Sterndale he ran back through the bushes and as he went

Sterndale could see the limp head of the pheasant bouncing stupidly against the side of Sam's mouth. He looked away in anger.

At the front of the wood Brock had watched the proceedings in horror. He could see the Urkku near him very clearly; he had seen the man pull the trigger, had been deafened by the explosions and felt sickened as he heard the sound all around him of falling birds. The last horror was when the man had spotted an injured pheasant, a young cock, dragging its wing along the ground and scurrying to get into the bushes near Sam. The man had laughed gleefully and run after it, to the great delight and amusement of his friends, who had jeered and shouted at him as he waddled clumsily through the snow trying to catch the terrified bird. Eventually he caught it and, after holding it up in triumph, had wrung its neck.

After this episode they had all proceeded to walk into the wood, still in their line, and Brock had had great difficulty in stopping himself from running out and attacking the man as he moved within paces of the sett. Slowly they had gone through the wood, passing the spot where Sterndale and the others were still hiding, and jumping over the brook to get to the other side. With every shot that came to him over the snow Brock felt a surge of pain and anger as he imagined the horror and hurt that some animal was going through. Time and again, the question 'Why?' echoed through his mind.

There were not too many more deaths that day. Three young and inexperienced rabbits, a buck and two does, had escaped Pictor's control and ventured out to see what was happening; no sooner had they come out of their burrow than a hail of lead cut into them, leaving the two does dead and the buck writhing on the snow with his back legs in tatters. He had pulled himself with his front paws into the cover of the bushes, where Pictor had found him later, still dying, after the Urkku had left. He had suffered horribly for a night and mercifully died the following dawn.

The other losses were five woodpigeons and a hare which had been startled as the Urkku were making their way back through the field. Eventually they had gone, leaving the wood raped and violated after their crude invasion. For days it was impossible for the animals to forget about it; the smells lingered on and the air seemed full of death: one would come across trampled undergrowth or traces of the

Urkku such as red cartridge cases still smelling of gunpowder or pieces of paper or the remains of the white sticks they used in their mouths. Sometimes there were the scattered feathers of a bird that had been shot or tufts of brown fur from a rabbit; mute testaments to the sufferings of their owners. The animals were frightened and nervous; they skulked in the shadows and ran to their burrows or flew off at the slightest noise.

As the line walked back over the field in the watery afternoon sun, Brock's mind went to the baby Urkku in the sett behind him; it was hard to believe that he was of the same race. He went back down the passage, sad and weary, to find the baby crying frantically and waving his arms in the air.

'It was the noise,' Tara said. 'I couldn't keep him quiet. Could you hear him?'

'No,' replied Brock quietly. 'No, I couldn't hear him.'

'Was it bad?' Tara said, getting up and coming towards him. She rubbed her nose against his and then pushed the side of her head against his neck, trying to comfort him.

'Yes,' Brock murmured, 'it always is; it seems to get worse. And what can we do? Nothing, Tara, absolutely nothing.' He lay down on the earth floor with his back curled against the wall and went to sleep. Tara watched him tossing fitfully for a while and then she went back to the baby which was quieter now the Urkku had gone. Soon there was silence again.

Outside the sky had clouded over and it had become warm. In the late afternoon the rain began to fall and on the white snow the crimson streak left by the young cock slowly spread until finally it disappeared with the last of the snow.

CHAPTER VI

The seasons changed and the baby grew into a young boy. They called him 'Nab' which, in the language of the Old Ones, means 'friend', and he became as one of the animals of the wood. He understood instinctively the joys and sorrows, the sadness and the beauty of each season: the two seasons of stillness; cruel winter, a time of survival when the weak fell and the strong grew weak as the icy winds scythed through the wood, and friendly summer, a lazy time of plenty: a time of drowsy afternoon sleeps in the fragrant green shade under the bracken. Linking winter and summer and leading each gradually into the other were the two seasons of change – spring, with its atmosphere of excitement and anticipation, full of the magic of birth when the trees showed their delicate new buds and the earth covered itself with the glory of flowers – carpets of blue and yellow and pink and white on the woodland floor; and autumn, perhaps, if it were possible to choose, Nab's favourite time when the wood turned to gold and the air was full of falling leaves and there was a constant smell of woodsmoke and the dankness of rotting vegeta-tion; and above all a feeling of intense and beautiful sadness so exquisite that it made Nab's heart ache as he watched the brown leaves drifting slowly in the wind down to the floor.

When he reached the age of three Brock and Tara built him a home in the rhododendron bush to the left of the Great Beech as he had grown too big for the sett. The layers of shiny leaves formed a large waterproof canopy over the large round open area inside the bush and when they had cleared some of the branches which ran through the middle there was plenty of space for the boy. Above all, it was well hidden: the branches and leaves were so thick that it was impossible to see through them from the outside although there were a number of places on the inside from which Nab could see out. The entrance to his home was at the back of the bush and it was only possible to crawl through it.

Brock and Warrigal would spend many hours in there with the young boy talking and explaining about the ways of the wood; and often the other animals would come in and spend time with him also, for the Council had decided that although Brock and Tara would always be his special guardians and protectors, he was also the responsibility of the entire wood and was not to be brought up as a badger, or any other animal for that matter, but was instead to be allowed to develop in his own way with all the animals helping him and teaching him in their own particular skills. Thus from Perry-foot the hare Nab learned the art of running and also a lot about humour. The boy laughed a lot naturally but with the hare he could play games like hide and seek and they would cuff each other in fun.

Pictor would come and have long serious talks with him about the art of organization and of running a community while from Sterndale the Fierce he came to understand the rightful place of pride and aggression. Often in the evenings Nab would be sleeping soundly in one corner of his bush when he would suddenly feel the presence of something and, waking up, would be thrilled to see the triangular face of Rufus the Red looking at him intently. After his initial doubts, the fox had become extremely fond of the boy and now delighted in spending time with him, teaching him the arts of cunning and stealth. The boy would sit spellbound as the fox recited tales of adventure and excitement about the amazing and daring tricks his ancestors had used to avoid the savage packs of dogs which the Urkku sent out to kill them. Rufus also spent long hours teaching him how to walk without making a sound, how to merge with his background, how to use whatever cover was available and how to freeze whenever there was the slightest sign of danger. Most impor-tant of all, perhaps, he taught Nab the art of alertness: how to remain constantly on guard and what sort of sounds to listen for as signals of Urkku. While Rufus was talking to Nab, the boy would sit close and run his hands over the fox's soft fur or bury his fingers in it and pull them backwards so that the fur stood up in little spikes on his back.

Nab also loved talking to Warrigal and sometimes, on summer evenings, Wythen himself. From them he learnt wisdom and wood-lore and they explained to him, slowly and gently, about the Magical Peoples and the Urkku and the relationship between them. The Elflord knew about him, they said, and it was he who was helping the animals to bring him up. At some time Warrigal would take him to meet the Elflord and they would have a long talk but that would not be for quite a few seasons yet. From the time he had left the sett Nab had been aware that he was not a badger and that in fact there were no other animals like him in the whole wood. The owls had ex-plained to him that he was of a quite different type of creature and that his race lived separately in their own area some distance beyond the hill they could see at the far end of the fields at the front of the wood. They told him he had been found under the Great Oak one snowy winter's night by Brock and that he had taken him in to look after him. Whenever he wanted to he could leave the wood to join his own race, they said, although of course the boy had no desire now to leave his home and his friends. They took him to the brook and showed him his reflection in the dark brackish water so that he would have some idea of what he looked like for he had not yet seen an Urkku. Whenever the shoot came they took him back down the sett where he stayed with Tara until it was all over. When he asked about the noise they told him that it was thunder and lightning and that they were keeping him in the sett to protect him from it, for they did not want to influence him in any way against his own race. This had all been explained very carefully to Wythen by the Elflord. 'We must let his attitudes and opinions towards the Urkku develop entirely independently; they must come from him,' he had said. And so, until he was slightly older, they had decided not to let him see the Urkku killing. There was another reason why they put him in the sett when the Urkku were around; although no one had come looking for Nab they were afraid that if he were found he would be taken away and

43

they did not yet think that he had enough skill to be able to escape detection while men were in the wood.

Nearly every night Brock would crawl through the narrow passage into the bush and Nab would see two great white stripes appearing out of the gloom. They would then go out together and Brock would take him all round the wood looking for food. All the animals had told him what they ate and explained to him how to find it but Nab did not like the idea of killing his fellow animals and then eating their flesh, so his diet consisted of berries, fruits, toadstools (which he particularly liked), bark, grass and other plants of the wood. In the autumn he would go round the wood with Digit and the other squirrels collecting acorns, beechmast and the fragrant hazelnuts and these would be buried in one corner of his room

to last the winter. He would also go with Bibbington the hedgehog to the dark damp places of the wood where the best toadstools grew and these would be gathered and hung all around the inside of the bush so that the air could circulate around them and they could dry for the winter. Bibbington told him to stay well clear of any white-gilled fungi because if he ate some types of those he would die a painful death, so he gathered only those which the hedgehog had assured him were good to eat: the yellow and ragged chanterelle with its delicate perfume and peppery flavour, the field and horse mushrooms which were his favourite and the oyster mushroom which grew in abundance on the old rotting silver birches in his part of the wood. Then there were shaggy caps, puffballs which Bibbington told him to 'be sure and gather before the brown powder comes' and boletus of all sorts which sprouted out of the decaying autumn leaves in their shiny oranges and dark browns and which the hedgehog had taught him to recognize by their tubelike gills and their smell. The dandelion provided him with both a vegetable all year round from its leaves and a root which, when dug up in the autumn, he could dry and use to add some variety to his winter diet. In spring he would rejoice in the abundance and variety of the new foods that were growing all around; the nutty flavour of the young hawthorn leaves, the slightly bitter wood-sorrel and the sweet young beech leaves which he would chew straight off the tree. He would also nibble the fresh young shoots of nettles and collect armfuls of the new season's chickweed which, although he could gather it all the year round, always tasted better in spring. Sometimes he would scamper down to the big brook over the fields with Perryfoot and there they would spend the afternoon enjoying the nutty flavour of the young burdock stems which grew in profusion all along the banks and collecting watercress to take back and eat in the evening. Perryfoot had shown Nab another very useful plant which grew by the big brook in summer and which was always easily found by its scent; this was mint, which he used to add variety to the flavour of some of his more staple foods. It could also be dried if hung up and he would use this in the winter with his toadstools. Often he found large patches of meadowsweet in the same area as the mint and he gathered clumps to lay on the sleeping corner of his bush and to give to Tara for the sett. Ever since he had first been taken in and laid down on the pile of meadowsweet, he had found it difficult to sleep unless he had that fragrant scent in his nostrils.

A particular delight of late summer was to wander on a balmy evening with Brock and Tara to the blackberry bushes that grew round a hollow in the bank in the fields at the back of Silver Wood and to pick these juicy succulent fruits and eat them straight off the bush until they had had their fill. They would then sit for a while looking down on the wood while Brock told a story and the moon moved slowly through the sky.

There were other fruits which summer produced; rosehips, wild gooseberries and, a rare delicacy, wild raspberries. Sometimes, when the first leaves were beginning to turn brown and the smells of autumn began to linger in the air, Brock would take the boy off over the fields to a bank where bilberries grew and they would spend all night picking the delicate black berries off the small bushes and eating them. They would then gather as much as Nab could carry and take them back to surprise Tara who would ruffle the boy's hair with her paw in delight.

CHAPTER VII

Nab's eleventh winter was long and cold; the snow had stayed for an age and there had been vicious frosts which had killed many of the year's young birds. On the very coldest nights, when the savage north-east winds threatened to cut the animals up and leave them on the frozen ground, both Brock and Tara would make their way from the sett into Nab's bush and lie down on either side of him to keep him warm in their fur. During the short days Nab would venture out for some fresh green plants to augment his supply of nuts and dried fungi and then, if the noon sun was warm enough, would sit outside the bush and look out over the frozen fields where only the rooks and the crows moved. At other times the rains would lash down so that it became impossible to stay dry; little drips would start to seep through the rhododendron leaves and wet the floor of his bush which was made up of a dark brown, peaty mixture of soil and leaves, so that it took the boy all his time to find a dry place to sit. He also had to make sure that the dried toadstools, which were scattered all over the inside wherever there was a little twig to stick them on or a flat surface where they could be laid, were kept away from the wet; otherwise, as Nab had discovered in a previous winter, they would begin to spoil and rot leaving him hungry. Sometimes Warrigal would fly down from his hole in the Great Beech and perch on a thick branch in the bush and talk to the boy or else sit with him silently as they both stared out at the sheets of rain falling down outside; there was something very comforting and cosy about being under shelter while outside everything was a torrent of wet. When the rain finally stopped and the heavy black clouds moved on, the sun would often come out and Nab would leave the bush to wander through the dripping wood and rejoice in the feeling of freshness with which the grasses and the trees and the bushes had been left; the sun would sparkle from all the little raindrops that lingered everywhere and Nab's mind would be lost in a magical world of golden reflections and sparkling silver crystal.

The cold March winds continued into April, dragging the winter out so that it seemed it would last for ever until, finally, one day the cry of a curlew echoed over the fields, and all over the wood hearts jumped with a thrill of anticipation at this triumphant clarion call of spring. Soon the plovers arrived and the fields were full of their liquid warbles as they strutted about with their magnificent plumed heads arrogantly turning from side to side or swooped and dived through the air, asserting their control of the sky over their fields. As the days grew warmer the larks began to sing their distinctive one-note symphonies as they hovered way up in the blue sky, so high some-times that Nab thought they had vanished until he would suddenly see a tiny black dot, fluttering delicately.

It was on one of these days of high spring that Nab first saw the race of which he was a member. He was sitting, with his eyes closed, on an extremely comfortable tussock of grasses, listening to the larks and feeling the warmth of the sun fill his body with energy and life, when suddenly he felt a little cuff on the side of his face. He opened his eyes to see Perryfoot jumping around in front of him with his great long ears cheekily erect and his black eyes sparkling with merriment.

'Hello,' he said. 'Coming for a walk?'

Nab gave a yawn and a stretch. 'I was enjoying that until you turned up,' he said and darted forward with a hand to catch the hare on his back thigh, at which Perryfoot skipped to one side missing the hand by a pace.

'Too slow, too slow,' he said and, as Nab recovered his balance, he nipped forward again and dealt the boy another smart blow on his cheek with his front paw. 'Come on; it will do you good – get some of that winter stiffness out of your bones.'

Nab agreed on condition that they try and get Brock to come with them. They both wandered over to the sett and Nab knelt down in front of the tunnel and gave a call, for it had been many seasons now since he had been able to crawl into the sett. There were only three badgers now; the two cubs had left and gone to Near Wood and since Nab had come there had been no more. Brock believed that this was the work of the Elflord; indeed Warrigal had hinted as much when they had been talking one evening. The reason, the owl had told him, was so that he and Tara could devote all their energies to looking after the boy.

Finally, after a number of calls had met with nothing but silence, Nab spotted the black tip and white stripes of the badger's face making its way up the passage and Brock agreed to go off with them for an afternoon walk. Nab picked a handful of the delicate young beech leaves which were just beginning to emerge and started to chew them as the three made their way from the sett to the old stile. Then they walked along the far side of the brook to where, in a bank in the middle of the new young birches, Rufus had his hole. When they reached the fence at the back of the wood they walked along it until they came to a hedge which ran out across the field and which they could use for cover until they got down to the stream. They stopped there for a while in the shade of a great ash tree and looked out at the wood basking in the spring sun. Nab went off to explore on his own leaving the other two meditating under the tree. He walked down to a thicket of rhododendrons and young birches, made his way through them and emerged on to a carpet of bluebells which stretched over the floor of the wood until they reached a number of enormous elms.

Nab knelt down and buried his face in the heady scent of the blue flowers; he felt he could almost drink their fragrance and as the smell pervaded his senses he could see, in his mind's eye, every perfect spring day he had ever known. He stayed there for a long while, kneeling with his face on the ground as if he were praying while the sun sent little shafts of golden light through the branches of the trees. He lifted his head and looked around exultantly; these were the times when his whole body seemed so full of energy that he felt he would explode and his soul sang with joy. He got up and ran like the wind back to the ash tree where Brock was sleeping and Perryfoot sat on all fours, his great ears laid flat along his back, quietly contemplating. They woke the badger up and made their way under the rusty wire of the old fence and into the field under the shelter of the hedge. They went past some warrens in a little sandy hollow, where the rabbits greeted them and asked for news of Pictor and the woodland rabbits, and then walked up a fairly steep slope until they reached the top of the bank. The wood was now quite far behind and below them and ahead there was a gentle slope down to the stream. It was a perfect afternoon; little white clouds scudded about in the blue sky and there was a gentle breeze which blew delicious gusts of warm air against their faces. Nab's heart was light and free.

'Race you to the stream,' he said, and he and Perryfoot scampered away down the slope through a belt of small willows and over a velvety green carpet of new grass while Brock pottered along behind. When they got to the bottom, Nab and the hare began dancing around, each trying to land little cuffs on the other's cheek. They often played this game although Perryfoot nearly always won; his huge back legs could shoot him out of range so quickly that Nab seldom caught him and then, while the boy was thinking about his next move, the hare would be in and out, cuff: cuff, before Nab could blink. Still, it didn't matter, they both loved playing, and this afternoon Nab was feeling so good that he managed to catch the hare once or twice. Brock sat under the cool shade of a willow next to the stream and enjoyed watching them. Since that night so many seasons ago when he had found the baby, Brock's life had been devoted to caring for and looking after the boy. There had been little talk of Elflords or saviours or any 'grand purpose' since that time, although Warrigal sometimes intimated that the Elflord was well pleased with the progress of the boy and Wythen occasionally came to visit Brock and Tara to see how they were managing and to guide them on difficult issues.

After a while, when Perryfoot and Nab had grown tired after their game, the three animals decided to wander a little further along the stream. On the other side of the stream there was another green field which sloped steeply down in a sharp bank, so there was little need to be cautious as they were well out of sight of any farm and in any case even if they did see an Urkku there was plenty of undergrowth in which to find cover. Thus they were ambling along quite carelessly, stopping every now and then to pick some berries or young leaves to nibble, when suddenly, upon turning a corner of the stream, they froze. Ahead of them the little steep-sided valley along which they had been walking opened out so that the slopes became far more gentle and on their side of the stream there was a little cluster of yellow gorse bushes surrounding three sides of a hollow. Inside this hollow they could hear the sounds of laughter and talk and there were other unfamiliar sounds which they could not recognize.

After a long time, the trio, satisfied that they had not been seen or heard, relaxed. They were in single file behind a large willow and a holly bush that had been seeded, probably by a bird, many seasons ago and which had flourished by the

water. The only sound, apart from that coming from the hollow, was the continuous tinkling of the stream as it meandered over the pebbles in their sandy bed.

'What shall we do?' said Nab quietly as he turned round to face the others, who had been walking behind him when they had heard the noise.

'It's the Urkku,' said Perryfoot. 'Come on, we'll go back. Come on Brock, turn round,' and he gave the badger a gentle push with his paw.

'No,' said Brock firmly.

'What do you mean, "No"? It's Urkku and they've probably got guns. Don't be silly. Let's go back,' the hare whispered fiercely.

'No. I'm pretty certain they aren't dangerous. I can tell; they aren't behaving like the Urkku we normally see. Besides the sounds of the voices are different; higher and softer. No, there's no danger. It's a good opportunity for you, Nab, to see some Urkku at first hand. Listen, here is what we'll do. Perryfoot, you go round the front of the hollow, as near as you dare, so that they can see you. Then while they're watching you, Nab can run across at the back and take cover

51

behind the gorse bushes. I'll stay here and watch.'

'Hmmm. I don't like it at all,' muttered the hare. 'Not one little bit. Still, if my learned friend says there's no danger, there's no danger. I just hope he's right. Why don't you go, Brock?'

'Because if I'm wrong, you can run faster,' said Brock, smiling mischievously.

'All right,' said Perryfoot. 'Wish me luck.'

The hare ran slowly over the grassy bank and, when he appeared in view at the front of the hollow, the two remaining animals heard little squeals of delight coming from behind the gorse bushes. Perryfoot had stopped and was preening himself and from the sounds of merriment Brock guessed that the Urkku had seen him and were fully engrossed in watching his antics.

'Right, off you go. But be careful and keep well out of sight,'

whispered Brock, and the boy scuttled along, bent almost double, until he reached the shelter of the bushes at the top of the little hollow. He sat silently for a moment, hardly daring to breathe and then, bursting with the most intense curiosity, he crawled along until he found a gap in the bushes through which he had a clear view. There he saw, for the first time in his life, another member of his own race. There were in fact two of them, both sitting watching Perryfoot with their backs to Nab. Even though they were sitting down he could tell that one was bigger than the other and he guessed that they were parent and young and, from what Remus and Bibbington had told him, he further believed that they were both female. He had not known what he had expected to see but he recognized himself in them and was not so surprised as he thought he might have been. Nevertheless he was fascinated by the way they talked and the way they looked and as he watched he found his attention drawn more and more to the little girl as she snuggled up close to her mother, holding tightly on to her arm with the thrill of seeing the hare so close. Perryfoot was obviously beginning to enjoy himself now as he found himself the object of such rapt attention and in no danger: he hopped a few paces and then stopped, raising himself up on to his back legs and putting his ears erect so that he looked like an arrogant monarch, and then he hopped a few more paces and repeated the performance. The little girl had now turned to watch Perryfoot, and Nab could see her face; judging by her size she had probably seen as many seasons as he had and, as he stared at her wide blue eyes and delicate mouth and the gentle pink of her cheeks framed by a tangled cascade of golden hair, he became entranced. All the magic of the spring day seemed to Nab to be captured in her face and when she laughed he could feel his heart miss a beat in sheer joy; she was a Princess of the Golden Afternoon and he would never forget the way he felt as he first saw her, through all the rest of his life.

The hare had begun to get bored now and, feeling he had carried out his duty, he hopped slowly back to where Brock was watching from behind the holly bush. Nab, however, was quite unable to tear himself away and indeed had hardly noticed that Perryfoot had gone. 'What is he doing?' whispered the hare crossly. 'Hasn't he seen enough?'

'I don't know; be patient and try to imagine how you would feel if you were his age and were seeing a hare for the first time.' Perryfoot grunted and stretched out to enjoy the full warmth of the sun and reflect on the story he would tell his doe. Meanwhile Nab's reverie was suddenly broken as the little girl jumped up, said something and ran off out of the hollow towards the stream, where she began to pick primroses. As she followed the meanders of the stream she was soon out of sight of her mother and had come fairly close to where Nab was lying; in fact he could approach her without being seen from the hollow. He was suddenly seized by an overwhelming impulse to talk to the girl and make himself known to her despite Brock's warning and in the face of all the animal instincts which told him to remain hidden. How could he approach her? How would she react? Would she call to her mother? A hundred questions like these raced through his mind as, with his heart beating so loudly that he was certain she would hear, he crawled slowly down the bank away from the shelter of the gorse bushes until he was in a shallow ditch that would lead him up to a large willow by the stream which was near the little girl. Behind the holly bush Brock had roused Perryfoot and they were both watching horrified as Nab crawled nearer and nearer to the girl. 'What's he doing? Shall I go and stop him?' said the hare.

'No,' replied Brock. 'It's too late now; he'll do what he wants and we can only hope it turns out for the best.'

Nab was now at the foot of the tree and he crouched among the roots hardly daring to breathe and listening to the stream just by his left elbow running over its sandy bed. Very slowly, as Brock had taught him, he raised his head so that he could just see over the edge of the ditch. The little girl was some eight paces away, humming quietly to herself and thoroughly involved in picking the primroses and red campion that were growing on a little tussock which jutted out slightly into the water. She was bending down with her back to him; across the stream the green meadows rolled gently upward until they met the great beeches that stood at the edge of Tall Wood. Sheep were grazing contentedly, their white fleeces standing out clearly against the green, and overhead the larks hovered, singing the songs of spring as they had since time began.

Nab stood up and walked silently over the grassy bank of the stream until he was only a pace behind her. Suddenly, sensing that someone was near, she stopped humming, stood up quickly and turned round.

'Oh!' she cried in alarm. 'You frightened me. Who are you? I don't think I've seen you in the village. Are you playing a game – dressed like that I mean? Come on, tell me, who are you?' She stared at him in growing amazement as she tried to understand what she saw. His hair, a dark golden brown, hung in gentle waves down around his shoulders and three or four fresh green rushes had been tied around his forehead to keep the hair out of his eyes. About his waist was a wide length of silver birch bark threaded through with a new willow branch, thin as a reed and fastened somehow at the side. His feet were bare and his hands were large with long fingers and broken nails, and they hung loosely by his sides. But his face! his face was the colour of the autumn beech leaves and out of it shone two smouldering dark eyes which roved ceaselessly around her and burned with a wild intensity. She felt she ought to have been scared but her instincts told her there was nothing to be afraid of and she was, in any case, too mesmerized by his restless eyes to do anything but stare.

'Who are you?' she said again, slowly and gently. 'Why are you frightened? Where do you come from?'

Nab was quivering with fear from head to foot and yet, he did not know why, he was bursting inside with the need to communicate with her and tell her about his home and his friends and the wood and the bad days of last winter and everything he had ever done or

seen or heard. But when he tried to speak in the language of the wood she shook her head and appeared not to understand; she simply kept opening her mouth and uttering strange sounds and noises which he had never heard before: this must be the Urkku language which he had heard about. But he loved the sound of her voice; he could have listened to that gentle happy sound for ever.

The little girl listened in astonishment to the series of barks and whimpers and yelps and growls that came from this strange boy. She thought he was trying to talk to her; it was obviously no game but she was puzzled beyond words by it. He apparently didn't understand her either; she must be kind and gentle and patient as she was with animals. She decided to try and take him over to meet her mother; perhaps she could explain everything. She moved slowly towards him with her hand outstretched and tried to grasp his arm; as she got close she realized that he smelt of moss and leaves and sunshine and grass and somehow she understood then that he was not from the village, or indeed any village. As she placed her hand on his arm he snatched it away and his dark eyes flickered.

When she touched him and he could smell her gentle fragrance Nab became so overcome with embarrassment, confusion and fear that he was finally panicked into a full realization of what he was doing. He pulled his arm away from her hand savagely and looked round to the holly bush where he had left Brock and Perryfoot; there was no sign of them. With a quick glance back to the little girl, who was looking deeply at him in a most strange way, he took off back along the ditch and up the gentle slope towards the top of the hollow and the shelter of the gorse bushes from where he had first watched the girl and her mother. He looked down into the hollow and saw the mother lying flat out on the grass enjoying the sun and he turned back to where he had left the girl. She was standing, looking straight at him; her red gingham dress was blowing in the gentle afternoon breeze and her hair glinted golden in the sun. She raised an arm and waved it at him, and Nab, not knowing what he was doing, responded by waving back and then sensed with a thrill of joy that he had communicated with her. Finally, after what seemed for ever but was only in fact a heartbeat, Nab took a last precious look at this delicate vision and, tearing his eyes away with an effort that made

56

him feel sick, he ran down the slope to the holly bush.

'Well, so you finally decided to break off your discussion with the Urkku,' whispered Perryfoot fiercely, 'and not, if I may say so, before time. We thought you were never coming.'

'Come on,' said Brock, 'but there's no panic; she hasn't told her mother yet. Go carefully, quietly and quickly.'

At the sound of his two friends' voices, Nab felt the sense of warmth that only arises from coming home after being away and, almost overcome with love for the two animals who were standing in front of him, he felt tears welling up in his eyes. 'Come on,' said Brock again, gently, and he turned round and began to make his way back along the stream with Nab following him and Perryfoot bringing up the rear.

It was late evening when the three weary creatures found themselves back at the top of the ridge that looked down into Silver Wood. They sat down and Nab told his companions about the events of the afternoon; at least, he tried to tell them but he found it hard to express the feelings that he had experienced and explain why he had so recklessly approached the Urkku. But Brock seemed to understand and, despite Nab's disobedience, he did not appear to be cross. In truth Brock was really very satisfied with the way things had gone; it had been purely accidental but it had solved the problem of how Nab was to learn about his own race in a most fortunate manner. There had been little or no danger and Nab had had face to face contact with an Urkku of his own age; the only worry was that the girl would tell her mother and news of his existence would go round the village. Still, they would solve that problem if and when it arose. Perryfoot had calmed down after his initial anger and was now enjoying going through in his mind his own part in the afternoon's adventure and working out exactly how he would relate it to his doe when he saw her later that night. It would make a good story.

And so it happened that when the moon began to shine that night it found a boy, a badger and a hare still sitting looking down on the wood; each of them silently lost in his own different thoughts. Across the fields a little girl was looking out of her bedroom window at the moon and thinking, as she had done ever since the afternoon, of the strangely beautiful boy she had met by the stream. It seemed like a dream but she knew that it had been real. She couldn't tell anyone, of course; that would spoil the magic, and it was her secret that she would keep with her always.

CHAPTER VIII

The fresh green days of spring passed all too quickly and turned into a hot, hazy, dry summer. Nab spent the long hours of sunshine drowsing in the shade under the tall bracken that covered all the top part of the wood or lying at the foot of one of the great beech trees where the ground always seemed cool and there was plenty of refreshing sorrel and chickweed to nibble at. As evening fell he would make his way slowly back home and then with Brock or Perryfoot or sometimes Rufus the Red he would go searching for food.

The incident by the stream had dominated everyone's thoughts all summer. At first it had been thought by the elders of the Council that it would be unwise to tell the wood of what had happened for fear of causing panic and even anger at Nab; but it had not been long before rumours had begun to spread and, as most of these wild and exaggerated tales were different, it had eventually been considered the best policy to call a Council Meeting and clear everything up by disclosing the truth. It had been a somewhat unruly meeting with Wythen having to use all his authority to control matters, but Nab, at his first Council and feeling extremely nervous, had given a good account of himself in his attempts to explain exactly what he had done and why he had done it. This, coupled with the fact that most of the woodland animals now knew him and liked him, eventually won the day and it was decided that the only danger was the possibility that the little girl would have told her parents and the Urkku would come searching for him. Thus the guardians of the wood, Warrigal and

Brock, were asked to keep an especially careful look-out, but since it was now almost the end of summer and there had been no Urkku in the wood since the affair, it was believed, to everyone's relief, that the little girl had kept the meeting secret.

The incident had had a particularly marked effect on Nab. Although he had been aware before that he was a different type of animal from any of the others in the wood, it had never before seemed to matter very much. Now he had seen other Urkku he was filled with a curiosity to find out more about them for himself. He thought constantly of the little girl and was unable to clear his mind of his golden image of her as she had stood waving at him and smiling from the banks of the stream with the breeze ruffling her dress and blowing in her hair. But his memory was  always bittersweet as he recalled the confused turmoil of emotions that had made him snatch away his hand and run off. He also began to realize, for the first time, that he had not been born in the wood and that he must have two parents somewhere of his own race. Why had they left him under the Great Oak so many seasons ago? Where did they come from? What were they like? These questions repeated themselves over and over in his mind and he spent much time thinking about them while he was walking through the wood in the evening or musing in the daytime under the bracken. One night Tara had gone into his bush for a talk and found him sitting in a corner looking completely lost in himself. She turned round and without being noticed made her way back to the sett. There she began to dig in the wall where, so many seasons ago, she had buried the multi-coloured shawl in which he had been found. The walls of the sett were rubbed smooth and hard but her strong claws soon felt the cavity in which she had placed it. Taking it out carefully she shook it to get any soil off and then, having repaired the wall, went back up the passage and once more into Nab's bush. She went up to him and rubbed her nose against his neck. He looked up slowly and stared into her warm black eyes; 'Hello, it's nice to see you,' he said.

'Nab, I've brought you something. It's for you, to keep.' She produced the large gaily coloured shawl and handed it to him. He took it and, standing up, held it so that it hung straight and the pattern of the colours could be clearly seen. His eyes widened in amazement the more he looked and he began to feel it, running his fingers up and down the soft silk and through the long fringes that hung down all around it.

'It's for me,' he said, 'to keep? I've never seen anything like it before. Where did you find it?'

'It's for you because it belongs to you. When you were left in the wood you were wrapped in many layers of cloth because, as Brock has told you, it was a cold night and the snow was heavy on the ground. When Brock carried you back to me I took the outer layers of cloth off until I found, next to your skin, this shawl, and I buried it in one of the walls of the sett, ready to give to you when the time was right. So you see, it was given to you by your mother and father; it belonged to them and they gave it to you. It is a link with your parents.'

Nab sat down clutching the shawl tightly against him and he began to cry softly to himself. Tara went up to him and put her paw on his shoulder.

'What were they like?' he asked. 'Brock saw them, didn't he?'

'They were good Urkku. Brock felt no sense of danger or fear when he was near them.' She described the events of the first night as Brock had told them to her. At this moment he was out with Warrigal walking round the boundaries of the wood; it was a pity he wasn't here now to tell Nab at first hand but the boy could talk to him later.

When she had finished, Nab put his arm around her shoulder and buried his face against her neck. He stayed like that for a long time and when eventually he raised his head he smiled and there was a sparkle in his eye. He removed the layers of bark which formed his clothing and, before replacing them, tied the coloured shawl around his waist.

Summer in Silver Wood seemed to last for ever. The days became too hot for the animals to do anything except lie in the shade around the edge of the wood where there was a breeze. In the centre of the wood there wasn't a breath of wind to relieve the intensity of the heat and the stillness hung so heavily one could almost touch it. The only sound was the constant buzzing of the insects as they hovered and darted over the tall canopy of green bracken that filled the wood. Sometimes, as Nab lay under it staring up at the sky, he would see the topmost branches of the tallest silver birch trees waving gently in a breeze that only existed in heaven and he would stare at the movement of the leaves until he fell asleep. Occasionally something would startle a blackbird and it would chatter loudly as it flew off to settle on another branch. Nab would then wake up and decide to go for a little stroll; it was impossible to walk through the bracken so he would crawl on all fours beneath it until he found another spot where he felt secure and there he would again fall asleep. Under the ceiling formed by the interlaced bracken leaves there was a different world, a cool subterranean jungle where the green stems of the bracken were like trees and the floor was of rich dark brown peat under a light brown carpet made up of the sharp and spiky remains of last year's dead bracken. As Nab made his way through this jungle he would find his hands and knees criss-crossed with their imprint and he had to be careful not to let them cause splinters. He would see spiders scurrying about their business and metallic green beetles walking slowly along the bracken branches. As he moved he could feel the bracken dust which he had disturbed catch in his throat and he could smell and touch the damp peat, still moist under its covering of dead bracken. Sometimes he would come across a cluster of wood sorrel with their delicate white flowers and would pick a leaf and chew it to refresh himself.

Eventually Nab began to notice the first harbingers of autumn; although the sun still shone and it was hot during the day, the evenings grew damp and chill where before they had been balmy, and now there was a dew on the ground. By the stream, meadow-sweet appeared with its tall stalks and clustered heads of creamy white flowers which scattered as they were knocked, and in the wood the autumn toadstools made their way out of the mat of damp decaying leaves on the floor; the blusher with its scarlet cap covered in little rough skin-like flakes and the great orange boletus which felt shiny and shone in the dew but whose flesh, when the spongy gills had been removed, was one of the treats of autumn. In the mornings and evenings the hollows filled with mist which disappeared as the sun fought its way through to light up the golden leaves; Nab would lie on his back in the warmth of the midday sun under the great beech and watch the leaves gently floating down; if they appeared to be drifting near he enjoyed trying to guess whether or not they would land on him, and he was always surprised at how few, out of the hundreds that fell, succeeded.

The animals feared autumn; not because of its natural sadness or because it heralded the beginning of winter but because it was the season in which, after a period of delicious peace during the summer, the Urkku amply compensated for the rest with a time of killing and slaughter which was the most terrible of the year. Nab was now allowed to watch the Urkku from the shelter of his bush, although Brock was always with him to make sure he did nothing foolish. Although Nab had been told, when he had seen animals that had been shot, that their death was the doing of the Urkku he had become confused this summer because he could not reconcile the image he had built up of them as a race of savage killers with the reality of the two he had actually seen. However, as he watched with mounting horror and shame the activities of members of his own race as they spread terror and pain throughout the wood, his confusion gave way to a seething anger. With every crack of a shot which echoed through the wood his whole body ached as he imagined the pain that was being inflicted, and Brock was always having to restrain him from rushing out of the bush to attack the Urkku.

That autumn the killing seemed to be particularly bad; more Urkku seemed to come and they came more often. The wood seemed to be constantly full of the lingering smells of gunpowder and cigarette smoke and wherever Nab went he found reminders of them. The undergrowth was crushed, branches were broken, toadstools had been kicked over and tufts of bloody fur and feathers lay amongst the withering brown leaves. The wood seemed defiled and, unable to escape the oppressive weight of their almost constant presence, Nab's moods wavered from a brooding silent depression to a seething rage.

The animals crept furtively through the bushes, moving quickly and quietly so that the whole wood seemed to have died. The rabbits, led by Pictor, had suffered particularly severely this autumn as the result of a new method of killing which meant that they were now no longer safe even at night. Nab had been out in the wood the first time it was used and watched it in operation. He had been crouching down behind the old rotten stump of a silver birch picking a toad-stool and examining it for worms when he had suddenly become aware of the most terrible noise, grinding and clanking, coming from the direction of the pond. Looking up he had seen an enormous Urkku machine lumbering and lurching its way ponderously over the field towards the wood. The clouds were covering the moon that night and it was dark but Nab could make out the shape of the machine; it seemed like an ordinary tractor with a large trailer behind such as he had seen in the fields on hundreds of previous occasions, but somehow, at night, it seemed terrifying, like an enormous beast. When it arrived in the middle of the field at the front of the wood it shuddered to a halt and suddenly Nab was blinded by a bright shaft of light that shone straight in his eyes; he could see nothing and do nothing; he shook his head and screwed up his eyes in panic but when he opened them again he found that the light had gone from directly in front of his eyes and was moving away to his left in a great white beam that came from the trailer and searched across the  field. As the light moved on, it found three rabbits who had been eating just to the front of the wood; they stopped exactly as they were when the light had caught them, paralysed with fear and unable to see just as he had been. Two shots split through the night and two of the three toppled over onto their sides, their legs kicking in the air. The third one was galvanized into action by the shots and began to scurry away but, instead of turning to its side and so getting out of the light, it ran down the path of light which shone from the trailer. Nab heard the guttural sounds of an Urkku as it whooped with delight at the prospect of some sport and the machine started to clank and grind on in pursuit of the rabbit, which was now hopping pathetically from side to side in its prison of light. The laughter and shouts of the Urkku as they tried to make it run faster filled Nab's ears and head and his stomach felt sick. He watched as the rabbit eventually became so tired and confused that it stopped and, turning round, ran back up the shaft of light towards the tractor in a last panicking attempt to escape from its torment. Nab's ears rang from the shot and the rabbit looked as if it had run into an invisible wall as it was suddenly flung over into a backward somersault and landed kicking on the grass. The boy watched as the tractor stopped and two Urkku jumped down and ran to pick up the dead rabbits. They threw them into the back of the trailer and then the machine went back the way it had come to disappear finally as it went behind the hill at the back of the pond.

The mellow autumn golds eventually turned into the cold grey shades of winter and the winds came to blow off the few remaining leaves from the trees; only the oak leaves clung stubbornly to their branches, the last to come and the last to leave. Nab was out with Rufus in the late afternoon not many moons after the incident with the rabbits. The fox had been showing Nab the spot where he'd seen some chickweed growing at the back of the wood by the little stream and the boy had gathered a handful to take back for his meal with a few hazel nuts from his store. The fox's head bobbed up and down beside him as they made their way back to the front of the wood.

'You'll be able to pick at that chickweed all winter; I've never seen it there before,' said Rufus.

'Yes. I had to go down to the big stream before. It will be a big help,' the boy replied. He didn't often go out with the fox who always foraged for food on his own, but Rufus often came to the rhododendron bush to tell the boy about places which none of the other animals had been to or else to recount legends of the Fox from the time Before-Man, when foxes lived, not as they did now in isolated individual holes but in a vast underground colony which stretched as far as the mind could think about and were ruled by the Winnat – three foxes whose bodies were covered in beaten copper wrought for them by the Elvensmiths in return for an alliance with the Elflords.

They walked in silence for a while until suddenly Nab felt a sharp tap on his leg as the fox knocked him with the side of his head. As he stopped Rufus motioned to him to get down. The boy dropped quietly to the ground and followed on all fours as Rufus silently led the way to some cover behind the base of an oak.

'Look,' whispered the fox.

Nab looked out over the bleak winter fields but could see nothing at first. Then he saw, just coming into sight on his left, two Urkku walking along the front of the wood, both with their guns tucked under their arms. They were talking very quietly and looking intently all around. Nab looked at the fox, who motioned him to lie down flat; he himself was crouched as if to spring, with his whole body quivering, his sharp ears erect and the black tip of his nose twisted to one side as it strained to pick up every scent on the air. The Urkku stopped and looked around them; for one long agonizing spell they seemed to be staring straight at the oak tree and then their gaze moved on. Suddenly, to Nab's horror, he saw one of them motion with his head to the other in the direction of the part of the wood where he and Rufus were. They took the guns from under their arms and held them with one hand under the barrel and the other by the trigger, ready to raise to their shoulders and shoot, then they began to advance slowly in to the wood. Nab looked at the fox in panic.

'Listen,' said Rufus. 'They don't know we're here but if they carry on as they are doing they are bound to find us. If they come too close I'll run off towards the front of the wood so that they can see me. That should take their attention away. You must stay here and not move until you feel it's safe. Then go straight for your bush and stay there. Above all, stay where you are until they've gone; I'll try and

66

get them to follow me.'

'But what about you?' Nab whispered.

'I'll be all right. They rarely manage to kill us with their death sticks. We're too quick for them. Now, keep quiet.'

They lay side by side on the earth behind the oak. Nab could feel the damp coming through his layers of bark and his knees were sore. As the Urkku came closer and he became more frightened, his hands reached out to feel the rough bark of the oak and he gained comfort from the power and strength of the tree. He looked at Rufus. The fox's eyes were staring at the Urkku with a black intensity and his quivering body seemed about to explode with energy. They were now barely twenty paces away and Nab's heart was pounding so strongly that he felt certain they must have heard his frightened rasps of breath. Rufus looked at him and put his paw on the boy's arm; then he burst out from behind the tree and glided noiselessly away through the tufts of grass and around the fallen logs that littered the floor, his great bushy tail flowing away behind him.

Nab watched as one of the Urkku caught sight of a flash of brown and shouted to the other, pointing excitedly at the undergrowth. They both raised their guns and the boy's heart stopped as two shots echoed through the wood; desperately he looked for the fox and then to his relief he saw him by the stile at the edge of the field running across to the other side of the wood where the trees were thicker and he would be safe. Then he heard another guttural shout and two more shots shattered the air. Rufus crumpled up and toppled over on his side; in a blind fit of grief the boy ran out from behind the oak tree and dashed across the wood until he fell on his knees beside his friend. His whole body was seized with uncontrollable spasms as he sobbed hysterically. 'Rufus,' he cried, and cradled his arms under the fox's head to bury his face against the warm fur. The eyes slowly opened; a few short heartbeats ago they had shone with life and energy; now they were liquid brown and still and they looked at the boy with sadness and love and hope. The boy felt his hand warm and sticky where it held the fox and then the eyes closed and the head sagged. Nab knew he was dead and a surge of sickness welled into his stomach as the full horror of what had happened suddenly hit him. Through a blurred veil of tears he looked at the black nose and the

67

mouth which was drawn back in death so that the teeth could be seen; he looked at the two triangular ears and he buried his hand in the deep fur around his neck. He was unable to accept that life had gone when the body was here exactly as it had been when they were both behind the oak. The eyes would never again look at him; he would never again see the fox's head as it poked its way through the rhododendron bush and there would be no more stories on winter evenings. He kept going over these things in his mind to try to make himself understand but he could not grasp it; it was too much to comprehend. Still shaking violently as the tears flowed down his face he threw himself over the dead body of the fox.

'Look, Jeff; I told you. It's a kid.'

Nab heard the Urkku behind him and felt pressure on his shoulder as a hand gripped him and tried to raise him up from Rufus's body. He had forgotten the fox's last words to him, that he was not to move until it was safe, and he realized with a shock of remorse that Rufus had been killed trying to protect him but now, through his own fault, it had been in vain.

The boy tried to jump up but found that he couldn't; the Urkku had too firm a hold of him.

'Steady, kid. Who are you? Chris, look at it! It's dressed in bark; and look at its hair. I don't think it can speak. What's your name, kid? See if the fox is dead, Chris.'

Nab watched in horror as the other Urkku put his boot under Rufus's body and kicked it over; the head pointed straight up for a second or two and then toppled over the other way. Then the Urkku pulled out a knife and hacked at the tail; when it had come off he kicked the fox over so that it landed nose down in the ditch, its once magnificent body spreadeagled and twisted crazily so that its back legs faced one way and its front legs the other. Suddenly all the sadness and grief that Nab felt turned into a searing anger and hatred and he tore free of the Urkku's hand and flew at him, biting and scratching at the man's face. The force and energy with which the boy charged were enough to knock him over and they rolled on to a tussock of grass as the gun went flying. Nab felt his nails sink into the man's cheek and as he drew his hand down he felt blood.

'Get him off! For God's sake get him off.'

The other Urkku grabbed the boy tightly around the waist and pulled him away; he struggled ferociously but the Urkku was too strong and he was unable to break free. The man on the ground slowly got up, cupping a hand over his cheek where three large gashes oozed blood.

'Come here, you little brat. I'll teach you,' and, while the other held Nab, he struck him across the face repeatedly with the back of his hand.

'Take it easy Jeff; it's only a kid.'

'I don't care – look at my face.'

'You'll be all right, it's only a scratch. Well, we can't leave him here. Best take him back home where Ma can decide what to do.'

Nab redoubled his efforts to get free as he realized with sudden panic that the Urkku intended to take him away from the wood. His mind swirled as hundreds of thoughts raced through it; images of the Urkku homes he had built up from conversations with Bibbington and Cawdor and Rufus; plans of escape; dreadful worries about where he would sleep tonight and what the Urkku were going to do with him; thoughts of Brock and Warrigal and Perryfoot and Tara coupled with terrible fears that he might never see them again. Then through all his panic would flash, clear and still, a picture of Rufus as he lay on the damp bracken dying, and the tears once again began to flood from him.

He felt himself being half dragged, half carried through the wood towards the stile and he was pulled roughly over it into the field. He was still struggling and biting and scratching but the numbness in his face and jaw and his desperate fight with the Urkku had taken their toll of his body and he could no longer muster the energy to do more than wave his arms around in a pathetic token gesture of aggression. He saw Silver Wood recede as he was taken across the field; the winter evening was now drawing in and the wood looked black, deep and impenetrable. Nab was somehow amazed that through all the terrible events of that afternoon it had remained exactly the same, nothing had changed; his rhododendron bush was still there and so were all the great trees. It had simply watched impassively as the horrors had unfolded before it and he felt vaguely resentful at its inability to help him.

They passed the pond as great black clouds began to appear in the grey sky bringing little spots of rain in the wind which stung his face and mingled comfortingly with his tears, as if all Nature were crying with him. As they reached the rise at the top of the little hill past the pond the Urkku stopped for a rest. Nab looked back at the wood standing aloof in the distance. It was his home, he had never slept anywhere else and now he was being taken away, perhaps never to see it again. His heart was heavy and his stomach felt as if a thousand butterflies were fluttering inside him; suddenly he felt the arms round his stomach tighten and he was pulled off again down the far side of the slope. Desperately he tried to fix a picture of the wood in his mind and his eyes clung to the treetops as they got smaller, until eventually they disappeared out of sight behind the top of the hill.

CHAPTER IX

The single spots of rain that Nab had felt before now turned into a downpour; great sheets of water seemed to be falling from the sky and the Urkku were running across the fields, each holding one of his hands and pulling him with them. The rain was beginning to seep through his bark and his hair was dripping down his back. Soon Nab saw, through the rain, a group of buildings clustered together on the near side of a gently sloping rise. He guessed that these were Urkku dwellings and that this was where they were heading. They came to a gate and, opening it, were now on a rough stone track which hurt his feet as they raced along. There were buildings now on either side and Nab could hear the heavy breathing and constant shuffling of the cows inside; occasionally one would moo loudly as they heard the clatter of the Urkku's boots on the track. Then suddenly they rounded the corner and the front of the farm faced them; racing up to it, the men stopped in the shelter of a porch.

'Take your boots off before we go in, Jeff; Ma will only grumble if we trail muck in. Damn rain, I'm soaked. Come on then, bring him in.'

They opened the door and Nab was met by a wall of heat and greasy cooking smells which made the air so heavy that he immediately began to gasp for breath. He was amazed to find it brighter than daylight in the room and he was forced to screw his eyes up to avoid being dazzled. Everywhere was full of a cacophony of noise; he could see two more Urkku and these two were shouting excitedly

71

with his two captors, who were still holding an arm each. Much of the heat seemed to be coming from a great red crackling glow in one wall of the room; Nab guessed that this was fire from the description Bibbington had given him and he was both frightened and fascinated by it. Steam began to rise from his bark as it began to dry and he could see the same thing happening to the clothes of the Urkku. They were all looking at him now, eyeing him up and down and turning away to talk to one another before turning back to him. Nab felt both exposed and trapped and he looked around desperately for a way out but there was none; he felt crushed by the weight of the walls around him and the thickness of the air. The woman began to speak. 'Get on with your dinner, Father; it'll go cold. Come and sit down, boys, and I'll put your supper out and then I'll see about him. You found him in the wood, you say, and he can't speak English; and look at his clothes and his hair. Jeff, go and wash your face and put some ointment on, you've got a nasty gash there, and look at his nails. He could do with a good wash. I bet he's starving, poor little mite. Father, get me a plate and I'll put some stew on it for him.'

The two brothers let go of him; one of them went out of a door at the back of the kitchen and then upstairs and the other sat down next to his father at the long table that ran down the middle of the room. Nab stood shivering with fear in a pool of water that had come from his hair; he stayed where he had been left because there was nothing else he could do. The woman went over to the range and opened the oven door to take out the pot of stew. She put a spoonful on a plate with some potatoes and sprouts and set it down on the table next to where she had been sitting. She then walked across to Nab.

'Watch him, Mother, you've seen what he did to Jeff,' said the brother.

'I know. He'll be all right with me. Come along, come and have a bite to eat,' she said, putting her hand gingerly on Nab's arm, and trying to pull him gently towards the table.

Nab felt from her tone of voice that the woman meant him no harm and he allowed himself to be led. He was then pushed on to a chair and found himself sitting, like the rest of them, at the table. His fear was now beginning to give way to curiosity; he gathered by the way the woman was pointing to the stuff on the table and then to her mouth that he was meant to eat it. He bent down to sniff it and heard laughter coming from the Urkku. Quickly he raised his head and the woman, still laughing, bent over him and put a hand on his shoulder.

'It's only a stew,' she said. 'It looks like he's never seen proper food before, Dad. Look at him. He doesn't know what to do with it. Well, I can't understand it, I'm sure. It's a funny business; I don't think he can understand a word I'm saying. After he's had a bite to eat, I must go and get some clothes for him. He must have lost his own somewhere and put together this affair with bark; it's clever though. Look at the way it's threaded through with bramble briars to keep it together.'

The woman gave Nab two implements, one in each hand, and once more pointed to the plate and his mouth. He was at a loss as to what to do with the things in his hands so he put them down where they had been before and pickedd up the only thing that he could recognize in any way. It was a sprout and, being green, was at least similar in colour to the leaves and plants which he was used to eating. He put it in his mouth and was surprised to find it warm but he chewed it and there was no denying that it tasted good. He smiled with satisfaction and was surprised to hear laughter once again. Slowly he picked up all the sprouts and ate them one by one. Then he turned to the mashed potato and began to scoop it up with his fingers. When he had finished he turned to the stew and picked a lump of something brown from the mixture on the plate. Again he placed it in his mouth as he had with the rest and chewed, but this tasted foul and the consistency was unlike anything he'd ever had before. He quickly spat it out to the obvious consternation of the Urkku.

'He must eat his meat; it'll do him good,' said the woman and she put a lump on a fork and, crooking her arm around the back of his

73

neck, tried to insert the meat into his mouth. Nab clenched his teeth shut and shook his head from side to side in an attempt to escape the pungent greasy smell.

'No, he won't have it. Pity, it would have built him up,' she said.

Just then the other brother, Jeff, came loudly through the door; the sight of him reminded Nab of all the terrible events of that night and he jumped up suddenly from the table and leapt back, cowering, into a corner. His chair went flying and the plate crashed on to the floor.

'He doesn't care for you much,' said the father. 'What have you done to him?'

'I paid him back for my scratches – he won't attack me again,' the brother said, staring aggressively at Nab.

'Well, sit down and eat your supper. Here!' and the woman put a plate in front of him at the table. 'I'd better take him upstairs and get him to bed. Father, will you phone the police and tell them what's happened. Come on, son, you and me'll go upstairs and find you some pyjamas.'

Nab got up from his crouching position in the corner by the fire as the woman took his hand and led him towards the door through which Jeff had just come. When she opened it all Nab could see was darkness but suddenly everything was lit up again and he could see another room opposite which was lit only by the red glow of a fire. Lying stretched out in front of the fire he saw, to his utter amazement, a familiar sight. It was the dog, Sam. Nab looked again in disbelief; he was certain that he was not mistaken; he could make out, in the flickering firelight, the golden coat and long bushy tail that he had seen so often making its way across to the wood. The dog suddenly raised its head and looked up. Sam was as surprised to see the boy as Nab had been overjoyed to see him but he quickly overcame his initial shock, and, leaping up, he bounded across the room and down the three stone steps into the hall where the woman was about to lead the boy upstairs. Nab squatted down and stroked the dog whose tail was going furiously from side to side. He put his mouth against the dog's ear and spoke quietly in the language of the wood.

'They've killed Rufus. You must tell Brock what's happened and get me away from here. Sam, it's lovely to see you, but look, you ought not to appear too friendly, we don't want them to think we've met before.'

'Well, you two seem to get on together,' the woman interrupted. 'Go and lie down, Sam,' and she pulled Nab to his feet before leading him slowly up the stairs. The boy watched Sam turn around and walk back to the fire. He couldn't believe his luck and his heart began to beat faster at the glorious prospect of escape and freedom.

When they reached the top of the stairs they turned right and walked down a long narrow corridor, past three doors, and then at the end they turned right again to stand in a little landing with just one door on the left. The woman opened the door and they went into a small room with one window looking out over the farmyard. The walls were white and there was a bed along one side with a little wardrobe at the end. Along the other wall was a small dressing table and kitchen chair. The light came from a bulb with no shade that hung from the ceiling and the only break in the monotony of white was provided by the dark wooden beams that were set in the walls and the occasional picture. The room smelt musty and unused and although Nab had been pleased to escape the stifling atmosphere of the kitchen he found this room chill and damp.

The woman did something with some contraption on the floor and it began to glow red and give out a welcome heat.

'Now take all that bark off and put these nice pyjamas on,' she said as if he could understand what she was saying. 'We'll soon have the spare room looking nice for you. Come on!'

Nab just stood looking at her. He recognized the Urkku language from the time the little girl had spoken to him by the stream last summer, but he was unable to grasp what she wanted him to do. She moved up to him and began removing his bark; he grabbed her hand as she put it to the end of one of the briars that held it together and refused to let go. He would not let her take this off him; it was a part of himself and frightened though he was he would fight to keep it. It had taken him a long time to put it all together and to treat the bark so that it remained supple and he was proud of the way it had turned out.

'All right, keep it on,' she said and, moving over to the windows, drew the curtains. 'Now, here's the bed – you want to lie down on it and get a good night's sleep. I'll leave the light on for you and come back later with a mug of cocoa to see how you are.' She moved to the door and looked round to see him still standing where she'd put him when they first came in the room. He was staring at her. 'You're a strange one and no mistake,' she said, and closed the door behind her as she went out.

When she had gone Nab remained where he was until he heard her footsteps recede along the corridor and down the stairs. Everything was now silent except for the battering of the rain against the window. He went over to the curtains and, pulling them aside, put his head against the glass and looked out at the night. At first he could see nothing until he discovered that by cupping his hands between the window and his eyes so as to shield the light from the room he was able to see quite clearly. Beneath him was the farmyard through which he had been brought that night; at the end of the yard facing the house was a large cowshed and to the left of that Nab could see the roofs of other cowsheds which stood on either side of the track into the farm. He tried to look over the roofs of the sheds but everything was pitch black beyond them and it was only because the yard light was on that the boy could see anything outside at all. He stood with his nose pressed against the glass for a long time; he somehow felt better looking out and his study of the cowsheds and the barns occupied his mind. Eventually he turned round and faced the rectangular room with its four white walls and wooden door. He felt an overwhelming sense of being trapped and confined; the walls seemed to bear in on him and he felt an uncontrollable panic well up inside. Out of instinct he began pacing round the room in an effort to control his pounding heart and he found that it helped to relieve him slightly. He was still pacing round the room when, four hours later, the woman opened the door to see how he was. He didn't even stop to look up at her, his mind was so numb. She watched his monotonous pacing for a minute or two and then put the light out and closed the door. Immediately Nab flew at the door and began screaming and yelling; he couldn't bear that total blackness. She came in again.

'All right, all right. I'll leave the light on. Now, stop your bawling, there's a good lad.' She watched him resume his circuit and then,

76

feeling sorry for this strange boy and puzzled at his odd behaviour, closed the door once again and locked it before she went down the landing to her bedroom, where she was unable to get to sleep for a long time because of the creaking of floorboards that was coming from the spare room. Well, she thought, she had done all she could. Perhaps when the police came out tomorrow they would solve the mystery; although they hadn't been able to tell Father anything over the phone. He had probably escaped from an institution somewhere and had to live rough for a few days. Yes, that would be it; and he couldn't speak or understand them because he was backward. Eventually she dozed off under this train of thought while Nab still paced endlessly round and round the little room.

CHAPTER X

When Sam had left Nab at the foot of the stairs and gone back to the living room to lie down by the fire, his mind had been racing. His main thought had been that Nab must be set free somehow and as soon as possible; that very night if it could be done. But how? He would find it difficult, if not impossible, to do it on his own and besides, if he failed, those animals who were still not sure of him would have their doubts confirmed. No; he must get to Silver Wood and tell Brock and Warrigal so that they could all work out a plan together; that way, if it failed, at least he wouldn't be solely to blame. He was amazed at the good fortune of the boy's being captured by the Urkku from his household, although the wood was on their land, albeit at the very edge, and as the two young masters had got older they had taken more and more to shooting, so perhaps it had been only a matter of time before they saw him. The fire felt warm on his face and stomach as he lay on the rug. He loved this time of early evening when he had the whole room to himself; when the Urkku came in he would be told to move back and lie in the cold behind the couch but until then he could bask in the full warmth of the fire and watch the flames flickering with a red glow on the walls. But tonight he would have to stir himself and go off to Silver Wood; blast the rain, he thought.

Reluctantly he got up from the hearth and went down the three stone steps to the front door, where he began to bark and scratch to be let out. The old master got up from his rocking chair in the kitchen where he'd been lighting up his pipe and, patting him on the head, opened the door, whereupon Sam dashed out into the rain.

He stopped for a second in the yard under the shelter of a wall and waited until he saw the chink of light coming from the house narrow and finally disappear as the door was shut. Then he raced off down the yard, turned left at the end to make his way along the track between the cowsheds and then, squeezing under the gate, he was out into the fields. Near Wood formed a barrier on his right and he ran along in the field, keeping to the edge of the wood so that it provided him with some shelter from the driving rain. Finally he was out of sight of the farm and when he reached the far corner of Near Wood he turned left to head across the fields to the pond. He was completely in the open now, fully exposed to the rain and to the wind which had just begun to increase in intensity and was blowing directly against him. He put his head down and willed his tired body to keep going; his coat was completely sodden with the rain and had begun to feel heavy and his paws squelched and slipped on the wet grass. Soon he found himself climbing the familiar rise and when he reached the top he saw below him the dark brackish waters of the pond looming out of the night and beyond it the tall trees of Silver Wood. He bounded down the little hill and, passing the pond on his right, headed out across the last two fields before the wood. The wind had now begun to blow the rain away and the night began to get lighter as the clouds broke up and allowed the moon to come through; looking up he could see the black clouds racing across the night sky, each one, as it passed in front of the moon, acquiring a silver border. He put his head down into the wind again and raced on under the fence that enclosed the field in front of the wood and finally through the old barbed wire fence that went around the wood itself. He stopped for a second, panting heavily, and then made for Brock's sett under the Old Beech. When he came into sight of the earth he was surprised to see the badger outside talking to Warrigal, who was perched on one of the lowest branches of the tree. They were both looking at him as if he were expected.

'I saw you coming across the fields and called Brock,' said the owl gravely.

The dog flopped down panting beside Brock and looked at Warrigal. The rain had now stopped but he was too exhausted even to be bothered to shake the wet off and he was trying desperately to get his breath back. His mouth hung wide open and little drops of saliva dripped down from his tongue on to the ground; his body shook with the effort of breathing. Brock put his paw on the dog's shoulder.

'All right Sam, take it steady,' he said. The dog was not getting any younger and whereas once he could have recovered from a run like this in a matter of seconds, now it took some time. 'We know that Rufus and Nab are missing,' Brock said. 'I saw them go off together in the afternoon and the boy at least should have been back by now. And Warrigal tells me he heard a shot in this part of the wood and the most terrible shouting going on; I must have been in the sett. By the time he had flown over he could see nothing.'

'A terrible commotion and I can almost be sure one of the voices I heard belonged to Nab,' added the owl, looking down unblinkingly at Sam.

Between pants the dog told all that he knew. Neither Brock nor Warrigal interrupted him and when he had finished they remained silent, each looking down at the woodland floor.

Finally Warrigal spoke. 'It's worse than I thought. Rufus is dead and not only do the Urkku know about Nab, they've actually captured him. Well, there's no doubt as to what to do; he must be rescued immediately – tonight. Brock . . .' he called to the badger. 'Brock,' he said again more loudly.

The badger was sunk in despondency. He had let everyone down; the wood, Bruin, Tara and, worst of all, Nab himself. He had been appointed as the boy's guardian and he had failed in his task. And how would the Elflord react? What a terrible night; he wished desperately that it was all just a bad dream and he would wake up and find everything normal and Nab safely back in his rhododendron bush. Even if they managed to rescue him, the damage had been done; the Urkku knew about the boy. What would they do with him? And if he escaped, he wouldn't be safe in Silver Wood; where could he live?

'Brock,' shouted Warrigal for the third time. The badger looked up slowly into the great round eyes of the owl. 'You must not blame yourself,' he said. 'It was not your fault, you could do no more than you did to look after him. It was impossible for you to be with him the whole time.' The owl leaned forward on the branch. 'As he got older he had to have more freedom.'

Warrigal saw from the expression in the misty eyes of the badger that he was not to be consoled and that the only thing to do now was to begin to take steps at once to bring the boy back.

'I'll fly over and inform Wythen of what has happened and ask him to call an emergency Council Meeting so that the others know. You, Brock, go across the field and find Perryfoot; we shall need him with us. Sam, you stay here and get your breath back, you've earned a rest. We'll all meet back here as soon as we can.' He blinked slowly at them both and then, moving his brown wings gracefully, he glided quietly back into the wood.

Without looking at Sam the badger padded despondently across to the old fence and, lowering his back slightly to get under the bottom wire, walked out into the field. When he got to the middle he gave a little bark. Perryfoot never stayed in one form for more than a night and at about this time in the late evening he could well be out feeding somewhere. There was no reply. Brock moved on a bit towards the pond. This time the hare heard Brock's call and came bounding across from a little hollow where he'd found some tasty grasses.

'What's up, old friend? I spotted Sam racing like a mad thing over to the wood earlier this evening and wondered. That's why I hadn't gone too far from the wood when you called.'

He sat squatting with his ears flat along his back and silently chewed while Brock related the events of the night to him. When he'd finished, the hare, subdued for once, made his way to the wood alongside the badger. They found Sam where he'd been left and Warrigal just flying down to land on a low branch.

'What did Wythen say?' asked the badger anxiously.

'Well, he wasn't as surprised or worried as I thought he might be. Still, he very rarely gets ruffled so it's not always easy to tell what he's really thinking. But the Elflord must be told, and Wythen is flying off tonight to Dark Wood as soon as he's told the rest of the Council leaders. However, he asked me to put your mind at rest, Brock; no one else blames you and you mustn't blame yourself. Now, enough time has been wasted already; we must get moving. You three should not walk together in case you're seen so leave quite a bit of space between you. Perryfoot, you lead off in front and, if you spot any Urkku, just stop where you are. I'll fly ahead and if there's any danger, I'll give the alarm call.'

So the animals set off with the hare in front, followed by Sam and with Brock some way behind. Ahead of them the owl flew slowly at hedge height. All four were lost in their own private thoughts; Brock felt slightly better after Warrigal's report of what Wythen had said but now he was worried at the confirmation of the fact that the Elflord would have to be told. Sam was thinking about the part he had played that night and about what they would do when they got to the farm. The formation of a plan would be largely left to him as he was the only one with any knowledge of the layout of the house. Perryfoot's mind was on that glorious day the previous spring when he, Brock and the boy had gone down to the stream; that had been a happy time, so different from the way they all felt now.

They were just passing the pond on their left and making their way through the gate into the next field when Brock became aware of some animal following them. As soon as he had got through the gate he suddenly turned to his right to hide behind the trunk of a large oak that stood at the side. After a few seconds he heard the sound of soft breathing and the gentle thudding of paw-steps on the ground. When he judged that they were level with the gate he suddenly sprang out and found himself, to his immense surprise, face to face with Bruin. The old badger stopped dead in his tracks and his hair bristled with shock.

'Young'un,' he said, 'don't do that again; you'll kill me! When Wythen told me what had happened I thought you might need some help so I followed you and I've been trying to catch up. But you go too fast for me. Now come on, or the others will wonder where you've got to.'

'You shouldn't have come, it could be very dangerous,' Brock said when he'd recovered from his surprise, but he couldn't disguise the pleasure he felt at seeing his grandfather. His confidence had been severely shaken by the events of that night and he was grateful for the fact that this experienced old warrior would be with them. They set off together quickly up the slope from the gate and soon caught sight of Sam and, some way ahead, Perryfoot and Warrigal. Many of the clouds had now broken up and gone and the fields and Near Wood on their left were bathed in moonlight but there was an icy wind that blew across from the hills and seemed to get into their bones. They were now running along the side of the wood, back the way Sam had come earlier that night in the rain, and soon they caught sight of the farm buildings in the distance. Warrigal flew down and perched on the low branch of a large oak whose boughs hung over into the field and as the others came up to it they gathered round the branch and the owl addressed them.

'We're pleased to have you, Bruin,' he said. 'We shall need your experience and courage.' Technically Bruin the Brave, full member of the Council, should have assumed leadership of the expedition now that he was here but Warrigal was known for his wisdom and tactical expertise and the old badger was happy to be led by him.

'Now, we must have a plan and we must all be clear about our part in it before we get to the farm. Sam; tell us where the boy is being kept and what you think is the best way of getting in:'

The animals huddled together with their backs to the wind while Sam explained the geography of the house to them, but he was unable to think of a way they could get into it, nor was he certain which room Nab was in. He himself was only able to go through the doors when they were opened for him by his masters; otherwise they were a solid barrier of wood. There was silence while the animals put their minds to this difficult problem; only the rustling of the few remaining leaves, brown and withered but still stubbornly hanging on, disturbed the peace of the night. Bruin suggested that they charge at the doors and break them down but Sam explained, with considerable deference, that the Urkku, although they slept at night, would be awoken by the noise that this would make, and the plan was discarded. Sam then recalled how, when he had been a puppy, he had scratched at things a lot and he remembered how when he scratched at doors his claws had made impressions on them and he had been severely scolded. Perhaps the badgers, whose claws were so much bigger and stronger than his, would be able to scratch a way through.

Warrigal looked thoughtful for a moment. 'Are there any other

ideas?' he said, leaning forward on the branch and looking quizzically at each one of them in turn. 'Well,' he said, when no further plans were forthcoming, 'that is the scheme we shall adopt. But it will still create a lot of noise. We shall have to work very slowly. When we get to the farm I will fly up to Nab's window and let him know what's happening. Perryfoot; while the two badgers are at the door you stay at the bottom of the yard and keep a lookout. But stay out of sight; if anything goes wrong you must run back to the wood and tell Wythen. Now, is there anything anyone would like to know before we move on?'

There was silence. Now was the moment of truth. None of these animals except Sam had ever been as close to an Urkku dwelling as they were even now, let alone going still nearer and then, eventually, actually inside the building. Until now they had had no time to think of the danger; they had simply been driven by the need to rescue Nab and the entire escapade had been a vague concept in their minds. Now, suddenly, it was real. Warrigal could sense the growing fear.

'All right then. Come on,' he said and, moving his wings very slowly, he took off and began to fly just above the ground across the field and towards the gate. The others walked slowly in single file behind him. Warrigal waited for them at the gate and then, when they had all arrived, beckoned to Sam to take the lead and they all made their way along the rough gravel track with the cowsheds on either side of them. They walked on the middle of the track where the weeds had grown through so as not to crunch on the gravel and as they walked they heard the sounds of the cattle inside, the occasional rattling of a chain or shuffle of hooves. Suddenly a loud cough came from one of the sheds and they stopped dead in their tracks but Sam motioned that it was simply a cow and the party continued on its way. Brock's fear was almost overcome by his fascination for all the

84

things around him, the buildings and the farm vehicles; some bales of hay heaped in a corner and a ladder leaning against a wall up to a hay loft. Then at the end of the cowshed on their right they turned the corner into the yard and faced the front of the house. They stood in a little group looking across at the huge building; it looked like a fortress, high and impenetrable and the six windows, dark now that most of the lights in the house were out, stared out at them like great soulless eyes, daring them to enter. Once again fear gripped them and they stood rooted to the spot, huddled against the wall of the shed.

It was Sam who, understanding nothing of their fear of the house, urged them forward and took them across the yard to the great wooden front door, leaving Perryfoot behind where he could see the whole of the yard and also the track down which they had come.

'Right,' he said. 'Now this is the door, Brock, you start scratching here,' and he indicated the bottom left-hand corner. 'I hope the window of Nab's room is up there, Warrigal,' and as the owl silently flew up, Brock sank his sharp claws into the door and, drawing them down, left four great scratches in the wood.

Warrigal could hear the work going on below him as he hovered outside the window looking for a place to perch. He spotted the large sill and delicately dropped down on to it. He could see nothing through the window except little slivers of light that peeked out around the curtains. The icy wind blew particularly fiercely around this corner of the house; he had forgotten about it in the shelter of the yard. He turned his head round and saw Perryfoot crouching in the shelter of a doorway. Turning back to face the window he put his head on one side to listen for any sounds of danger from inside the house but all he could hear was the creaking of the floorboards in the room as Nab paced restlessly to and fro. He leant forward and gently tapped the glass with his beak twice; there was no response. He tapped again and this time the pacing stopped and he heard footsteps come towards him. He tapped again and this time there was a rustling inside as the owl saw the curtains start to move. He walked quickly along to the end of the sill from where he could see in but couldn't be seen himself in case he had come to the wrong place; it had only been Sam's guess that Nab would be in the spare room. Suddenly there was

86

a flood of light as Nab succeeded in drawing the curtains apart. Warrigal saw the boy's face with relief and walked back until he was once again in the middle of the sill. The boy was frantically looking out into the night, searching everywhere with his eyes except where the owl was perched. His face was pale and streaked where tears had traced their way down his cheeks and his eyes looked red and sore from crying. Warrigal tapped again and Nab looked suddenly down directly at him. As he saw the owl and realized who it was, his face lit up and relief shone out from it so intensely that Warrigal was afraid he might shout with joy, but all the woodland instincts that had been ingrained in him signalled extreme caution and silence and instead the boy simply put his smiling face to the glass and watched as Warrigal indicated to him that the others were down below and that they were now planning his escape. The boy was transformed; a minute ago he had been a pathetic trapped creature lost in the depths of self-pity, degraded and debased by capture. Now, with the prospect of freedom before him, he regained his dignity and self-respect and became alert and vibrant with energy.

When Warrigal was certain that Nab was fully aware of the situation he indicated to him to pull the curtains shut so as to prevent the light pouring out; if any of the Urkku saw it they would definitely come to investigate. Then he flew back down to the door, where Bruin and Brock were making good progress and Sam was waiting for him anxiously. He told them in hushed tones of what had happened and that everything had gone smoothly; Nab was now waiting for them. Brock was particularly thrilled at the thought that Warrigal had actually seen the boy and that he would soon be with them again and, while Sam went down to tell Perryfoot and Bruin carried on at the door, he plied the owl with questions as to his appearance and how he seemed in himself. Warrigal was pleased for his friend; he knew how hard the effect would be on the badger if things turned out badly.

Soon it was Brock's turn at the door again; the pile of splinters and shavings had now grown quite large and there was a definite indentation into the wood. He leant forward to bite off some large splinters that were getting in the way and then, sinking his claw into the wood again, he felt it go through. Overjoyed he went to work with renewed energy and soon there was a small jagged hole through which he could see the little entrance hall and, leading from it at the back, the stairs up which Sam had said they must go to find Nab. He wanted to carry on but the muscles of his shoulders had begun to ache and the pads of his paws were very sore. He pointed out the hole to the others and then limped painfully to one side to allow Bruin to carry on. It shouldn't be too much longer now, he thought; all they needed was a hole big enough to squeeze through. Sam stood by the hole watching carefully and listening for any sounds inside that might tell him whether any of the household were awake. There was silence except for the rhythmic scraping of Bruin's claws against the door as the hole grew wider. Soon Sam saw that the job was done and he put his paw on the old badger's shoulder to tell him to stop. It was time to go on in.

Warrigal gathered them all together and whispered quietly. 'Sam, you know the way so you lead us to the room. Brock, you go next and I will follow you. Bruin, I think you should stay just here, by the door, so that if the worst happens and the Urkku spot us you may be in a position to help. Now, is that all right with everyone? Good. Off we go then.'

As Bruin took up his position by the door Sam went through the jagged opening and found himself once again in the familiar surroundings of the house where he had lived for as long as he could remember. Their familiarity made the danger they were in seem unreal. There were no lights on. He walked gently across the few paces of tiled floor to the bottom of the stairs. Brock was squeezing himself gingerly through the hole, taking care not to get caught on one of the jagged splinters that were left around it. He could see Sam waiting for him. He realized with a shock of excitement that he was in an Urkku dwelling for the first, and probably the last time. His paws found it difficult to get a grip on the smooth floor and his claws made a slight rattling noise as he walked slowly across the tiles; he looked carefully all around him, into the kitchen on his right and the living room with chairs, tables, pictures and the red dying embers of a fire: the strange smells made his nose wrinkle and some of them threatened to catch in his throat and make him cough. When he joined Sam he turned round and watched Warrigal hop up and perch for a second in the hole before flying silently across to sit on the bottom stair. 'Right,' he whispered softly, and Sam began to make his way up the stairs with Brock following and Warrigal waiting behind. Brock found climbing these strange angles difficult at first but he watched Sam and copied the way he moved and before they reached the top he had got the hang of it; putting his front paws on the next stair, gripping and then bringing his back legs up to join them with a little jump. Once or twice the stairs creaked and to the animals it sounded like a thunderclap but luckily none of the Urkku seemed to have been woken, and Sam, having listened attentively for a few seconds each time, beckoned them on. Brock's paws now felt as if they were on something soft, like a very coarse moss, and he found it easier to move than on the tiles. He watched Sam arrive at the top of the stairs and walk along the landing a few paces, where he stopped and waited for Brock to catch up. Then Warrigal took off from the bottom and flew up the space over the stairs to join them. Sam thought how strange it was to see the owl flying around the house like a brown shadow and he had to blink his eyes to make sure it wasn't all a dream. But no; when he opened them again there was Brock by his side and Warrigal perched on a banister rail, both animals looking to him for guidance as to the next move. He led them along the landing past the three doors on their left which led into the bedrooms where the Urkku were sleeping and finally turned the corner on to the small landing where Nab's room was. They stopped outside the door and Sam indicated that this was it. So far, so good, he thought, but now the really difficult part of the operation would begin; if the noise of Brock's scratching at the door didn't wake his master or mistress it would be the work of the elves. Warrigal walked back along the little landing until he reached the corner where there was a banister post; he flew up and folded his talons around the top of it to perch there and keep a watch along the main landing. When the badger saw that he was in position he started once again the painful process of gouging away the door. As soon as he had started he heard footsteps inside the room and his heart lifted with joy at the realization that Nab was just on the other side. He worked very slowly; partly to make as little noise as possible and partly because of the pain in his paws which had started while he was working on the main door and which now had become almost unbearable. It was made worse by the fact that he was on his own now and couldn't have a rest while Bruin took over. His pads had started to bleed and as he scratched he left smudges and streaks of red behind. Sam indicated to him that this door was less thick than the other and luckily the wood was nowhere near as solid. Nevertheless, as the work progressed painstakingly slowly, he wondered how he was going to finish. He had to though; he felt responsible for letting all this happen in the first place, despite what the others said, and it would be totally unthinkable for him to admit defeat with the boy just the other side of the door. This was Nab; whom he had found as a baby on that snowfilled night long ago; whom he had taken back to his earth and whom Tara had suckled and looked after as a cub. No; if anything happened to the boy, life for him would lose all its purpose.

As these thoughts filled Brock's mind his paws grew mercifully numb; he lost all sensation of pain and the work was now mechanical, a matter of moving his claws to the correct place and using his shoulder muscles to pull them in the right direction. Sam stood half-way between Warrigal and the door; his head cocked on one side and his ears erect, listening for any sounds. After what seemed to all the animals to be an age, Brock finally saw that there was a small hole right through the door and he gestured to Sam to come over and look. While they were both examining the hole they became aware of a light thumping noise coming up the stairs. They turned round and saw Perryfoot turning the corner of the small landing and stopping to talk to Warrigal. He looked anxious and had obviously sprinted from his post outside in great haste. The dog and the badger walked quietly along the landing to meet him.

'I heard an Urkku vehicle coming down the track. We're trapped! He's bound to see the hole in the door and come looking to see who has done it.' Suddenly, as Perryfoot was talking, the darkness on the landing was split by a great shaft of light which shone through a window at the end, and outside they could hear the unfamiliar but unmistakable sound of a car. The beam of light seemed to move across the landing as the car turned in the yard and the engine stopped and then after a few seconds it went out. Sam spoke in a hushed whisper.

'It'll be one of the two young Urkku. They often go out at night and come back at this time but they rarely go together so with luck there will only be one. I'd forgotten about it. Brock, you've nearly finished the hole. I will try and keep him downstairs for as long as I can while you complete it and bring Nab out. I'll try to keep him in the kitchen, so when you go out through the front door I'll be on your left. Don't wait for me.' He paused, and they all heard footsteps coming across the yard. Sam turned away from them and ran along the main landing and down the stairs while Brock went back to Nab's door and continued the familiar routine of scratching and biting while Perryfoot and Warrigal remained on the corner.

As Sam bounded down the stairs his head was in a turmoil trying to think of a plan to keep his master from going upstairs. He decided he would just have to take things as they came. As he reached the tiles at the bottom the door was just opening. It was the one they called Chris; of the two, this was the brother Sam preferred. He seemed to have less of a streak of cruelty in him than the other. Sam decided that he must appear overjoyed to see him; that way he would be noticed more and could play for time. He began to wag his tail furiously and jump up, panting in an attempt to try and lick his face.

'Hello, Sam. What's up with you tonight? You're very pleased I'm back. You're normally too lazy to stir yourself from the fire. I wonder what's got into you. I don't suppose it's anything to do with this door is it? It's mighty odd.' He bent down to examine the hole more closely. At least this was giving them time, Sam thought, but he must get him into the kitchen otherwise they wouldn't be able to escape from the house. As the Urkku got up Sam wagged his tail again.

'What do you want? Perhaps it's a drink you're after. Come on; I'll give you one in your bowl in the kitchen,' and he patted Sam on the head as he led him through. This was easier than Sam had anticipated even though it hadn't been planned. They went over to the sink and Chris filled Sam's bowl from the tap and put it down in a corner.

'Oh, well. I can't leave that door like that all night; it'll be freezing in the morning. I'll just put some carpet over it and then I'm off. Goodnight, Sam,' and he started towards the open kitchen door.

This is it, thought Sam, who was standing between his master and the door. He's going to go upstairs.

'Out of the way, Sam. Let me get past.'

The dog continued wagging his tail.

'You can't be hungry; I fed you myself earlier on this evening. I've given you water. Now come on, don't be silly, I'm tired,' and he tried to walk round the dog.

I'm going to have to keep him here by force, Sam thought, and he suddenly sprang back so that he was barring the doorway and began to growl with all the menace he could muster. He thought of Rufus and of all the times he'd seen this Urkku killing and maiming his friends from the woods and fields and his anger grew so that his hackles rose into a great spiked ridge along his back and his lips pulled up into furrows on either side of his mouth, showing his two great fangs and the rows of teeth behind them. He stood there with his feet set squarely apart and his body quivering, ready to pounce; little drops of saliva began to fall on to the floor. The Urkku was frightened; Sam could smell the fear and the smell stuck in his nose and made him more angry.

'Sam!' Chris said. 'Get back. What's got into you? Let me get past.' But there was no authority behind the orders; the supreme confidence that all commands would be unhesitatingly obeyed had evaporated before this transformed creature.

Upstairs Brock was frantically tearing at the hole with his mouth and on the other side, he could see, to his great relief, Nab's fingers also pulling at it. Suddenly the night was shattered by a loud cry from downstairs.

'Jeff, come and get this dog off me; it's gone mad.'

Nab would have to try and get through the hole now; there was no more time. Warrigal and Perryfoot looked desperately at Brock, who called to the boy.

'Come on,' he whispered hoarsely.

Nab put his head down and pushed it through but when he tried to follow up with his shoulders they stuck on the sharp jagged splinters at either side. He pushed harder, trying to contract so that his shoulders were hunched forward.

Inside the two bedrooms, the Urkku were waking from their

restless sleep. The cry from downstairs had finally broken into the fitful state of half dreams which had kept them tossing and turning for the past two or three hours and, when it came again, the Urkku Jeff pushed the bedclothes back, cursing quietly to himself, and got out of bed. Pausing only to reach under it for his gun he put his slippers on and ran downstairs. When he got into the kitchen he saw his brother cowering in a corner with Sam snarling ferociously in front.

How much longer would they be, thought Sam. It was impossible to keep both of them in here and, besides, he had seen what that gun could do.

Upstairs the boy was still squeezing his shoulders and arms through the hole but as he pushed, the splinters cut into his arms and scraped away the flesh. At that moment, round the corner, the old Urkku came out of the bedroom to be confronted by an owl perched on the banister post in front of him and a huge hare crouching on the landing. Warrigal stared at him, blinked twice and took off silently to glide down the little landing while the hare followed.

'Mother, come out here,' he said. 'I don't believe what I'm seeing.'

Nab was just pulling his feet through the hole when Warrigal and Perryfoot came up to them. The owl spoke.

'Come quickly. There are two Urkku on the landing blocking our way. We shall have to charge past them. Brock, you go first; you're big enough to knock them over if they are in our path. Then you, Nab, then Perryfoot and I'll come last. Don't stop for anyone and don't look back. Now, run!'

Brock steeled himself to forget about the pain in his lacerated pads and with all the energy he could gather he bolted off down the small landing, turned the corner and hurtled straight into the legs of the old farmer, who fell back against his wife as she was coming out of the bedroom door.

'Look, Mother!' he shouted, and they both stared in amazement from where they had fallen on the floor as Brock dashed past followed by the boy and then a hare and an owl. 'Stop them, Jeff!' the old man shouted. 'They're coming down the stairs.'

In the kitchen Sam, to his relief, heard the sound of the animals pounding down the stairs and saw the Urkku known as Jeff look round towards the door and begin to walk towards it. If Sam didn't move quickly the animals would be caught before they could get through. The dog sprang forward and seized his master's ankle in his teeth, pulling and wrenching at it to try and topple him over. With a cry of pain Jeff swung the rifle butt down and it caught Sam on his head so hard that for an instant he was dazed and let go. At that moment he saw Brock in the doorway followed by the others as they all dived through the hole in the front door. He dashed out into the hall just as Perryfoot's brown furry back disappeared outside.

'Quick,' said Warrigal, hovering just above him. Sam looked back into the kitchen to see Jeff limping towards them with his gun raised to his shoulder.

'I'll get you for this, you damn mongrel,' he yelled, but he was prevented from shooting because the old Master and Mistress had just appeared at the bottom of the stairs.

'Out of the way, Dad,' but Sam was through the hole and the owl had followed.

Outside the door Warrigal looked for Bruin. He was standing crouched in the shadows to the right. 'Run, Bruin,' he called. Suddenly the door opened and the yard was bathed in light; the Urkku Jeff dashed out and stood with his gun to his shoulder about to fire at the animals who were halfway towards the cowshed at the end. Bruin sprang forward, knocking him on to the ground and the gun clattered as it fell to the concrete. The old badger stood with his great weight on the man's chest so that he was pinned down and unable to move.

'Help me, Chris,' he shouted and the brother ran over and put his hands on Bruin's two front legs to try to pull him off. The badger quickly sank his fangs into the Urkku's left forearm and with a squeal of pain he staggered back. Bruin looked up and saw Sam and Warrigal turning the corner at the end of the yard and disappearing out of sight. 'They should be safe now,' he thought to himself, and he jumped off the Urkku and began to run as fast as he could after the others but his old limbs no longer had the speed of youth and, though he knew he was moving, the corner of the yard seemed to get no nearer. By the time he was halfway down it his legs had begun to ache and feel heavy with tiredness. There was plenty of time for the Urkku

Jeff to pick up his gun, take careful aim and empty both barrels into the old badger.

CHAPTER XI

When Brock had turned the corner of the yard he had waited until Nab was at his side and then they had both run without looking back until they reached the edge of Near Wood at the side of the field and they waited there, at the same tree where the animals had gathered on their way to rescue Nab, until Sam and Perryfoot joined them. There was no sign of Bruin or Warrigal. They waited, huddled up against the oak tree for shelter from the biting wind, but as time went on their hearts began to get heavy with the awful realization that something terrible had happened. Eventually out of the darkness they could see, to their relief, the shadow of the owl gliding towards them. He flew down and perched on a low branch.

'They killed him,' he said simply, as the animals looked up at him. 'I stayed behind on one of the roofs in the dark where they couldn't see me and saw everything. He died so we could escape.' Warrigal told them what had happened by the farm door and in the yard. When he had finished they all remained silent for a long time, nursing their grief until Warrigal roused them out of their state of shock by reminding them that they were still far from home and much too close to the farm for safety when dawn arrived. Wearily the animals started to walk along the side of the wood, back the way they had come earlier that night when Bruin had been with them. Contact with the Urkku had left them all emotionally shocked and the loss of Bruin had been the final horror. Brock, of course, felt his grandfather's loss more keenly than the others but he had been an extremely popular and highly respected member of the wood and none of them could grasp the fact that he was dead. And Rufus, killed as well, two of the most important members of the Council lost in the space of a day. As the animals trudged slowly homeward each became lost in a fitful daydream in which confused visions of Rufus, Bruin, the farmhouse, the doors and the Urkku all became jumbled together into a waking nightmare. Brock, Nab and Sam were also badly injured; Brock from his pads which were now so numb he could hardly feel them except for the fact that the blood made them stick to the grass as he walked, Sam from the blow on his head which was now throbbing painfully in the cold wind, and Nab whose arms and shoulders had great open cuts in them. For Nab, the joy he felt at seeing the animals again and his immense relief at being free were overshadowed with sorrow at the loss of Rufus and Bruin, both of whom, he realized, had died for him. As the sun began to rise in the grey wintry sky they were by the pond: they could see the familiar trees of Silver Wood and they began to realize that, despite the death of Bruin, they had been successful in a venture that had seemed almost impossible when they set out. Soon they were crossing the field, which was covered in a sprinkling of frost, and when they had crawled under the fence into the wood, they gathered outside Brock's earth under the Great Beech. Warrigal said that he must go off and tell Wythen but that the others should get some rest. They would meet again at dawn the following day.

'Where shall I stay?' asked Sam. They had forgotten that it would be quite impossible now for him to go back with the Urkku; he would have to remain in the wood. It was decided that the best place for him, at least temporarily, was in Nab's rhododendron bush. The animals then dispersed; Warrigal to the Great Oak, Perryfoot out to the hedge in the field, Sam and Nab to the rhododendron and Brock down the earth to face Tara with the sad news of Bruin's death but also to give her the good news of Nab's safe return. When he told her of the boy's injuries, she took Brock back up with her and the two badgers joined the boy and the dog. While Nab was sleeping she licked his wounds clean and then carried on licking so that they would heal more quickly.

The animals slept all that day and all the following night and, as they still showed no signs of waking at the appointed time, Warrigal, who had gone into the bush to see where they were, let them sleep on until the evening, by which time Brock and Sam were awake and stretching themselves to try and ease their aching limbs of the stiffness which had come over them. Sam's head and Brock's paws still hurt but now that they were refreshed after their delicious sleep they felt far more able to cope with their injuries. Just then Perryfoot came in to join them and Brock went over and licked Nab's face. The boy sprang up in fear but when he realized where he was he almost cried with joy and he went round greeting all the animals in turn and thanking them for rescuing him, for he realized he had not had time before. He told them everything that had happened from the time he and Rufus had spotted the Urkku in the wood until he'd heard the knocking on the window and opened the curtains to see, to his amazement and relief, Warrigal perched outside.

'I have called an emergency Council Meeting for tonight,' said the owl when everyone had settled down. 'The wood must be told of events; rumours are going round already of a mass slaughter of all the Council leaders. No Urkku have been seen near the wood since we got back so it would seem that, for the time being at any rate, you are safe here, Nab. Wythen has been to see the Elflord and he has indicated that the time has now come for you to meet him. Brock will go with you and I will take you there. I have been once before, as is the custom when an owl reaches his maturity, and my father feels that, as he is getting older, I should make myself better acquainted with the Elflord. We will set out immediately after the Council Meeting.'

So, thought Brock, this was the time he had been dreading ever since Warrigal had told him that the Elflord was involved. In fact it came as something of a relief in a way, that the moment had finally come. Nab was extremely excited at the prospect although he also felt little butterflies of fear fluttering in his stomach, not so much at the prospect of meeting the Elflord but at the thought of what might be revealed to him about his future. Ever since he could remember veiled references and allusions had been made about his part in the destiny of the animals and how he was the fulfilment of a legend. Now perhaps he would learn what they all meant.

Warrigal interrupted their thoughts.

'Come on,' he said. 'It's time to go.'

Most of the animals had already arrived at the familiar semi-circle on the far side of the little stream, eager to learn the true story of what had happened two nights ago for fantastic tales had already begun to circulate about the rescue. The Council were all sitting in their places along the far side of the old fallen tree trunk although the vacant places at the end of the log where Bruin and Rufus usually sat made it painfully obvious that the events of that night had been fatal to two of the most respected members of the wood.

Everywhere was covered with a silver coating of ground frost which winked and sparkled in the moonlight and made the dead bracken on the ground hard and crunchy so that as Brock, Tara, Sam, Perryfoot and, last of all, Nab, walked into the meeting the sound of their footsteps made all eyes turn towards them and a sudden murmur of conversation rippled among the animals. Feeling very embarrassed, the animals sat down just to the left of the entrance in a space hurriedly vacated for them by some rabbits at a ·sign from Pictor. Warrigal had flown into the clearing over the top of the bushes and was perched on a silver birch branch to the right of the log. Wythen's head turned slowly round until he saw his son and then he looked back at the semi-circle where all the woodland animals were now waiting expectantly for him to open the meeting.

'Welcome to you all,' he said, as he always did whenever he first addressed a meeting. 'I have called this emergency Council together so that the wood may be informed of certain dramatic, and indeed tragic events which took place two nights ago. In the broadest terms they concern the capture and, as you can see, the successful rescue of Nab from the hands of the Urkku.' He waited until the shuffling of the animals as they all turned to look at the boy had stopped and then he continued. 'As you may also see, these events led to the deaths, caused by the Urkku, of Bruin the Brave and Rufus the Red, both of whom will be sorely missed, both by myself personally for they were my friends, and by the wood as a whole. I feel sure, however, that their names and exploits will live on for ever in the annals of legend and myth so that they will never die and their spirits will watch over us.' He paused and there was an expectant hush. 'I will now call upon

99

Nab to give an account of his capture and the killing of Rufus.'

The events of the past two days and nights had been so swift moving and shattering that Nab was still half-dazed by them and, when Brock pushed him forward, he had no time to be nervous and gave a vivid account of everything that had happened since he and Rufus first spotted the Urkku outside Silver Wood. Indeed, as he was recounting the events he began to live through them again so that the story became alive and at the end when he'd finished there was silence.

As he sat down again, exhausted with the emotional effort of reliving that night, Brock, Perryfoot and Sam were almost speechless with amazement at the full realization of what had happened and at the part they had each played. When everyone had calmed down, Wythen called on Sam and Brock to relate their sides of the story and finally Warrigal gave an account of Bruin's brave death. The picture was now complete and the tale would become legend as it was told and re-told in burrows or earths, holes or nests on balmy summer evenings or on wild winter nights. It would lose something in the telling but it would also gain something and the animal who told it would be proud to say, 'I knew Sam,' or 'Brock and I used to have long talks together.'

When Warrigal had finished speaking, Wythen, sensing that there was no more to be said, slowly turned away from the meeting and flew up to join his son. All the animals, at this sign that the meeting was over, then began to disperse. They were lost in thought, each with his own private ideas, but when they returned to the privacy of their homes there would be endless discussion and analysis of the story and of the serious consequences to which it might lead. When Nab had first come to the wood many of them had felt that they were on the threshold of history and some of them now believed that this was the beginning.

Warrigal flew down while the rest of the animals were making their way back through the entrance or through the trees and told Nab and Brock that Wythen wanted to speak to them under the silver birch at the edge of the semi-circle and that then they would have to leave. The badger and the boy sadly turned to the others to wish them farewell. Warrigal then said that the whereabouts of

Brock and Nab should be kept secret at all costs; it was a matter that must not be disclosed until the time was right. Brock and Tara rubbed noses affectionately; she was very proud of him now as he was about to leave the wood to meet the Elflord, and she was pleased for him that his disappointment with himself in not preventing Nab being captured seemed to have gone. He was back to his old self; confident, a little arrogant, and full of excitement about the future. Nab then came up to her and, putting his hands deep in the fur around her neck, he rubbed his forehead against hers. She was full of apprehensions and fears about the safety of this boy, whom she loved dearly. All the early times in the wood; when he had been little and they had played together and she had told him stories as she held him in her forepaws; they all seemed so long ago now. The prophecies of legend and the paths of destiny had then seemed to belong to another world. Now it seemed that world was coming closer to draw them in and there was nothing she could do about it; the stage was set and the actors already chosen and all she could do was watch and play her part as best she could.

After what seemed a long time but was in fact only a few seconds, Nab let go of her fur and stroked Sam and Perryfoot before turning away and walking off towards the birch with Brock and Warrigal. The dog and the hare also felt an affection for Nab which they found hard to explain; they had already risked their lives once to rescue him and they knew that they would do it again and again if necessary without a thought. They would dearly have liked to go with the others but Warrigal had told them that Wythen had been given precise instructions by the Elflord as to whom he wanted to see and that they were to remain in Silver Wood in case they were needed.

When Brock and Nab arrived at the silver birch where they were to meet Wythen they stopped and looked back across the empty clearing to see the others standing by the entrance gazing over at them. For a second the two groups stared at each other and then, with Perryfoot leading, the three turned away and disappeared through the gap in the trees. Suddenly Wythen appeared with Warrigal at his side. He spoke very slowly and his clear voice had an almost mesmerizing effect, as if he was willing his audience to remember every word.

'I have given Warrigal directions and he will take you. None of you has been to Tall Wood before. It is where the Elflord resides. In the language of the old ones it is named Ellmondrill, the Enchanted Forest. It is not a perilous place but for the first time it may be frightening in that all is not what it may seem. Do not be afraid; once you are there you are safe. The Urkku do not go into the wood for it has the reputation amongst them of being a dangerous place; those that have ventured in have come out with their minds turned for the Elflord works strong magic to retain his refuge. It is now Moon-High; if you travel carefully, keeping well hidden, you should arrive on the outskirts of the wood by dusk tomorrow. Do not hurry; it is vital that you are not seen by anyone, for the suspicions of the Urkku must not be aroused any more than they already have been. Now, farewell.'

They turned and walked slowly away through the wood, their minds preoccupied with Wythen's words. Warrigal of course knew all of what his father had just said for they had been talking almost continuously since he had returned after the rescue of Nab. Although the young owl had possessed a vague knowledge of these affairs before (and had pretended he knew more), this was the first time that Wythen had spoken to him directly about Elvenlore in a deliberate attempt to pass on his knowledge. The fact that Wythen was not going himself with Nab and Brock was a further indication that he appeared to be sharing the Patriarchate of the Owls with his son. Warrigal was flattered and pleased but also a little afraid at the thought of his new responsibility.

For Brock and Nab, walking together through the moonlit wood, the references to danger and the innuendoes of magic and legend had served to strengthen the grip of the apprehensive fears they both felt.

It was a wonderful night; the air was full of the keenness of the frost and all the damp leafy smells that frost brings out. Nab breathed it deeply and became almost intoxicated by it so that his whole being hummed with vibrant excitement and his mind seemed to float. All the excitements and tragedies and pain of the past few days came together in a confused blur that filled him with a feeling of limitless energy which seemed to fit perfectly the spirit of the journey they were now making. He looked at Brock and, as he watched the wonderfully familiar black and white figure plodding along beside him, his nose snuffling along the ground, lost in the smells of the night, he felt the warm glow of love surge through him. Suddenly in a burst of exhilaration he fell on the badger and they wrestled together joyfully on top of the frosty bracken which crunched and crackled under them. Then Warrigal's hooting from an oak tree at the edge of the wood reminded them that they should be on their way and they raced each other to where the owl was sitting perched on an exposed length of root, watching them and chuckling quietly to himself with pleasure at seeing his old friend so full of fun again after the sadness of his self-recrimination when the boy was captured. Something about the night and the sense of adventure they felt about the journey they were on had affected them all.

The badger and the boy crawled under the bottom strand of old rusty barbed wire which fenced off the wood and then they were out on to the moonlit fields, walking up the slope at the back of the wood and following the silent shadow in front of them as he turned and flew along the top of the rise. Every so often Warrigal would stop at a convenient tree and wait for the others to catch up and then they would move on again through the night.

As the first rose-pink streaks of dawn appeared on the lightening sky the three were down by the big stream, near the spot where Nab had met the girl. For a time he walked along in silence thinking of her and wondering whether he would ever see her again and then slowly he realized that the countryside around him was strange and new and with a thrill it occurred to him that he was now outside the boundaries of his previous experience. This was further than he had ever been before. He looked around him intently as the morning sun slowly came up beyond the hill away to his left and filled the sky with a brilliant mass of orange and dark flaming reds. The steep-sided valley through which they had followed the stream had now gradually opened out so that they were in a shallow basin with the fields sloping away upwards very gently on either side. There were not many trees now to break up the rolling meadows: only the thick thorn hedges dividing the fields into squares or rectangles and providing refuge and a home for birds and sometimes rabbits. The stream on Nab's right had now widened slightly and it meandered less, running along its sandy bed almost straight for a while until suddenly for no apparent reason it began once again to twist and curve and water willows sprang up at either side growing thick and dense along the banks. Warrigal stopped at one of these and showed the others where two of the trees had fallen across the stream and so formed a convenient bridge.

'We go across here,' said Warrigal. 'Then we cross two fields and make for that belt of trees you can see straight ahead. Behind those trees lies Ellmondrill. I think you two should stay at the side of the hedges where possible from now on; Urkku may be around and we can't be too careful. There's a farm on top of that hill to the right. Can you see it?'

They looked and saw a collection of buildings clustered around the top of the rise in the distance. Then they gingerly inched their way across the fallen willows and set off along the far bank of the stream until they came to a thick hedge which ran in from the field to meet it, and then they turned and moved along the side of this as it took them out into open country.

They travelled like that for the rest of the short winter day, keeping well under cover of hedges and moving slowly, constantly looking round and sniffing the air for scents of danger. The sun shone brightly out of the clear blue sky and the early morning frost soon disappeared, giving way to a day that was so warm that the animals occasionally had to think twice to remind themselves that it was the middle of winter. The feel of the sun and the smells that it produced as it warmed up the ground filled them full of yearning for the spring and, as they walked, Nab and Brock chatted quietly about past springs and their times together. Nab also asked the badger to tell him once again the story of that night so many years ago when Brock had found him in the snow; he never tired of hearing it and it sounded different every time it was told. And when the story was finished there were always endless questions of detail, particularly about the two Urkku who had brought him. Somehow the story always made him feel secure and warm and comforted him whenever he was anxious or worried. It had that effect now and the nervousness which had been building up inside him as they got closer to Ellmon-drill subsided and was replaced with a feeling of quiet confidence and certainty.

Around the time of Sun-High they were delayed by a flock of sheep. They had been walking quietly along the hedge of the field in which the sheep were grazing when suddenly, hearing strange sounds and seeing the badger and the boy, they had bolted and an Urkku had come down to the field from the farm on his tractor to investigate. They squeezed through a gap in the hedge and watched him as he drove around the field. His tractor chugged loudly and pushed out puffs of grey smoke which hung in the still air for a long while after he'd gone, growing bigger but less dense so that in the end they became so thin that they disappeared completely.

He drove around the field two or three times and then, having satisfied himself that there was nothing to worry about, he turned his tractor around and drove back up the fields to the farm.

The travellers waited a short time to make certain he wasn't coming back and to let the sheep settle again, and then they resumed their journey. They had been walking towards the distant trees since early morning and had seemed to be getting no nearer, but now, as the afternoon wore on and the blue sky began to turn grey and wintry, the trees became clearer and more distinct even though a mist had appeared which filled the fields with a grey haze and blurred the outlines of the hedges. The fields now seemed to be smaller and the hedges thicker and soon they found themselves walking along a narrow path bordered on either side by hedges which were so dense that they could see nothing through them. They walked on as if they were in a tunnel towards the patch of grey they could see at the far end until, suddenly, they were out in an open meadow, standing at the top of a steep slope and looking down at a stream which moved restlessly along at the bottom. It chattered and gurgled in the still-ness, and beyond it stood Tall Wood, shrouded in the evening mist, dark and impenetrable except for the occasional burst of gold as the evening sun, perched just above it, managed to breach the blanket of mist. The trio stood for a long time, gazing in awe and wonder at this magical sight, until finally Warrigal broke the silence.

105

'Come on,' he said. 'We must cross the stream before it gets dark so that we can spend the night in the wood. Once we're there we are safe and the elves can contact us. Wythen said that we don't go to them; they will find us. All we must do is simply to be there.'

The owl took off and flew slowly down the slope and the others followed him, too exhilarated to be nervous. As they walked towards the wood the trees loomed out of the mist and seemed to grow taller. It was very damp and the stream rushed along so loudly that they had to shout to be heard. Warrigal was looking for a fallen oak that Wythen had said could be used to get across. They waited while he flew along the stream and then walked along the bank to join him when he indicated that he'd found it. Nab went first, sitting astride the tree and shuffling along with his hands in front to support and steady himself. When he was halfway across he looked down at the stream below him; it was very full after the recent rains and it swirled and eddied along with furious determination and purpose. Then he looked back up and stared into the darkness of the wood ahead of him before gingerly inching his way across the last half of the slippery bridge; the constant damp from the stream had coated the tree with patches of slimy green mould and the mist had made them extremely treacherous so that once or twice the boy almost slipped, but his strong legs managed to hold him on. Finally, with great relief, he arrived on the far bank and stood watching Brock, who was looking extremely precarious as he approached the halfway stage. Brock's claws would normally have been a great help as they would have sunk through the slimy surface into the bark of the oak but they were still sore and he found it difficult to use them properly. Suddenly, on a particularly bad patch, he began to teeter and in moving his feet to try to obtain a better grip he fell over and plunged with a loud splash into the stream. The sight of the badger toppling into the water struck Nab as so funny that, against all his better instincts, he was unable to stop himself laughing and, when he clambered down the bank to help the badger out of the water and saw the thick coat plastered down around his body, the boy's laughter only increased until the tears came to his eyes. In fact, he was so busy laughing that he failed to notice the badger manoeuvring himself into position at his side so that when Brock began to shake himself vigorously the first shower of icy cold water that hit him came as a complete surprise and he stood still in a state of shock while Brock soaked him; much to the amusement of Warrigal, who was still standing on the far bank laughing to himself.

When Nab had got himself as dry as possible by rubbing his body with some old ferns that he gathered from the bank and by jumping up and down, the three animals turned their faces to the wood and began to make their way through the undergrowth which consisted of the debris from last year's summer: dead bracken and ferns and briars that scratched Nab's legs and made them itch. The floor of the wood was a thick carpet of rotting leaves; not golden and crisp as in the days of autumn but black and slimy as they began to decompose.

Every three or four paces about them, on every side, was a tree, tall and black, and sometimes an elder or a small holly would bar their way so that they were forced to go round. Warrigal flew low from tree to tree and the badger and the boy followed. They hadn't gone far before Nab looked back to the stream and was surprised and a little dismayed to find that he could not see it. He could not even see where the edge of the wood was, for in no one direction was there any more light than in any other. With a little jolt of fear he realized that, if he had wanted to go back the way he'd come, he wouldn't have been able to. They were totally lost. He listened for the stream but could hear nothing; everywhere was completely still except for the gentle rustling of the tops of the trees as they swayed in the wind high above them and the sound of their footsteps as they padded over the damp leaves or occasionally cracked a twig. Even these sounds were quickly absorbed by the silence so that they appeared muted. After a while another thing struck Nab; there were no animals or birds anywhere to be seen and the only indication that there might be any living creatures in the wood at all were the huge, squirrels' dreys way up in the tops of the trees. He began to grow a little afraid; it was no

107

wonder that the Urkku never approached Ellmondrill.

As they walked on through the mist Nab became aware that the undergrowth, which normally reached no higher than his knees, was brushing against his chest and, rather than walk through it or over it, it was easier to go under. He stopped for a second and looked up; he could hardly see the tops of the trees now and the sky appeared as little specks of grey between the distant foliage. When he looked back down at the trunks of the trees, they seemed enormous and he found himself staring at the protruding roots which were as high as he was. In desperate panic he looked for the others; Brock was still walking slowly and calmly along at his side while Warrigal was perched on top of a huge fern ahead of them. He thought of Wythen's words before they left; 'all is not what it may seem; do not be afraid', and resolved to try not to show his fear.

Further and deeper into the wood they went and Nab wrestled more and more to keep his panic under control. The trees now seemed altogether different as he walked in a subterranean under-world where the woodland fungi reached to his shoulders and the chewed-up remains of the nuts from a squirrel's hoard presented an obstacle which could only be clambered over with difficulty. The huge oaks and elms, towering way above, seemed to be watching him as the gods watch the creatures on earth; the furrows and cracks on their bark looked like deep valleys cut into them, each one unique in its pattern and colour and each with a different character. Nab also grew aware of the silent sound of the earth; a constant whisper and hum as if it were the noise of life itself.

Then the character of the wood changed, the undergrowth stopped and instead they were walking on a carpet of pine needles and the smell of fir was all around. This was a different world where the trees were always green and the changing seasons left no mark; a constant world of twilight. Here, even their footsteps could not be heard and the wind seemed unable to penetrate the hushed atmosphere. Nab began to feel tired but his fears were subsiding as he grew more used to the wood. Warrigal had perched on an exposed tree root and was staring in front while Brock and the boy caught him up. The owl's eyes were shining, unblinking and filled with a strange light that they had not seen before.

'Ellmondrill,' he said slowly under his breath, and then he repeated the word louder, taking a long time to say it and intoning it as if it were a magical chant. They stood still for a while; the owl looking straight ahead and the other two behind him, neither wishing to break the silence and content to let their minds wander where they wished. After a period of time which would have been impossible to measure in the world outside the wood, Nab became aware of Brock whispering fiercely at his side.

'Look, look ahead,' he was saying, and he pointed in the direction that Warrigal was facing. Nab did not find it easy to collect his thoughts and focus his eyes but when he looked hard he could just make out in the far distance, through the mist and the gloom, two bright lights like stars, silver and twinkling, and moving towards them slowly.

'It's the elves,' Brock said, and there was wonder in his voice.

The two silver stars bobbed and weaved towards them and then suddenly they were directly in front. Warrigal turned to the others.

'We have to follow them,' he said, and, as if on a word of command, the lights moved back again into the distance. Mesmerized, the animals set off after them. Soon they left the area of the pines and were in a part of the wood which was more open and less cluttered than that which they had so far gone through. The undergrowth here was a mixture of mosses and ferns and grass and the trees seemed very old. Often they came across a huge fallen trunk and had to decide whether it was easier to climb over it or go round while Warrigal perched on top patiently. The two lights always seemed to stay the same distance away and sometimes they would appear to be chasing each other round and round in the air as if playing a game. Watching them closely Nab sometimes thought that he could make out little figures inside the lights but then, when he blinked, they vanished until he screwed his eyes up so as not to be dazzled by the brightness and once again the figures would appear. He became completely engrossed in this and his tiredness and fear were forgotten. Brock, at his side, was caught up in the wonder of it all and seemed fired with a hidden energy that he had not known since he was a cub. They had no idea how far they were walking nor how long it was taking them; time seemed to have been suspended ever since they entered the wood and the deeper they had gone the more difficult had it become to imagine any world outside. It seemed an eternity since they had stood at the top of the slope in the field and looked down for the first time at Ellmondrill.

The lights had now stopped and were dancing in front of a belt of trees which seemed so thick to the animals that they were unable to see how they could get through; the trees were so close to one another that the trunks almost met. The lights then began to move slowly off to one side and the animals followed until after a short distance they stopped again and Nab could just make out a gap between two great oaks. The lights disappeared through it and then Warrigal indicated to Nab that he was to go first. The boy got down on his hands and knees and began to crawl slowly along what was in fact a tunnel between the trees. Inside it was dark, but the light that came from the far end enabled him to see where he was going and to make out very dimly the dark polished wooden sides. Under his hands the wood felt smooth and reminded him of the roots around the inside doorway of the sett in Silver Wood: worn smooth by generations of use. The light behind him was cut off as Brock and then Warrigal entered the passage and the three animals shuffled slowly along; the sounds of their breathing echoing loudly inside it.

Soon they emerged from the darkness of the tunnel and found themselves in a large clearing. The belt of trees continued all around it and the edge of the clearing was filled with lights similar to those which had guided them, all dancing and leaping around and through the air. The floor was covered with mosses and lichens, merging and blending into one another so that they formed a continuous carpet of velvet so soft that Nab's feet sank in it up to his ankles. Mist lay everywhere but unlike the mist in the rest of the wood which had been grey and swirling this was still and golden as if the evening sun were shining through it and it blurred the edges of the trees and grasses with a soft, gentle haze.

In the middle of the clearing was a pond, dark and black as night, whose waters shone like a jewel and, at the very centre of the pond, stood a small island on which stood a huge oak tree whose gnarled fingers swept low over it, casting their shadows in the deep waters.

Nab looked at his two companions, who were standing at his side

111

entranced by the sight, and laid a hand on Brock's head. He felt in need of some reassurance that his body had not melted away in the golden haze all around.

Two lights suddenly appeared in front of them again, although Nab could not be sure whether or not they were their guides. He could see the elves inside quite clearly now and realized that the light was simply the silver glow which came from their bodies.

'Come, the Lord Wychnor awaits,' said one, and in a flash it had vanished down to the shore of the pond. The animals walked slowly and carefully through the moss, which grew spongy as they approached the water so that at times they were afraid of sinking. Nab noticed that even Warrigal was walking; a sight he had never seen before, and he guessed that the owl had not taken to the air out of respect.

At the edge of the pond floated what looked to Nab like a huge brown oak leaf which bobbed gently up and down on the water and whose edges curled up slightly.

'Please step in,' said the elf. Overawed as they were by their surroundings and impressed as they were by the elf this was a request which the three animals were extremely wary of complying with. They guessed now that the Elflord dwelt on the island in the middle of the pond and that somehow they had to get there, but the thought of floating across those black waters on the flimsy looking vessel that the elf had indicated was a prospect which they did not relish.

'I am not going over the water in that,' whispered Brock fiercely to Warrigal. He had had quite enough of falling in water for one day, and besides, the stream was only narrow compared to the size of the pond they had to cross now. Warrigal, however, appeared less than sympathetic to the badger's fear and told him to get in.

'Come on,' he said to the badger, and Brock, using extreme caution, clambered reluctantly into the vessel and settled down on one side.

'You next,' Warrigal said to Nab, and the boy, whose fears equalled his excitement, climbed in the other side and then Warrigal followed him and settled down in the rear. Finally the elf hopped in and went to the front, where he stood with his face raised to the sky and began to sing in a strange voice which seemed to fill the clearing.

The language was one with which the animals were completely unfamiliar, although Warrigal thought that he recognized some of the sounds from the words that Wythen sometimes used in conversation.

'It's the language of the Old Ones,' he said quietly to the other two, who were staring at the elf, completely enraptured.

The song ceased as abruptly as it had begun and the animals saw a large ripple moving across the water from the far side of the pond. They watched as it came nearer until finally it stopped at the front of their vessel and the elf leant over the edge and busied himself with some activity in the water. Finally he finished and turned around to face the animals, at which point the leaf started to move slowly and steadily towards the island.

The elf smiled at them. 'In return for taking us across the water he demands a song,' he said, and the three animals nodded in understanding, none of them wishing to show his ignorance by asking who exactly it was that demanded a song.

'Who does he mean?' whispered Brock to Warrigal, but the owl pretended he hadn't heard. Nab looked over the side into the black depths beneath them and thought he could make out a large oval shape under the water moving along with them, but he couldn't be sure and it may only have been a reflection.

Soon they were right out in the middle of the pond and a long way from the shore. Now that they had settled down the animals felt safer, and had begun to enjoy the feeling of being afloat, an experience none of them had ever had before. What they found particularly strange was the feeling of moving while sitting down and doing nothing. They were travelling quite fast now and, although it was so still in the clearing, their speed gave the sensation of a light breeze which ruffled Warrigal's feathers and blew through Brock's fur; Nab turned his head directly into it so that his hair was blown back from his face and when he closed his eyes his mind seemed to float away behind him. Then when he opened them again and looked back at the shore he got a shock when he saw how far away it seemed. He watched the wake which the leaf left behind it; a series of little waves which disturbed the smooth calm surface of the water for a short time and then slowly disappeared as the pond became still again. He looked over the side and delicately put a finger in so that it cut a bubbling gash in the water, the crest of which danced with little silver jewels before they melted back into the pond. Looking up he saw that they were now very close to the island and the leaf seemed to be slowing down. Suddenly they were shaken by a series of little judders as it came to rest in the shallows; the elf once again leant over into the water and then the ripples moved away to where they had come from on the far shore.

They got out of the leaf with a strange feeling of regret that the journey was over, for contrary to all their expectations they had enjoyed it. It had also taken their minds off the meeting with the Elflord, about which they were extremely apprehensive. Now that they had finally arrived they began to grow afraid.

'Follow me,' said the elf, and he walked up the short bank from the pond towards the huge oak. Unlike the far shore the ground here was covered in a mass of dead leaves all of which were the size of the one that had served to carry them across the water. When they were almost at the foot of the tree the elf told them to wait and went out of sight to the far side of the trunk. The three animals turned back to look across the water at the clearing. It was growing dark now and on the opposite shore the silver lights of the elves showed up clearly as hundreds of little stars, like the dew sparkling on an autumn morning. The mist had gone now and the patch of sky which they could see above them was turning from light to dark blue; it was that indefinable magic moment when a winter evening becomes night. Soon the elf was back.

'Come with me,' he said, and they followed him round the trunk of the tree.

CHAPTER XII

The entrance to the tree, for it was hollow, was a large pointed archway, the edges of which were framed with moss. The elf led the animals through it into a circular hall, the floor of which was again covered in a carpet of green moss. Around the walls seats had been carved into the wood and they were taken across to one side of the hall and asked to sit for a short while.

'Welcome to the Elvenoak,' said the elf. 'My name is Reev and I will be your guide and friend while you are here. I have spoken to the Lord Wychnor and he wishes you to spend the night with us for he will see you on the morrow. I must now go and arrange some sustenance; I am certain you must be hungry. I will call you shortly,' and he walked lightly away over the velvety carpet to a circular flight of steps which had been cut into the wall and which wound round the inside of the hall until it disappeared through the ceiling above them. When he had gone the animals relaxed and looked about them, talking amongst themselves and exploring. What seemed strange at first was that though it was dark outside now, there was still plenty of light in the hall but on looking round the walls Nab discovered little patches of bright orange lichen which gave off a warm glow and it was these, combined with the light that came from a number of small fungi growing out of the moss, that enabled them to see as if it were a summer twilight. As they walked around they found strange carvings sculpted into the wood, some portraying the mythical events with which old Bruin had made them so familiar and

others that related legends and stories they had never heard. As their eyes grew more used to the light they saw that even the stairs and the seats were decorated with ornate and intricate patterns which Warrigal said were ancient runes. There were a number of doors set flush with the walls and twice while they were waiting an elf came out, gave them a greeting and walked through the front archway into the night. When the door was open they could see stairs behind leading upwards which were smaller than the main stairway.

While they were looking at a particularly large carving which Warrigal was attempting to explain, Reev called to them and they turned around to see him standing halfway up the stairs.

'Your room is ready now,' he said, and the animals, who had not eaten since they left Silver Wood, gratefully walked across the hall and climbed the stairs. The last time they had seen stairs was in the

116

Urkku dwelling where Nab had been captured and they shuddered with fear and revulsion at the memories that came back to them. These were different; the dark wood had been worn smooth and the edges of the stairs were rounded and shaped so that walking up them was a delight. As they got higher they looked over the side at the hall below and saw the orange glow flickering against the burnished wood of the carvings. Suddenly they were standing at the end of a winding corridor with doors on either side, and Reev led them off the stairs, which continued to wind around upwards, and took them down the corridor and round some corners until they came to a door which he opened and ushered them through.

'This is where you'll stay tonight,' he said. 'I think you will find everything you want; food is on the floor in the corner; but if you require anything just pull that briar that you see hanging from the roof. I will call you in the morning when the Elflord will speak with you.' He paused and smiled at them. 'I bid you goodnight; may your dreams be touched with silver.'

The room was small but extremely comfortable. Along one wall was a mass of fresh meadowsweet for Brock and Nab to sleep on and a stout branch had been provided for Warrigal's perch. It had been placed on the dark wood floor next to a small round hole in the outside wall through which the moon was shining, sending in a shaft of light which bathed the little room in silver. The animals went over to the window and looked out at the clearing. Warrigal was of course used to looking down at things from a great height but for Nab and Brock it was wonderful to survey a scene from above. The moon seemed to be shining out of the pond, so brightly was it reflected in the still, black water, and the trees sparkled as the frost brushed their branches with glitter. They stood for a long time, gazing out at the picture below them until its memory was so firmly implanted that, whenever they wanted to later, they could recall every minute detail and always with a feeling of calmness and serenity.

Eventually their stomachs began to remind them that they were hungry and they reluctantly turned away and went over to the corner in which Reev had said there was something to eat. There in carved wooden bowls and dishes they found a selection of food and drink that was bewildering in its variety. There were all the usual things which they were accustomed to, but they came from all the seasons, not just winter, and Nab marvelled at their exquisite flavours and the odd fact that they seemed to taste so much better than they did at home. There were some dishes which contained familiar things but which were warm as if they had been heated in the sun; hot portions of puffball and boletus that seemed to melt away in the mouth without the need to chew and which tasted completely different from when they were cold. There were other dishes which contained foods they had never seen before, and they took a long time cautiously exploring these new flavours and textures, each reporting to the other his views on the contents of a certain bowl and being advised in return to try a bowl which the other had just investigated. Interspersed among the foods were bowls of crystal clear water which sparkled and seemed to fill the drinker with energy. The animals discovered that even these were different; some were of a delicate pink and had the sweet savour of rosehips while others were more of a

reddish hue and reminded the animals of clover. There was one of which Brock was particularly fond; it was a rich golden colour and tasted how the badger imagined meadowsweet would taste in a drink. He found that it went particularly well with the flavour of the hot portions of puffball and he spent a long time by the two bowls that contained these delicacies taking a mouthful of the white fungus and following it with a sip of the golden water.

Finally, when the moon was high up in the night sky, the animals stopped eating and, feeling as content and secure as they had ever felt, settled down to sleep; Brock and Nab with the fresh scent of meadowsweet surrounding them to remind Brock of Tara and the sett and Nab of the days when he was young and would curl up against Tara's warm fur at night, and Warrigal perched on the branch, his liquid brown eyes closed, thinking of Wythen and the number of times his father must have stayed here on previous occasions. Their long journey and the excitement they had gone through had left them more exhausted than they had realized and immediately their eyes closed they were off into the light but restful sleep of the wild animal, and whether it was the food or the drink or the moon they could not be sure but their dreams seemed touched with silver as Reev had wished them.

They were woken next morning by the sunlight pouring in through the window and when they looked outside they could see a thick layer of hoar frost on the trees and the ground, covering everything in white. At that moment Reev came in.

'Welcome to the day,' he said, and the sing-song sound of his voice chased away the shadows. 'Have you glanced outside? We are blessed with a frost; a wonderful day. A good day for you to meet the Lord Wychnor.' He danced over to the empty bowls on the floor and began to chuckle quietly to himself. 'My, you were hungry. You enjoyed your food.' He pulled the bramble briar and three elves came in carrying more bowls full of food and put them down in place of last night's, which they then took away on wooden trays.

'The morning is yours,' he said. 'When you have eaten you may do as you wish; walk around outside, explore the pond; and I will meet you at Sun-High in the hall downstairs whence I shall take you to meet the Elflord.' He went out as suddenly as he had come in, and the animals, to their surprise, found themselves as hungry as ever and began to eat once more.

'I shall forget what it's like to have to go and find food,' said Brock with his mouth full of bilberries, but in spite of himself and all the wonder and magic of this place he found himself thinking of Silver Wood with a little ache of homesickness.

'I suppose once we have seen the Lord Wychnor we shall leave,' said Nab, who knew how the badger was feeling but whose excitement did not allow him any room to think of home. He knew that he was about to learn about himself, and his apprehension at the thought of this, coupled with an intense curiosity, made him begin to feel terribly nervous and to realize that, in their fascination with everything around them, they had forgotten the main purpose of their visit.

When the bowls were empty again and the animals were replete, Nab pushed open the door to their room and they walked back along the corridor and down the stairway into the hall where they had waited last night. It looked different now with the sunlight streaming in through the entrance, making the corners it didn't reach seem dark in contrast and throwing great bands of light on to the mossy floor, turning it into a bright emerald green: the colour of the young beech leaves when they first start to unfurl in the spring. There was much coming and going with elves rushing in and out through the doors leading off the hall, meeting and talking and laughing as they went about their business, going outside and coming in again. To the animals they gave the impression of always being on the move; full of a restless vibrant energy with quicksilver minds and bodies that danced about ceaselessly. Their voices filled the hall with music and reminded Nab of the sound of the stream behind Silver Wood as it chuckled and tinkled its way over the pebbles on its sandy bed. In the sunlight the glow from their bodies seemed less bright than it had done yesterday evening but it was still there and as they moved it seemed to leave a trail behind so that it was difficult to see exactly where they were at any single moment except when they were standing still, which was never for very long.

The animals made their way through the hall slowly, feeling ponderous and slightly clumsy as well as extremely conspicuous. The elves all seemed aware of their presence and none showed any surprise as they walked past; each one giving them a different greeting but all bade them welcome before going on their way.

Nab emerged first into the sunlight and had to screw up his eyes for a short time until he got used to it. Then they all walked down to the shore, scrunching over the oak leaves on the ground which were still crisp with frost, and made their way around the edge of the pond. They found themselves strangely relieved when they realized, after walking for a while, that they were out of sight of the entrance and they settled down on a stone behind some tall rushes and sat for a long time without saying a word, staring down at the water and listening to the sound of some little waves, stirred up by a light breeze, as they lapped gently against the shore. It was good to be on their own again and eventually they all felt more relaxed and began talking about everything that had happened to them since they first entered Ellmondrill. Soon they were all talking at once, each with his different ideas and views and opinions, until Warrigal interrupted.

'Come on, we'd better be making our way back. It's almost Sun-

High,' he said, and a little sadly they got up and, with the sun on their backs, went back to the entrance and through it into the hall.

The bustle of the morning had subsided now and there were just a few elves passing through. It seemed very dark inside after being out in the bright sunshine and it took a while for their eyes to adjust so that they could see clearly. Reev had spotted them from the other side and he came over to address them before they had had a chance to see him.

'You enjoyed your morning,' he said. 'You smell of sunshine. Come; Lord Wychnor is waiting,' and he walked off up the main stairs. The animals followed him as he went up the way they had gone to their room last night, past their door, along to the end of the corridor and then up a new flight of stairs which seemed to go on for ever. Every so often there was a crack or a hole in the wall and, when they peeped cautiously out, they realized that they were climbing higher and higher as the clearing grew smaller beneath them and soon they came level with the tops of the trees on the other side of the pond. They could see the great squirrels' dreys nestling amongst the stark black winter branches and sometimes they saw a squirrel sitting patiently on the twigs and staring out over the tops of the trees in the rest of the wood to the fields beyond.

'They keep a constant vigil for signs of danger, approaching Urkku and so on,' said Warrigal, when Nab asked him what they were doing.

A door suddenly appeared before them; a great door set in a high curved archway, heavy and laid across with bands of silver which formed a criss-cross pattern. A rope made of many bramble briars woven together hung down to one side, and Reev pulled it while the animals waited nervously. Then the door opened and they were ushered into a high circular chamber by two elves dressed in green and brown who led them along an aisle which ran straight through the middle towards a raised dais at the far end. Nab, his heart in his mouth and his stomach fluttering with nerves, stole a glance around him and saw elves gathered in little groups; some were dancing, others were seated on the floor and appeared to be working with their hands while still others were making music from strange instruments, some of which were composed of strings which they plucked with

121

their fingers and others which they held to their mouths to produce cascades of high pure crystal notes. Nab felt the music take his soul and send it soaring through the air until it felt as if it had broken through the roof of the chamber to fly off into the grey, winter sky; it filled him with energy so that, as he moved, the rhythms of his body coincided with the spirit of the music and he found himself dancing in time with it as he followed Reev. He also became aware of the fact that they were all being looked at with some curiosity by the elves, and there was a sustained level of animated discussion as the elves stopped what they were doing and put their heads together to talk excitedly amongst themselves. Nab felt that he in particular had been singled out for special attention and, as he walked down the centre of the enormous chamber into which the sun was sending streams of light through the little windows in the outside walls, he could feel hundreds of pairs of eyes watching him and hear the hubbub of voices rise as he got near and then fall as he passed by. Eventually, after what seemed like an age, they reached the dais at the end. They went up some steps to it and then walked nervously across until they came to where the Lord Wychnor sat waiting for them.

'Welcome,' he said, and the music of his voice sent shivers down their backs. 'I apologize for their rudeness; they should not have stared but you understand that they were curious to see you. Come; we will go through into my own room where we can be private and talk.'

He stood up and his great green and silver cloak fell to the floor and swept along after him as he walked towards a little door and, opening it, ushered them through. Nab glanced back at the huge throne where he had been sitting; made of black oak it seemed to grow out of the floor. In fact it did not seem to have been made at all but rather to have always been there; there was no decoration except that which was in the wood itself, and the ends of the arms shone where the Elflords' palms had rested on them since the beginning of time, polishing them so that they glistened like water. The throne was bathed in a pool of sunlight which poured through a window high up in the roof. The sun shone against the black wood and brought out the colours; blues, purples, and reds from deep within.

The little room in which they were now standing was panelled in green moss all around the walls and here and there patches of the orange lichen that served to provide light were buried amongst the green. The wooden ceiling was low and gave the room a cosy atmosphere quite unlike the grandeur of the great chamber outside; it reminded Brock and Nab of the sett. There were two small round windows in opposite walls and through them could be seen the whole of the clearing; Brock looked out and saw that the sun was starting to grow pale and the mist beginning to rise from the water and spread out amongst the trees.

The Elflord sat in a seat that had been carved in the wooden wall next to one of the windows and Nab and the animals sat on the floor at his feet. He smiled at them for a long time, looking from one to the other, and his smile had the warmth of age. They looked deep into his misty grey eyes and became lost in the mysteries of time until they felt as if they were swimming in a sea of cloud. Finally, as the sun sank in the winter afternoon and shone through the window casting a halo of gold around his head, he began to speak, and his voice was grave.

'The time has come,' he said, 'for you to learn something of our world. In the beginning were only the Efflinch, by name Ashgaroth and Dréagg; and Ashgaroth the Great One, Lord of Good, had fought Dréagg the Mighty, Ruler of Evil, since time itself had begun.

'And the Universe rang with the sound and fury of the Efflinch Wars and the nature of them may not be contemplated by us though their horror may be perhaps guessed at and glimpsed in the darkest and wildest of our nightmares.

'And in their struggle for supremacy the Efflinch wrought matter out of themselves and hurled it through the endless darknesses of space.

'And after aeons of time too infinite to grasp Dréagg the Mighty wearied and became subdued and Ashgaroth trumpeted in the heavens his glorious victory. And Dréagg he banished to the Halls of Drāgorn in whose foul atmosphere he was to languish for ever. Dréagg, he nursed his wounds and brooded long over the bitterness of his defeat.

'And Ashgaroth looked at the wreckage of war and saw the Universe full of the missiles of battle; and in celebration of victory he

chose such a one and vowed to transform it, to make it his jewel and glory to shine as an everlasting memorial to the triumph of the Lord of Good.

'And he blessed it with the gifts of life and he gave colour, shape and form to this life.

'He first created the green growing things: the trees, grasses, mosses and lichens; then the flowers and the vegetables of the earth and their colours glowed and shone so that he was well pleased.

'And he created the mountains as pinnacles of his power to reach up to the sky; and he gave them a savagery and power to reflect even his own.

'And he created the sea and the blue was of a depth and brilliance that defied the eye to meet it; and in joy at his creation he invested it with a fragment of his own might so that it heaved and rolled even as he breathed.

'And lastly he peopled the oceans and the land with the creatures of life, the animals, the birds and the insects, to live among them and to survive by the fruits and the berries. And there was harmony and peace amongst the life he had created and they were at ease with one another so that it was even as he had wished, for Earth shone out as the creation of the Lord of Good.

'And the light was strong so that it came to Dréagg where he lurked in the Halls of Drāgorn which are outside the Universe and his fury welled within him even as the light goaded him, seeming to taunt him with the bitter memories of his defeat so that he fed from the eldritch and steaming fluids that lie within the Halls and slowly regained his strength and power.

'And his sojourn amongst these noxious vapours had made of Dréagg a more cunning adversary and the more dangerous for it so that he returned slowly and insidiously with great stealth and deceit and he turned the animals one against the other so that they fought one with the other and lived off the flesh of their fellows, and the creatures of the Earth were afflicted with much suffering and torment as the waters ran red with their pain.

'And Ashgaroth in his renewed struggle with the Lord of Evil created a race to fight the influence of Dréagg and to restore peace and innocence to his chosen jewel. And this race is named the Elves and they are of Magic so that they were formed from the wind and the stars and their essence is of the depth of the mighty sea and their spirit is amongst the green growing things of the woods and the trees and their souls are of the wild forgotten mountains.

'And three Elves he put over all the Earth according to the three great vastnesses of creation, so that there was Malcoff, Lord of the Mountains; Saurélon the Lord of the Seas and Ammdar who was Lord of the Forests and the green growing things.

'And the Elflords fought the power of Dréagg for many moons and the stories of their struggle have passed into legend for great was the bravery of the Elves and mighty were their Heroes. But greater still was the power of Dréagg and Magic alone was not enough to combat his dread evil so that his influence waxed strong and the Earth was rendered hideous by the horrors that abounded.

'And the Elflords beseeched the Mighty Ashgaroth to render them aid in their time of need. And so it was that he bestowed upon the Elves, the second of the Duâin Elrondin (or the powers of life) which is Logic, and of the two, which are Magic and Logic, this second is the most dangerous. But there was great fear in the heart of Ashgaroth at the bestowal of this gift and he warned them of its danger and that it was to be used most sparingly for if it were allowed to gain ascendance, then it would destroy the Earth.

'So that none of the Elves should be able to use the power without the others, Ashgaroth divided the power into three, which are the Three Seeds of Logic, and each seed he placed in a casket wrought from burnished copper from the deepest Mines of Mixon; and each casket he gave into the possession of one of the three Elflords. Thus it was that the power of Logic could not be used unless the Three Seeds were brought together and released as one and once they had been released they could be used no more.

'And it has been seen that there were three Lords over all the Earth; but of these the greatest was Ammdar, Lord of the Forests whose power was such that the grass turned to silver where he walked and the leaves changed to gold when he wished it. And he walked the forests, his domain, and all bowed down and marvelled at his might and he fought Dréagg and many times he won.

'And Dréagg watched the powers of Ammdar and saw in their very greatness the chance for which he had been waiting. And in the darkest nights, when the Earth slept, he whispered to Ammdar from afar so that he might not know that the words were the words of Dréagg. And as time passed so did Ammdar, the Silver Warrior, become vain and proud and conscious of his strength; and so also did he grow greedy and Dréagg nurtured this greed and fed it until it grew so that Ammdar rejected his Lord Ashgaroth.

'And finally, when Dréagg sensed the time was right, did he make himself known and plant his scheme in the mind of Ammdar. "With the seeds of logic in your possession," he said, "then would you indeed be supreme over all the Earth. And I will help you in this task if you will accept me as your Lord so that together we may conquer Ashgaroth."

'And the lust for power, which had been gnawing away at the soul of Ammdar like a disease, was such that he welcomed Dréagg willingly as his Lord.

'And so began a saga of deceit and treachery in which Dréagg assisted Ammdar to find Elflings of his own and of the two other Great Lords who would help him in his quest for the seeds. And he promised them power if they would reject Ashgaroth and their own Lords in favour of the Ruler of Evil. And many who were approached refused Ammdar and were destroyed most horribly but some there were who accepted him and these are called Goblins for they are Fallen Elves.

'The Goblins were granted the powers of evil by Dréagg and became reviled and feared, and mighty was their cunning so that they wormed their way into positions of trust with Malcoff and Saurélon and the Keepers of the Seeds.

'And so finally it came about that Ammdar Lord of the Forest had at one time in his possession the Three Seeds of Logic. The power could not be granted to the Goblins for they were of Magic and Magic and Logic would not lie together. Thus he conceived of the idea that if the gift of Logic were to be given to the animals in return for their acceptance of him and the Rule of Evil then would he truly be supreme over the Earth and the overthrow of Malcoff and Saurélon would be complete.

'So on a night when the moon did not shine and the air was still he did summon the Leaders of the Animals to his lair in the deepest forests of Spath and there he offered them this mighty gift if they would pledge themselves to him alone.

'But the powers of Ashgaroth were strong in the animals and they rejected the offer of Ammdar so that they might remain in the light of Ashgaroth.

'And a great fury came over the Lord of the Forest at his rejection so that his wrath was terrible to see and the animals fled in fear and the trees shook till they were rended from the earth and the mighty boughs tore and broke like blades of grass.

'And Dréagg watched the ravings of Ammdar with much satisfaction for the Lord of the Forests was now as clay in his hands to be used as he would.

'"Let us take revenge for your rejection," he whispered in the mind of Ammdar, "on these creatures which scorn your might."

'And it was thus that Ammdar and the Ruler of Evil, the mighty Dréagg, created a race of beings which they called Man; which we call, in the language of the Old Ones, Urkku which means "The Great Enemy".

'And in them was all the wrath of Ammdar against the animals so that they had no regard for them and Dréagg planted the root of cruelty deep within the Urkku so that they were cruel in their ways towards them for Man had been made as an instrument of revenge.

'And Man was created with the power of the Three Seeds so that he was of pure Logic; and Magic, the gift of the Mighty Ashgaroth to the Elves, was denied to him. Clever was the work of Dréagg for even as Ashgaroth had bestowed upon the Elves fragments of himself so did Dréagg give to Man, alongside the root of cruelty, the evil nature of arrogance so that he believed himself to be supreme over all the Earth and over all the Creatures of the Earth. And in his logic, this justified his treatment of the animals.

'So Man began his reign over the Earth and Dréagg was well pleased for the jewel of Ashgaroth was torn asunder and the colours faded and the green growing things withered and died and it became as a barren waste. And only what was necessary for the support or pleasure of the Urkku was allowed to survive.

'And the creatures of Ashgaroth, the Elves, whose powers were of

Magic, were driven out by Man and began to dwell in the secret hidden places deep in the fortress of the Earth; known only to the animals.

'And Ammdar also was well pleased as he watched for truly a terrible revenge was exacted on the animals and great was their suffering.

'And the Tale of their Persecution and Abuse is as known to you as is the air you breathe.

'But some there were among the Urkku who cast out the influence of Dréagg and in whom the root of cruelty and the nature of arrogance failed to grow. And they turned towards Ashgaroth and he opened their eyes so that they had glimpses of the Earth even as the Elves and the animals do and they saw the magic in the mountains and the trees and the sea and they were as one with the animals so that they are called Eldron or The Friends.

'And throughout the reign of Man have been the Eldron but in numbers they are few. And for their ways have they been laughed at, scorned and ridiculed, and a great anger is in them as they see the suffering and horror inflicted by their fellow race on the animals whose pain they feel as they would feel pain inflicted on their fellows for with them is all cruelty vile.

'For Ammdar, Lord of the Forests, the taste of power was to be bittersweet and brief, for Dréagg had no more use for him and in him Dréagg sensed appetites to rival even his gargantuan tastes. So did the Ruler of Evil sow the seeds of discontent among Ammdar's lair in the Forests of Spath, and a Goblin, Degg by name, was given the power to destroy Ammdar, which is to say that the sword of Degg was woven with the spell of time; for in his fall from Ashgaroth Ammdar had lost the immortality of the Elves, and Dréagg now could destroy the Goblins as he wished by halting the flow of time within them.

'And the sight of the destruction of Ammdar was truly horrible and the sound of his wailing at the anguish of his betrayal, even by Dréagg who had sworn to make him great, rang out from the Forests of Spath and sounded long and loud throughout the Earth for many moons so that the Elves trembled even as they rejoiced at his ending.

'And since that time the smells of corruption, deceit and trickery have lingered around the Goblins' lair in the Forests of Spath and they have fought and quarrelled constantly among themselves, for-gotten even by he who spawned them, using each the other to indulge their vile games and appetite for cruelty. Yet sometimes will Dréagg use them in the struggle against us so that they are not to be ignored.

'And with the destruction of Ammdar, I, the Lord Wychnor, was appointed by Ashgaroth to become Lord of the Forests and the Green Growing Things.

'And thus it is that in the Shadow of Dréagg dwells the Earth. The Elves and the Animals cried out to Ashgaroth that they had been abandoned, for truly they were powerless against the Elrondin of Pure Logic. And they beseeched Ashgaroth that he might help them. And he answered them and said, "Be patient" for it was as he had said, truly Logic was the most dangerous of the Elrondin and in Man it had been used with no regard for its power and was pure and undilute so that in it are the seeds of self-destruction.

'And Ashgaroth further promised them that when the time was right and the stars in the heavens were in their true place then would he send a Saviour who was truly of the Duâin Elrondin, so that in him lay both Magic and Logic and to this Saviour he would show the way and through him would they be saved.

'And the Tale of his Coming is even as has happened; he would be born of two of the Eldron so that he would be possessed of Logic yet would his spirit come from Ashgaroth so that he would have Magic. And in him would the influence of Dréagg not exist so that he would be afflicted by neither cruelty nor arrogance. And he would be raised among the animals to be with them and to be of them.

'And so it is, Nab, that we believe you to be this Saviour and I, Wychnor, as the Elflord who dwelt nearest to you, have watched over you since the day your parents, the Chosen Eldron, left you in the snow.

'But you must travel to meet the two other Elflords so that they may recognize and know you. They dwell in other Nations across the seas but they will journey here and meet you in a part of their Kingdom which is in this Nation.

'So the Lord Saurélon will meet you by the sea where it thunders and rages in the westernmost part of this nation in a place I shall direct you to and then you will journey to meet the Lord Malcoff in a high place amongst the towering mountains which border our nation in the far north.

'And Ashgaroth has directed that from each of the Elflords will you be given a small casket within which will be found the essence, The Grain, of their Kingdom, called the Faradawn, and when you have these three, then will the Mighty Ashgaroth reveal to you alone what is the Way.

'You will travel by the Old Ways, the Secret Pathways which only the Elves and the animals know but which you also with your powers of Magic may now know. And you will not be alone as you journey for with you will be your companions of Silver Wood; Perryfoot the Fleet and the dog Sam, you, Brock and you, Warrigal.

'And there will be a sixth traveller, known to you now as an Urkku but in fact one of the Eldron; the girl you met by the stream. She will be a friend of your own race and you will learn much from her, as you travel, of the ways of Man.

'When you leave here you will journey to where she lives. She will be waiting, for Ashgaroth has touched her mind as she slept to prepare her for your coming. And so that she may know you for the one sent by him, you will give her a Ring.'

He stopped talking and there was silence for a long, long time as the three travellers continued to look at him, their minds racing furiously with all that they had heard. He sat in the windowseat, looking gently at them, framed by the light of the early moon, for the sun had now gone down. Nab wished that he could sit here for ever, listening to that voice, and remain secure in this little room. Somehow he was afraid to leave, for while he was in the room he retained some part of him as he had been before he entered; when he left, he would be in some way different. He felt as if before he had been safe; wrapped in a cocoon of ignorance, but that now the world was a different place and his role in it frightened him terribly: from being a mere bystander watching from the outside, he was now at the centre. He looked at Brock and Warrigal and found that they were looking at him and he wondered if their attitude towards him would change.

For the badger and the owl, in fact, the Elflord's words as to the place of Nab amongst them had been no surprise, rather a confirmation of something which they had felt from the night he had arrived in the wood. What their minds were trying desperately to cope with was the wealth of knowledge which they had just been given and the incredible story behind it. Brock soon gave up, his mind submerged under it all, but for Warrigal it was like the completion of a puzzle as all the little fragments of stories and legends that he had picked up over the years finally came together as one.

The Elflord's voice broke in upon their thoughts.

'You will dine with me tonight, as my guests,' he said, 'and tomorrow before you leave I will present you with the Ring and the casket of the Faradawn. Come with me.'

He stood up and beckoned to them to follow him as he walked back across the little room and opened the door into the hall. As they emerged into the vastness of the huge chamber a wonderful sight met their eyes. Down the centre stretched a long mat woven with rushes of greens and browns and interlaced with fronds of fir, and on the mat, which stretched almost to the far end, was a vast selection of foods and drinks all arranged in little silver and copper dishes, each one carved with a different pattern and each illustrating a part of the story which they had just heard. The Lord Wychnor led them across to the head of the mat, where he sat down on a brilliantly coloured cushion and motioned to Nab to sit on his left with Warrigal and Brock on his right. When these four were sitting, the host of elves who had been standing alongside the mat also sat down and all turned towards Wychnor, who stood up, raised the silver chalice which was in front of him and turned to Nab looking deep into his eyes. Then he drank from the chalice and the elves all cheered and likewise raised their bowls and drank. When Brock leant forward to take a sip from his bowl, which he guessed he was supposed to, he saw with a thrill that around the outside of the bowl was carved a delicate picture of a badger moving backwards through a snow filled wood with a bundle nestled under his two forelegs. He looked excitedly at the other bowls around him and saw that they too represented different scenes from his life with Nab; a carving of the sett with him and Tara playing with Nab, the first Council Meeting, and others, all bringing back warm and satisfying memories. He looked across at Nab and then turned to Warrigal and they too were looking in

132

wonder at their silver bowls, lost in thought. The boy raised his head and looked back at Brock and a tear oozed from his eye and trickled slowly down his cheek until it fell on the mat. Then the Elflord sat down, the cheering stopped and everyone began to eat and drink.

'Do you like them?' said Wychnor, pointing to the carvings and speaking to the three companions. 'Our craftsmen were finishing them even as you were walking past them this afternoon to meet me. See, here is one of the three of you walking through Ellmondrill and here is another of you coming across the water with Reev. Ah, here is some music and the dancers. This will be a new dance, performed in honour of you all; even I have not seen it before.'

The great door at the end of the hall had opened and a stream of elves were dancing in, some carrying instruments from which came the sounds of music and others clad in costumes from which hundreds of little lights shimmered and sparkled in the orange twilight glow that shone from the patches of lichen on the walls. The owl, the badger and the boy watched in wonder as the musicians settled down around the outside walls and began to play and the dancers moved in time with the rhythms, echoing in their movements the memories and timeless images which the music evoked in their minds. Nab recognized little snatches of sound from the walk through the hall that afternoon when they had been practising and, as these more familiar sounds came to him, he once again felt the impulsive urge to dance. He watched the dancers as they moved around the hall and their costumes formed a dizzy whirlpool of colours in which he became lost, and then dimly, through the haze of sounds and lights, he felt himself get up from his cushion by the mat and dance across to join them. Once he was up and had given himself to the music his body seemed taken over; he seemed to fly through the air up to the rafters, which were festooned with evergreens, across to the far wall and then down to crouch on the floor in a tiny ball only to explode again into separate pieces each of which flew away to different parts of the hall.

Brock and Warrigal watched in amazement and the elves cheered and laughed and soon the cushions around the mat were vacant as the floor was filled with dancers, each joyously lost in his own world of movement. The badger and the owl sought out Nab and the three of them frolicked and spun and laughed and leapt until they could move no more and then when the moon was highest in the night sky the visitors returned weary and happy to their little room below, and the elves all retired to sleep. All except Wychnor, who went to his private room and sat alone staring out through the window at the moon shining on the clearing; and his mind was lost in the past.

The next morning the animals were woken by Reev as he came into their chamber, bringing, as he called it, their 'travelling food' on a large tray. The sun shone very brightly through the window and they knew what that brightness meant; snow had fallen in the night. They went over to look outside and could hardly recognize the clearing, covered as it was by a thick layer of white, making everything round and smooth and soft. The elf stayed with them as they ate, talking about last night; he had been one of the dancers but none of the animals had recognized him in his costume. Indeed, in the myriad of wonders that had so mesmerized them, they could remember very little, but when they thought back to their talk with Wychnor a little cold chill sent itself shuddering into their hearts at the recollection of his words. In the magic of last night they had been able to forget, but now, in the cold light of a new day, the things he had told them came flooding back in a rush so that they no longer felt hungry.

'You must eat; finish your food. You need all your strength for the times ahead,' said Reev in a quiet comforting way. 'When you have finished I will take you once again to the Lord Wychnor and then you shall leave us.'

When they had eaten their fill, Reev led them back along the winding corridors of the Elvenoak and through the hall, empty now and very different from the way it had been last night, until they arrived once again outside the door of Wychnor's little room. Reev pulled a cord and the Elflord opened it and bade them welcome, closing the door behind them as Reev walked away.

'There are things I must give to you,' he said, 'and words I must say. Here, Nab, is the Belt of Ammdar, which he used to keep the three seeds of logic safe; you will see it is woven of young willow saplings and interlaced among them are three silver lockets. I have placed the Faradawn of the trees and the green growing things in the

134

one furthest away from the fastening. It is good that the belt should now be used to help defeat the evil that Ammdar brought upon the world. Wear it as he did; close to your body under your garments.'

Nab looked at the wide belt with amazement and fear; the idea of wearing this belt, which had been worn by and belonged to the dread and mighty Ammdar, the fallen Elflord, was not one that appealed to him. He looked at Wychnor, who knew what the boy was thinking.

'Take it,' he said. 'It will help you on the side of Ashgaroth even as it helped Ammdar in the cause of Dréagg.'

The Elflord passed the belt over and Nab received it with trembling hands. Despite its width and the three silver lockets which he could now see clearly embedded amongst the green sapling strands, it was amazingly light; in fact, if he hadn't seen it lying in his hands, he would not have known he was holding it. He looked at it in wonder, and Brock and Warrigal crowded around to gaze at this fragment of living legend, reaching out cautiously to touch it to make sure it wasn't just a figment of their imagination.

'The Belt of Ammdar,' intoned the owl under his breath, as if reciting a magic spell.

Finally, when Nab had managed to pluck up courage, he lifted his clothing and placed the belt over the multi-coloured shawl that lay always next to his skin. Then he brought together the delicately carved copper fastenings and found to his surprise that, when they came close to each other, they seemed to spring shut of their own accord. It fitted him perfectly and felt strangely comforting fastened securely around his waist.

'Here is the Ring which you are to give to the chosen lady of the Eldron,' said Wychnor. 'Put it for safe keeping in one of the lockets.'

The Ring was a deep translucent gold colour with threads of silver inlaid inside it, so that they appeared as wisps of mist on an autumn morning. In the top was set a silver jewel, the base of which was buried deep within and it shone through the gold with a light that lit up the whole ring. As he handled it Nab became aware of a vague scent of pine and, when he mentioned this to Warrigal later, the owl said he believed that the gold was resin from the pine trees that had existed first upon the earth and which the elves used to mine when these trees had long since died and become part of the ground. How the silver threads were put inside he was unable to say. As Nab looked at the ring he thought he saw them moving, as the mist does in a gentle breeze, and the golden light seemed to wax and wane as if the sun were reaching midday and sinking to evening.

Wychnor showed the boy how to open one of the lockets by pressing a catch at the back which caused the top to fly open and Nab then dropped the Ring inside before pushing the top down again so that it clicked shut. Nab then rearranged his top garments so that the belt, with its precious contents, was hidden and looked up to see the Elflord's great grey eyes fixed upon the three of them.

'And now it is farewell. Reev will travel with you back through Ellmondrill and he will take you to the dwelling of the Eldron. There he will leave you and you will return with her to Silver Wood to collect Perryfoot and Sam. Then you will start your journey. The reasons for your going and the matters I have disclosed to you must be kept secret, although of course the members of the Council know already: Dréagg is now, after your capture by the Urkku, aware of your existence, Nab, although not yet aware of your significance. Beware, then, for he will be watching and when he thinks the time is right he will strike: the minute he learns the purpose of your journey he will act but, in ignorance of it, he will wait and try and learn by following your travels. Take the utmost care therefore not to be seen by the Urkku, for they are the eyes and ears of Dréagg. Keep to the secret paths and the ancient places which you will know from the magic in your bodies.' He paused and they waited as he turned to look out of the window for a second before turning back and addressing them once again.

'There is one final matter,' he said. 'I have told you that the seeds of logic that were used in the creation of the Urkku contain the means of self-destruction. Thus it is that the world of Urkku, and with it our world, the world of the jewel of Ashgaroth, is drawing to an end. Your task must be accomplished before that happens otherwise we shall all perish with it; yet even now it is rumoured that there

136

is great trouble amongst the Urkku and that their fragile world is breaking down. Do not unduly delay therefore. Be steady and sure in your purpose and as swift as caution permits. Now, farewell; may the light of Ashgaroth go with you.'

They turned around slowly and with an immense sadness in their hearts followed Reev as he led them out through the hall and down through the Elvenoak, until they once more found themselves gliding back over the water, doubly black now in contrast with the snow all about them on the ground and in the trees. On the far bank they alighted and made straight for the gap in the wall of trees through which they had come. They paused before they entered the tunnel and looked back at the clearing, standing serene and peaceful, glistening white under the blue sky. There was no sign of movement anywhere and no sound of activity; were it not for Reev standing waiting for them, his green and brown doublet blowing gently in the breeze that came across the water, and the belt which Nab could feel as he walked, the whole episode could have been a dream. Then they looked away and were soon on the far side of the tunnel and walking once again amongst the enormous trees and deep undergrowth of the wood. The going was more difficult now with the snow covering everything and Nab and Brock found themselves frequently falling through a pile of bracken or a small bush although Reev seemed to dance on top as if he weighed no more than a feather and Warrigal had once again taken to the air and was swooping and gliding ahead of them with obvious enjoyment at being back in his element.

Nab did not recognize any of the areas through which Reev led them; in fact the whole wood seemed different – the trees not quite so enormous and the atmosphere more friendly. The owl and the elf were constantly having to wait while the others caught up and Nab would see them ahead in a clearing, bathed in the shafts of sunlight that came lancing through the trees as he and Brock plodded through the snow towards them. The sun was thawing it and every now and again the branches of a tree would shed its load with no warning, and the wood echoed with the crashing noise it made as it fell down through all the lower branches bringing the snow on those tumbling down as well; then there would be utter stillness once again, broken

137

only by the panting of the boy and the badger who were now warm with the effort of walking through the snow.

Finally they reached the stream and they rested for a while just inside the wood and looked out at the white fields on the other side rising up gently to the corridor-like path through which they had come just two days ago, although it seemed an age. The stream, swollen now with the melting snow, rushed on its way, gurgling and spluttering past them, knocking folds of snow off the banks as it went which seemed to struggle bravely for an instant to remain white and whole but then sank beneath the black waters as they rapidly dissolved. The midday sun was at its height, shining down on the snow and filling their world with silver light. Reev produced a selection of nuts, toadstools and berries from a little pouch which he wore on his belt and gratefully the animals munched on these as they sat. Nab began to think of where they were going and he realized that until now his mind had been so busy with everything that had been happening around them that he had given very little thought to this part of the Elflord's revelations, and the full impact of it now slowly began to dawn on him. They were travelling, right at this very moment, to meet the Urkku girl whom he had seen three summers ago and whom he had never really forgotten; and she was, according to Wychnor, a part of his life and would share his journeys with him, although what was to happen to them then not even the Elflord knew. The more he thought about it the more excited he became and he found himself longing to see her again; he thought of how he had last seen her, standing waving to him from the banks of the stream, her red dress and long golden hair ruffling in the springtime afternoon breeze and in her hand the posy of yellow primroses and pink campion she had picked for her mother. All the wonder and magic of that day came flooding back to him in a rush of exhilaration, but with it came the doubts, the anxieties and the fears which had also been a part of it and he felt himself getting nervous again. It was impossible to believe that she would simply leave her home and her parents and her friends and go with him on a journey to places even he had never been to before; and then it occurred to him, with a sharp stab of panic, that he would not even be able to tell her where or why they were going because she did not speak the language of the wood.

Suddenly his gloomy thoughts were broken into by Reev who was sitting next to him and had guessed from the intense look on Nab's face and from the intuition that comes with magic what was going through the boy's head.

'Have faith in the powers of Ashgaroth and remember, she is of the Eldron,' he said, 'and you have the Ring.'

Nab turned to look at him and the elf smiled warmly so that all the boy's fears seemed to vanish.

'Come,' said Reev. 'It is time we made a move.'

They got up feeling greatly refreshed and walked the few paces to the bank; to the animals' surprise they had come out exactly where the fallen log formed the bridge from which Brock had fallen when they came across the other way. This time there were no incidents except for the amazing way in which Reev appeared to jump over the stream; one minute he was in the wood and the next he was on the far bank waiting for the animals to cross and grinning broadly. The strange thing was that they had not actually seen him in the air as he jumped.

Soon they were walking briskly up the slope towards the entrance to the two thorn hedges that formed the corridor and then they were walking along inside it once again, leaving Ellmondrill glimmering majestically in the sun. The rest of the walk back took place in silence; each of the animals buried deep inside the comforting cocoon of his own mind, letting little fragments of what the Elflord had told them enter their thoughts one at a time to be thoroughly absorbed and digested before the next piece was allowed to enter and be, in turn, mulled over and put in its place. Now that they were away from Ellmondrill and walking back towards familiar territory they felt more confident and more in control of their own destiny, and this gradual sifting and sorting out of all the new things they had learnt and experienced allowed them to understand things that before had buried them beneath a deluge of bewilderment. For Nab and Warrigal, understanding was easier than it was for Brock, who found much of Wychnor's tale confusing and vague, but he understood above all that he had been right in the feelings of destiny which he had experienced from the first time he had set eyes on Nab although he also realized that he would be leaving Silver Wood and

Tara for a long time. When he had questioned Reev about this, the elf had replied that any more than six animals travelling together would be far too conspicuous to the Urkku; six itself was really too many but Wychnor felt that the advantages in terms of safety of the combined skills of all those who were going outweighed the disadvantages. Besides, Reev had added, Tara was not as strong as were the rest of them; the strain of bearing cubs had left its mark on her. Then Brock had understood why, but it had not helped to ease the pain he felt at the thought of being parted from her.

Eventually by the time the sun was beginning to sink on the short winter afternoon they arrived back in the fields which led, over the rise, to the back of Silver Wood and they could just make out the tops of the trees in the distance. Reev called them to a halt and told them that they were now about to make directly for the home of the Eldron and that therefore rather than go through the wood it was quicker to take a path to the right of it. At the sight of the familiar trees and hummocks the animals were filled with pangs of homesickness but, comforting themselves with the thought that they would be back once they had collected the girl, they steeled themselves and followed the elf as he headed away across the fields at an angle that took them, once again, away from the wood.

It was evening by the time Reev stopped again. They were just under the summit of a small rise in a field.

'The dwelling of the Eldron is on the other side of the hill,' he said. 'I will leave you now; you have no further need of me. When you leave Silver Wood with the girl, take the way that leads towards that copse of fir trees in the distance; that will set you on the right path. Farewell.'

He was gone before the animals had a chance to say goodbye; the silver light that glowed about him dancing off into the darkness of the evening until it vanished on the far side of a hedge. Their last link with the wood elves had gone and they were on their own again.

'Come on,' said Nab, and they crunched their way over the frozen snow until they reached the top of the rise. They looked down and there, nestling in the fold between two little hills, stood a small cottage. The hill they were standing on was at the rear of the cottage and in front was a thick wood. Light shone from three of the downstairs windows; from two of them the light was a warm orange colour and from the third, at one end, it was tinged with a flicker of red. Smoke drifted straight upwards in the stillness from a chimney at this end and the smell of woodsmoke hung heavily in the chill air, reminding the animals of autumn. Nab looked around him at the steely grey evening sky, the white frozen fields and the wood which lay dark and forbidding under the first stars. For an instant he was consumed by an inexplicable longing to be inside the cottage, warm and secure and locked away from the cold of the night. It came from somewhere deep within him and passed as quickly as it came but the yearning was so intense that whenever he thought of it afterwards a great sadness welled up inside him.

They walked quietly down the slope towards the cottage and were soon scrambling through a rough wooden fence that separated the field from a garden at the back. This back garden was only small and there were some trees forming a border round it which were so close together that they formed a tall hedge. The animals gathered under it to work out what they were to do.

'I think it would be better if I approached alone,' whispered Nab. 'She might be scared if she saw all three of us together at first; after all, she has seen me before.'

Warrigal and Brock agreed; the owl flew up into one of the trees, where he perched on a branch from which he had a good view of the whole of the back of the house, and the badger melted back into the shadows, watchful and tense, ready to dash out and render help the instant it might be needed. To his surprise he realized that he was quite enjoying himself; there was not too much danger, he didn't think, but what there was took his mind off the future and enabled him to live for the moment for a while. These sorts of adventures were the kind he was used to from the times before Nab had come and he felt more in control of himself than he had for quite a time. He settled down, under the overhanging branches of one of the trees, right back against its trunk and, looking out, saw that Nab had reached the end of the hedge of trees and had started to creep along the wall of the cottage towards the first of the windows. The last of the evening light had almost gone and the night was nearly upon

141

them; against the darkening sky the badger saw a lone rook flying home and suddenly he was filled with a wish for the old days when he would have been emerging at about this time for his evening walk. Now all that had changed; their lives had been taken over by the hands of destiny.

CHAPTER XIII

Beth was in the middle room decorating the Christmas tree. They were late doing it this year because everyone had been so busy; her father at work, her mother with the new baby and she herself had been unable to find the time because of all the little things that need to be done at this time of year; buying presents for the family, visiting grannies and grandpas and seeing friends. There had also been a lot more for her to do in the house because her mother's time seemed totally taken up by little James and she had found herself making meals, washing and cleaning somewhat more than usual. So now it was Christmas Eve, snow was on the ground outside, the atmosphere in the house was full of excitement and anticipation and she was hanging tinsel and coloured balls on the tree. Life was perfect; and yet she was not content. She had not felt truly at peace with herself since the spring day when she had come face to face with that extraordinary boy down by the stream. She had told no one and the secret had burned away inside her with the effort of not telling but to her surprise she had succeeded in keeping it quiet. Something about the boy had sparked off within her a restlessness that had troubled her ever since and she had taken to going for long walks by herself through the woods and fields; at first in the hope of meeting him again but, when this seemed to become more and more of an improbability as the days passed and there was still no sign of him, she had simply walked because it was only while she was out amongst the trees and fields that she felt content. Eventually though, she had fought this feeling within herself and had settled down to her school work again, which had begun to suffer terribly from her inability to concentrate on any one thing for more than a few seconds at a time. She had then become more like her old self to everyone around; her mother, her father, her elder brother, her teacher and her friends. Once more she was a pretty, studious, diligent, polite and cheerful little girl. She was pleased because she loved all these people and it hurt her to worry them but she knew that it was only an act, a façade put up for their sakes, and that behind it she still burnt with energy and felt as restless and bored as before. Still, she hoped that if she worked at it hard enough, the feeling would eventually go away and, as time went on and the memory of his face and those dark eyes began to fade, she even started to believe that she was succeeding. She had been to some parties this autumn and winter and had quite enjoyed them and was due to go out tonight to a dance in the Village Hall. She was looking forward to this and as soon as the tree was finished she would go upstairs to her bedroom and get ready.

However, just a few weeks ago she had had a dream; it was not an unpleasant dream, in fact quite the reverse, but it had brought all her old feelings of unrest flooding back. She had dreamt of his face, and it had been as vivid in the dream as if he had been standing in front of her; his vibrant eyes had searched hers the way they had that day and she had felt strangely drawn to him. Then there were disconnected snatches of other pictures; in one of them she was walking at his side along a mountain path and they were followed by a dog, a badger, a hare and a large brown owl; in another he was giving her a ring, a beautiful ring of a deep golden amber with silver wisps inside it.

These dreams had recurred almost every night since then and, although the images of his face and the ring remained constant, as did the animals, the others changed so that in some of them they were walking along a beach and the sea was crashing against the shore and in others they were in a marsh, lonely, desolate and lost in the middle of the night. The dreams occurred so often and were so real that she sometimes felt as if they were her real life and it was her daytime life that was a dream. She began to exist in a strange twilight world where the two became confused and intermingled to such an extent that she was frequently surprised to find, during the day, that she was not with the boy and the animals and she found herself referring to incidents in her dream life when she was talking to her mother or to friends.

Now it was Christmas and she was hoping that the excitements and joys of this time would help her to return to normality. She hoped for this and yet the strangest thing of all was that although the dreams made her muddled and uneasy she longed for the end of the day when she would once again inhabit their world and be with the little band of companions as they journeyed through the countryside.

She was just putting the finishing touches to her arrangement of the lights on the tree when her mother called through to her from the kitchen.

'Beth, lay the table would you, dear? Your father will be home soon and the meal is almost ready. Get some sherry glasses out for us; you can have a little glass as well.' There was a pause and Beth heard the clatter of pans in the kitchen. 'Have you finished the tree? I suppose we'll have to get your father to look at the lights again. They never work; it's the same every year.'

Beth switched them on at the plug socket and nothing happened.

'No, they haven't come on, Mummy,' she said, and stood back to admire her handiwork. 'The tree looks nice though,' she called.

She went over to the big oak dresser which stood against one wall of the room and pulled out the cutlery drawer so that she could lay the table. The mats she fetched from a ledge which ran along the bottom of the dresser and she then walked across to the middle of the room and began to lay four places on the large oval dining table which smelt of polish and shone in the flickering light of the candles which she had lit and placed in the centre. Upstairs she could hear sounds of movement as her elder brother who, at fifteen, was two years older than her, though he sometimes acted as if it were ten, got up from the desk where he had been reading a book and walked over to the door of his room.

'What time is it, Beth?' he shouted down.

'Five o'clock,' she told him. 'Come and fix these lights before Father gets home.'

'Fix them yourself.'

'Pig!'

'Children, don't bicker tonight. I've got enough to cope with feeding James and getting the meal ready without you two going on at each other.'

Beth finished laying the table.

'I'll go upstairs and get changed now,' she called through to the kitchen, 'so that Daddy can take me to the dance as soon as we've had the meal.'

'All right, dear. I've ironed your new dress; it's over the back of the chair in your room. Don't be too long; Daddy should be home any minute.'

The girl walked across to the open wooden staircase which ran up one side of the little room. She loved this room; this was the old room, the one that had always been here ever since she could remember, unlike the new room at the end which had been built as part of an extension to the house four years ago and which, although it had been designed to be in keeping with the rest, she had never taken to as being a part of it. It was too well-planned and neat. But the old one seemed to have grown out of the earth itself and she never felt shut in inside it because it gave her the feeling of being outside in the woods. When the winds blew and the rain poured down on winter evenings she felt as if she were underground, and the rough and gnarled black oak beams in the ceiling which glimmered in the fire-light were the roots of a large tree. Even when her restless moods were on her she felt content here and would often sit alone, reading, when the others had gone through to the new room to watch television. The magic of the books she read seemed to be intensified by the room with its flickering shadows and atmosphere of secret history.

146

Beth had reached the stairs and was about to start climbing them when her eye was caught by a movement through the window in the wall behind the stairs. She stopped and bent her face to the glass to look outside. There, to her disbelief, was the face which had grown so familiar to her in her dreams, the face of the boy from the stream. She closed her eyes, counted to ten and opened them again to make sure it wasn't a dream but the face was still there, looking at her, the smouldering eyes searching into her soul. Now the dream had become reality and she felt strangely calm for she had been with the boy so often in her dreams it was as if she had known him for a long time. This was a moment she had lived through on countless occasions in the twilit world she had been inhabiting, so she knew exactly what she would do.

Outside, Nab was a mass of doubts and uncertainty. He had been to the first window and when he had seen no one in that room he had moved cautiously along to this and had been standing watching Beth for quite some time while she set the table. At the sight of her again, he had been unable to do anything except stare, transfixed, as she moved around the room. She was of course older than that spring day when he had first seen her and she had begun to acquire a grace and delicacy in the way she moved which captivated him; the way her hair flowed around her face as she walked and the way she tucked the sides behind her ears so that it would not get in the way when she bent her head to put the cutlery on the table; the way she had folded her arms when she called upstairs and the way her lips had set when the voice came back down; and the way she had stood talking to her mother with both her hands tucked in the back pockets of her jeans. There were a hundred little mannerisms, indefinable and unconscious, all of which came together to weave a spell under which Nab became entranced so that when she looked through the window and he knew she had seen him he was unable to think what he should do. Then he remembered the ring and he fumbled under the layers of his garments until he found the second locket on the belt. With hands that were shaking in confusion he pushed the catch, the top sprang open and he placed his two first fingers inside to draw it out.

When she saw the boy delicately hold out the ring to her on a hand that was dark and seamed with use Beth knew without any doubts

147

that she had to go with him. It shone with the colours of an autumn morning, just as she had seen it in the dreams. She looked up at the boy's anxious face and their eyes met. She knew he was nervous and tense, as he had been when they first met. He stood there, ragged and wild, the breeze gently moving the layers of bark that hung around him and blowing his hair over his face so that only his eyes were uncovered. He was as a wild animal; the tension in his body filling him with the energy which is at the source of life itself, magnetic and powerful, his entire being tuned to the rhythms of the earth and the sky. At the same time his eyes, which burned so desperately into hers, were full of sadness and mistrust, of constant persecution, but deep within them was an anger, the perception of which frightened Beth, so resolute and enormous did it appear. 'I would not like to be the cause of that anger,' she thought to herself. 'It would destroy the world.' She did not know it and neither did Nab but what she was seeing was the fury of Ashgaroth.

Their eyes held each other for a long time and, because it was the only way they could communicate, worlds passed between them. Suddenly Beth became vaguely aware of her mother calling from the kitchen. It sounded far away as if it came through a room filled with cottonwool but Nab heard it and his face froze with tension.

He watched her, through the window, as she called something to her mother; then she turned back to him and placing her finger over her lips in the universal gesture of silence she pointed up the stairs and then down again, and then out to him.

While Nab was thinking about this she began to climb the stairs and he then realized what she had meant. He crouched down under the window up against the back wall to wait for her.

Beth passed the door to her brother's room and opened the door to her own which was next to it along the corridor. Thankfully she closed it behind her and went to sit on the bed for a minute or two to gather her thoughts. Now that the boy was no longer in front of her she began to wonder again whether it was just one of her dreams; even if it was not, was she mad to think of running away on this freezing snowy night with a boy whom she had known for no longer than ten minutes in her whole life. And the boy! The more she thought about it the more incredible did the idea seem. Every possible rational argument was against it and there was no way in which she could logically justify what she was thinking of doing. Then she remembered the ring and somehow the thought of it filled her with a strange feeling of security. That had been no mere coincidence; neither had it been part of a dream. Something was calling her and she had to go; what it was she did not know but that it was there she could not doubt. There was no real choice, for if she did not go she would be unable to live with herself for the rest of her life.

With her mind resolved into certainty she began to think about what she should take with her. She got up and went over to her little dressing table in the corner and ran her hands slowly along the front edge and then, when they reached the two corners, back along the sides until they came to the wall. She loved this dressing table; it had been given to her last Christmas and was the first big thing of her very own that she had ever had. She sat at it for hours, staring into the mirror and thinking about everything and nothing. At the front was a small crocheted woollen mat that had been made for her by her grandmother and given to her last birthday, and along the back and sides were all her bric-a-brac and personal things; bottles of different types of perfume and scent, hairslides, tubes of make-up, bottles of nail varnish. In the middle was a wooden jewellery box, made for her by her father when she was a little girl; she opened it sadly and looked at the jumble of rings, bracelets and necklaces that spilled over the edges on to the surface of the dressing table. Pushed into the frame around the mirror were rows of little photographs; some were with friends from school and there was a column of four that had been taken with a boy she had known. He was the son of some friends of her parents and had taken her a few months ago to see a film in the city, miles away. When they had come out he had taken her to a restaurant and they had had a meal with some friends of his. She had learnt a lot about herself that day and had lain awake in bed all night, thinking. In this way, as she looked at all the things on the dressing table, fragments and images of the past flashed through her mind.

She was leaving them now and, although for months she had been dominated by insatiable restlessness, now that she was actually going, she was unable to leave without sadness. She smiled ruefully to herself at all the things she saw; there would be no need for any of them now, she thought, and turned away quickly lest she start to cry. She must write a note for her mother and father; they would be bound to worry but perhaps she could ease their fears a little. She picked up a pen and paper but the words she searched for did not come; how could she express what she felt and explain why she was going away? She sat wrestling with the sentences and then suddenly, from nowhere, they came and seemed to write themselves. The words were the words of poetry, gentle magic words filled with awe and beauty so that when her parents later found the note pinned on to the front of the dressing table they were glad, even in their sorrow at losing Beth, for there was no doubt in their minds but that she was safe and happy and would always be. They knew, for they were of the Eldron.

When the note was finished she opened the drawer of the dressing table and out sprang her clothes. She selected three tee-shirts; green, red and black, and three jerseys, starting with a fairly closely knit cardigan and ending with the enormous chunky polo neck sweater which she had bought this winter; it was a dark muddy green colour and had a red and white patterned band around the chest. When she had put these on, she got a large brown corduroy jacket from the wardrobe which stood at the side of the dressing table and finally, over everything, she put on the dark brown tweed cape with the lion's head fastening which had been her grandmother's. Beth had been given it on her tenth birthday after admiring it constantly every time she had gone for a visit. It was perfect, she thought. Apart from the purely practical point that it was the only thing that would go over the top of all these layers of clothing and that it was wonderfully warm, she felt that it was the right sort of thing to be wearing for walking over moonlit fields; she had always had a feeling that there was something special about it, an aura of mystery and magic, and for that reason she had never worn it before, preferring to wait until an occasion which would warrant it. She placed the heavy cape over her shoulders, pulled the fastening chain across from the lion's head on one side to the metal tongue behind the head on the other and slipped it over. The cape fell around her and lay, draped in heavy folds, all the way down to the carpet on the floor. She buried her hands amongst the rest of the clothes in the drawer, found the fawn coloured woolly hat she had been looking for and, when she had put it on, pulled the hood of the cloak up and was ready.

She took a last look in the mirror and then turned away to go towards the door. The pretty little red dress that her mother had ironed for her ready for the dance lay over the back of a chair on the other side of the room; it's funny, she thought, how only half an hour ago everything had been so normal and ordinary. The dress looked lost and forlorn lying there waiting to be put on and Beth too felt sad even in her excitement. Then she suddenly remembered the Christmas presents and she reached under the bed, where they had been hidden, and laid them out on top. Luckily she had wrapped them last night and put on little cards with names. There was a pewter bracelet for her mother and a pen for her father; a record for her elder brother and for the little baby James she had bought a big brown teddy bear. Both grandmothers had been given the same to stop possible accusations of favouritism, a wildlife calendar, and both grandfathers had been given socks. The sight of all these presents laid out in a row in their gay Christmas paper and the thought of giving them out around the tree tomorrow morning was almost too much for her and tears began to run down her cheeks.

She had to go now, without thinking any more about anything. Resolutely she made for the door, opened it and walked out without once looking back. Silently she walked down the stairs and went over to the cupboard opposite the back door where she kept her wellington boots. There was a pair of thick white woolly socks pushed down one of them and she put these on before she pulled the wellingtons over her jeans. Then she heard, with a stab of pain, the familiar miaow of Meg and felt the black furry body of the cat rubbing up against her leg. She bent down and picked her up and Meg closed her eyes and began to purr loudly. Beth held the cat closely to her and then lifted her up so that they were face to face.

'Look after yourself, little friend,' she said softly. 'I'll never, ever forget you,' and she gently put the cat down on the floor where she sat upright looking at Beth. 'I'll have to go now,' she said, and without daring to look at Meg again, she put her hand on the back door knob and turned it. The door creaked as it opened slowly.

'Is that you, Beth?' her mother called from the kitchen.

'I'm just going out to get some coal for the fire,' she shouted back, her heart thumping with the fear of being discovered. How would she explain all the clothes she was wearing?

'Well don't be long, dear; your father will be home soon.'

As she stepped outside, the icy air of the freezing winter night hit her and she shivered involuntarily. Then she slowly shut the door and it was only when she removed her hand from the knob that she realized the full impact of what she had done. She put her hand back on it as if to make sure of an escape route if things went wrong and looked frantically in the dark shadows under the window for the boy. 'No, it was all a dream,' she thought, and suddenly felt very stupid. But then, as she was about to go back inside, she saw him stand up and move nervously towards her. At the sight of him all her doubts and fears instantly vanished; this was her world now and he, whoever he was and whatever he did, was her life. He stopped unsure of himself, and she began to walk slowly towards him. When she was just a pace away she smiled and then with a sudden rush of emotion she flew to him and flung her arms around his neck. Tightly she clung to him and the more she held him the more she found that all the restlessness and the anxieties she had suffered since she first met him flowed away. While holding him like this, she was also able to forget her worries and her deep sadness at leaving home and leaving all the people she loved. This was the only way they could communicate; through her body she was trying to transmit all these emotions and fears to him and, along with the fears, the great joy and happiness she felt at seeing him again and being with him. It was as if a dam, against which water had been building up for three years, had suddenly burst and all the water was gushing out.

Nab, who when the girl had first put her arms around him had been unable to understand what she was doing and had grown even more tense and afraid than he already was, now began to relax and respond by slowly lifting his arms and closing them around her. Like all animals his senses were very highly attuned to emotions and he understood what she was trying to tell him, so that he equally, in the only way he could, tried to reassure her and comfort her in her uncertainty and sadness. Beth, when she felt his body relax and his arms around her, could have cried for joy and relief. For the first time

152

since she had been very young she felt totally at peace with herself; the cold night air that she breathed went to her head, and the trees in the back garden which stood stark and winter-bare silhouetted against the dark sky, their twigs like the long bony fingers of an old wizard, seemed to be her friends and guardians.

They stood like that for a long time in the shadows at the back of the house, each trying to reassure and comfort the other; so lost in their own world that nothing mattered except the moment which was timeless. Then suddenly their world was shattered by two great beams of light that cut away the darkness on their left then moved across to catch them in its glare for a moment and finally vanish inside the garage to the right of the cottage.

'Daddy's home. We must rush,' she said and, although Nab could not understand what she was saying, he detected the note of urgency in her voice and in any case he also felt that they should leave as quickly as possible. As they heard the noise of the car engine stop they were halfway across the back garden and by the time the garage door slammed shut they were passing the belt of trees under which Brock had been waiting anxiously and with not a little irritation for them to come away from the house. How much longer they would have stood there if the car had not arrived he did not know nor did he like to think but he was thankful that Nab was here at last, with the girl, and they were safe.

Beth wondered what the boy was doing when he uttered some sounds in the direction of the trees but when the badger emerged stealthily from the shadows she was not altogether surprised as she had seen him so often in her dreams. Nevertheless she was very excited; despite all her time spent in the woods, particularly at dusk which was her favourite part of the day, she had never before seen a live badger. Now here was one walking beside her and never even giving her a sideways glance. Then she saw the owl perched on the fence apparently waiting for them. She heard the boy make some more noises to it and to her astonishment the owl responded. Then the truth occurred to her; although he could not speak the human language he was able to speak in the language of the animals and they likewise spoke to him. The noises that he made to her were in their language and that was why she could not understand them.

153

They were just crawling under the wooden fence when they heard the crunch of footsteps walking along the gravel drive from the garage to the house and then the sound of the front door opening and closing and, muffled from inside the house, the traditional evening greeting from her mother to her father and his to her. 'Hello dear; had a good day?' 'Yes thanks; and you? Any post?' Then a pause while he looked at any letters that had arrived. 'What's for supper?' he would add finally before he went up the stairs to change out of his work clothes.

Beth heard each piece of the familiar jigsaw pattern of her life and wondered whether it would be for the last time. The security of that routine had been the foundation of her life; now she was scrambling up the hill with a badger on one side of her, this strange and beautiful boy on the other and a large brown owl flying low ahead of them over the field leading the way. Where she was going she did not know nor even why, but now that she was on the way she was hardly able to contain the exultant feeling of joy and freedom which surged through every part of her body. And then finally, when they were at the top of the hill, she heard a different note in the house and knew that the jigsaw, for a while anyway, had been broken. It was the sound of her father she heard, calling down in panic to her mother, 'Where's Beth? Have you seen her?' and then the back door flying open, releasing a stream of light into the darkness, as her mother dashed out to see whether she was still by the coal-shed and stood framed in the doorway shouting her name out loud over the fields. 'Be-eth, Be-eth,' a long drawn out cry which cut the girl through with guilt and remorse and almost made her run back down and tell them she was all right and safe and that she loved them. But she knew that she could not. She had caught hold of Nab's shoulder when they heard her father shout and they were both standing now looking down at the scene of panic below them. Nab understood the pain she was feeling; it was as if he were to leave Brock and Tara, never, perhaps, to see them again, and he found her hand where it lay hanging limp and cold by her side, and clasped it in his. She turned to him and her eyes were misty and sparkling with tears and once again they held each other tightly for comfort until the voice of her father, calmer now, came down to her mother calling her in to look at something. He had found the note in her bedroom. Beth could do no more; she turned away quickly from the sight of home and, still holding each other's hand, the two walked slowly away over the frozen snow until they found Brock and Warrigal waiting for them under a large ash tree at the side of the field. Then the four set out under the moonlight for Silver Wood.

CHAPTER XIV

They did not rush to get back to the wood. Instead it was a slow and lingering amble under the stars which seemed to last for ever for they felt that the night was full of magic and had been made especially for them. There was little wind; instead the air was still and the moon shone down out of a night sky that was of such a deep blue that it was almost black. It reflected up from the white fields so that if it had not been for the shadows under the hedges and trees which showed up darkly against the snow and stood like silent watchers of the night, everywhere would have been as bright as day. The sorrow that Beth had felt at leaving home began to evaporate as she lost herself in a world that was as new to her as if she had just been born. She had been out at night before into the fields but somehow she felt as if her eyes must have been closed for it had never seemed like this. Before, she had been on the other side; now she was on this side, their side, the side of the badger and the owl and all the other creatures of the wild. Instead of being an observer, she was now a participant looking at their world from within. For Nab, seeing the wonder and joy in her eyes as she looked around at the night, it was as if he himself was seeing everything anew and her happiness became his. Every so often they would stop and the girl would bend down to stroke Brock and bury her face against his neck the way that he loved. Then she would hold his head and look straight into the badger's eyes and talk to him in her strange language with a voice that was full of music and gentleness. Afterwards she would stand up and look at Warrigal as he

157

perched on a branch and the owl would stare back at her with his great round eyes for a long time without blinking and then he would emit a very low hoot as if to tell her his pleasure that she was with them. She would smile at him and lift her hand up to his head to stroke it carefully and gently so that the lids closed over his eyes for such a long time that Brock and Nab would think he had fallen asleep. Thus it was that she captured their hearts as she had Nab's so that soon she was to them almost as Nab and they did not see her as an Urkku, for this is the way of the Eldron.

At other times on the walk back to the wood they would have fun racing one another to a gate or a tree or a hedge and when they got there they would be laughing for joy; Warrigal, of course, always won, and Nab would have come next but with an instinctive sense of good manners he always let the girl beat him. Brock however was not so polite and would do his utmost to beat her, sometimes running under her legs so that they both toppled over on to the snow; she laughing and he uttering little barks and yelps of amusement.

Beth also taught Nab the joys of snowball fighting. He had been walking slightly ahead of her and when suddenly he realized she was not by his side and turned around to find her, an icy cold lump of snow hit him on the chest. Then when she bent down to scoop up another handful he copied her and with some delight hit her squarely on the shoulder only to find he had been hit on the neck again and the cold snow was beginning to creep down inside his garments. From then on they had a running battle until their hands grew cold. Then Nab copied her again as she cupped them around her mouth and breathed very hard on them and found to his surprise that this warmed them. There was so much he would learn from her, he thought, his curiosity at the ways of the Urkku awakened, but first he would have to try to learn to speak her language. He looked at her and smiled and his heart lifted again for joy when she smiled back.

So lost were they all in the happiness of that walk that they did not realize how far they had come until suddenly they were by the gate near the pond and with a thrill of anticipation saw in the distance the tops of the trees of Silver Wood. The thought of home put a new lightness and urgency into their step and they were soon going under the fence into the flat field at the front of the wood. It was at that

158

point that they first began to realize that something was wrong. The wood was too quiet; not a sound was to be heard and not a movement was to be seen, neither the hooting of Wythen nor the scurrying of rabbits around the front of the wood as they played and ate as they always did in the evening. But it was not just the absence of any signs of life that caused the hearts of the animals to start beating faster; the appearance of the wood seemed different as well. Even at this distance they would normally have been able to make out the large looming shapes of the belts of rhododendron and the familiar sight of the Old Beech standing at the centre of the front of the wood, but with a growing sense of panic and horror they could not find them. The nearer they got the more they lost their bearings so that they did not know which part of the wood to make for. They were running

now, fast, blindly, and the silver moonlight which had before seemed magical now shone down coldly and cruelly to expose the dreadful sight before them. Now they were at the old fence which surrounded the wood and before them they could clearly see the remains of their home. With the blood pounding in their ears and their stomachs heavy and knotted with the sickness of despair they looked at the tracks left by the tractors in the soft ground as they had pulled the rhododendrons up and left them in a pile on one side, and they saw the stumps of the trees where the saws had cut through them sending them crashing down to the ground where the ones that had not yet been sawn remained lying uselessly amongst the debris which had once been the floor of the wood. Not all the trees had been felled yet; the men had started at the front and were working back so that the trees they had seen in the distance were those which had been in the back part of the wood beyond the little stream. Everywhere the smell of the Urkku lingered on the air; the fumes from the tractors and the cloying smell of cigarettes, and pieces of paper littered the ground, either frozen to the earth or floating on the gusts of wind that blew across from the hills in the distance. And then Nab saw the first of the familiar red tubes which he dreaded; cartridges were strewn everywhere and as the animals picked their way over the great ruts left by the diggers they found dark streaks of blood on the black earth and tufts of hair and fur lying on the floor.

Slowly now, for they were numb with horror, they walked amongst the mess that had been their home. When an area had been cleared of trees the diggers had moved in to grub up the bracken and any remaining shrubs or saplings and in these areas there was no trace left of the wood for them to recognize, just a churned up expanse of muddy earth, but where this had not yet been done they could just about get their bearings and so eventually they came to the Old Beech, lying half sawn up on the earth. The freshly cut flat top of the stump was a very light pink colour and showed up clearly in the moonlight. They stood staring at it for a long while, unable to believe their eyes. Beth stood behind them, realizing that the wood had been their home and understanding their grief at what had happened. She herself had often looked at the wood from afar and thought how beautiful it was, and when she had heard in the village that it was to be cleared she had felt deeply sad for the animals that lived there.

Brock, Nab and Warrigal looked at the entrance to the sett, open now and exposed for all to see and the thought of Tara drove itself through the numbness of their minds until finally Brock slowly dragged himself across the unfamiliar ground at the front of the sett, scarred and cut by the tractor that had pulled at Nab's rhododendron bush. He was just about to go down the hole when a movement caught his eye amongst the heap of bushes piled up just beyond the sett. The others had also seen it and they looked round as Sam slowly emerged from cover. His head was bent low and his tail was tucked round under his back legs so that as he walked he appeared to be hunched up. His tan coat, which normally shone with life, was now all matted with mud and the front of his shoulder on the right was covered in a dark red cake of dried blood. There was also a graze across his nose which showed up as a red stripe running from the black tip and ending up on his forehead in a deep gash. He limped heavily towards them without even raising his head, stopping when he got to where Brock was standing. Warrigal and Nab went forward but Beth stayed where she was, shocked by the transformation of this night from one of the greatest joy to the misery she now saw before her.

Sam's voice was low and unsteady as he spoke and the others edged closer to catch what he was saying.

'They came soon after you'd gone,' he said. 'First with the guns; hundreds of them, killing everything that moved. It was terrible; the cries of the wounded as they tried to escape, and the noise; hundreds of explosions, deafening until I couldn't think. Everywhere there was terror, panic, blood, the smell of death, the smell of their guns. No one could escape; they were all around the wood; beaters at one end and guns at the other. Rabbits with their legs blown off twitching, bleeding into the snow, pheasants thudding down like rain. The smell of blood.' He stopped, unable to continue – the nightmare was more than he could recount. Finally, after a silence which no one broke, he went on.

'Then when the guns had gone they came with the long white tube; round all the holes, earths, setts, warrens. And the silence that hung over everything was broken only by the muffled cries and thumpings underground. Finally they came with the machines and began to tear up the wood. All day, clanking, grinding and banging and shouting. I got out of your bush just before they dragged it away, Nab; it's over there somewhere amongst that heap.'

There was another silence and then Brock said quietly, 'Tara?'

Sam looked up for the first time and the misery in his deep brown eyes told Brock the worst. He turned away slowly and walked off into the field. Nab followed him and they both walked until they got to the fence at the far side, when they stopped and began to walk back. There was nothing to say; grief burned in both of them, and the shock of the final loss which death brings held them in a state of trance. As if in a dream they walked unbelievingly up and down the field trying to grasp the fact that she had gone and that they would never see her again. Pictures of her flashed into their minds but when they tried to focus on one and keep it there it began to fade away. Memories flooded back; for Brock the early days, setting up home, having the cubs, life with Bruin, the way she would scold him after one of his escapades, the warmth of the love in her eyes. And then the arrival of Nab, the excitements and anticipation of those first days; the joy in her face when she suckled him, the laying out of the fresh beds of meadowsweet that first night. Nab thought of winter evenings with her in the sett when he was young, snuggled warm into her deep soft fur, and summer evenings when they would sit together outside the sett under the Great Beech and talk while the pigeons cooed and Brock was out foraging. Then, when he was older, the warmth and understanding of pure love which was always there whenever he was worried or had a problem. Now she was gone and it was as if the sun had gone for ever and there would be no more summers. He thought he had got used to coping with sudden and violent death after losing Rufus and Bruin but, he realized now, it was impossible to ever get used to that sickening sense of absolute loss that burns through every part of the body at the death of someone you love. Tears misted his eyes as he tried to focus on the ground while they walked together, he and Brock, up and down the field. They would never see her again; the thought churned itself around in their minds, over and over until it became a mere form of words, and then suddenly the sense of loss would surge back to hit them physically in the stomach and a wave of grief would once again engulf them, forcing burning tears down Nab's face and sending him once more into sobbing convulsions of despair which hurt his throat and turned his stomach sour.

They walked like that for a long time while the others watched them, miserable and lost, from the mess that had been the wood. Finally when the sense of unreality and the shock of death had given way to anger, the boy and the badger came slowly back to join their friends. Gone now from their eyes was despair and in its place the others could see a towering rage. Hatred emanated from them like heat from a fire; hatred for the obscenity of what had been done to their home and hatred for the revolting death of Tara. Brock was unable to go down and see her for when he put his nose into the entrance the gases flung him back coughing and choking; and this was the final indignity, that she should be down there twisted and broken and alone. He imagined her lying amongst the meadowsweet, strewn around in panic as she fought for breath, with her lips drawn back against her teeth in that hideous half-smile, half-snarl that is the mark of death by poison. At that moment the words of Wychnor came back to him, '. . . and Dréagg planted the seed of cruelty deep within the Urkku so that they were cruel in their ways towards the animals, for Man had been made as an instrument of revenge.' Nab also thought of these words and they were a help in that at least now they knew the reason for their suffering.

They stood by the stump of the Great Beech for a long time, huddled together in the cold, lost in misery and not knowing what to do. Then they heard a noise in the field and looking up saw an animal moving slowly towards them in the moonlight. It was Perryfoot. As he got closer they could see that he, like Sam, had been wounded. He dragged his back leg behind him leaving a trail of red in the snow and movement appeared to be painful. But they were immensely pleased and relieved to see him, as he was to see them.

'You've been a long time,' he said, and they smiled ruefully at him and the fact that even at this, their most desperate hour, he could produce some spark of his old self, filled them with new hope. Then he saw Beth standing behind them looking at him with gentleness in her eyes and he recognized her as the little girl before whom he had performed that spring day with Brock and Nab. Warrigal then attempted to explain to both Sam and Perryfoot that the Elflord had told them that she was a part of their mission and would be with them on a long journey they were all to go on.

'There is much to explain to you,' he said, 'but we shall tell you later. Suffice it to say that she is not of the Urkku but of the Eldron and that therefore she is a friend.'

Beth did not know what they were saying but guessed that they were talking about her from the way that the dog and the hare, which she thought she recognized from somewhere, were both looking at her as the owl seemed to be talking to them. She went forward and, kneeling down, began to stroke Sam's head with one hand and Perryfoot's with the other. At first they were tense and wary but soon, as she continued to stroke them and talk to them gently, they gained confidence in her and relaxed. She looked at their wounds; they really needed a good wash before she would be able to tell how bad they were. She did not know what their plans were nor whether this awful destruction of their homes had changed them but if they were staying she could perhaps find a little stream.

While these thoughts were going through her head she suddenly became aware of a dark shadow swooping down out of the sky and, looking up, saw another brown owl landing on the stump of the tree and starting to speak to them.

The animals were relieved to see Wythen still alive. He explained to them as best he could what had happened since they had left but even he, who was normally so dispassionate and objective, found it hard at times to relate the atrocities he had witnessed and he had to stop frequently and swallow hard before carrying on. He told them how Sam had been shot charging at the Urkku who were putting the long tube down the sett and how even though he was wounded he had got one of them on the ground before the other one knocked him out and left him for dead; that was what had caused the gash on his head.

The owl then recounted how Perryfoot, to try and draw the attention of some of the Urkku with guns away from the wood, had brushed up against their legs and then run slowly out into the field, so that they followed him. He had led them right to the pond, running in a zigzag so that they were unable to get a good shot at him, but then an Urkku had suddenly appeared in front so that he had momentarily stopped. That had been enough and he had been shot in the back leg; he had then crawled away and taken cover in the hedge and the Urkku had been so afraid of missing good sport back at the wood that they had not bothered to look for him.

Wythen told the other animals these two stories because, although in normal times they would have been told by Sam and Perryfoot themselves, he knew that at the present time of grief and sadness they would be too modest, and stories like that must be told and remembered.

He went on sadly. 'Very few of the other animals have survived. Pictor was gassed after herding his rabbits down their warrens during the shooting; I don't think any of the rabbits are left. Thirkelow was shot on the wing while trying to urge the other pigeons faster away from the wood, and Sterndale, having failed again to keep his pheasants from flying up, was shot while attacking one of the Urkku; he is still alive though barely and I am staying with him on this, the last night he will see. He sends you all good fortune; I have told him your mission and he will die happy, confident of your success. Digit, Cawdor and Remus are all dead and Bibbington has left the wood. All the other survivors have fled although there is nowhere for them to go. I shall stay while there is a tree left for me to roost in although that will not be for much longer.'

There was a pause as the old owl looked down at the ground and when he looked up his huge round eyes were full of sadness; yet when he spoke again there was no despair in his voice.

'But now there is hope,' he said. 'You have been to the Lord Wychnor and know all there is to know. You have the girl from the Eldron; your mission has started well but there is one thing I would say to you. Let not your anger and hatred at what you have seen this night interfere with your resolve, for if you do it will cloud your judgement. I understand well enough how you must feel; yet channel your hatred into determination for success in what you must do, for that will lead to the ultimate victory. Now I wish to see you go, for you cannot stay here any longer. It is for the far hills that you head; I will stay here watching until you are out of sight.'

The travellers filed past him singly and as each one walked by he looked them deeply in the eyes as if to transmit some part of his enormous wisdom to them, and indeed, as they left his gaze and walked out into the field, they did feel somehow different. They turned to their left when they were out of the wood and walked along the front of their ravaged home. When they reached the corner they stopped and looked back. Wythen was still there, perched on the stump, looking at them with the breeze ruffling his brown feathers and his head upright and proud. Then they turned away and without looking back again struck off across the frozen fields with Wythen watching them until they went behind a hedge in the middle distance and were finally out of sight. He remained perched on the stump for a long while, thinking, but his head now was bowed and he looked old for he had called upon his last reserves of strength and energy to fill them with courage for their journey. Now there was no need and the scenes of carnage he had witnessed and the destruction of his home bore down upon him once more so that his shoulders dropped and his eyes clouded over with sorrow. Finally he gathered himself together and took off from the stump to fly back to the hollow in the bracken where he had left Sterndale dying. As he dropped down by his friend the midnight bells were ringing in Christmas and the sound echoed over the fields and into the desolate wood. Sterndale heard it through the mists of pain which submerged him from the wound in his chest and was thankful that he would not be alive to witness the final destruction of the few surviving animals at the big killing which the bells always foretold.

Wythen looked down into the eyes of the pheasant, which were glazed with suffering and whispered quietly to him. 'Old friend, you may die with hope in your heart for they have gone and I believe they will succeed. And then all our suffering, and the suffering of those before us will not have been in vain. Do you hear me, old friend? There is hope.'

Sterndale's eyes then lost their panic and became calm and as he sank beneath the waves of death he held on to the hope in Wythen's eyes so that he died with a heart that was, finally, at peace. Then the owl left the side of his dead friend and flew up to the Great Oak. There he perched on one of the high branches to look out over what was left of the wood and wait for the end.

CHAPTER XV

The animals walked through the frozen fields in silence, each nursing his grief privately like a wound. With the loss of their home they felt as if they had been cut adrift and were floating aimlessly in nothing; the lifeline that had always reached out to them wherever they might be had gone for there was nowhere to go back to. They walked in a dream; their only security now was the security of the journey, and their only home wherever they happened to be at any particular moment. They had just lost everything and were not yet able to appreciate the safety of having nothing more to lose. They would never forget the pain of their grief that night but in time it would become less sharp and would become simply a part of themselves instead of this huge dark cloud which dominated and threatened them constantly, hanging over them so that they were unable to escape its shadow. And Brock and Nab, although they could never think of Tara without the tears coming to their eyes, would eventually be able to talk about her and their times together with some happiness at their recollection.

They had to walk slowly because of Sam's injured leg, which was getting worse the farther they went so that now his limp was very pronounced and the wound had opened up and begun to bleed again. Worse even than that was the fact that the cold got into the gash on his head, making it throb terribly and giving him a splitting headache.

Perryfoot had found it impossible to walk at all and very early on, when they had just passed out of sight of the wood, Beth had torn off part of one of her tee-shirts and fashioned a makeshift sling which she tied around Nab's neck and then placed the hare in, much to the boy's surprise and Perryfoot's delight. At first he had been apprehensive but as he got more used to the idea of being carried in this way he began looking around with some of his old arrogance and Nab detected a familiar twinkle of mischief in his black eyes. When he was alert like this his ears stuck up erect and now they kept getting in Nab's face, but after a while the combination of utter exhaustion and the rhythm and warmth of Nab's body as he walked, lulled the hare into a deep sleep so that his ears fell flat along his back out of the way.

Warrigal flew ahead of them, low over the fields at about hedge height and it seemed to Nab, watching him swoop and glide like a shadow, that he had spent the last half of his life travelling like that with the owl always just in sight leading them to their destination. He looked down at Perryfoot's closed eyes and smiled inwardly at the thought that the hare at least was in peaceful oblivion. Beth, holding his hand by his side, had long since given up trying to make any sense out of what she was doing and abandoned herself to the rhythm of the walk. It seemed a long time now since she had left the cottage, and the image of her mother crying frantically for her as she stood in the doorway flashed back into her mind as a memory from a forgotten world. Even the magical happiness of their walk to Silver Wood seemed to have taken place an age ago so dark was the cloud of misery that now hung over the animals. And she shared their grief for, in a sense, she too had lost her home and her loved ones as well as having seen the ruin of theirs. Already she felt as if she had known the boy for years, so easy and relaxed did she feel with him and despite the fact that they had not been able to say two words to each other which could be understood. Yet this did not seem to matter, so close was the empathy and understanding which for some miraculous reason seemed to exist between them. She turned her head slightly to the right to look at him as he walked by her side. His head was bowed now and the anger that had filled his dark eyes seemed to have given way to a dull sorrow which had even touched the way he walked so that instead of the limitless energy which had seemed to propel him before, his steps seemed plodding and tired. She suddenly felt an enormous wave of sympathy towards him and a wish to protect him and look after him and make him happy again. She had no idea of where they were travelling or why but she sensed that in some way they were involved in the making of history and that the boy was somehow in the centre of it and that he would need all the love and care she could give him in the days ahead. She gently squeezed his hand and he looked at her as if he understood all that she was thinking and was grateful. She smiled and he returned her smile and for a moment he escaped the clutches of the nightmare that was pulling at his mind. When she smiled it was as if a shaft of sunlight had pierced a darkened room, providing hope and encouragement for the future; a glimmer of joy at the end of a tunnel of gloom, urging him to go forward to meet it and to become lost in its brilliance. Nab wondered whether or not, without her, he would have had any will to carry on. He glanced quickly behind him and saw, some way behind, the limping figure of Sam and by his side Brock, looking old and worn. In the sling at his front lay Perryfoot, unable even to walk and only Warrigal, in front, seemed remotely capable of undertaking the enormity of the task which they had to accomplish.

When the Christmas bells tolled at midnight, sending peals of music over the moonlit fields, Beth's heart was touched by a pang of homesickness but the animals stopped and looked at each other grimly in anticipation of the slaughter it foretold.

In Silver Wood, in the old days, a Council Meeting would have been called to discuss tactics and to prepare the wood in readiness. 'They have nearly all gone now,' thought Brock. 'Only Wythen is left.'

His mind flashed back with a little thrill of recollection to that Council Meeting, so many seasons ago, when he had broken the news of the arrival of a baby Urkku in the wood. And then he realized, as did the others, that although by the time the killing began they would be a long distance away from the wood nevertheless they would still have to be extremely careful, wherever they were, for the slaughter went on all over the land.

And so they trudged on slowly with their thoughts drifting between the past, the future and the present, and the only sound the crunching of the frozen surface of the snow as they walked. The trees, dark, shadowy and mysterious in the moonlight, seemed to move in acknowledgement as they passed, the boughs dipping slightly, and the sound of the breeze in the branches seeming to greet them and wish them good fortune on their journey.

In the distance the little copse towards which their eyes were fixed stood out clearly on the skyline where it stood encircling the top of a large hummock which grew like an enormous molehill on the relatively flat stretch of moors surrounding it. Soon the colour of the sky behind the copse grew lighter and the animals found themselves among the gently rolling foothills which led up to the flat summit of this small range of hills and, as the first rose-pink streaks of dawn began to appear in the sky to herald the beginning of a new day, Christmas Day, they stood looking across a bleak expanse of moorland in the middle of which was the copse. The snow here was deeper and the wind was quite strong so that it had drifted in the little hollows and against the tussocks and the walking was difficult. Brock and Sam could now only go very slowly because of the dog's injury and the others had to keep waiting for them. The wind was much colder up here and Beth was thankful that she had brought so many clothes; looking at Nab's bare legs she gave a little shiver and huddled deep into her grandmother's cape. They saw no other animals but there was the occasional track of a hare in the snow and once or twice they heard the chuckling of a grouse in the distance. Finally, as a pale watery sun appeared in the clear morning sky, they climbed up the slope of the hummock and entered the copse. They carried on climbing through firs and the occasional twisted oak until they reached the top which was bare of trees and through which sharp angular outcrops of rock showed, where the wind had blown away the snow. The snow had also been blown off the heather and clumps of it clung on to the patches of earth between the rock or else seemingly grew out of the rock itself, its roots finding a precarious foothold in the cracks. It moved with the wind as seaweed moves with the waves and the strong gusts seemed to be trying to pull it away, yanking at it savagely.

Amongst these rocks each of the travellers found a sheltered spot and sat looking down across the bleak expanse below them where the moors stretched away into the distance before dropping down sharply into the valleys and clefts of more foothills and then finally levelling out into a huge plain; and although they could not see it they knew that at the far end of that plain was the ocean towards which they were heading. As they sat with the wind blowing in their faces and making their eyes water and with what seemed to be the whole world laid out beneath them they felt the power of the place fill them with strength and energy. Each of them seemed to grow inwardly until their spirit was bigger than their body and escaped the physical confines in which it had been trapped for so long to leap out into the mountain air and dance joyously in the wind. No longer did the sufferings of their bodies seem important; they seemed to be outside themselves, looking down as they soared into the sky and flew on the wind. This place was one of the Scyttels or places of power, guessed at by many, and whose existence is hinted at in legend and song, but known only to the elves and those with the power of magic. It is at the Scyttels that the elves gather for rejuvenation of their magic and at the greatest of them it is said that the Elflords are visited by Ashgaroth. Thus it was that the Lord Wychnor had chosen this copse as their starting place, for there Nab, as one with the power of magic, would be enabled to get his bearings and to follow the currents of the earth to the Elflords of the Sea and of the Mountains by means of the secret ways, or Roosdyche, which join the Scyttels one to the other.

Nab and Beth were perched together in a little rocky crevice between two enormous boulders, their bodies braced against the wind, exulting in the power of the place and the warmth of each other as they huddled close. They sat like that until the sun was high in the blue sky and then weariness overtook them and they lay down together behind the rock out of the wind and went to sleep. Nab had dropped straight off as soon as his eyes had closed but Beth had lain awake for a while thinking and staring at a sparrowhawk hovering way above them in the distance. She was marvelling at the deep contentment which she felt within herself and luxuriating in the peacefulness of it. Finally when the sparrowhawk had swooped away out of sight she turned to look at Nab lying beside her, his body moving rhythmically as he breathed the deep breath of sleep and his legs curled up into his chest with his head resting on his two hands clasped together under it for a pillow. Then smiling to herself she gently wrapped her arms around him from behind, snuggled up against him and went off to sleep.

The rest of the animals had also gone to sleep; Sam, Brock and Perryfoot together in a little hollow behind a boulder just beneath Nab and Beth, and Warrigal perched on an old root of heather which he had found on one side of the hollow. They slept all the rest of Christmas Day and all that night, finally waking up the following dawn feeling marvellously refreshed; the cloud of sorrow which they had carried with them from Silver Wood seemed to have been blown away in the wind, leaving them with sad memories but freeing them from the claustrophobia of their earlier misery. Now they felt ready and eager to press on; they got up from the warmth of their sleeping places and, looking back fondly at their first home of the journey, they began to make their way back down from the rocks.

They had just reached the bottom of the belt of trees and were about to emerge on to the heather covered slope at the base of the little hill when, ahead of them, Warrigal stopped and, perching on a low branch moved his wings slowly up and down. That was the signal to wait and, an instant later, they saw a line of Urkku come into sight walking slowly along the flat stretch of moors at the bottom of the hill beneath them. They all held guns resting in the crooks of their arms so that they pointed out from their bodies and down to the ground. They were just like the organized slaughterers that the animals had seen coming through Silver Wood and they made those same funny shouting and whooping noises to frighten the animals into showing themselves. Nab and the others froze where they were and then sank down slowly behind the trees; Beth felt her wrist gripped tightly and she responded as quietly and carefully as she was able to the boy's gestures. The line slowly passed by them, hardly looking to left or right, and to the relief of the animals not turning and coming towards them up the hill as they had dreaded. Soon all that could be seen was a row of backs retreating into the distance but then they heard the rapid frightened chatter of some grouse and, a second later, the cracks of the guns as the morning yielded up its toll of death. Then Perryfoot, lying at Nab's side, saw to his horror a large mountain hare suddenly jump up from its night time resting place and race off in front of the guns. The shots, as they were fired, seemed to jerk the hare back as if there was a length of string attached to its neck which had suddenly run out and pulled it up short. They watched as it lay twitching and crying on the ground until one of the Urkku came up to it, kicked it over with his foot and then beat it over the head with the butt of his gun. Perryfoot was whimpering and shivering uncontrollably with fear at the sight of what had so nearly happened to him and at the other side of him Nab could feel Beth trying to free her hand and get up. She was not yet used to sights such as this, as were the others, and the anger in her burnt fierce and keen like a flame which has just burst into life. Nab motioned to her to get down and stop pulling but she took no heed. However she was no match for the iron grip of the boy and soon she gave up and began to sob quietly. Nab and the others found to their surprise that Wythen's parting words enabled them to control their emotions; '. . . yet channel your hatred into determination for success in what you must do, for that will lead to the ultimate victory.' So their anger became submerged in their overall purpose; they were fighting the Urkku now in the pursuit of their wider goal. This was merely a battle; they were fighting the war. What they had just seen, and would doubtless see again many times before the end, merely strengthened their resolve to succeed.

And yet, watching the magnificent creature that a second ago had been vibrant with life and grace being clubbed to death slowly over the head, it was impossible to remain totally detached and objective and Nab felt tears start from the corners of his eyes and trickle down his face.

Eventually the Urkku vanished into the far distance and the animals felt able to relax again. Warrigal flew back to them where they lay amongst the trees and they all decided to stay where they were until after Sun-High to give the Urkku plenty of time to get clear.

'We shall rest here, then, until mid-afternoon,' said Warrigal, 'and then we shall have to travel through the night.' This of course suited him and Brock but Sam and Perryfoot felt more at home in the daylight. Nab did not mind travelling by day or night as he was equally comfortable in either, but on balance it was agreed by them all that it was generally safer in the evening and at night as there were less likely to be Urkku abroad. The sky was still bright and clear and the mid-morning sun was quite warm in any shelter they could find from the cold wind. So once again they settled down behind clumps of heather and tree trunks and were soon lightly sleeping with the warmth of the sun on their eyelids.

Sam was the first to wake up in the afternoon and he roused the others. It was quite a different day to the one they had closed their eyes on. The sky was full of large ominous black clouds and the wind had died down slightly and changed direction so that it was also warmer.

'Rain,' said Brock as he lifted his nose and sniffed at the air, and just as they left the trees the first large wet spots began to fall. Beth put up the hood of her cloak and felt grateful for its cover as she heard the rain pattering down on it. They headed out over the stretch of moors through which the Urkku had walked that morning with Warrigal once again in the lead. However, he had to keep stopping now and conferring with Nab for it was the boy who was able to feel most strongly the currents in the earth which told them the way to follow. The rain soon began to turn the hard crisp surface of the snow into a wet soft slush and the going became more difficult as they departed from the route along which the shoot had gone and headed into an area of bog where the green spongy surface of moss and rushes squelched beneath their feet and Beth found her wellingtons sinking in almost to the top. Perryfoot, although he was much better, was still unable to keep pace with the others so he was being carried again by Nab but Sam was having great difficulty behind them as his legs kept sinking in the mulch and Brock had to help him out.

Fortunately they were soon clear of the bog and now they began to descend through the foothills. It was less sharp and craggy here; instead gentle green slopes and soft valleys surrounded them and here and there they saw flocks of sheep grazing, seemingly oblivious to the weather. Soon they were walking through a particularly deep valley with a rushing stream on one side and they were completely hidden from view by the steep banks on either side which were covered with gorse bushes, thorn trees and the strewn remains of last year's bracken, standing out dark brown with the wet. The sky ahead was full of the pinks and crimsons of sunset and the dark clouds had broken up allowing shafts of cold winter sunlight to break through. The rain had stopped but with its departure the cold wind had returned adding to the discomfort they all felt at still being soaked from the rain. In a way the sunlight made them feel worse as it gave the illusion of warmth and made them even more aware of how cold and damp they were. Wearily they trudged on through the valley along a muddy path that ran next to the stream. Sam's wounds had begun to ache badly again and he and Brock were falling further and further behind until, as dusk drew in, the others had to keep stopping to let them catch up or they would have been out of sight. Gone now was the magic euphoria of the Scyttel when the power of the rocks and the wind had filled them with a feeling of limitless energy and invincibility. Now the thought of plodding on through the night filled them with unutterable despair. To make matters worse the rain had started to fall heavily again and it was so cold that the drops were coming down as hail, stinging their faces and necks and making them smart with soreness where they hit. And they were hungry. The animals had not really stopped to eat since they had left Ellmondrill so long ago and Beth had not eaten since lunchtime two days ago. Strangely she had not realized it until now and was only at this moment beginning to feel hungry; the excitement of everything had allowed her no room for thoughts of food; but now she became scared as her stomach began to rumble and feel hollow and empty. 'What am I going to eat?' she thought to herself. She would have to eat what the boy ate, whatever that was. She wondered when they would stop for food, if ever, and, gripping Nab's hand tightly to make him look at her, she pointed a finger to her open mouth. To her relief he nodded and stopped.

Softly and very low, Nab called to Warrigal and the owl flew back and perched on a branch of the alder tree under which they had stopped. There the four of them waited for Sam and Brock and when they had arrived it was arranged that Perryfoot and Sam would stay under the shelter of the tree and try to keep as dry as they could while the others went off in search of food. Warrigal would bring something back for Sam and Brock for Perryfoot while Nab and Beth would look after themselves. Then they separated and Beth found herself being led by the boy down into the stream where they splashed along looking minutely at the damp dripping banks and picking out little green shoots and roots which he handed to her and she ate. The tastes were mostly strange: some were vaguely familiar and reminded her of salad vegetables, like the water-cress which he found and which she had had many times before, but others were tangy and acidic or else bland and tasteless. Sometimes she recognized the plant but had never eaten it before, like chickweed, but more often she had no idea what she was eating. Occasionally he would find a fungus growing and hand it to her with a look of pride and satisfaction, for edible fungi were difficult to find at this time of year. Then she closed her eyes and chewed little bits off and swallowed them without thinking. She loved mushrooms but some of these were slimy as they slid down her throat and she had to fight hard to avoid being sick even though they tasted of very little.

When they had walked along the stream for some little while they clambered up the steep bank and Nab led her to a patch of scrubland where he again proceeded to produce little pieces of green foliage and leaves for her to eat. Finally after what Beth guessed must have been about two hours of searching for food, he stood up and they began the long walk back to the alder where they had left Perryfoot and Sam. She felt very little better and just hoped that what she had eaten would keep her going through the night. She thought with longing of the meals at home and the wonderfully satisfied feeling of warmth and fullness after a good supper and began to panic a little. Still, if it kept the boy going it must be all right for her, she thought, and tried to put all thoughts of food out of her mind although to her intense annoyance visions of large chunks of whole nut chocolate kept appearing and making her mouth water and her tummy rumble.

When they got back they found that Warrigal and Brock had returned and that Perryfoot and Sam had gratefully finished the food that had been brought for them.

'Come on then,' said Nab. 'We must put some distance behind us

176

before dawn.' Then he looked at Perryfoot who had put his ears down so that they hung limply on either side of his face. He looked indescribably miserable. 'I suppose you still want to be carried,' said the boy, and the hare visibly brightened. Sam looked on enviously as Perryfoot was again hoisted into his sling and the little procession set off once more. It was dark now so they moved more slowly and kept closer together. To their relief the rain had stopped and nearly all the snow had been washed away but the wind was still very cold. Above them the moon occasionally peeped out from behind a black cloud and sometimes a star could be seen twinkling merrily. The rest had done Sam's leg good and they made steady progress through the night until, by the time that dawn broke through on another grey wintry day, they had almost reached the bottom of the foothills and could see a huge plain stretching as far as the eye could see with only an odd hummock dotted here and there to break the flatness. On the very far edge of the plain, almost out of sight in the distance, one of these hummocks stood out larger than the rest and they could just make out, on the summit, a number of large standing stones.

'There is where we make for,' said Nab.

They were standing on top of a small hill which fell away steeply in front into a sheltered grassy hollow. The travellers made their way down into it and curled up close together at the bottom so that they were well out of the wind. They all fell asleep almost immediately, exhausted as they were, and did not wake up until late afternoon. Beth felt terrible; her legs were shaky and she was so dizzy and faint that she could hardly stand. Nevertheless she was afraid to show the others; she must persevere and start walking: perhaps once she was on the move she would feel better. Speed was obviously important and she must not hold them back from their destination wherever it was. She was also worried deep inside about how they would react if she became a burden to them, and for the first time she began to wonder why they had brought her with them in any case. Perhaps it was just as a favour to the boy because he wanted her with him after their meeting by the stream and if she became ill he would choose, or perhaps be forced, to go on with them and leave her behind.

She moved forward slowly and carefully so that she would not stumble and fall but instead of feeling better her legs felt more unsteady than before. They started walking and she steeled herself for the ordeal but after a few paces Nab looked at her and there was anxiety and compassion deep in his eyes. Then suddenly her legs collapsed under her and she felt herself falling to the grass; it was as if she were outside her body watching somebody else fall and it all seemed to happen in slow motion. The last thing she remembered before she blacked out completely was a circle of worried faces framed against the yellow evening sky as they looked down on her.

'We must get her somewhere warm and dry, quickly,' said Nab.

'I saw a stone building just over that ridge,' Warrigal said. 'I'll go and see if there are Urkku around and whether it would be safe,' and he flew off.

While he was gone Nab tried to nurse the girl back to normal by cradling her head on his lap but her face remained pale and ashen and he was scared. Sam spoke quietly.

'She's not used to living outside. They live differently from us; they have different food. It even took me some time to learn how to live like you. You were all born to it; I wasn't and neither was she.'

They waited in silence until the dark shape of the owl flew back over the ridge of the hollow and settled on the grass beside them.

'Perfect, perfect,' he said. 'It's full of hay so it will be warm and there is a smaller building on one side where there are a number of hens. They will warn us if any Urkku come near. I didn't tell them about the girl or you, Nab, so you must stay out of sight with her. They are probably trustworthy but we can't be too careful. I gave them a story about looking for new homes; I think they believed me. It took a long time to get through to them though; they found great difficulty understanding our language and I couldn't follow much of theirs. Still there was an old cock there who seemed brave and wise so we should be all right.'

Sam broke in, 'We could give her some eggs; they like eggs and it will do her good.'

Greatly relieved, Nab hoisted the limp body of the girl over his shoulder and they set off for the hay barn. They were soon there and they pushed open the great wooden door at the front which, luckily, had been left ajar, and found themselves at the bottom of a flight of stairs which led up into the hayloft. The ground floor was full of farm machinery and there were other oddments lying around which were obviously not used very often judging by the cobwebs that hung on them. Gingerly Nab climbed the stairs and when he got to the top lifted Beth carefully up on to the pile of hay. Climbing up after her he then dragged her away from the edge until he found a little hollow in the middle and there he made her comfortable. All the others except the hare had waited downstairs and Nab left Perryfoot beside her before going back down to rejoin them. He found that Warrigal and Sam had been next door to where the hens lived and had brought some eggs; the dog had carried one in his mouth and the owl had gripped one in each talon and placed them very carefully on the floor of the barn before landing.

'We took them when no one was looking,' said Sam, a little note of secret triumph in his voice for this had been his idea.

They all followed Nab back up the old wooden stairs and over to where Beth was lying in her nest of hay.

'Cover her over to keep her warm,' said Warrigal, and they pulled folds of the hay out of the surrounding bales and laid them on top of her so that only her face showed and, around it like a pool of gold, her tangled hair.

'All we can do now is wait and hope she gets back to normal,' said Warrigal. 'I'll go and perch in that open window at the far end to keep a look out,' and he flew off in the narrow space between the top of the hay and the roof.

'I'll go and keep watch at the bottom,' said Sam, and he limped back over the hay and made his way slowly down the stairs, which were open-backed, a bit slippery and rather awkward.

Brock curled up against the girl on top of the hay and was soon asleep while Perryfoot nestled up against Brock's deep fur where he too was soon lost in oblivion, his nose twitching and his leg occasionally jerking as he dreamt. Nab sat, feeling strangely at peace. The smell of the hay barn was new to him; he had smelt hay faintly on the wind before as it had been drying in the hot summer sun on the fields down by the stream but they had never made hay in any of the fields near Silver Wood. Now he found himself almost overpowered by its sweet, almost sickly scent. There was not a sound that could penetrate here either and the unreal stillness contributed to his sense of being in a different world. And it was warm. If warmth was what she needed then she should soon be better. He looked down at her face and wallowed in the luxury of being able to really look at every part of it closely and for as long as he wanted. He became absorbed in the delicacy of her features; her mouth, her nose, her chin, every aspect of her face entranced him. Suddenly he was overwhelmed by a desire to kiss her; it seemed the only way in which he could express all the tangled emotions towards her which he felt. Slowly he bent his face over hers and in his gentle kiss all the warmth, compassion and love he had seemed to flow out and fill her with new strength and energy. As he drew his face away Nab saw her eyelids flicker and then to his joy they opened and she looked at him and smiled.

Beth found it hard to focus at first and she had difficulty for a second or two in appreciating where she was. The last thing she could remember was waking up feeling faint in a deep green hollow; now here she was in a hay loft. Oh and it was so beautifully warm! The warmth under the hay brought life back to every part of her body and she closed her eyes again for a second or two to bathe in the luxury of it. Then she vaguely recalled Nab's kiss and looking at him she reached her hand out from under the hay and grasped his where it lay by her side. She felt peaceful, content and happy. They stayed like that for a long time; looking deep into each other's eyes with their hands squeezed tightly together. Nab's other hand gently stroked her cheek and straightened her hair where it lay spread out in its tousled fan under her head. Only the grunts and snuffles of Perryfoot and Brock as they slept broke the stillness of the loft. The only light came from the little window at the far end where a fitful moon threw the occasional shaft of silver on to the hay and silhouetted Warrigal where he stood on the sill looking out into the night. Finally the warmth and their exhaustion spread over them and they both fell asleep with Nab curled up in a ball by her side.

When they awoke next morning Beth felt a lot better and the colour had returned to her face. Nab showed her the eggs and she forced herself to eat them raw; breaking the shells carefully and then pouring the contents quickly down her throat. They would do her good anyway, she thought and indeed as the day progressed she grew stronger. In the afternoon Sam and Warrigal fetched three more and, later, three more for the evening. It poured with rain all day, pattering down on the roof and dripping off the eaves. In the morning Beth and Nab went over to the window where Warrigal had kept lookout and they stared out at the sheets of rain as they bucketed down from the heavens and swept across the green fields and valleys, filling the rivers and streams and saturating the ground. There was something very comforting and cosy about watching the rain from inside; Beth had loved to look out through her bedroom window at home when storms broke, and it reminded Nab of the times he had stared out from his rhododendron bush in Silver Wood. As they sat together by the window Beth decided that she would begin trying to teach Nab her language and perhaps she could learn his. Now would be a good opportunity to start when there was nothing else to think about and there were no distractions. She pointed outside and then cupped her hand under a drip from the eaves. 'Rain,' she said and then pointed to Nab's mouth hoping he would understand that she wanted him to repeat it. He did so slowly and carefully and then she pointed to him to tell her his word for it. Nab quickly understood what she wanted. 'Ashgaroth ∮ Draish,' he said. To Beth it sounded like a lot of squeaks and grunts for there are no alphabets and letters as the Urkku know them; only sounds. Nevertheless, difficult though it was, she attempted to copy the noises made by Nab and her attempt sent him into a fit of laughter which was so infectious that she too began to laugh. Then she tried again and Nab nodded and smiled to show that she was nearer.

After this she taught the boy her name which he found easy to say and he taught her his which, because it was short and only consisted of one sound, she found relatively simple. They went on like this for most of the rest of the afternoon, pointing to or touching things around them. Generally Nab found it easier to learn her words than she did to repeat his, and she found his even more difficult to remember, if not virtually impossible. Still she made up her mind to persevere; at least they had made a start and she was surprised at how quickly and easily Nab had taken to human speech.

When evening came the skies began to clear and the rain finally stopped. Warrigal flew down from the rafter where he had perched, sleeping all day, and spoke to Nab.

'We should be making a move,' he said. 'How is she, do you think?'

'Much better,' Nab replied. 'I'll try and indicate to her what we think and ask if she's ready.'

He did so; pointing outside and then to all the animals and then outside again. Beth understood. She nodded her head to show him that she thought she was all right now although she would really have liked another night in the barn. Still, she definitely felt much improved and since the night was clear it was probably as good a time as any to start out again. The three of them went back to where Perryfoot and Brock were still sleeping, roused them and then, after Beth had carefully put the three remaining eggs in an inside pocket of

182

her cape, they went down the stairs, with the hare once more in his sling, and, fetching Sam who had been lying on the bottom step, squeezed through the partly open door and went out into the night.

CHAPTER XVI

All through the cold crisp days of January they trudged on across the plain. The cloak of winter was heavy on the land; the trees were bare and stark, the grass cropped short and the fields frozen. There was some snow but no rain; it was too cold for that and the animals were grateful, for rain brings damp and damp is the enemy of every wild creature. So the snow froze, coating the trees with glitter which glinted in the moonlight and covering the fields with a crisp white surface which was easy to walk on and left no footprints. But although they were free of rain there was an icy cutting wind which swept down from the hills they had just crossed and nagged at them until it found a way through to their bodies. Beth was grateful for her cloak and all her layers of clothing which, although heavy and cumbersome to walk in, kept her at least moderately warm.

They kept to the same pattern as before; by day sleeping under hedges or in hollows and then as the sun started to go down in the late afternoon, setting out to walk through cold clear nights when the stars twinkled at them and the moon lit their way. For much of the time the Scyttel of standing stones which they were heading for was out of sight but Nab had no difficulty in feeling the currents of Roosdyche. Sometimes as they travelled they would come across a smaller Scyttel quite accidentally; it would perhaps have been marked by a stone or else it would simply be a little mound or a copse of trees or a place where water welled up from the earth. At other times it took the form of a grotto by a stream or a collection of huge rocks. They would stop by these places for a while and feel the power of the Scyttel giving them energy, strength and clarity of thought and, if they were lucky enough to come across one around dawn, they would sleep there for the day and awake feeling marvellously refreshed and invigorated.

Sam's injuries were almost perfectly healed now and he was in the peak of condition; his coat a deep shining gold and his eyes clear and bright. Perryfoot too was better and had been ejected unceremoniously from his sling by Nab one night when it was thought that things had got to the stage when he was simply cadging a free ride. In fact, without his lift he would never have got better or even survived but now, although he still had a bad limp and would never be able to recapture his former speed, he was very nearly back to normal.

Beth found that she had got used to the grasses, roots, berries and toadstools that Nab found for her and had even begun to enjoy some of them. They at least now kept her going and she looked forward to the spring and summer when she knew there would be far more variety and choice. Now she was able to recognize some and, although Nab always insisted that he look at them before she ate in case they were poisonous, she gathered most of her food herself.

The teaching and the learning of each other's language, which had begun in the hay barn, continued as they walked along together through the nights and it was not long before Nab had enough command of Beth's language to be able to tell her of his life and of the purpose of their mission together. She listened in amazement and fascination as he told her of his early days with Brock and Tara in the sett and of how he had been found, and of his adventures and friendships with the other animals in Silver Wood. He related to her the tales and legends of the members of the Council; Rufus, Bruin, Sterndale and Pictor, all of them now dead, and he told her the stories which he had been told of the great heroes of the past and of the early days when the Urkku were first on the earth and of the myths of the time Before-Man. Slowly, as their journey together continued, Beth felt a whole new world revealed to her; a world of whose existence she had previously been almost totally unaware and a world over which the shadow of the Urkku loomed, omnipresent, dark and forbidding. She felt as if her eyes were being slowly opened and when finally Nab retold to her, as best he could, the saga which had been related to him by the Lord Wychnor, then the answers to so many questions which had worried her and puzzled her for so long became clear; now the jigsaw became complete. She felt humble and proud to have been the one chosen by Ashgaroth to accompany Nab and she was pleased that the significance of her dreams had been explained. And she was to play a part in this saga; a part which she and the others would only fully understand at the end when they had completed their mission and Ashgaroth revealed it to them. When Nab had finished he buried his hand beneath his raiments of bark and, finding the casket on the Belt of Ammdar which contained the Ring, he pressed the catch and put his fingers inside to pull it out.

'Here; this belongs to you. It is your gift from Ashgaroth; given to me as a sign for you by the Lord Wychnor,' Nab said tenderly.

Beth took the precious ring, which she remembered so clearly from her dreams, and as she did so the silvery threads of mist deep inside it shimmered and moved gracefully in the golden light given off by the jewel deep in the shank. She placed it slowly and carefully on the long middle finger of her right hand and it seemed to cast an aura of light around her, so powerful was its glow. There it remained for ever, never to be removed, and the strength of its beauty never failed to fill Beth with wonder whenever she looked at it, and to help her through the difficult times ahead whenever she felt doubt or fear or uncertainty. It was her link with the world which Nab had shown her; her proof that she was truly chosen, and a constant reminder of the power and magic of that world and the depth of its mysteries.

The country through which they were going was not as flat as it had appeared from their first view of it; little streams and valleys cut it up and there were large areas of woodland and these they passed quickly in case they were seen by any of the travellers living in them. The existence of Nab and Beth must be kept secret until the end, and talk within a wood would soon find its way out to Dréagg through careless conversations. As they passed on across the plain the land became more fertile, the fields smaller and the Urkku dwellings more numerous. Farms were everywhere and sometimes it was impossible to avoid being within sight of one and they would find themselves crawling along ditches or by the side of hedges as lights from the farm windows blazed out across the fields and the noise of the cows being milked in the shippens, the hum of milking machines or the clatter of pails drifted out on the frosty air. At other times a dog would bark and the travellers would freeze where they were as a door opened and an Urkku stared out into the night to see what had caused the disturbance. Then they would wait until the door had closed again before venturing forward like silent shadows.

It was also at this time that they came across roads; the great bands of concrete which cut across the face of the land. Beth explained the purpose of them to Nab and he in turn told the others although they had all seen them before. Beth told them of the dangers if they were crossing when one of the Urkku vehicles was travelling along, and she always led the way over them, standing on the verge looking out for headlights and beckoning them to go over one by one when she thought it was safe. Sometimes two of them would be safely on the far side, normally Perryfoot and Brock as they went first, and then a stream of cars would appear from nowhere and the animals would lie terrified behind a bank, or hidden in a ditch by the verge, while the cars roared past in a thundering storm of noise and light, choking them with dust and fumes and leaving them shaking with fear. Once they had been crossing on a bend and Beth, thinking it was safe, had motioned Perryfoot across. He had just hopped on to the tarmac when a car screamed around the corner trapping him in its lights. The hare had frozen, mesmerized as Nab remembered from the incident he'd seen in the field at the front of Silver Wood, but fortunately Beth had just had time to leap out and pull him back before he was crushed under the wheels. The driver had seen the girl in the glare of his headlamps and had pulled to a halt further up the road. Beth had gone up to him when he got out and told him that it was her little dog he had almost run over and that she had left him tied to a tree at the side of the road in the ditch. He offered her and her dog a lift home as it was a cold night and it was past eleven o'clock, but she had politely declined the offer explaining that she did not live far away and was just taking the dog out for its last walk. The man had then wished her goodnight, walked back to his car and driven off, feeling slightly bemused by the sight of the wild-looking pretty young girl in the brown tweed cape whose eyes had seemed to transfix him with their depth and intensity and whose blonde hair had tumbled like a mane around her shoulders. She did not live far away, she had said, and yet the nearest house he had passed was eight miles back. Once back in the familiar surroundings of his own car, it was almost as if he had dreamt the entire incident.

Some time later they came across their first town. The previous night they had noticed a red glow in the dark sky and had wondered where it came from. They had stopped at dawn by the base of a huge oak tree and rested all day. That evening they set off again and the glow had still been there ahead of them until, towards midnight, they became aware of a constant hum coming to them on the wind. It was such an indistinguishable mass of sound that it could almost be forgotten about and it reminded the animals of a strong wind rushing through trees. As they got nearer the glow became brighter and the noise louder and more jagged so that now, over and above that level hum, could be heard the occasional horn of a car or the sound of a heavy lorry churning its way through the streets or a motor cycle buzzing along an empty road.

They were approaching the summit of a sharp rise in a meadow: suddenly they were at the top and there, stretched out in front of them, lay the town. It was not particularly big but to the animals it seemed as if it went on for ever. Their ears now felt as if they were being assaulted by the noise and the sky was ablaze with light; gone now was that comparatively gentle red glow, this was a maelstrom of reds, oranges and whites which carved away the darkness of the night in a huge arc above; and all around, like the crooked spokes of a giant wheel, stretched out ribbons of red as the street lights followed the roads out into the suburbs. Sometimes they could see twin pairs of lights travelling along as a car returned home late or a lorry made its lonely way through the town. As they turned a corner, these lights would sometimes, if they were on the outskirts, beam out into the darkness of the surrounding countryside and swing round as the car turned: once or twice they shone straight out at the animals, blinding them momentarily until they continued on their way.

The air was heavy with the sickly cloying smell of fumes and chemicals from a large industrial estate on one side; here also the lights were brighter and there was more noise and activity. The smell stuck in their nostrils and put a strange metallic taste at the back of their mouths; they felt unable to draw their breath properly and they became a little desperate and frightened as every time they breathed they felt this unfamiliar air go through their lungs and make them feel like retching.

They stood at the top of the rise for a while, scared but also fascinated by what seemed like a huge beast breathing fire and smoke and which even at rest was unable to stop the ceaseless turmoil within itself. Nab asked Beth lots of questions and she answered them as best she could because she was not very familiar with town life. As she told him all she knew he became cold with fear for he realized that he would be totally unable to survive in it; to live in the middle, surrounded by that mass of concrete and lights and noise, would be for him a nightmare.

'We cannot go through it,' he said to Warrigal, who was standing at his side. 'I would not be able to feel the Roosdyche and we would lose our bearings. We shall have to go round and hope to pick it up on the other side.'

'It will take us a long time,' replied the owl.

'We have no choice. If we got lost in there it would take us far longer. We should never get out. And we would be certain to be spotted. Beth has said untold numbers of Urkku dwell inside it. No; we must go round.'

They set off on a detour around the town, keeping the same distance away from it all the time. It took them fifteen nights; fifteen nights during which the town was their constant companion. By the end they almost felt as if they had come to know it; to become aware of its changing moods as the week wore on from the desperate gaiety of Saturday through the busy workday clatter of the week to the docile slothful slumber of Sunday, before the pattern began again, to repeat itself over and over, inexorably.

They had to go very slowly because of the

multitude of outlying dwellings around the town and the busy main roads down which the cars screeched and thundered but there were no mishaps even though sometimes they were forced to go so close to a house that they could hear voices. When Beth heard the familiar household noises drift out through the night air, the clatter of plates in a kitchen or the whistle of a kettle boiling on a cooker or the thump of a pair of feet going upstairs, she felt very strange. They took her back to her other world, the one of which she had been part for so long and which she had now abandoned, and she was reminded of her parents and her home. At these times waves of nostalgia would sweep over her to vanish quickly in the tension of the moment as they crept behind a wall or through a hedge in a garden.

So, while people watched television or lay asleep in their beds, outside in the cool clear night the little band made their slow and careful way round the town until finally they caught sight of the Scyttel in the distance. It was not long then before Nab detected the earth currents which told him that they were once again on the old way and they set out towards the distant mound with excitement and relief; they felt that they were now well and truly on their way and that it would not be too long before they arrived at the place of the Sea Elves where they would meet the Elflord of the Sea and the first part of their journey would be over.

Soon they reached the mound which they had kept in sight for so long. It was smaller than they had imagined from far off and was simply a large flat-topped hummock with a circle of large standing stones set in the grass. Some of the the first Urkku had, by means of logic, been able to recognize the magic power of these places and had attempted to concentrate and magnify their strength by placing these stones on them for, because magic had been denied to them, they were forced to use logic in order to be able to extract and make use of the power. It was only where the magic force was strongest that they were able to perceive the power of the place so there are myriads of lesser Scyttels totally unknown to them and of whose existence only the elves and the animals are aware, for it is only those who possess magic who can feel intuitively where they are. Thus it was only occasionally on their journey that the animals came across one of these larger and more powerful Scyttels. The day they spent at this one was a wild blustery day in early February when the sky was heavy with enormous dark clouds rolling after each other as the wind howled over the plain. They sat huddled behind one of the stones out of the wind, mesmerized by these armies of cloud passing overhead and letting the strength of the Scyttel flow into them. So aware were they of the energy of the place that they were unable to sleep and in fact they felt no need of it. Stretched out behind them they had a view of the entire plain over which they had travelled while ahead of them was a further small range of foothills to cross and they sensed that beyond those lay the sea.

When night-time came they set off across the small stretch of plain which lay between them and the hills and by midnight they were climbing. Soon the lush green pastures of the lowlands had been left behind and the ground became rocky; the grass poor and short, and instead of cows they saw only sheep picking at the sparse patches of green between the rock and the scrub. The following day the winds brought in snow and they awoke in the late afternoon to find everywhere covered with a thick blanket of white. Fortunately the snow had stopped and the sky had begun to clear so that the moon was shining clearly down on the hills. The going was easier now because the snow was freezing on top of the heather and scrub and they made good progress, particularly as up here there were no Urkku dwellings or any other sign of them.

It took them two more nights to reach the other side of the little range of hills. Eventually they found themselves standing on the top of a steep slope looking down on to a carpet of mist below. It was almost dawn so they rested and slept behind a crag before setting off in the evening down the slope. To their disappointment it had begun to rain again as the weather had grown warmer and soon the exhilaration of the clear crisp nights walking over the snow-covered heather with the moon and stars lighting up their path had evaporated under a pall of dampness.

There was no moon and the rain made it difficult for even Warrigal and Brock to see far ahead. They descended slowly down narrow paths turned slippery by the rain, which had not yet melted the ice but instead had polished them with a layer of water, making them treacherous. Several times Beth slipped and once she went rolling down a steep bank until she came to a halt at the edge of a little stream. From then on Nab kept hold of her hand for some of the paths took them along the edge of deep drops falling into inky blackness which they guessed went a long way down.

When they reached the lowest of the foothills and were almost at the bottom, the visibility became suddenly much worse as they found themselves in the middle of a thick swirling mist. The rain had now stopped but the cold clammy dampness of the mist soaked them to the skin. They carried on for a while with Nab in the lead for he was able to follow the Roosdyche even more strongly than Warrigal, who was perched on his shoulder peering into the murk ahead and steering him as best he could along what seemed to be raised green footways on either side of which the ground appeared to fall away and become black and broken.

'We cannot go much further tonight,' Nab said suddenly. 'I have lost the Roosdyche. We'll wait here until dawn when we might be able to see where we are.' Warrigal flew down and perched on an old rotten treestump in front. His eyes were red-rimmed and raw with tiredness and his feathers rough and bedraggled with the wet. Behind them the others gathered in a little group, miserable and silent as the mist blew in wraiths about them.

'We've decided to stay here until the morning,' Nab announced, and without saying a word they all lay down on the saturated ground. It was impossible to sleep. Somehow an air of evil hung about the place; the mist seemed to form itself into figures which danced and leered at them through the gloom, racing on to be replaced by another and another, each one different to the last until their minds became numb with a kind of dull sick horror. Tiredness eventually overcame Beth and she fell into a restless fitful sleep in which the evil figures which had paraded before her in the mist assumed gigantic proportions. They laughed down at her from the heavens and their long fingers wrapped themselves around her body and picked her up, tossing her like a rag doll from one to the other. Their flesh seemed to be made of some sort of slimy gelatinous substance so that where they touched her she felt terribly wet and cold and the dampness went right through her body, wrapping its icy fingers around her soul and tugging at it as if trying to shake it free. She struggled and fought to release herself from their grip but they only laughed and threw her up in the air again where she waved her arms about in panic until she was caught by another. A terrible fear spread over her, freezing her heart and turning her legs to jelly as the utter helplessness of her situation forced itself into her consciousness. She was about to give up her struggles and abandon herself to despair when she felt herself shaken by another warmer grip and heard her name called insistently by a familiar voice. 'Beth, Beth,' it said, and slowly she shook off the webs of the nightmare as the voice brought her back to wakefulness. She opened her eyes to see Nab's anxious face looking down at her. Although it was so cold she felt little beads of perspiration mingling with the damp on her forehead.

'Hold me,' she said in a small frightened voice and he did so, reviving her body with life and melting the chill in her soul with the warmth of love.

'You were tossing in your sleep, and crying out. We were afraid for you,' he said.

She told him of her dream and the others sat around and listened in fear. There was silence when she finished; they sat in the damp half-light of the early morning not knowing what to think or to do. Soon a pale watery sun began to try to filter through the mist and around them they saw a bleak landscape of twisted, stunted trees and flat bog which lay dark and oozing for as far as they could see in the unreal light. They had been walking along one of a number of raised paths on which grass grew but the one they were on now came to an end just a few paces further on and sank back into the quagmire. The heavy dank smell of decaying vegetation hung over everything, and they could see, protruding from the bog like fingers, the dead rotten stumps of old trees covered in fungi and lichens and mosses which dripped continuously into the bog.

'This is an evil place,' whispered Warrigal quietly to himself as if he was afraid that the bog might hear.

'We must go back and try to find another path,' said Nab, but he didn't move for his body seemed to be sunk into a deep trough of despair and apathy from which he was unable to raise it.

Suddenly Brock exclaimed loudly, 'What's that! Look; walking through the mist.'

193

They could faintly see a tall white figure walking slowly and deliberately through the bog towards them and they could just about make out the regular splashing of delicate footsteps in water.

'It's a heron,' Brock said. The bird walked towards them picking up its long spindly legs and placing them down carefully in the bog and as it did so its head, with the deadly sharp pointed beak, moved backwards and forwards in time with the rhythm of its walk. The animals had occasionally seen such a creature before as herons had sometimes come to the stream at the back of Silver Wood but that had been a rare occurrence and they had never been this close to one before. It stood before them, its long white wings folded in on either side of its body and reaching down at the back to a little rounded peak, reminding Beth of an old-fashioned tail coat. From each eye to the top of its head stretched a narrow spherical black marking that seemed to continue on into its plume which now was held down so that it pointed from the back of its head at an angle to the ground. To Beth it looked as if it was wearing a pair of glasses with thick black rims. When it spoke the long neck, which was tucked in between its shoulders, quivered slightly.

'I am Golconda, the Great White Heron; Guardian of the Marshes of Blore. I have been awaiting your arrival for some time since the Sea Elves warned me of your coming. My task is to see the traveller safely through the marshes. We must beware, for with your presence here the atmosphere is thick with goblins. A band of them reside in the marsh and normally we live in an uneasy truce. However they are aware of your importance if not of your purpose and they will do all they can to stop you.'

'But no one saw us,' said Nab. 'We took the greatest care. How could they know we are here?'

The heron laughed; a deep rasping noise which seemed to grate its way up from the bottom of his legs.

'You cannot escape the eyes of Dréagg. His spies are everywhere. He knew where you were from the moment you left your wood. Do not underestimate him. Now follow me, but be extremely cautious. There is but one way through the marshes. If you step off the way you will swiftly be submerged in the ooze.'

They set off through the marsh, each of them following exactly in

194

the footsteps of the other except for Warrigal, who once again sat perched on Nab's shoulder. As they walked Nab asked the heron why he was unable to feel the Roosdyche here.

'It is because Dréagg has blighted this place,' Golconda said. 'It belongs to the goblins who have no need for light nor for the power of the earth. Ashgaróth and his gifts are unknown here, it is an empty space for him and does not exist. Can you not feel the Evil One all around you?'

'Why do you then stay?' asked Warrigal.

'I have told you; someone must show travellers across. There is no other way to the sea without going through an enormous detour over the high mountains and that would take far too long and be even more dangerous. In any case it is impassable in winter. And I can survive on what is to be found in the marshes. The goblins do not suspect that I work with the elves; I am a solitary bird and they leave me alone. I am too unimportant for Dréagg to waste his efforts on so I stay and no one bothers me. That is the way that it has been.' He paused while they walked under the overhanging branches of a small oak tree which swept down almost to the ground. The trunk of it was covered in thick green lichen, and on the roots which stuck up out of the green sludge, grew hundreds of little orange fungi that contrasted strongly with the dull greens and browns all around.

'But you,' Golconda went on. 'I know all I wish to know about your journey and your mission and I bid you the greatest of good fortune for you will need it. But tell me of your wood and of the animals in it, and of your early days, Nab; and the Urkku with you, who is of the Eldron: tell me of her. I see that she speaks to you in our tongue. I would like her to talk to me of the ways of the Urkku.'

The time passed quickly as they talked; they forgot the evil around them as they related the stories and legends of Silver Wood to the heron, and when Nab told him of the early days, sunshine and laughter seemed to fill his mind. But when they got to the end the heron stopped them and asked Beth to tell him of her life and they listened in fascination and amazement as she told them haltingly of how she had lived and of the ways of man.

They enjoyed talking to him for he was a good listener, only occasionally interrupting to ask a pertinent question or add some observation of his own. He reminded them all, in his stature and bearing, of Wythen and they wondered sadly if they would ever see the old owl again. Soon, before they realized it, the darkness began to fall and night started to set in.

'We must press on, make haste,' Golconda said when Warrigal asked him if they were going to rest for the night. 'There is no knowing what the goblins are planning, and the sooner you are safely through the marshes, the better I shall feel.'

The swirling, writhing mist had not lifted all day but the darkness made it appear thicker and more dense so that it felt like a heavy drizzle and their coats once again became soaked with wet. They went in silence now, concentrating on following the heron as he walked ahead of them for they could see very little. Suddenly Nab, who was immediately behind him, heard a muffled thud and a little cry which was stifled almost as soon as it began so that he could not be certain whether or not he had imagined it. He stopped for a second and whispered to Warrigal.

'Did you hear that?'

'Yes,' the owl replied quietly.

'What was it?'

'Just some creature, I would think. I heard a splash as well. Come on or we'll lose sight of Golconda.'

Nab peered ahead through the murk. For an instant or two he could see nothing except the shapes formed by the mist but then to his relief he saw the familiar form of the heron, striding ahead, his tall white figure appearing almost wraith-like as it gathered shrouds of mist around it.

'Hurry up,' said Warrigal urgently and Nab felt the talons of the owl tighten on his shoulder. 'He seems to have got a long way in front. Better not call him in case the goblins are around. Come on.'

Nab moved forward quickly and the others followed and soon they were once again trudging along in silence, sunk in thought, with the heron just visible in front. The little nagging feeling of panic which Nab had felt when he had heard that cry soon passed as he concentrated on following Golconda. Nevertheless there was still something bothering him and as time went on and the figure ahead of him kept going forward resolutely without ever turning around or getting

any closer, Nab felt little prickles of fear creep up his spine until he felt as if the hair on the back of his neck was standing on end. No matter how quickly or how slowly they walked the heron always seemed to remain exactly the same distance in front of them. Why did he not wait for them to catch up? If only he would turn round and they could see his face or if he would just say something. The marsh seemed to be getting thicker and thicker and the smell of damp rotting vegetation was now so heavy on the air that they could almost see it lying like a cloud above the surface of the dark brackish waters and bog moss which lay on each side of their raised path. Around them the swirling clouds of damp played tricks with their eyes, making it seem as if the dead stumps of the trees were moving; every so often one would loom up at them out of the mist like some malevolent creature of the bog.

Nab's eyes were fixed so much on the figure ahead of him that he failed to see the ending of the path. Suddenly his feet were enclosed in a mass of green sludge and when he tried to lift them out he found that it was impossible; the more he tried to free one, the further in did the other one sink. Warrigal had flown back on to the path and he called to the others to hurry up. Beth was only just behind but by the time she had arrived the quaking mire was up to his knees. Brock, Sam and Perryfoot ran the few paces to the spot where the path fell away into the bog and saw with horror the scene before them as Nab frantically waved his arms about trying to throw himself towards the bank, but the more he struggled the further he sank. He could feel himself being sucked down with a strength that was impossible to fight: soon he could not move his legs at all for the sludge was halfway up his thighs. Beth lent over as far as she could but still she could not reach his hand and then, through the haze of her memory, she recalled scenes from films and books in which someone had been caught in quicksand. Quickly she took off her cape and rolled it on the grass so that it formed a rope of cloth and then she lay face down on the path as near to the edge as she dared until the stench of the bog filled her nostrils.

'Brock, let me hold on to you and Sam, you lie across my legs,' she said.

The animals understood what she wanted and so with her left hand gripping Brock's front leg as he stood at her side and with the weight of Sam holding her down she threw the cape out with her free hand, but it did not fall straight and dropped well short of Nab's clutching hand.

'Hurry,' he shouted and as he did so he felt the sludge force itself up over his waist.

Beth drew her right arm well back so that the cape was stretched out straight on the path behind her and then with all the strength she could muster she flung it out across the bog. This time the whole of its length was used up and her arm lay out at full stretch. With her heart pounding beneath her she hardly dared raise her head to look, but when she did, to her enormous relief, she saw that he had just managed to grasp the end. Then she could feel him pulling on the cape and her arm felt as if it was being torn out of its socket. She closed her eyes and gritted her teeth as a wave of pain swept over her. The problem now was how to haul him out of the bog. She tried to bend her arm to pull him but it was impossible; she did not have enough strength. Then she felt her hand begin to slip on the cape but she managed to wedge her fingers against the lion's-head buckle to stop it sliding. Next she began to wriggle back on her tummy in an attempt to drag him out but that also proved impossible. Desperately she thought for a second and then she called to Brock and Sam to grab hold of her by her legs and pull. They did so, gripping her jeans in their teeth and pushing away from the edge with all their strength. At first nothing happened but then slowly, inch by inch, Beth felt herself moving back.

'We're doing it,' she yelled exultantly to Nab. 'It's working.' She prayed that the cloth of her jeans would hold. Very gradually, Nab felt himself being pulled out of the mire. Soon only the lower part of his legs was left in and he was able to move his hands along the cape to heave himself out more quickly. He would never forget the delicious feeling of freedom as each part of his body fought itself free of the clinging mass that had engulfed it.

Finally he lay on the firm grass path with Beth at his side, panting breathlessly with the effort of her exertions. The joint where her right arm joined the shoulder throbbed terribly with a pulsating ache and the mouths of Sam and Brock were bleeding but they were almost delirious with relief. When he had recovered a little from his ordeal Nab got up slowly and, having thanked them all solemnly picked some handfuls of grass and began to wipe some of the foul ooze from his body. Everywhere was deathly quiet. Then suddenly, for in the drama he had just been through he had completely forgotten him, his thoughts turned to Golconda. Surely he must have missed them by now and turned back? But there was no sign of the great white heron. Nab peered desperately into the darkness but all he could see were the shapes in the mist, dancing joyfully. For a moment the tiredness of his eyes played tricks and he almost believed they were laughing at him. Had the heron been a figment of his imagination? No; they had all seen and spoken with him. Worse still then, had he been in league with the goblins; leading them all into the middle of the bog by gaining their confidence and then abandoning them to wander about for ever in this terrible place to be swallowed up one by one by the marsh as he almost had been?

His thoughts were suddenly interrupted by the voice of Warrigal, who had perched on a stump at his side.

'We have no guide,' he said simply. 'We have no alternative now but to go back along this path until we find another and then see where that leads us.'

'Where is Golconda?' asked Nab.

'I do not know but I fear we shall never see him again. You rouse the others; we must be on the move.'

Beth's eyes were closed and the other animals were asleep. It seemed a great pity to disturb them while they were still enjoying the exhilaration of success and before they realized the desperateness of their situation, but Nab agreed with Warrigal that they dared not delay.

Eventually, after Nab had woken them up gently, they started walking back along the path down which Golconda had led them that evening. The relative happiness of that earlier walk was difficult to believe in now; it was almost as if they had dreamt it. Suddenly, when they came to the spot where Nab had heard the cry, he

stumbled over something on the ground and almost fell over, toppling Warrigal off his shoulder. He bent down and saw a bolt lying
across the path; the shaft was made of rough wood and the head was a
jagged rock. Then he looked up and saw that the others were all
staring at a tree stump on the other side of the path. He followed
their gaze and then he saw Golconda. His head had been severed and
stuck on the top of the stump; the eyes wide and staring and the long
sharp beak gaping open. The rest of his body had been dismembered
and each part had been attached to a different part of the stump so
that the whole represented some ghastly caricature. The snow-white
feathers were speckled and streaked with deep crimson where the
blood had run. They all stared for what seemed an age, transfixed
with horror, and an icy fear gripped their hearts and froze the blood
in their veins so that they were unable to move. Then the physical
manifestation of that horror took over and they all began to retch
violently, their stomachs heaving and churning till they were shaking with weakness. Beth, summoning up from within her a reserve of
emotional strength she was unaware she possessed, pulled herself
together and shouted at them to move and, when there was no
response, she went round to each animal and shook him fiercely by
the shoulder until the daze of horror was shaken free. Finally, they all
began to move, slowly at first, stumbling as if in a dream but then as
the fog in their minds cleared they walked faster and faster until they
were almost running in their efforts to get away from that dreadful
place. How long they went on for or how far they went they did not
know, but finally, and all at the same time, exhaustion overtook
them and they slumped down. The awful truth now occurred to Nab.
The splash and the cry which he and Warrigal had heard had been
when the bolt had struck home and the goblins had pulled Golconda
off into the marsh. The figure that they had then followed had not
been Golconda at all but some creature of the marshes controlled by
the goblins; it may even have been the mist itself summoned up by
the goblins to do their bidding and taking the animals further and
further into the depths of the bog while they did their grisly work
knowing that any survivors would be bound to come back that way.
The thought came to him that they were being played with and a
feeling of utter and complete hopelessness swept over him. He

looked round at the others sitting or lying down on the sodden strip of ground which kept them from being sucked in by the bog. Their coats were saturated and matted with mud and on their faces Nab saw only utter misery and despair. Even Warrigal was staring down at the ground, his eyes dull and listless and his shoulders hunched over in an attitude of weariness and apathy. Beth lay face down with her head buried in her arms, and her body quivered slightly as she sobbed quietly to herself. Next to her sat Perryfoot, staring out over the marsh with his ears flat along his back and at his side lay Brock and Sam like two ghosts. They could go no further, thought Nab. This was it; the goblins had done their grisly work well. Any will to continue had been extinguished completely by the sight they had seen back along the path.

For some time, as these thoughts went through his mind, he had been growing gradually more and more aware of a sound coming over the bog. At first he thought it was no more than the wind blowing through the rushes but as it grew slowly louder he could distinguish an underlying conglomeration of noise which sounded very much like the murmur of low conversation and the splashing of footsteps. The others had also heard it for they had looked up and were staring in the direction from which the noise was coming; the expression on their faces having changed from despair to terror. Nearer and nearer the noise came until suddenly, abruptly, the murmur stopped and all they could hear were splashes as the footsteps continued over the marsh towards them. Then even those stopped and they saw through the darkness and the mist a long line of shadows standing silently and still, just within their sight but too far away to be able to distinguish any features.

'Goblins,' Brock whispered to himself under his breath but so quiet was it that they all heard him.

The line of shadows stood like that for what seemed an age to the terrified animals and then, once again, it began to move forward. They could just make out, now, the separate figures as they walked. Then suddenly, like a shaft of sunlight, they heard a cry echo over the bog and shatter the dreadful silence. It was a pure liquid cry which pealed out through the darkness and seemed to fill the air with light and beauty so that the travellers felt their hearts instantly freed from the cold terror that had gripped them. In it was the happiness of the first call of the curlew after the winter and the warmth and comfort of the first sunshine in spring. Dawn was just breaking and in the golden iridescent light of the early sun as it shone through the mist the animals could see the dark ominous line start to break up and divide as a host of elves fell among them, their swords glinting and flashing in the sun. They watched spellbound as the goblins fell back in disarray and the air was filled with the sounds of battle; the clashing of sword against sword and the terrible cries of the goblins as they were wounded or killed, for they did not accept defeat easily and fought with a dreadful strength, their short squat bodies wielding massive swords and maces as if they were feathers. But they were slow and clumsy and the elves danced around them confusing and taunting them so that they became angry and lunged wildly until they grew tired and their strength left them. Then the elves would quickly and deftly finish them off. The battle raged all morning but eventually the last few goblins fled away over the marsh and the air was once again still. Then the animals saw the elves coming towards them out of the mist. They walked slowly for it had been a long hard fight and they were weary. They were also sad, for killing is not in the nature of an elf and they will avoid it if at all possible. Even the killing of goblins is to them an evil and victory in battle was never a glorious time for them.

Soon the elves were standing on the path and their leader spoke.

'You are safe,' he said. 'Welcome to the land of Sheigra. I am Faraid, battle leader of the sea elves and I have come to take you to Saurélon, Lord of the Sea. It came to us that you were assailed by the forces of Dréagg and you were long overdue. Come now, drink this; it will revive you until you can rest and eat in the caves of Elgol.'

From under his garments of spun silver Faraid produced a flask and handed it to Nab, who raised it to his lips and drank deeply of the sparkling liquid inside. The colour he could not see but the flavour reminded him of the sweetness of sun-ripened clover and he could feel it coursing through his body, reviving and refreshing him. He passed it to Beth and then Faraid took the flask back and poured it into a large bowl-shaped shell inlaid with mother-of-pearl for the animals to drink from.

When they had drunk their fill and vitality and life had begun to appear once more in their eyes, Faraid led the little band out over the marsh with the elven army following behind. They shuddered with repulsion as they walked through the area of battle and saw the black blood seeping out of the goblins' wounds and mixing with the stagnant oily waters of the bog. The whole area was now thick with the foul stench that escaped from these wounds and the animals found great difficulty in getting their breath. They picked their way between the fat ugly bodies lying where they had been felled and could hardly bear to look at the faces which in death were even more vile than in life. The hideous puffy features were twisted and contorted and the slavering viscous lips had pulled themselves into such an attitude of hatred and contempt that even in death they still made the animals feel afraid. The sight of death reminded Nab of Golconda and he told Faraid of the goblins' treatment of the heron but the elves already knew because they had passed the awful spectacle on their way.

'He is once again whole, and will rest content,' said the elf, and Nab was relieved for he felt guilty that he had ever doubted Golconda's allegiance and could not help feeling in some way responsible. This was yet another animal who had laid down his life for him and the thought of their love and faith made him feel intensely humble.

Slowly, as they walked, the mist started to become less dense and the ground less marshy and then suddenly they were dazzled by the sunshine of a warm March afternoon. The golden light seemed to bathe them so that all the evil and horror of the marsh was washed away and became a memory. Now they were standing on the edge of a small flat area of trees, heather and tall grass, a patchwork quilt of browns and greens, and at the far end of it they could see, glistening and sparkling in the sun, the sea. None of them except Beth had ever seen it before and that first magic glimpse of blue vastness was something that would live for ever in their minds. For Beth, to whom the sea was as precious as the land, it was like a homecoming, and her heart beat in excitement and anticipation as her memory was stirred by the cry of the gulls and the salty breeze that blew against their faces, and into her mind and soul came recollection of all the enchanted moments she had ever had by the sea in the past.

CHAPTER XVII

The animals stood on the clifftop, gazing out in wonder over the sea. There was a strong wind and the surface was quite rough and choppy so that hundreds of little white horses raced towards the shore, gaining speed and strength as they got nearer and finally crashing down on the little rocky beach below where they were standing. At either end of the beach a huge column of rocks jutted out into the sea and as the waves smashed against them fountains of spray were thrown up violently to fall in little harmless showers all around. Sometimes the sun caught the spray and shone a rainbow through it which lasted for no longer than the blinking of an eye and then was gone. Nab and Beth stood with their arms around each other for the wind that blew their hair back from their faces was cold and the dampness of the marsh still clung to their bodies. The savage strength and might of nature, which is perceived inland but rarely seen, was here exposed, visible and awesome and, standing next to this vast, constantly moving mass, Nab felt very humble and small. His problems and worries seemed to be taken from him by the ceaselessly changing blue-green depths to be lost in the ripples and eddies of the water as it rushed in among the rocks. He was mesmerized by all this movement and he lost himself in the patterns and rhythms of the waves charging in and then retreating, charging in and retreating, on and on until he became one with the sea.

Beth, very cold but happy and relieved that their ordeal in the marsh was over, found herself looking at the elves as they stood scattered in ones and twos along the top of the cliff. Although Nab had told her about the wood elves of Ellmondrill she had been unprepared for the intense fascination which she felt towards them. She was entranced by them. 'Elves,' she said slowly to herself as if it was a magic chant, and then again, as if in disbelief that they were really there: 'I'm with the elves'. Their existence, of course, is rumoured amongst the Urkku and Beth recalled some of the stories she had heard from her mother when she had been read to at night, but no one, not even the Eldron, believed that they really existed. Where the idea of elves came from no one could say but nevertheless they were dismissed as fantasy. Fantasy! Here they were with the golden sun glinting off their helmets and shields and their faces turned into the wind. The battle with the goblins had taken its toll and they were regaining their lost energy and strength at this, their Scyttel, so that they stood or sat in stillness and silence and let its power break over them. Beth stared at them, amazed that she could have been unaware of their existence for so long, and the sight of their fragile and delicate beauty pulled at her heart and brought tears of melancholy to her eyes. The other animals were sitting in a row alongside, all quietly looking out to sea, feeling the magic of this place and moment wash away the evil of the bog until they felt clean again and the awful memories had been blown away. Only the tall white figure of Golconda striding through the darkness like a bright star on a moonless night remained in their thoughts from their time in the marshes. He was whole again and, as they looked towards the horizon, sometimes, far out to sea, they thought they could see him flying low over the waves, his great wings slowly beating up and down and his long beak pointing forward to carve a way for himself through the air. Then, as they blinked, he was gone to reappear somewhere else.

Eventually, as the sun began to descend in the sky, Faraid stood up and producing a large horn-shaped shell from his belt, he blew upon it to produce a long low mournful sound which seemed to boom out over the sea long after he had removed the horn from his lips. He waited a while and then blew again and the call echoed and bounced off the cliffs and on to the rocks below and then rolled over the waves until it faded in the distance. This time there came an answering note from out at sea, forcing its way through the roar of the waves and the cry of the wind until it came to them where they stood; a sound full of sadness and suffering but not despair, for within its deep tones lay hope. The elves then stood up and began to move off along the cliff and Faraid came over to them.

'You look better,' he said happily, for their eyes, which when he had found them in the bog had been flat and dull with misery were now sparkling and bright. The wind and sun had also dried them out and the mud and dirt on their coats and on the garments worn by Nab and Beth had turned to little flakes which they had easily removed. Brock, who hated to be dirty, had spent a long time cleaning himself and then he and Sam had groomed each other so that now their fur shone; the one deep and black, the colour of ebony, and the other, the gold of the sun on an autumn afternoon. Warrigal's feathers lay even and perfectly placed and Perryfoot stood on his hind legs with his ears erect and his body quivering with alertness.

'Come,' Faraid said, smiling. 'Saurélon is waiting for us on the Isle of Elgol,' and he pointed to a little rocky island a short way out from the beach against which the waves did not pound with the fury they showed elsewhere but, rather, lapped against the sheer rocky sides. It reminded Beth of a three-tiered cake; the lower one, always under the water, was dark brown and shiny with seaweed; the middle layer was fawn-coloured from the barnacles which encrusted it and set in amongst the fawn were little blue-black clusters of mussels, like currants. The third layer, on top, was dark green from sea mosses, lichens and mildews. At one end a group of black and white oyster-catchers was sitting on an outcrop of rock until suddenly they all took off uttering their shrill angry cries. Elegant long-necked cormorants flew fast and low over the water between Elgol and the shore and then vanished out of sight around the headland as quickly as they had appeared, and always, overhead, the white gulls wheeled and cried, floating on the air currents and circling high up in the blue sky.

The elves had now reached a spot on the cliff from which a steep, narrow path descended to the beach and they were already going down it.

'Come,' said Faraid again, and he led the animals to the path. At first it sloped away quite gradually over a bank of short grass but then suddenly it fell away very sharply as it took them down the rocky cliff. Faraid went first to lead the way and the others followed in single file as the path zig-zagged down along little ledges and outcrops. Warrigal flew down alongside them with a slight air of superiority for he was relieved not to have to use the path; in a number of places fresh water seeped out of the rock and ran across it leaving it very muddy and slippery and he watched as the others gingerly stepped across. Of all the animals Beth was the most frightened for she hated heights and at times, crossing over these treacherous patches of mud on the narrow path with a sheer drop on one side, the wind blowing at her from the sea and with only tiny little handholds in the cliff on the other side for her to hang on to, she was terrified, even though Nab, who had gone first, waited with a hand outstretched to grab hers as soon as she came within reach.

As they got further down the path the roar of the waves grew louder and they felt the presence of the sea like a great protective barrier in front of them. Their hearts quickened with excitement as they descended the last few steps and finally, with a sense of relief and joy, they jumped down with a clatter on to the rounded stones and pebbles of the beach. The sea looked very different at eye-level; up on the cliffs they had observed it as if they were looking at a painting but now they were in the painting, a part of it, totally absorbed in the sounds and smells all around. The limitless energy and strength of the sea seemed to fill them until they felt as if they would explode. They were seized by an irresistible urge to run along the beach, and suddenly Sam took off, racing as fast as he could down to the edge of the sea and then speeding away through the shallows where the waves broke on the shore. The others ran after him; Perryfoot racing Brock and Nab chasing after Beth. They splashed along through the water with the wind and salt spray in their faces until they reached the rocks at the end of the beach and then they ran back to where Warrigal and Faraid were standing waiting. Their eyes shone with happiness and Faraid laughed at them as they stood panting in front of him.

'I am pleased that you enjoy the sea,' he said, and the sound of his laughter mingled with the waves and the cries of the sea birds until it seemed as if the whole beach was laughing with him. He led them off in the opposite direction from where they had run and took them towards the rocks at the other end. The pebbles under their feet rattled as they walked and nearer to the sea they were still shiny and wet from the retreating tide so that, unlike the dull greys and blacks and whites of the large stones higher up the beach these smaller pebbles, worn rounded and smooth by the sea, shone like jewels. There were deep reds and greens, oranges and jet blacks; some were speckled or lined or were all black except for a broad or narrow band of purest white running around them or forming a circle or an oval at one end. Others were special because of their shape; perfect rounds or ovals or else shaped like miniature mountains. Nab and Beth kept stopping to pick them up and look at them, each one unique and precious, and wished that they could have kept them all. Reluctantly they threw them down, to be lost for ever to the sea.

Finally they reached the rocks and began to clamber over them. At first they were dry and the barnacles gave them a good grip so that the animals found no difficulty, but as the rocks reached further into the sea they became covered in brown and green seaweed which made them wet and slippery so that Perryfoot, Brock and Sam particularly found them very hard to walk on. They were used to the woods and the fields and they had no idea of the techniques to use in this vastly different world. Nab and Beth were able to reach and stretch so that for them it was relatively easy, but they had to keep waiting for the others to catch up or go back to help them, much to the animals' distaste, by lifting them down or carrying them from one rock to another. Their pads, which were used to the earth, became sore and hurt from the sharp barnacles and sometimes they stood on a limpet by accident so that the conical shell stuck up into their foot painfully and they almost slipped in their efforts to get it off. Soon they were so far out on the rocks that they were able to look back on the beach behind them and see the waves racing past at their side. Between the rocks, the pools left by the sea got bigger and deeper as the tide came further in, and when they turned round, rocks which they had walked across had become covered by the water so that they were cut off and could not have gone back even if they had wanted to and the thought of this gave Nab a thrill of excitement. In the pools the seaweed swirled and danced with the rhythm of the sea and as they clambered round, little fish darted quickly for cover under its protective fronds. Some of the pools now were so wide that it was easier for Nab and Beth to wade through carrying the others and this they did; Beth anxious that the water would not go over her wellington tops and Nab enjoying the sensation of the swirling water round his ankles.

Eventually they rounded a large boulder and saw Faraid standing just ahead with a few of the elves gathered at his side. The rocks had come to an end and ahead of them was only sea stretching out to the horizon; a long straight line in the far distance which was tinged with gold where the sun had just started to sink down behind it. Then to their surprise, they saw the seals, their grey heads bobbing up and down in the water. The seals were equally surprised at seeing the animals and, being intensely curious, were unable to take their eyes off them and stared until, feeling they had overstepped the bounds of politeness, they swung round in the water with their backs to them, but then seemingly unable to contain their insatiable nosiness they turned round and began to stare again, their round black deep-set eyes peering out from shiny domed heads. Faraid called to them and they came up close to the rocks, whereupon the remaining elves clambered on to their backs and the seals sped off across the sea to Elgol.

'Is that how we get across?' Brock asked Faraid anxiously as he carefully made his way across to the rock where the others were standing. The elf turned and smiled.

'There is no other way unless you can swim,' he said, and the badger groaned inwardly.

'I'll carry you with me,' said Nab, laughing, but Brock replied forcefully:

'I'll manage on my own.'

Perryfoot had been carried for most of the last part of their walk over the rocks and Sam with his longer legs had been able to manage more easily than the badger but Brock had declined any help, determined to make it on his own. Now here he was confronted by

211

another situation which taxed all his fortitude. It was all right for Warrigal, he thought as he looked at the bird perched on a rock staring out to sea. Warrigal, however, was not as unconcerned as Brock thought: he was thinking to himself that he had never before flown over such a large expanse of water and with such violent and gusty winds ready to pull him off balance. He watched a group of gulls and tried to pick up any hints he could, admiring the way in which they used the wind rather than trying to fight against it.

Nab and Beth sat down together on a rock at the very edge of the sea and stared down into the grey depths. They were so far out that the waves did not break against the rocks; instead the water rose and fell, reminding Nab of the words of Wychnor which he seemed to have heard so long ago: 'And in joy at his creation he invested the sea with a fragment of his power so that it heaved and rolled even as he breathed.' He watched hypnotized by the movement as the water funnelled between the rocks where they had been worn smooth and round, rushing in furiously and then being sucked out again almost as fast as the waves withdrew for another onslaught. Then out at sea he heard once again that long mournful sound they had heard on the cliff top answering Faraid's horn and looking up he saw the seals returning. So it was they who had made that noise: somehow it suited them for these graceful creatures seemed to Nab to be the embodiment of all the suffering of the animals while at the same time containing within them their essential qualities: purity, innocence and strength and now, perhaps, a new element – hope. Swimming on their own they spent a lot of time under the water; their heads disappearing suddenly and then reappearing a little while later somewhere else, totally unexpectedly. Soon they were by the side of the rocks, breathing heavily and occasionally snorting out of their nostrils so that their long whiskers quivered, and all the time staring at this strange but very interesting assortment of land creatures who, for some reason, seemed rather nervous and wary of the water.

Nab turned to Beth. 'I'll help you down,' he said, trying to appear brave and unconcerned but in truth as apprehensive and frightened as everyone else. Beth in fact was perhaps the least nervous because she had been out in a yacht once or twice with her father when they had been on holiday with some friends who lived by the sea, and also she was able to swim quite well. Holding on to Nab's hand she climbed backwards down the rock until she felt her boots in the water and then she managed to get one of her legs on the other side of the seal who had swum over and was using his flippers to keep himself steady alongside the rock. She lowered herself down on to his back and then with her legs wrapped tightly round him she let go of Nab's hand and found herself bobbing up and down very comfortably except for the fact that her jeans were wet up to her knees and felt cold and clammy against her legs.

'I'll go with you,' said Perryfoot urgently and Beth smiled up at him.

'All right, you lazy old thing: hop on,' she said, and Nab handed him down to her. Beth held him cradled underneath her while she bent down and put both her arms around the seal's neck so that her face was resting on his back just a few inches from the water.

'No pride,' thought Brock to himself, but of all the animals Perryfoot was the one who, with his short legs, would have been least able to cling to a seal and cross alone.

Beth tried to say something to the seal but he appeared not to hear her. Faraid called down, 'They don't speak your language; they only know the language of the sea. I'll tell him when to go. Are you ready?'

She replied that she was and Faraid spoke to the seal which suddenly took off across the water. At first Beth found it hard to hang on because he was so slippery and she panicked when she got a mouthful of salt water but once she had got used to the powerful rhythm of his swimming and was able to more or less guess when they would hit a wave so that she could hold her breath, she began to enjoy it. The sea under her face sped past in a blue-green mass of ripples, and looking back she could see the white foaming wake left by the seal's flippers. She turned her head sideways so that she could just see the sky where it met the sea on the horizon and as they got further out she was able to see other bays and beaches along the coast. It appeared to be deserted except for the occasional cottage perched up in the mountains which rose from the sea like towering fortresses. She wondered whether anybody might be looking out over the water and what they would think if they spotted her; a girl in a brown cloak riding on the back of a seal. Pinch themselves to make sure they were not dreaming, she thought; but they were now too far out to be seen clearly anyway.

'How are you feeling?' she called to Perryfoot, but he could not hear her above the roar of the sea. His eyes were shut tight and he was shivering with fright; his legs splayed out across the seal's dark slippery back and the nails of his paws fully extended to try to get a grip.

She turned her head so that she could look back at the others on the rocks. They appeared to be just about to set off. Brock, having tried to sit on the back of one of the seals, had fallen off and had to be hauled out of the water by Nab, so he had now condescended to ride with Faraid and was sitting astride the seal looking extremely uncomfortable with the elf behind him holding him on. Sam was riding with Nab. Like Beth he had been to the sea once before with the Urkku who had owned him and so it was not altogether strange. In fact he used to swim in the ponds around Silver Wood and he had been thinking of trying to swim across to Elgol but he did not like the look of the waves and it was a long way from the shore. The knowledge that he could swim if he fell off, however, gave Sam a lot of confidence and this helped Nab feel better as he sat shakily on the seal's back behind him.

'Ask him to go slowly,' he shouted above the waves to Faraid, and the elf called something to the seal before they moved away from the rock.

'Sam,' shouted Nab, 'sit still,' for the dog was wriggling around in front of him trying to get his mouth in the water so that he could play at catching the waves.

'Don't worry; I'll hang on to you if you slip,' Sam said, laughing.

Overhead Warrigal was flying against the wind and experiencing some difficulty with the strong air-currents until a cormorant came up and helped him by showing him how to fly low over the water where the wind was less gusty and more constant. The owl felt that the nearer the water he flew the less room would he have to correct any errors before he was in the sea, but when he tried it he found that it worked and soon he was skimming above the waves with enormous pleasure, alongside the others who looked at him enviously.

214

Soon even Brock and Nab relaxed a little and began to enjoy the ride. They became exhilarated with the sight of nothing in front of them except the vast ocean twinkling in the late afternoon sunlight and their hearts lifted with the feel of the wind in their hair and the spray on their faces. They anticipated the slight thud as the seal met each wave and braced themselves with excitement for the next one. Only Perryfoot, small and completely out of the element of which he was master, remained so frightened that he was unable to even open his eyes.

Soon they were close to the landward side of Elgol and began to ride around the edge of it slowly, causing other seals who were basking on little ledges in the rock to look up as they passed and call out to their companions. The travellers stared with fascination at the steep sides of the rock; thickly encrusted with layer upon layer of barnacles and the mass of seaweed that floated like a protective curtain around its base. Soon they rounded a corner so that they were completely out of sight of the shore; ahead of them lay a tiny bay surrounding a pebbly beach on which a number of elves were standing. The seals swam towards the beach and as they got nearer the visitors saw, standing a little taller than the elves and surrounded by them, a figure who began to wave to them slowly. He had long white hair falling around his shoulders and down to his waist and his white beard tumbled like a waterfall over his chest. The seals were unable to swim right up on to the beach and they stopped a little way out; Nab and Faraid got off their backs into the sea and, while Nab carried Brock and Beth took Perryfoot, who had begun to recover from his ordeal, Sam swam alongside them. Warrigal, not wishing to arrive on the beach before the others, flew next to them slowly, enjoying his new-found skill and just missing the tops of the waves.

Finally they splashed their way out of the water and stood wet and shivering in the cold March wind that blew off the sea. Faraid led them up the slight slope over the pebbles until they met the host of elves. The crowd parted and through the passage left for him came the tall white-haired figure. He walked slowly and with a slight stoop and as he came they saw that his face was brown and weatherbeaten and the skin creased and seamed like an old apple. He stopped in front of them and looked at them through two bright blue eyes which sparkled and shone with wisdom and merriment so that the youth which was in his soul seemed in some strange way to complement the age of his body.

Around his shoulders and down to the beach hung a long cape which seemed to match the colour of the sea exactly so that at that moment it was of a deep dark greyish hue interspersed with flecks of white. Later they learned that it did in fact change as the sea changed so that out at sea he was almost invisible. Around his head he wore a thin band of silver with a simple dark green stone set in it at the front.

'Saurélon; Lord of the Seas,' said Faraid, and he ushered the animals a little closer to him so that they were standing, rather nervously, in a line. Although Saurélon's figure represented an awesome and intensely magical image, they were not frightened of him. He came to each one of them in turn and put his hand on their heads or held them by the shoulders while he looked into their faces and when he smiled at them their bodies seemed to glow with warmth as if the summer sun were shining. He came to Nab last and stood for a long time in front of him until it seemed as though he would stay for ever, and Nab thought that he could see tears forming in the corner of his eyes; but he never told anyone and it may only have been the reflection of the sun against the cloak.

'We have waited for you a long time,' he said, and in his voice was the music of the sea. 'A long, long time. Come; follow me. You must be cold, hungry and tired after your ordeal in the marshes.'

The sun was now going down over the horizon and the sky was filled with the gold of evening. The white clouds that had been scudding about in the blue all day had now gone and the heavens were darkening. They followed Saurélon up the beach with the elves coming behind, and he led them into a large cave. It was dark at first and the crunching of their footsteps over the pebbles echoed loudly. Further in, the place smelt more and more strongly of wet seaweed, for the sun never reached here to dry out what the tide had left. Their eyes had grown more used to the darkness now and they could see the glistening walls of the cave and make out, running along both sides at about the height of Nab's shoulder, a wide ledge in which the sea had gouged out little hollows. These now formed rock pools in which

crimson and green sea anemones waved their delicate fronds and strands of red or brown seaweed floated gently. The bottom of many of these little pools was bright pink so that the mixture of colours was like a miniature garden and Nab and Beth were unable to resist stopping to look into them. They explored them with their fingers, delicately moving the forests of green seaweed and watching the little fish dart out to find another hiding place. Little bright yellow periwinkles crawled slowly along the bottom as if burdened down by the weight of their shells and once they saw a hermit crab tentatively sticking his pincers out of the empty whelk shell in which he had made his home.

The cave now opened out and became slightly larger. Saurélon stopped and the elves went off into various dark corners around the walls about their own business. Although they were quite a long way from the shore and were unable to see the beach the cave was remarkably light and the animals saw that the rock itself contained streaks of yellow and silver which shone and it was from these that the light came. On the far wall, the sea had carved a seat in the rock, the back and the arms of which had been worn smooth by innumerable tides.

'My seat, when I'm here, which is not often enough,' said Saurélon, and he took them over to it and sat down. 'I am fond of it here,' he continued, 'it is one of my chosen places. I was pleased when it was learnt that I was to meet you here in the land of Sheigra on the Isle of Elgol for little enough do I get the chance to come and I always enjoy it so.' He stopped as if his mind had drifted off and he stared down at the ground in silence until the elves came over carrying food and drink in little shell bowls and handed them to the visitors before going back and fetching their own. As the elves moved to and fro Beth noticed that the silver light which had shone from them in the darkness of the cave entrance had faded in the light of this main part of the cave so that now they no longer sparkled but rather gave off a faint white glow similar to the light of the moon when it lingers on into morning or appears in late afternoon. Soon they were all sitting down on the damp pebbles of the cave floor eating and drinking busily for they were hungry, and the only sound that could be heard was the distant crashing of the sea on the shore and the clink of the shell goblets and plates.

The food was plain and simple, unlike the vast array of different dishes which had been presented to them by the wood elves and which had made Beth's mouth water when Nab had described the feasts to her. Now they were given simply a bowl in which had been placed some carragheen and some kelp both of which had been turned into a kind of mulch and which tasted rather bitter, but there was also some delicate green sea lettuce which was crisp and had a touch of sweetness so that, eaten together, they were pleasant. The drink in their goblets was the same as that which Faraid had given them when they had first been rescued in the marsh and it tasted as good now as it had then, warming them through and through and washing the last vestiges of darkness from their minds. The travellers were more hungry than they had had time to realize for they had not eaten since before they entered Blore, and they had soon finished the contents of their bowls and finished their drink. Faraid, who was sitting next to them, beckoned to two other elves nearby who jumped up and took away the goblets and bowls to refill them. Once more this happened until finally they felt full.

When Saurélon was sure that they had eaten enough, he spoke. 'Tell us of yourselves,' he said. 'Let us hear your story from the beginning, for although parts of it have come to our ears they are like parts of a mosaic which need to be fitted together to form a picture.'

The elves had stopped talking and were looking expectantly at the animals, and Saurélon was smiling down at them from his seat in the rock. Nab looked at Brock. 'Come on,' he whispered. 'You must start. We'll take over for the bits we each know best.'

Brock was reminded of the time he had had to speak at that Council Meeting so long ago in Silver Wood. He had had to tell the same story then as he was about to tell now but little had he known then how it would all turn out. If someone had said to him that he would eventually be relating the story to Saurélon, Lord of the Sea, and a group of sea-elves on the Isle of Elgol in the land of Sheigra, he would have laughed at them. Tara would have been proud of him now; how he wished she was still alive and could be with him for it was her story as much as his. He looked across at Warrigal as he had that first time, and the owl, knowing what he was thinking, nodded at him in encouragement for he too remembered that Council Meeting very clearly when they had been trying to persuade Wythen and Bruin and Rufus and Sterndale and Pictor and the others to allow Nab to stay in the wood. He thought of them now, nearly all dead, and he wondered what had happened to old Wythen. Brock started his story and the owl listened carefully, trying hard not to interrupt if the badger missed something or got something slightly wrong, for amongst the animals it is the height of bad manners to interrupt a story while it is being told.

By the time the tale was finished the sound of the waves was echoing loudly in the cave for the tide had come a long way in. They had all told a part of the story, even Beth, who had talked about her life as an Urkku and of the times she had met Nab and of her flight with him away from her home to Silver Wood. There was silence when the tale was over and all that could be heard was the lapping of the sea against the sides of the cave. The elves, still lost in the wonder of the story, remained sitting motionless and quiet, staring in fascination at the travellers until finally Saurélon spoke.

'The sea will soon be upon us. Come; you must be tired. Faraid will lead you to your cave and we shall meet again tomorrow. May you sleep the sleep of the dolphin.'

He got up slowly from his seat and made his way up some step-like grooves in the wall of the cave until he reached the wide ledge. He moved along this until he came to a spot where there was a groove for a seat and there he sat down. Faraid followed him up the steps and then beckoned to the visitors to follow him. When they reached the ledge there was a small opening in the rock and they saw the elf disappearing down it along a narrow passage. The roof was so low that only Warrigal and Perryfoot were able to walk upright and the others had to crawl along on their stomachs with only the silver glow shining from Faraid to show them where they were going. Perryfoot was last down the tunnel and before he went he looked back at the cave. All the elves were now sitting along the ledge looking down at the sea beneath them which was washing over the area where, a little while before, they had been sitting eating and telling their tale. The sound and smell of the sea filled everywhere. He turned away and instantly the roaring sound became muffled as he followed the others. The tunnel was only short and soon he emerged on to the floor of another cave, far smaller than the one they had left and much less deep, for although they were now standing against the back wall they could see out of the mouth of the cave quite clearly to the dark night sky outside and the waves crashing down on the pebbles just outside the entrance.

'The sea never reaches this far,' said Faraid.

'When you awake tomorrow you will find that the rhythm of the waves has become as much a part of you as the sound of your own breath. I bid you a peaceful sleep.' He smiled at them and was gone and the travellers were once more on their own, for the first time since the marshes. Now that they could relax they felt utterly exhausted and no sooner had they lain down than they sank into a deep and tranquil sleep with the sound of the waves outside on the shore soothing away their worries and the black curtain of the night sky, with a few twinkling stars shining brightly out of the darkness, forming a veil over the cave mouth.

CHAPTER XVIII

When they woke up next morning and looked out of the cave mouth, they saw that the clear blue sky of the previous day had gone. Instead the clouds loomed grey and forbidding over the sea and the air was full of a fine misty drizzle. The tide was out and they went for a walk on the small beach. They ambled slowly along the line of seaweed which had been left by last night's tide and found pieces of driftwood, stripped of their bark and bleached silvery white by the sea, which Beth picked up to take back to their cave. They also gathered up some of the pebbles and shells from the beach which were of a similar type to those they had seen but had to leave behind on the shore of the headland.

Warrigal ventured out over the water using his new found skills, and Sam, Perryfoot and Brock raced one another along the shore before they very gingerly joined Nab and Beth on the rocks where they were sitting looking out over the grey sea. It was as Faraid had said; no longer did they actually hear the waves crashing on the shore, instead the sound was a part of them which they would have missed had it suddenly stopped. They sat for a long time watching the sea come in and fill up the spaces between the rocks on which they were sitting, bringing new life to the seaweed which hung down flat and dull until it began to float again and colour came back to it. Then when the drizzle became too heavy for them and they started to get very wet they called to Warrigal and ran back to their cave. The elves had left them some food and drink and sitting just inside the cave mouth with the rain dripping down outside, they slowly and thoughtfully ate the warmed up seaweed and drank the hot contents of the shell goblets. It was the same as they had had last night but it tasted different hot and any feeling of cold or dampness seemed to vanish as the warmth of the drink spread through their bodies.

The sea air and the sound of the rain had made them feel dozy again and very soon they were all curled up against the back wall sleeping soundly, whilst outside, the sea pounded against the rocks sending great fountains of spray showering up into the air. When Nab woke up he saw Beth standing in the entrance looking out and he quietly got up and walked over to her. The others were still fast asleep. As he moved across the floor of the cave he saw that the pebbles and the driftwood they had gathered had been placed carefully all around the walls on little crevices and ledges. She looked round with a start as she heard his footfall behind her and then she smiled when she realized who it was. Nab saw with dismay that her eyes were red and tears were trickling down her cheeks.

'What is it?' he said gently, and without saying anything she flung her arms around him and buried her head against his shoulder, sobbing. He tried to comfort her, stroking her hair and holding her closely to him. Eventually her sobs died away and she looked up at him through eyes that glistened with tears, and spoke.

'I was thinking of what will happen to us. What will happen in the future. I'm afraid. I don't know, somehow the feeling of happiness and security here with the elves on Elgol makes everything else seem like a nightmare. I want to stay, Nab. I don't want to go. And I want a home for us; will we ever have a home? Where will all this travelling end?'

'I don't know,' he said, 'but I know what you mean. I was happy in Silver Wood; that was my home. I think about it all the time. It's easier for me though, I know. I was prepared through nearly all my life for this, and in my case my home is no longer there. But for you! To leave everything for this.' He stopped speaking for he felt responsible for her pain; it was he who had taken her away. There was no doubt in his mind as to what he had had to do and the story told by the Lord Wychnor had been simply the final piece in the puzzle. But she had been brought up amongst the Urkku; how could

223

she be expected to believe the truth of what they were doing?

Beth sensed what he was thinking and it was not the reason for her tears. 'Nab,' she said, but he would not raise his eyes. 'Nab, look at me. It's not that. I know it's true as much as you do. I feel it in my heart. And I would go anywhere with you. It's just like I said. I want us to have a home together, some time in the future and I'm afraid of how things will turn out. We don't know the end; we don't know what is supposed to happen. That's what is difficult.'

They held each other close for a long time, silhouetted against the grey sky. Then, as if Ashgaroth had seen their fears and was giving them strength, the grey clouds started to break up and, through the gaps, patches of blue began to appear and shafts of golden evening sun shone through. Suddenly a beam of sunlight caught them in the cave entrance and they were bathed in gold: looking up they saw that the mist had cleared and the sea was sparkling in the sunlight. All their doubts and fears seemed ridiculous now; how could they ever have been uncertain? They looked at each other and laughed with joy and then they ran out and dashed across the beach down to where the waves broke on the shore and, arm in arm, they walked along, splashing in the water and letting the wind from the sea blow in their faces and through their hair.

When they got back to the cave they found the other animals pottering around outside. Brock, who through the mists of sleep had dimly perceived the sound of Beth crying, was relieved and happy to see the laughter in their faces. What they were doing was not easy for any of them but he understood that it was hardest of all for Beth and he had been restless and disturbed in his sleep at the thought of her unhappiness, for he had grown to love and respect her almost as much as Nab. He ran up to them and they both bent down and stroked him. Then they joined the others at the cave entrance.

'Come on,' said Perryfoot, 'let's go and find the elves. They aren't in the cave. We had a look while we were waiting for you.'

They walked over the top of the rocky island and found the elves gathering seaweed on the other side. The seals were there as well, playing in the water or basking on the rocks, and the elves were talking to them in the language of the sea. Saurélon was sitting a little apart from the others and when he saw the animals he beckoned them over to speak to him. He asked them about their day and how they were feeling and he asked Nab to tell him more of Wychnor, Lord of the Wood-Elves.

'It is many, many seasons since I saw him,' said Saurélon. 'He was young then, and mighty in his powers. There was no one else worthy or even capable enough to put right all the damage caused by Ammdar and to sort out the chaos left behind. Ashgaroth called myself and Malcoff together and asked us who we thought should succeed after Ammdar had been destroyed. It was a stormy night. He had called us to the Forests of Smoo, in the east, and the rain fell down in torrents so that everything was saturated. We stood waiting under those vast trees heavy with creepers and vines while the water dripped from the leaves and great claps of thunder cracked in the sky. Then Ashgaroth appeared to us. It was only the second time I had seen him. We talked of Dréagg and Ammdar and of the evil they had spawned. He was filled with grief but he swore to us then that one day he would send a Saviour. "Be patient," he said, and we have been patient.' He looked at Nab, who was sitting next to him, and put his hand on the boy's shoulder. Nab looked up at him and Saurélon smiled. 'We have been patient,' he said again, almost to himself.

They sat on for a little while in silence until the sun had almost disappeared beyond the horizon. Then they all walked back to the elven cave where they ate and drank their fill. When they had finished, Saurélon told them stories and legends of the lands in the far frozen north from which he came, where the great white bears roamed over the icy wastes and huge whales played in the freezing waters among the icebergs. The magic of his storytelling was great, and such was the spell he cast upon the animals that they lived the sagas as they heard them and became a part of the stories. Finally, when the moon outside was high in the night sky and the tide was nearly upon them, they crawled through the little tunnel to their own cave where they fell asleep straightaway, relaxed and contented, and their dreams were all in white.

Their stay in Sheigra was perhaps one of the happiest times any of the friends had known. The moments they had there seemed particularly precious because, in a way, they were stolen. There was no question of their staying for very long and they knew that when they left they would once again be living with fear as their constant shadow, but here they felt secure and safe, sheltered from all the evil of Dréagg, and so they lived for each moment – exploring the rock pools or wandering along the beaches or simply sitting, looking at the mighty sea. Once or twice they went over to the headland on the backs of the seals and there they would walk amongst gorse and heather and dead brown bracken talking of the past and of Silver Wood and of those they had known. Then they would lie on the soft grass, looking out at the cliffs and rocks below and at Elgol, its outlines blurred by the spray from the waves and the seals basking on its rocky ledges. When evening came Nab would blow on the shell-horn that Faraid had given him and they would watch some of the seals flop off the rock into the sea. Then the animals would make their way down to meet them and soon be back at their cave, where bowls of warm laver bread and goblets of sparkling drink would be laid out to refresh them before they joined the elves. Every evening one of the elves would tell a story while the others listened, and sometimes Saurélon himself would tell them of the Ancient Days, the days Before-Man when the elves had fought with Dréagg; and mighty were the elven heroes of those times but great was their tragedy. He told them of Embo and Druim, of Urigill and Mowen but most of all did he tell them of Ammdar, The Silver Warrior, before the time of his fall, and the animals listened in wonder and awe as they heard the stories of his greatness in the struggle against the Lord of Evil. Then, with their minds still wandering in those misty far off days, they would go back to their little cave and sleep until they were woken by the morning sun streaming in.

They stayed on Elgol almost until the end of spring. The weather was mostly bright but it was cold and the mornings were very often wet and misty, clearing up towards the middle of the day. For some time now the animals had been trying to prepare themselves for the idea of leaving but none of them wanted to go and it was not easy. Finally Saurélon had spoken to them and said gently but firmly that, if they were fully refreshed, they should think about moving on to find Malcoff and the mountain elves. Then he had taken Nab to one side and placed a little shell-like phial containing the Faradawn of the sea into the casket on the Belt of Ammdar. 'You should leave tomorrow,' he had said. 'Travelling will be quite good and time is short. There must be no more delay. When you see Malcoff give him my greetings.'

That was yesterday and now they were waking up to their last day on Elgol. A damp misty drizzle hung over the sea making everywhere appear grey and miserable and covering the sea with little spots and circles where the rain fell on the water. It was the worst day for leaving that they could have chosen. They were just about to walk out of the cave on to the beach when they heard strange sounds coming to them over the water. They sounded far-off and after listening intently for a second or two the animals realized that they were coming from the beaches on the headland and were able to distinguish Urkku voices above the sound of the sea and amongst other less familiar sounds. Then suddenly the noises grew louder and it sounded as if there was some sort of struggle or fight going on with things being dragged over the pebbles, and the voices of the Urkku took on a familiar harsh triumphant note as they became intermingled with little grunts, cries and whimpers. The most persistent sound however was a heavy crunching thud which seemed to punctuate all the other noises, so that every time they heard one of these sickening thuds there would be a flurry of cries and whimpers which would then be followed by the sound of the pebbles rattling as something was pulled over them.

They stared hard across at the headland but could see nothing. For some reason, though, their hearts went cold and fear, which they had forgotten about during their days on Elgol, spread its icy grip around their stomachs. They stood listening, mesmerized by the pattern of noises and not knowing what to do, until Nab caught sight of Faraid and Saurélon coming towards them.

'What is it? What's happening?' Nab asked, when they were standing next to them.

'It is the Urkku,' replied Saurélon with anger in his voice. 'Every so often they come and slaughter the young seal pups while they are still on land and before they are able to take to the water.'

227

There was a lull in the noise and then they heard something being pushed into the sea and the sound of a motor coughing into life. Then all was quiet except for the high-pitched drone of the engine and the splashing of the little boat as it pushed its way through the waves.

'It sounds as if they're coming across to Elgol. They haven't before. You must get back in the cave quickly. I shall come with you. Faraid; you take the elves and disperse them among the rocks. Nab and the others will wait until the Urkku have gone but they may have to leave sooner if things go wrong. I want to know where the Urkku are the whole time they're on the island. Get five seals together and keep them hidden around this side and tell them to be ready to move quickly. I want a report as often as possible from you.'

Faraid went back into the elven cave to fetch the other elves and Saurélon led the animals quickly into their cave. The mouth was smaller than the cave itself so that there was quite a large area of rock wall on either side where they could hide and look out on to the beach without being seen. Saurélon put Nab, Beth and Perryfoot behind one side of the cave mouth and Brock, Sam and Warrigal behind the other. He himself stayed in the shadows at the back so that he could move from side to side and have as wide a view of the beach as possible.

They waited, saying nothing, their hearts pounding with fear. Then they heard the scraping of the boat on the rocks round to their right and out of sight, followed by the sound of its being pulled up on to the shore. The voices of the Urkku were loud and sounded very close but from neither side could they be seen. The boat was dragged up further and then the voices grew fainter as they heard heavy footsteps tramp off along the beach and then go up over the rocks.

'They've gone,' said Perryfoot with a sigh of relief.

'They'll be back,' replied Nab. 'Their boat's still here.'

It was not long before they began to hear the same noises that they had heard previously from the mainland, only much nearer and more vivid. Knowing what was happening, the animals were filled with sickness and anger. Faraid ran into the cave.

'They are at the back but working round towards this beach.

Saurélon; can we not do something? They are butchering all the pups. We cannot stand by.'

Just then they became aware of a tremendous commotion outside. They peered cautiously out of the cave mouth and saw that one of the Urkku had gone ahead of the others and was chasing a little white seal pup along the beach. They watched numb with horror as the mother flapped along clumsily behind, trying in vain to catch them up and stop what she knew was going to happen. Then the Urkku came alongside the baby and, raising a huge wooden club above his head, brought it down on the skull of the pup which whimpered and cried before the club came down again and it flopped down twitching as blood poured from the gashes on its head and a stream of red ran down into the sea. The mother was still trying to reach her baby when the Urkku produced a knife and began to skin it while its tail still flapped with life.

The whole ghastly scene had been over in seconds. Beth was sobbing behind Nab, her face covered in her hands and her shoulders shaking, and he was just turning round to comfort her when he saw Sam charging out of the cave.

'Sam, no,' he called, but it was too late; the dog had leapt at the man's arm and was pulling him down. The Urkku shouted and tried to shake him free but Sam refused to let go. The man tried to use his knife but he was unable to because it was the knife arm Sam had got hold of and eventually as the dog's teeth sank deeper into the flesh he dropped it and it fell with a clatter on to the pebbles. He shouted again and this time the animals in the cave heard footsteps running over the rocks and Urkku voices shouting across to the man on the beach.

'Get this dog off. It's mad,' he yelled desperately. 'Don't shoot; you might hit me. Use the clubs.'

Saurélon was now at the front of the cave trying to stop the others from going out to help Sam.

'No,' he said. 'I command that you stay. If you go you will be killed and we shall be lost for ever.'

'But Sam will be killed,' said Brock, angry and frustrated and determined not to let his friend die while he stood by.

Saurélon did not answer him. Rarely in all his long life had he been faced with such a difficult task, but there was no doubt in his mind that he was right to stop them from going even though it filled him with the utmost pain to have to do it.

They did not see the club come down but they heard it and they heard the growl of pain as Sam let go of the arm and rolled over on to the pebbles. Then the club came down again and they heard a little whimper.

Through a daze of grief they heard the voices of the Urkku outside.

'Bloody dog. How did it get out here? How's your arm?'

'It came from that cave. I wonder if it's the one from that pack of animals that have been causing all the trouble. You know. They've been on the news, chasing sheep and stealing food and they say there's two runaways with them.'

'Could be,' said a different voice. 'Come on. Let's go and look in the cave.'

The animals were too numb with pain to hear what had been said but Saurélon had and he heard the heavy footsteps crunching over the beach towards the cave mouth. It was at that moment that the storm arose. The wind which had begun when the Urkku first arrived on Elgol and which had blown much of the mist away, now suddenly increased to a frightening intensity so that, instead of blowing, it seemed to pull. It pulled at the sea to form great waves and the tops of the white horses it drew up into the air so that the bay was full of fine misty spray. Then the rain came, lashing down in torrents on to the shore and the sea. The Urkku were bent over against the wind and had to shout to make themselves heard.

'We'd best get back before it gets any worse. Come on,' said one, and another one, the one with whom Sam had fought, called back.

'We'll take the dog. It may belong to somebody on the mainland. I'll have something off them for what it's done to my arm.'

Then a third voice broke in. 'No. The storm's too bad. Look at the waves. Let's shelter in the cave until it's died down. We'd never make it in this.'

The others agreed. They picked up Sam's wet bedraggled body and Nab's stomach turned over as he heard it land with a heavy thud when they tossed it into the boat.

'We'll take the skins into the cave. Keep them dry,' said the third voice again and then came the clatter of running footsteps over the pebbles.

Saurélon spoke. 'We must hurry into the elven cave. Come quickly. The Urkku are almost upon us.'

It was too late. The animals, dazed and bewildered, were slow to react to Saurélon's command and the men ran swiftly over the beach to get out of the storm. Suddenly everything in the cave went dark as the five Urkku stood in the entrance and the animals realized with a jolt of horror that they were trapped. At first the Urkku were unable to see anything inside for their eyes were not used to the darkness but then one of them spotted the little huddle of animals crouched against the wall and the boy and girl staring up at him with big frightened eyes in their dark, brown, weatherbeaten faces, quivering with tension. He gave a shout of triumph.

'Look. It's them. Come here, kid. Let's have a look at you.'

As he moved towards them, the animals' trance of fear was broken and they sprang out from behind the rock. Then they heard Saurélon call to them from the shadows at the back of the cave.

'Run. To the seals. Run,' and, with Faraid leading them, they dashed out past the astonished Urkku, banging into their legs as they ran, and found themselves racing down across the beach with the full force of the rain in their faces. Through the roar of the wind they heard a yell from the cave mouth.

'Come on. Let's get after them,' and, glancing back quickly, Nab saw the Urkku running down the beach. Faraid was now at the rocks and Brock and Perryfoot, who were close after him, had to slow down because the rain had made them very slippery. When Nab and Beth caught up they helped them and very soon they were all standing at the edge of the sea and Nab was holding Beth's hand as she clambered down a rock on to the back of one of the seals waiting in the water. Then he handed Perryfoot to her and, holding Brock between himself and the rock, he half climbed and half slipped down until he and the badger were also safely down in the sea. Finally just as the Urkku reached the rocks, Faraid sprang down and with one leap was sitting astride his seal, Eynort, named after the great elven warrior. The storm was too fierce for Warrigal to risk flying so he flew down and joined Faraid and then the seals flicked their tails and they were off, cutting a way through the water or else bucking and leaping over the waves while the animals shut their eyes and clung on. Nab looked back and saw the Urkku standing on the rocks looking at them and he could vaguely hear snatches of shouted voices above the wind and the sea. The storm was too fierce for them to risk following in their boat and when Nab looked again they were running back to the cave.

Nab could see very little ahead through the torrents of rain that lashed across his face. He looked down at Brock, whose wet fur clung to him in little spikes and who hadn't moved a muscle since they started out, and he knew what the badger was thinking. One thought filled his mind also: they were leaving Sam. He could see in his mind's eye the familiar brown shape as it was tossed into the air and he could hear again that awful thud as it landed on the wooden boards of the boat. He was filled with guilt and remorse; looking back now he was unable to sort out how it had all happened. It seemed to be over so fast; one minute they were inside the cave and the next Sam was lying on his side on the beach. Then he remembered; Saurélon had stopped them from going to help Sam while he was fighting with the Urkku: if he had not stopped them perhaps Sam would be with them now. As this thought pounded away in his mind and his stomach turned to jelly with the realization, a wave of anger and bitterness against Saurélon and Ashgaroth and Faraid and Wychnor and his 'mission' and everything to do with it seemed to well up inside him and he gave a great shout in an attempt to release his churning emotions.

'Why,' he shouted at the storm again and again, until the sobbing ache in his throat became too painful; but the wind took all the force of his shouts and they were lost in the gale almost as soon as they left his mouth, and he fell into a deep brooding melancholy. In the days to come this feeling of anger and betrayal became submerged in the urgency of their task, but it was a long time before Nab was truly able to understand why Saurélon had stopped them.

The journey through the raging storm-lashed sea was one of the most terrifying experiences they had ever had. The rain and the wind beat against them with a frightening force as if trying to drag them off the backs of the seals to be lost to the sea, but some other force seemed to keep them on almost against their will; for they were all so frightened, depressed and miserable that they would almost willingly have abandoned themselves to the storm.

Finally, after what seemed an age, they could see the vague outlines of land ahead of them and very soon the seals slowed down in an area of sea which was quite sheltered by outcrops of rock on either side and where the waves were not so high. They swam slowly up to a small shelf of rock which jutted out into the sea and the animals gratefully climbed off their backs and stood shakily once more on dry land. It felt wonderful to be on firm ground again but it took them a little while to get used to the idea that they were not still rolling and plunging over the waves. At first they were unable to get their balance properly and they swayed around with their heads spinning as they tried to stand up straight and walk around the rock ledge. The seals bobbed up and down in the water and stared inquisitively at them. Then the animals bade them farewell sadly and followed Faraid up a steep path, almost awash with the rain, which wound its way precariously up the cliff to the top of the headland, where they stopped and looked out to sea. The rain was still coming down in torrents and hundreds of little streams and rivulets were running everywhere, but the sky had begun to clear a little and on the far horizon they could see the beginnings of that eerie golden light that always comes after a storm. Elgol was just visible, its outlines blurred by the rain, but they could not see the Urkku or the boat as they were at the seaward end of the island. They would remember Elgol with a mixture of great happiness and terrible pain and in their memories the island would always belong to Sam. They watched now as the huge waves raced in and crashed against it, sending great spumes of spray showering over the rock, and it seemed to the animals as if all the anger of Ashgaroth was contained in those towering blue-green breakers with their jagged crests of white foam.

Faraid, who had been standing a little away from them to let their minds run freely through the events of the day, approached them now gently and, in a voice humbled by the thought of all the sufferings these animals had been through, spoke to them. They heard his voice as one hears the first lark in spring after a long hard winter and it brought them back from the brink of despair.

'Come, my friends. It is time for the last stage of your journey. When it is over, then will be the time for you to rest and to rejoice.'

The animals wearily and reluctantly turned away and followed the elf as he took them back across the bracken and heather of the headland until they reached green meadows full of sheep where they had to climb over many stone walls as Faraid led them once again towards the Marshes of Blore. When they reached the edge of the marsh it was late afternoon and the storm had blown itself out. Everywhere was dripping with wet and the grass smelt fresh and clean. The light they had seen earlier on the horizon had now spread to fill the sky so that everything was bathed in a gentle golden light. Looking up, the animals saw that the sky had almost completely cleared and lots of little snow-white fluffy clouds were racing across the blue.

Nab asked Faraid whether they could rest awhile before they entered the marsh but the elf thought it advisable to press on as it was likely that the Urkku had now left Elgol and were back amongst their people. He told the friends what the Urkku had said outside the cave about the 'pack of animals' and the 'two runaways'.

'Every Urkku in the land will now be looking out for you,' he said, 'and if you are spotted they will pursue you relentlessly until they find you. Dréagg is feeding them with lies and rumours which will fester and grow as they spread until the stories of your misdeeds are known by all. It is the way the Evil One works; he uses deceit and trickery to play on the minds of the Urkku. You are near the end of your mission and he will do everything to stop you. If you were careful before, now you must be doubly so, for he will use the goblins again and they have the power to transform themselves into Urkku when they wish so that they may work with the Urkku against you. There is, then, no time to waste.'

It took them until the following evening to cross the marsh and somehow this time it did not seem so terrifying. They saw no goblins and although they went along the same path as that by which they had travelled before there was no trace of Golconda nor of the tree on which he had been left. They emerged out of the mists of the marsh into a calm golden evening at a place some way from that by which they had entered when they came. They stood for a little while looking out over a landscape of rolling foothills gently sloping up- wards towards distant moors. It was the end of spring and the beginning of summer, and the trees, huge elms and sycamores and ash, were covered in a multitude of different greens from the deep dark emerald of the elms to the delicate lime green of the ash trees. They towered up into the blue, their leaves gently moving in the evening breeze; rows of them like giant guardians of the earth stretching along the narrow valleys between the hills where little streams gurgled their way down through banks laden with primroses and bluebells and little green shoots of bracken poked their way up through the rich dark peat moss.

Faraid turned to them and pointed to a little hummock on the skyline.

'There is your first Scyttel. From there you will know your way to the lair of the mountain-elves by the feeling of the Roosdyche. Farewell, and may Ashgaroth guide you safely to the journey's end.'

So saying he turned and quickly vanished into the mists of Blore so that even as they looked after him, he was gone. Then they looked at one another in silence for a few moments before Perryfoot pricked up his ears.

'Come on,' he said. 'It's spring and the earth is full and green,' and he set off up the slope with the others following behind.

CHAPTER XIX

It was a perfect evening as they made their way up the green bank alongside the stream towards the Scyttel in the distance. The air was warm and scented with bluebells which covered the ground under the giant trees in a blue haze, and further down, near the stream, there were splashes of vivid orange from the marigolds that sprang up in clusters wherever there was a marshy piece of ground. The sun was almost down behind the far hills but it seemed to shine with a particular fierceness as if hoping that its light would last after it had gone so that its warm, magic glow flooded the little valley along which they were walking and sent shafts of gold through the huge green leafy tree canopies overhead. Then, suddenly, it was gone and the shadows of dusk filled the valley and soon the dew fell everywhere and their feet became wet as they walked through the long grass. The dampness on the ground filled the air with the smell of wet green leaves and grass: the unmistakable smell of a spring evening, and the animals drank it in as if it were elvenwine and indeed it had the same effect, filling their tired bodies with fresh energy and vigour so that they felt they could have walked for ever. The air stayed warm late into the night and a little breeze came up, blowing gently against their faces as if it was trying to cleanse their memories of that last morning on Elgol. The agony of walking without Sam was almost more than they could endure. They would keep forgetting he was not there and then, on turning to speak to him or look for him, would once again be hit by the shock of realizing what had happened. If it was worse for any of them, then it was worse for Brock, because he had known the dog the longest and had walked alongside him for the whole of the journey. Nab had asked Perryfoot to walk with him and the hare had willingly obliged but it did not seem to have helped much; the badger would walk along with his head down and then suddenly look up and stare at Perryfoot with blank, uncomprehending eyes until he remembered and then his head would once again slump down and he would urge his tired body to resume its shuffling gait over the grass. First Bruin, then Tara and now Sam; they had all felt the losses terribly, particularly Nab, whose life had been so intertwined with Brock's, but it was undeniably hardest on the badger, for two of them had been his family and one his best friend and Nab now had Beth to live for so that he was able to look forward: for Brock the past had died and the future was uncertain and lonely.

They reached the mound that night and slept under the shade of a huge sycamore until the following evening when they awoke feeling refreshed after a deep dreamless sleep. Even Brock felt a bit better as they started out once again towards a range of mountains in the far distance. They were quite high now and they walked through green fields cropped short by grazing sheep which were criss-crossed by white stone walls. High up in the clear blue sky larks sang while lower down plovers dipped and swooped over the ground and curlews sent out their liquid warbling cries into the still evening air. Behind them, from the valleys through which they had walked the previous night, they heard the occasional screech of an owl or the bark of a fox or else a cuckoo calling out his spring song. The daisies and dandelions which in the heat of the day had sprinkled the meadows with whites and oranges were now closing up and drawing their petals in for the night.

On they walked throughout the remainder of the spring; then summer came, and the hot sun beat down on them, making their throats dry and parching their mouths so that they walked from stream to stream, but as the days wore on and rain refused to fall the ponds and streams got low and the water that was left in them was brackish and musty. They were still making for the far mountains, which appeared hazy and bluish in the distance, but they had dropped down again now into the lowlands where there was little if any breeze to relieve the unrelenting heat which poured down from the blue sky into the lanes and between the hedges along which they cautiously made their way. They slept only in the afternoons now for Nab was anxious that they should move as quickly as possible and he and Beth each carried a share of her winter clothes: the brown cape and the jerseys which had helped her to survive the cold. Nab had wanted her to bury them under a hedge somewhere but she had been adamant in her refusal.

'They're all I have left of my old life,' she had said, 'and of my home. I could no more part with these than you could throw away your bark from Silver Wood.'

So, because he loved her, he reluctantly agreed and had ended up carrying her heavy cape and two jerseys while she took the remaining one and thanked him for being so thoughtful and kind.

It was in the height of summer, one hot morning when they were trudging along a dry dusty cattle track through a field, that they saw for the first time a thick black column of smoke rising in the distance. It went straight up in the humid windless air and the animals could smell the acrid stench of its fumes from where they were standing. They stopped still and looked at it; they had all seen smoke before from the chimneys of the Urkku but this was somehow different. The smoke was blacker, thicker and more dense, and the smell was sickly-sweet and nauseating; it reminded Beth of the smell caused when people put chicken carcasses on fires to burn them after the Sunday dinner.

'Look, there's another,' Brock said, and he pointed to a thicker column round to their right and as they looked around they saw more and more until there must have been a dozen fires, all with their black plumes drifting up into the sky. There was something ominous and evil about them and Nab felt a chill go down his back as he watched.

'Come on,' he said, 'we can't stay here all day.'

'What are they, Nab?' said Beth.

'I don't know but there's something about them which makes me afraid. We must move on.'

'It's almost Sun-High,' said Perryfoot. 'Couldn't we stay here for the afternoon by the hedge? It seems as good a place as any.'

Nab looked at Warrigal and the owl spoke.

'It may be our last opportunity to rest for quite some time. I think we should stay here and move on in the early evening.'

So the animals walked over the field towards a thick hedge which ran along one side. Growing in the hedge were a number of large oak trees and they settled down in the shade of one of these, huddled around the trunk with Warrigal perching on one of the high branches to keep a watch for any signs of danger. It was beautifully cool in the green shade of the oak and they were soon asleep.

When evening came and the dusk began to fall they awoke and moved on. In the darkness they could not see the black smoke from the fires but they could smell them and occasionally they caught sight of red flickering flames in the distance and heard noises of shouting and crying coming from the direction of the fires.

As dawn arose they were walking along a little grassy ridge with wooded heathland on one side and meadows on the other. The ground was blackened and scorched so that there was very little grass left in the field and all that remained of the heath was an expanse of charred black scrub and bushes. The smell of burnt wood was every-where and their feet became sooty as they walked. They could see now that the countryside all about was the same and the air was full of black smuts.

It was mid-morning when they saw the Urkku. They had been making their way up the scorched slope of a little hill when suddenly they froze at the sound of two shots from the far side followed by ferocious guttural shouts as if an argument was going on. They crawled through the blackened grass until they could just see over the top. There was quite a deep valley the other side and halfway up the far slope stood a number of Urkku, all with guns, yelling at one another. On the ground were some dead rabbits and the Urkku seemed to be in two groups, one on each side. Beth looked in amazement at the men, for she had never before seen any like them. Their clothes, if that is what they had once been, hung off them like strips of dirty rag and their bodies were so emaciated that the ribs stuck through their puny barrel chests and the skin hung in loose folds. They were wearing what appeared to be trousers and out of the bottom of these protruded thin bony ankles like matchsticks, and bare feet. She looked in mounting horror at their faces and was transfixed by what she saw. The hair was long, dirty and matted so that it hung down in tangled knots or else stuck out in greasy spikes, and beneath this filthy thatch, deep-set sunken eyes stared out of a face so covered in grime and dirt that as they shouted their teeth seemed to flash silver in the sunlight. Their cheeks were sunken and hollow and the cheekbones appeared to be all that held the covering of skin from falling away. Beth held her nose and had to stop herself from retching when the stench from their bodies, exaggerated by the heat, was carried over in the breeze.

The cause of the argument seemed to be the rabbits for each group was pointing at them and then gesticulating wildly and shouting. Suddenly an Urkku from one group ran forward and, flinging himself on one of his adversaries, began wrestling with him on the ground. They rolled around spitting and biting and kicking and a cloud of dust rose up around them. The others transferred their attention from the rabbits to their mauling companions, each side yelling encouragement to its own until finally one of them, whose hair under the grime was a ginger colour and who looked the bigger and stronger of the two, grabbed hold of a rock on the ground and brought it smashing down on his opponent's head. There was silence while the one who had been hit went still and rolled back on to the grass with blood pouring from his head. The ginger one was just disentangling himself from his grip when one of the other group shouted at him and, raising his gun to his shoulder, shot the victor in the chest and sent him flying back to end up lying on top of his opponent. The friends then looked on in amazement as the two groups began blasting away at each other from where they were standing. It was over in seconds and the crashing noise of the guns seemed to have only just started when it had already finished, the echoes dying away in the still silent air and the smell of gunpowder clogging up their nostrils for a fleeting instant before it blew away in a little cloud of light brown smoke. Eight Urkku lay dead on the grass and the survivors from the winning group were running away across the field carrying the rabbits by the back legs so that as they ran the heads jerked crazily up and down as if they were rag dolls. They were laughing in a high-pitched, hysterical way.

The animals remained where they were for a long time, in silence. The sun beat down on their backs and the smell of burning was heavy in the air. Finally Warrigal broke the silence.

'Most odd. Most peculiar,' he said. 'Something is happening in the world of the Urkku. I've never seen them look or behave like that before. Beth, what do you think?'

'I don't know. Those men. They seemed so – I don't know – so strange. And that fight; all that shooting. It was horrible. I don't like it. Let's move on quickly; get away from here.'

The girl felt a cold chill all over despite the heat of the sun. She was horribly afraid; more so than she had ever been before, and she, who had lived nearly all her life with humans, had felt it more than the animals. Something was going terribly wrong. She turned to Nab. 'Hold me,' she said, and he put his arms around her and she closed her eyes for a second and with her head snuggled against his shoulder she felt better.

On they walked but they could not escape the ghastly black columns of smoke nor get out of the scorched blackened landscape which seemed to stretch for mile upon mile around them in every direction. The sickly stench from the fires grew steadily more unbearable until even the act of breathing became something which they dreaded. Their hands, faces and feet were ingrained with black from the soot and the charred ground, and nowhere was there enough clean water to wash it off properly. When they came to a pond now it was almost certain to be dried up, its bed split open and cracked in great mud fissures, and they would search for a little corner somewhere where there might be a remaining puddle of foul-smelling brackish liquid with which they would attempt to slake their ravening thirst.

Every day now they saw two or three bands of Urkku like the first,

241

wandering ragged and aimless on the burnt ground, guns under their arms and eyes constantly moving as if they were afraid of being seen. This made it harder for the animals to avoid them as they were far quieter and less easily spotted than they used to be and the travellers were only able to move slowly with Warrigal flying ahead to make sure everything was clear to go on. Often now he would come back and report Urkku in front and they would have to wait for agonizing hours until they had moved on and it was safe to go ahead. They slept during these waiting periods and travelled when they could rather than sleeping every afternoon, and they found that they made better progress after Sun-High because the heat was so intense then that there were fewer Urkku around. The sound of shooting was also common, either a single crack or a battery of shots such as they had heard that first time, and then they would come across the casualties of these random fights and be careful to avoid going too close to them for fear of disturbing the flies and because of the smell. There was very little shade from the searing heat of those afternoons because all the green foliage from the hedges and trees had been burnt off. Giant oaks and sycamores, whose leaves had once cast a fragrant cool green shade on the grass, now stood gaunt, black and naked, their charred limbs standing out starkly against the clear blue sky.

One afternoon they saw a city in the distance. No smoke came from its factory chimneys and no hum of traffic from its roads and streets. Instead it lay like a huge slumbering giant and sizzled under the heat; the sun baking the concrete and sending out dazzling reflections from the empty office block windows. A shimmering heat haze hung over it and the unearthly silence was only very occasionally shattered by the wailing of a siren.

While the animals stood on the brow of a little hill from which they could see the sprawl of concrete stretching away into the far horizon, they suddenly became aware of a column of smoke just beginning to claw its way up into the sky on their right.

'I'll fly over and try and see what's happening,' said Warrigal. 'It'd be quicker and safer for me than any of you and I think we ought to find out.'

'Yes, that's a good idea. But take care,' Nab replied. 'We'll wait for you back in that little hollow.'

The owl flew off slowly and quietly and the others went back down the hill. It did not take Warrigal long to come within sight of the fire and he went as close as he could, perching on the branch of one of a number of what had once been sycamores situated around the outside of a clearing. Inside the clearing a large number of Urkku were milling around and shouting and in the middle a fire was crackling and spitting fiercely. The flames were hard to see in the bright glare of the sun but he could feel its heat even from where he was perched and there was no mistaking the sickening smell of the thick black smoke as it billowed its way up from the fire. Through the smoke Warrigal could see two large mounds from which the Urkku kept feeding the fire but it was too thick for him to make out what they were so, very cautiously, he flew round to the other side of the clearing. The sight that met his eyes filled him with horror. The mound furthest away from him was composed of dead Urkku and the other of dead animals; but it was when he forced himself to look more closely that the full impact of what he was seeing made itself felt. Warrigal was the least emotional of any of the animals but even he was unable to contain a flood of terror as he realized that the dead animals on the second pile were all either badgers, hares, fawn-coloured dogs or owls. They had been thrown together carelessly on to the pile as if they were pieces of wood and their heads and limbs stuck out at odd angles.

Suddenly the owl's trance-like state, caused by the horror in front of him, was shattered by a piercing shout from an Urkku who had come over to the pile to collect some more carcasses for the fire.

'There's one. Quick. Kill it.' There was a roar from the other Urkku who all began to rush forward to the tree where he was perching and then the crack of a gun sounded above the noise of the fire and Warrigal heard the thud of a bullet as it hit the branch above him. He flew quickly back through the belt of trees that surrounded the clearing while behind him the mob of yelling Urkku crashed their way through the undergrowth below and the air around him hummed and whistled with the sound of bullets. Swiftly he sped through the branches, using every trick he knew to gain extra speed and keeping an eye on the ground below to lead his pursuers through the thickest undergrowth. Eventually, to his intense relief, the sounds of pursuit began to fade away into the distance and the cracking of the guns stopped. Nevertheless he did not slacken his speed until he arrived back in sight of the little hollow where the others were waiting. He did not fly straight back to them but perched for a time on a tree at the edge of the field they were in, in case he was still being followed. There was no sight of Urkku anywhere and the smoke from the fire was getting thicker so he assumed they had returned and were continuing to feed it with its grisly fuel. He put his head on one side and listened intently but, apart from the shouting in the distance, everywhere was still and quiet. Then, certain that he was not being followed, he rejoined the others.

Ever since they had heard the commotion and the shooting from the direction of the fire the others had been frantic with worry and when the owl's familiar silhouette glided gracefully over the edge of the hollow, they were overjoyed with relief. Perryfoot jumped up and down and standing on his hind legs danced about, tapping the others with his front paws and chanting 'Warrigal's safe, Warrigal's safe,' over and over again.

The owl looked at the hare with affection and then said sadly, 'I'm afraid I don't bring good news.' Slowly he recounted every detail of what he had seen and when he had finished his tale Perryfoot was sitting slumped against the bank with his ears drooping along his back and Brock, Nab and Beth sat quietly staring at the ground. They did not understand the meaning of the dead Urkku but they slowly began to realize the awful significance of the pile of animals by the fire. Finally Warrigal spoke again.

'Until they're certain they have found us they will kill every badger, every owl, every hare and every dog like Sam that they can find. The longer we delay, the more will die.'

Silently they got up and climbed to the top of the hollow. The mountains, towards which they were heading and where they would find Malcoff and the mountain elves, were shimmering in the haze and appeared soft and grey in the late summer afternoon.

'How long will it take to get there?' Beth asked Nab.

'I don't know. Perhaps two days.'

They made their way, as quickly as they dared, in the direction of the mountains, but they saw nothing. No Urkku, no animals, no birds; the countryside was empty and desolate. When darkness fell they welcomed the coolness that came with the night although there was still not a breath of wind and the air was heavy and thick with heat. From the earth beneath their feet they could feel the day's sunshine coming back up at them and their mouths became dry and parched. By Moon-High their exhausted sweating bodies were demanding a rest but in the animals' minds was a vision of the pile of dead bodies which Warrigal had seen and it haunted them, spurring them on and on. Any delay now was unthinkable.

It was in the deepest hours of the night, between midnight and dawn, that they first heard the noise. It came from a long way behind them and at first they paid no attention to it, their minds being so intently fixed on the path ahead, but soon it grew louder and the blur of sound became distinguishable. They could make out the yelping and barking of dogs and mingled with them the shouts of the Urkku. They had all heard the sound before when Rufus and the other foxes of Silver Wood had been chased by packs of hounds and Urkku riding on horseback, whooping and cheering. But it had always been in the daytime; never at night. What were they doing out now?

They tried to ignore the noise in the hope that it would go away, and they tried also to quell the chill of fear that was fluttering in their stomachs. Dawn finally broke and a vivid gash of orange appeared over the mountains ahead of them but the barks and yelps, far from disappearing had grown louder and eventually Warrigal voiced their unspoken dread.

'I fear we are being followed,' he said.

'They're bound to find us with the dogs,' said Perryfoot. 'They never fail. How far behind us are they, do you think, Brock?'

'I used to hear them starting out from the village for Silver Wood and they were louder than this so we still have some time.'

Then Nab spoke. 'We shall have to hope that we can find Malcoff as soon as we get to the mountains. Otherwise they'll be upon us. We must move quicker.'

Beth shrank inwardly. She was already utterly exhausted and had been hoping that they could take a little break some time soon. Now they were going to have to move faster, perhaps even to run. The sun had now appeared in the clear blue sky and it looked as if it was going to be another scorching day. She could not go on, yet if she insisted on a rest or on taking the pace more slowly she would be holding them up and once again becoming a burden to them. No; she would not give up! She would go with them until she dropped.

'Come on, Beth. We shall have to run.' Nab smiled down at her where she sat on the ground. Her long hair was tangled and streaked with soot from the smuts that floated everywhere and there were smudges of black on her nose and her cheeks and forehead. Her arms and legs were red and blistered from the sun and her face was flushed with the heat. She still wore her black wellington boots but she had torn her jeans off above the knee. He thought back to the first time he had seen her, looking crisp and clean and fresh in the red gingham dress she had worn that wonderful spring afternoon down by the stream so many seasons ago. He stooped down, put both his arms around her and gently lifted her to her feet.

'We'll soon be safe in the mountains,' he said. 'Don't worry. Everything will be all right.'

She clung on to him as if trying to draw some of his energy and strength to her own worn-out body. Then suddenly she straightened up and looking deep into his dark eyes she said, laughing, 'Come on then, slowcoach,' and began to trot away over the fields.

All that day they ran at a steady loping pace over the flat burnt out meadows and all that day the yelps and barks and shouts behind them grew louder and clearer. By late afternoon they had reached the foothills of the mountains. As they climbed the gradually sloping fields they noticed that the grass became greener and soon they left the charred and blackened landscape of the lowlands behind them. Mercifully also the air became cooler and a little breeze began to blow against them, lifting their hair from their faces and blowing through Brock's and Perryfoot's fur. The fragrance of the long summer grass and the coolness of the breeze went to their heads like wine and their spirits lifted as they ran through little green valleys and up alongside gaily tinkling streams. After the desolation they had been through everywhere seemed so fresh and the greenness all around seemed to envelop them with its lush protection so that they felt safe and comforted. The sound of the pack was muffled by the trees and when they stopped to listen it seemed as if the barking was receding into the distance so they went more slowly, often stopping to drink from one of the cool clear streams or to nibble at something tasty. It was late summer now and some of the early autumn toadstools were beginning to appear in the dark and shady places.

It was just before dawn when they emerged from the trees and valleys of the foothills into the beginning of the mountains. Before them stretched a vast sea of purple heather interspersed with clumps of cotton grass waving their white heads gently in the breeze. It was very hard travelling over the heather and at first they kept to the little narrow sheep tracks, but Nab was afraid that if they strayed too far from the Roosdyche they would never find it again so they had to strike up and leave the paths.

They had not travelled far when suddenly they heard the sounds of the pack again, only this time it seemed as if it was just behind them. It had emerged from the trees and, now that there was nothing to smother the noise, the closeness of their pursuers was revealed to the animals with a shock of horror. They could not see them but the frantic baying was so near that it could only be a matter of minutes before they were spotted.

Desperately they ran over the heather urging their tired worn-out bodies to go faster until the breath rasped in their throats and their legs went numb with pain. Then suddenly Beth's knees buckled under her and she fell face down on to a large clump of heather. For a second or two, with her eyes closed, she luxuriated in the wonderful feeling of lying there and giving in to the demands of her body but then she dragged herself back to reality as she felt herself being shaken and heard Nab's frantic voice calling to her. She looked at him and his face seemed far away. She forced herself to speak.

'I can't go any further. Leave me here. You go on. I'll be all right.' Then she closed her eyes again and a haze of swirling blackness engulfed her.

'Beth, Beth,' shouted Nab but it was no use; her eyelids did not even flicker. He looked at the others; they were all stretched out panting on the heather, their bodies heaving with the effort of drawing breath. It was useless to think about going on but where could they hide? Suddenly Warrigal swooped down and landed beside him.

'Where've you been? I didn't even know you'd gone,' said Nab.

'I've been scouting around the hillside. There's an Urkku dwelling nearby; just a little way down the hill and across. We shall have to take a chance that they are of the Eldron and will help us; I saw smoke coming out of a chimney so it is definitely occupied.'

'We've got no choice, have we? We either stay here and get torn apart by the dogs for certain or else we take the risk of being handed over to them. I can carry Beth but I can't carry these clothes as well. Brock'll have to take them in his mouth.'

They cut off across the side of the hill with the sound of the dogs growing louder all the time. Then just below them they saw the dwelling. It was a croft. The walls were of rough white stone and they supported a roof of turf out of which grew a green haze of moss. There was a hole for a window and a hole for a door and out of the little chimney came the sweet smell of burning peat. The long low dwelling seemed to have grown out of the earth and this impression was confirmed by the heaps of peat squares piled up against the two end walls and the fact that the building itself was in a little hollow. There was a stone wall around it enclosing a garden and at the back the animals could see a small vegetable patch while at the front were a few pink and white flowers. The ground immediately outside the wall was dotted with troughs and squares from which the peat had been cut and a few sheep grazed around the outside of these while others lay inside hoping for some shade from the sun. Two white goats munched away vigorously just outside a little gate in the stone wall through which the garden was entered. There was something about the croft, and the scene below them, that was so peaceful that for a second they forgot their danger; it seemed impossible that anything bad could happen there. The place filled them with a feeling of trust and calm so that they felt no fear or doubt as they made their way down the slope. The latch on the gate made a loud click as Nab lifted it and the goats looked up and bleated, staring at them curiously for a second or two before resuming their grazing. Brock and Perryfoot walked quietly across the little garden and sat down against the wall of the croft to wait and see what happened while Warrigal flew up and perched on the roof. Still carrying Beth, Nab slowly walked up to the front door. As he got nearer he heard low voices and the clink and clatter of cups and plates. Finally he reached the door, which was open, and stood wondering what to do next. Gently he laid Beth down on the ground. What was the human word for greeting which she had taught him? Then he remembered.

'Hello,' he said quietly, but the sounds and voices in the kitchen carried on unchanged. They haven't heard me, he thought, and repeated it again more loudly. This time the sounds stopped and the voices took on a different tone.

'See who that is, Jim. I can't think who it might be. It's very early. Look! It's only half past seven.'

Nab heard the sound of a chair being scraped back across the floor and then the pad of footsteps came towards the door. It was so dark inside that he could see nothing until suddenly a man stood in front of him. He was old and his hair was white and sparse but out of his wrinkled brown face shone two blue eyes that danced with light. He wore a collarless shirt with a blue pin-stripe waistcoat and on his legs a pair of baggy blue serge trousers tied around the waist by a piece of string. He stood with one hand on the door and in the other he held an old briar pipe.

'Hello, young feller. What can I do for you? You're a long way from the road.' Then he spotted Beth on the grass. 'Oh, I see. Your friend's ill. Well, fetch her in then and we'll see what we can do. Probably the heat.'

'Danger. Hide,' said Nab and lifted three fingers of one hand.

'What? There are three more of you? What danger?'

Frantic with frustration at not being able to find the words he wanted, Nab called to the others.

'Well, blow me down. Ivy,' Jim called into the kitchen. 'Here a minute!'

The owl, the badger and the hare stood in a line outside the front door while the old couple looked at them in amazement. Then Ivy spoke. She was small with grey hair and wore a navy blue dress with a faint white flowered pattern on it. When she spoke her hands shook a little with age, but her eyes, like Jim's, were bright and merry.

'You know who they are, don't you, Jim?'

'Yes.'

'Well let's get them inside quickly and hide them. Listen!' She paused and waited while the barking and shouting got louder. 'Come on, young man. Hurry up, and bring your friends in with you. Jim; put them in the bedroom.'

The old man led the animals through the front room and the kitchen until they came to an old wooden door which he opened. In the middle of the room was a large bed and around the whitewashed walls were a few pieces of furniture; an old wardrobe, a chest of drawers and a beautiful carved dressing table with photographs of Jim and of Ivy's parents on it along with her brush and comb and one or two bottles of lavender water and scent.

'Now, don't worry. Get behind the bed and keep very quiet. We'll see to them.' He closed the door and there was silence except for muffled voices from the front room and the barking of the dogs. Nab lay Beth down gently on a piece of matting which was on the floor and sat beside her. Perryfoot and Brock squeezed under the bed and Warrigal perched on top of one of the brass bed-posts. It seemed to the animals as if they had only just settled in their places when the little house was suddenly filled with the sound of a loud thumping and banging on the door. They held their breath and their hearts quickened. It had all happened so fast that they had not had time to think whether or not they could trust the old couple; yet as soon as the seed of doubt entered their heads they dismissed it with a certainty that they could not explain. The old couple were of the Eldron; of that there could be no question. The animals had felt the goodness and warmth which flowed out towards them.

The knocking came again, only louder this time. Then a voice shouted out harshly. 'Anyone in?' Nab felt a tingle of fear rush up and down his spine and lodge, prickling, at the back of his neck. He instantly recognized the voice, it came to him as a terrible ghost from the past. The voice belonged unmistakably to the Urkku called Jeff; the one who, with his brother, had captured him from Silver Wood and taken him back to be locked up in the little room and, worst of all, the one who had shot Bruin. There were now voices at the door; the old man had finally answered it and his deep gentle lilting voice

250

contrasted sharply with the jagged staccato tones of the other. 'I must hear what they are saying,' thought Nab, and he crawled forward very slowly and quietly until he was up against the bedroom door with his ear pressed to it. He could not understand all the words but the sense of their conversation came across to him. The old man was speaking.

'I'm sorry I didn't hear; I'm a bit deaf. What do you want?'

The Urkku Jeff replied harshly. 'We're looking for the animals. They were seen a while back; at least the owl was, and the dogs have been following them ever since. Right up here to your front door. They must have gone past. Did you not see them?'

The old man replied steadily.

'What animals? We've seen nothing other than the occasional rabbit all morning.'

There was a silence which was almost menacing in its stillness. Even the dogs stopped their barking and growling.

'Don't play games with me, old man. You live a long way out but don't pretend you don't know what's going on. If you had seen them, you would tell us, wouldn't you?'

'You mean the little group of animals who are rumoured to have a boy and a girl with them. The ones who are supposed to have started the plague. I have heard something of it on the wireless when they have been able to broadcast. No, I haven't seen them. I didn't know they were in this area.'

'They were seen and followed here. To your house.'

'Well, I shall look out for them; though myself, I don't believe the stories that have been put round. There's no proof that the plague began with them.'

Again there was a silence. When the Urkku spoke his voice was low and guttural.

'Take care, old man. That kind of talk is dangerous. You had best forget it. Have you not had the government circulars? They must be found and destroyed, as must all their kind, for they too may be carriers and only in that way will we be sure we have got rid of it. The boy and the girl must be found and questioned as to all they know. Then they will be cleansed and educated; at least the boy will, for it appears that the girl may have led a normal life until she left her home. Apparently the disease does not affect them though they are the carriers. Now, old man; let's not hear any more of this foolish talk. Your attitude has been noted. If you see them you will have to walk down to the village and contact the police who will inform the authorities. As you must know, very few phones are still working.'

Then the dogs began barking loudly again as the Urkku moved off down the hill. It was only when the noise had faded into the distance that the door opened and Ivy came in. 'Well, they've gone for now,' she said, half to herself and half to Nab. 'Let's see how your friend is, shall we?' She knelt down beside Beth and raised her so that the girl was sitting up. She moaned and her eyelids fluttered but still she did not come round.

'Thank you,' Nab said and pointed outside to the door to show what he meant. Ivy looked at him and smiled gently.

'It's all right,' she said. 'Here, you hold her up while I go and get some cold water to bathe her face.' Nab was longing to ask her and Jim what the Urkku had said exactly but his command of human language was not yet such that he could put his questions into words. He would have to wait until Beth was better.

Ivy came back with a white enamel basin full of water and began splashing the girl's face. Perryfoot and Brock came out from under the bed and watched anxiously while Warrigal surveyed the proceedings curiously from his vantage point on the bed-post. Outside, through the window, he could see dark banks of cloud beginning to gather in the distance beyond the far peaks and he smelt rain in the air. The atmosphere was heavy and close and there was not a breath of wind.

Soon Beth was showing signs of regaining consciousness and Ivy called out, 'Jim, bring in a cup of tea for the poor girl.' He fetched the kettle off the range where it always sat and poured hot water from it into their little brown tea pot to warm it. Then he refilled the kettle and put it back on the hot plate to boil. The tea was in a caddy in the sideboard and as he went across to it he looked outside through the open front door and noticed that a sudden wind was getting up. 'Storm won't be long now,' he muttered. 'About time it broke. Should clear the air a bit.' He put four spoonfuls in the pot and then

252

called out. 'I'll just go and fetch the goats in, Ivy; before it rains. Kettle will have boiled when I get back.' He went quickly out of the front gate and called the two goats over. They came running across when they heard him and he led them back through the garden to a little stone shed at one end of the house. 'Keep your eyes off those,' he said as the goats strayed over to the little flower bed under the wall. 'Come on, you rascals. Let's get you in before it rains.' He had just put some fresh straw down ready for the coming winter and the shed smelt sweet and clean. 'Stop chewing my trousers. Go on, get in.' They looked at him quizzically as he began to shut the door and he laughed and gave them a friendly pat.

Great spots of rain were just beginning to fall as he went back in through the door and he heard the distant rumble of thunder. The kettle was boiling fit to burst so he quickly made the tea and took it into the bedroom. Beth was just regaining consciousness and was trying very hard to understand what they were doing in this beautiful little croft with a kindly white-haired old lady who fussed over her and now this lovely old man who had brought in a cup of tea. Tea! How she had longed for a cup of tea. Ivy poured it into a delicate little cup with a pale blue, yellow and red flower pattern on it and handed it to her. She took a sip and closed her eyes. It was like nectar. 'It's beautiful,' she said, and Jim and Ivy chuckled.

'How about your friend?' said Jim.

'He's never had it before. I'm sure he'd love to try some though. Nab,' she changed to the language of the wild, 'try this drink. It's a little hot but I think you'll enjoy it. It's very common among the Urkku and the Eldron. I used to drink it a lot. And try one of these to eat,' she said, pointing to a plate of chocolate digestives.

Between mouthfuls of biscuit and sips of tea, Nab explained to her all that had happened since she had passed out, and told her of the way Jim had kept their presence secret to the Urkku whom he had recognized at the door. Beth was amazed. 'Jeff Stanhope. Here. But he's miles from his home. As we are.' Then Warrigal spoke.

'Remember what Saurélon said about goblins taking Urkku form. This may well be one such case. I remembered his voice as soon as he spoke.'

'And I did,' said Brock. 'He killed Bruin. How could I forget?'

Jim and Ivy listened unbelievingly as the animals and the humans talked away together in this strange language.

'I'm sure you've a lot to tell us,' said Ivy, whose curiosity was growing by the second. 'Come into the kitchen and we'll have a good old chat. What do the animals want to eat?'

'Well, I'm sure the badger, Brock, would love one of those biscuits if you don't mind to much.' Ivy nodded and Beth told Brock to try one. The badger was delighted, and wolfed down two or three, whole, in quick succession. Perryfoot and Warrigal decided to wait until later when they would go out and forage amongst the heather and made do with a bowl of water each, which they drank greedily for they were very thirsty.

In the kitchen Jim pulled up two easy chairs for Nab and Beth; Ivy sat in her high backed chair opposite him on the other side of the range and he sat down in his old wooden rocking chair on a cushion, the cover of which had been crocheted by his mother years ago. He took out his pipe and, cutting a plug of twist, began rubbing it in between his palms. He had pulled the front of the range down and the red glow of the ashes cast shadows on the low beams of the ceiling for it had gone very dark outside now although it was only mid-morning. The rain was coming down in torrents, spattering against the window-panes and running down them, and through the window they could see the wind driving great sheets of rain across the heather-covered moors. The sky was black and occasionally they saw a flash of lightning or heard thunder rolling around high above them in the clouds. Nab felt that same secure feeling of cosiness that he remembered from the times he'd watched the rain while in the shelter of the rhododendron bush in Silver Wood. He looked all around him at the kitchen; the pictures on the walls, the stove, the pots and pans, the great dark oak chest in the corner and the carved oak dresser with plates on it. Everything fascinated him; from the taps over the sink to the brass ornaments on the mantelpiece over the range. Warrigal perched on the back of his chair looking round at everything slowly; his huge round eyes resting first on one object, then another. Perryfoot and Brock were sitting in front of the range on the maroon and black rag rug that Ivy had made three winters ago

254

and the heat of the fire with the exhausted state of their bodies had sent them both to sleep.

Jim lit his pipe and the smoke drifted languidly up and disappeared into the room. 'Now,' he said to Beth. 'Tell us your tale,' and Beth started, from the beginning; at first telling what Nab had told her and occasionally breaking off to ask him a question and then, with more confidence, talking about the time since she had left home and joined the animals. Nab understood most of what she was saying and sometimes he broke in to add something which she had forgotten or perhaps to correct her. This happened particularly over the part where she was trying to relate what the Lord Wychnor had told them and Nab felt instinctively that it was very important to Jim and Ivy that they properly understand it. They listened intently without once interrupting and the only sounds apart from Beth's voice were the crackling of the logs in the fire, the rain outside and the quiet popping noise Jim made with his lips as he puffed steadily on his pipe while rocking slowly to and fro in the chair.

It was halfway through the afternoon when she had finished and it was still raining. No one spoke for a long while and no questions were asked. The old couple were thinking deeply and quietly about this strange story which they had just heard while Nab and Beth stared at the dancing flames in the fire and the animals dozed. Jim and Ivy were quite startled to find that they were not really surprised by what Beth had told them. Rather they felt fulfilled and in some strange way, gratified by it in that it seemed to be the inescapable, logical conclusion to the beliefs they had held all their lives and a warm glow of satisfaction spread slowly through them. The dark sky outside was still heavy with the promise of more rain and the heather was dripping with the wet. Ivy looked across at Nab and Beth and she smiled at them with such warmth and love that Beth got up and went across to her and, kneeling down, laid her head on the old lady's lap, the way she used to with her grandmother. Jim looked at them and saw a little tear come out of the corner of Ivy's eye and trickle slowly down her cheek. Nab also felt the love in the old lady's smile and for him it was a strange experience. The only ones of his own race that he had known before, apart from Beth, had been figures of fear or hatred, to be avoided and despised. He had never known any Eldron and so had not experienced the goodness and warmth they were capable of. Now here he was with two of them, in their peculiar dwelling and sitting on their seats, and yet he had rarely felt more secure and safe and contented. He looked down at the rug in front of the range and chuckled to himself. Brock was curled round in a tight little ball, snoring loudly and wheezing in his sleep while Perryfoot was sitting snuggled up against him with his eyes closed, his head down and his ears pressed flat along his back. Turning his head he looked up at Warrigal who was still perched on the back of his chair and saw that he too was sleeping; his great round eyelids closed like shutters over his eyes.

Eventually Ivy broke the silence. 'You must be starving,' she said, and then, after gently lifting Beth's head off her lap, she got up and began opening drawers and getting out pots and pans.

'Can I help?' said Beth.

'Well, you can peel some potatoes if you don't mind while I get on with the beans,' replied Ivy. 'Would you like a glass of wine? I'm sure you would. Jim,' she called, 'get out the elderflower and some glasses.'

The old man got up and, opening the doors of a small oak corner cupboard, fetched four glasses and a decanter cut with pictures of barley stalks and wheat around its bowl. He poured the clear light golden wine into the glasses, took one over to Nab and then two across to Beth and Ivy where they were standing by the sink. When he had picked up his own he turned round and said, 'Let's drink a toast.' They all turned to face each other and then when they had lifted their glasses and Beth had explained to Nab what to do, Jim said in a quiet steady voice, 'Let us drink to every creature, whether human or animal, that has ever suffered at the hands of any other creature.'

They were simple words but they were all deeply affected by them and as they drank the wine and considered them they each became lost in their own thoughts. For Nab, the pain of thinking was almost too much to bear. He thought of all the animals he had seen mutilated and ripped apart because of the Urkku and then into his mind, slowly and clearly, appeared pictures of Rufus, Bruin, Tara and lastly Sam. He saw them as if they were there beside him and he felt a flood of tears begin to well up inside. But then his sorrow turned to anger and his anger into resolve and an iron certainty such as he had never felt before. He lifted his glass again and said quietly to himself:

'For you. We shall succeed for you,' and took another mouthful of the wine.

Jim and Ivy thought not only of all the animals they had seen abused and tortured by man but also of all the hungry and the poor and the oppressed of their own race. They thought of those who were dying of illnesses which could be cured but were not and they thought of the stupidity of war and the misery and suffering of its casualties. They thought until they could think no more and then suddenly Jim spoke and his voice trembled slightly with emotion.

'Nab. Come and give me a hand to milk the goats and get the eggs in.'

The boy was glad of the opportunity to break free of the cloud of depression which had filled his mind and he got up and followed Jim through the front door and into the dark wet evening.

'Here; put this over your shoulders,' said the old man and handed Nab a big blue tattered greatcoat. 'And put these on your feet,' he said, handing him a pair of wellingtons. The rain spotted against their faces as they walked along the path at the front of the house until they came to the door into the goats' shed. Inside it was warm and smelt of hay and Jessie and Amy came rushing across and began nibbling and snuffling at Jim's hands.

'Give these to them,' Jim said to Nab and handed him three thick crusts of bread. The goats immediately turned their attention to him and Nab broke the crusts up and tried to share them equally between the two as they pushed against him and jostled him in their anxiety to get more than their fair share. The bread was gone in an instant, wolfed down greedily, but still

they nuzzled and pulled at the pockets of the coat which Jim usually wore.

'Show them your hands; like this,' he said, and opened his hands so that the palms were flat to indicate to Nab what he meant. The goats sniffed disconsolately at Nab's empty hands and then, with a look of crushing disappointment, they turned away and went over to the buckets of bran which Jim had ready for them. As they ate, he milked them and Nab watched fascinated as the old man squeezed the frothy white liquid rhythmically out of the two teats; first one, then the other, then back to the first and so on, and the jets of milk splashed into the bucket underneath. Amy was milked first and then, as Jim moved round to Jessie, he beckoned to Nab to come over and tried to show him how to milk her. It took a little while and a lot of fumbling but eventually the boy succeeded in getting a thin stream of milk out of one of the teats into the bucket. Jim shouted 'Hooray' and clapped his hands in applause while Nab laughed.

The old man then took over as it would have taken too long if Nab had carried on and soon he had finished.

'We'll take this back to the house,' he said, picking up the buckets of milk, 'and then we'll go and get the eggs in and feed the hens. Goodnight, you two,' he said to the goats and Nab gave them a stroke and a pat but they were too concerned with finishing off the bran in the bottom of their buckets to pay much attention and they only looked up when the door closed, whereupon they gave a little bleat of farewell and carried on eating.

They dropped the milk off at the house, leaving it just inside the front door, and then, pausing only to get some corn out of a little stone lean-to, they made their way around to the back and walked over to a large hencote which nestled at the side of a stone wall. The rain was still pouring down and the high craggy mountains behind them were shrouded in low cloud. It was too wet for any of the hens to be out and as they opened the door of the shed and went in there was much squawking and fluttering.

'They're not used to strangers. That's why they're making more noise than usual,' said Jim as he went round the boxes, carefully picking up the eggs and putting them in a little brown wicker basket which he had brought from the house. 'Put the corn in the bucket into that trough in the middle, could you,' he said to Nab and, as he did so, the hens all flew down off their perches around the shed and began pecking away furiously. The rain pelting down on the roof sounded very loud in contrast to the muffled quietness inside as the hens concentrated on eating and Jim looked for eggs.

'Well,' he said, when he had walked all round and come back to the door where Nab was standing, 'I don't think I'm going to find any more. They've done well though; we've got plenty. I'll just fill up their water trough and then we'll go.'

They walked back round the other end of the house and Nab looked at the neat little vegetable patch around which Jim had put a tall fence to keep the goats and the sheep out. It was a mass of green; the fern-like tops of the potatoes, not yet dug up for the winter, rows of broccoli and sprouts and curly kale to see them through the long cold days ahead; smaller rows of autumn and winter cabbage and then at the end the high stakes on which the runner beans climbed. Jim had taken the onions in only yesterday and they were drying in one of the outbuildings.

When they got back in through the front door Nab took off his dripping coat and passed it to Jim who shook it outside and then hung it on a peg alongside his own on the back of the door. They left their muddy wellingtons on a mat at the side.

'You're just in time,' Ivy called out. 'I'm putting the soup on the table.'

'Come on,' Jim said to Nab. 'I'll bet you're starving.'

Four steaming bowls of vegetable soup had been laid out on the kitchen table and Beth and Ivy were just about to start. Nab sat down on the chair next to Beth and she showed him how to use a spoon to drink his soup. He remembered, with a shiver of fear, the last time he had done this, so long ago. They all laughed as the soup dripped from his spoon over the table or else dribbled down his chin but he soon learnt the knack of it and began to enjoy the delicious flavour. On a plate beside the bowl, Ivy had given him a thick slice of freshly made brown bread which was still warm and he copied the others who were breaking chunks of it off and eating it between spoonfuls of soup. Soon he had reached the bottom of the bowl and was spooning up all the pieces of vegetable that were left; cubes of tender young carrot and potatoes and turnip, peas and beans and barley. He and Beth had another bowlful and then Ivy went over to the range and fetched out of the oven four plates, on each of which stood a golden yellow green pea omelette garnished with sprigs of parsley and tomatoes.

'Jim,' she said. 'Can you get the fried potatoes and the vegetables.'

The old man got up and brought across a huge bowl full of crinkly fried potatoes and another bowl, in one half of which was a heap of french beans and in the other a little mound of green sprouting broccoli spears.

'Help yourselves,' said Ivy. 'I hope I've done enough. Anyway, have as much as you want. I'm sure you'd like some more wine. I'll go and get the glasses and fill them up.'

Nab found handling a knife and fork a lot more difficult than a spoon so after a few awkward attempts Ivy fetched another spoon and he used that. He savoured and enjoyed every single mouthful, as did Beth, who could never remember a meal tasting so wonderful before. Jim kept topping up their wine glasses as they became empty until by the time they had finished eating they not only felt gloriously satisfied but also rather lightheaded so that they found themselves laughing with each other and with Jim and Ivy at all sorts of little things which they found inexplicably and hilariously funny. For that short magic spell of time they forgot the horrors of the past and the frightening uncertainty of the future and were suspended in the present; totally carefree and living only for the joy and happiness of those moments of laughter.

When they'd finished the omelette they had gooseberry pie and then finally cream crackers and cheese; a lovely soft goat's-milk cheese which Ivy had made early that morning.

'Now, to finish off, have a piece of cake,' she said, and although Nab and Beth were full to bursting they were unable to resist the rich dark chocolate cake that Ivy pushed towards them.

'Just a little slice,' said Beth. 'We're really only being greedy.'

'No. You mustn't say that. It may be a long time before you're able to eat properly again. This will have to last you.'

'Well, it was delicious,' said the girl, taking a bite of the cake. How she had enjoyed the evening! She wished with all her heart that they could stay here with these two warm and gentle old people in this beautiful little house. It had been like a dream from which she never wanted to wake. She looked at Nab sitting next to her with a smile all over his face and his big dark eyes twinkling with laughter in the candlelight and knew that he too would have liked to stay. Then Jim asked the question she had been afraid to ask herself all night.

'When will you have to be leaving, Beth? You know that you're welcome to stay for as long as you want but we don't want to hold you or keep you.'

She turned and spoke to Nab.

'How do you feel now?' he said.

'A lot better,' she answered reluctantly.

'Well, I think we should leave in the morning. We'll get a good night's sleep and then leave at first light. We don't know how far away the Urkku are and anyway I have a feeling that time is running out.' He reached out and put his hand over hers. 'I want to stay as well,' he said, 'but you know we can't.' He smiled at her tenderly, wishing that he could promise her that some day they would have a little home like this. 'Perhaps . . .' he started to say, but then stopped.

Beth turned back to the old couple.

'We'll have to go in the morning,' she said.

'Well, if you're sure you're up to it. You know best. I'll make you some sandwiches.'

Beth laughed. 'You're very kind,' she said. 'That would be lovely.'

Now suddenly, the wine, the food and the warmth hit the exhausted bodies of Nab and Beth all at once and a great wave of tiredness engulfed them. The animals were still fast asleep around the fire and it was all Nab could do not to join them then and there, although he was unable to stifle a huge yawn.

Jim saw it and smiled. 'You're worn out,' he said. 'You must get to sleep now. We'll be in here for a bit washing up and so on so you two had better sleep in our room at the back, where you hid this morning. We won't disturb the animals. If they wake up we'll see what we can find for them to eat. Otherwise we'll leave something out.'

Wearily Nab and Beth pushed back their chairs and got up from the table. Then Beth, moved by a sudden impulse of affection, went round the table to where Ivy was sitting and, putting her arms around her neck, kissed her on the forehead.

'Goodnight,' she said, 'and thank you, for a lovely day.'

Ivy looked up and her eyes were misty with tears.

'Goodnight, dear,' she said. 'Sleep well.'

Then Jim got up and led them through into the bedroom. To her delight Beth saw a washbasin and towel in one corner of the room.

'Can I have a wash?' she said. 'It's a long time since I've used soap. Oh, and talcum powder. Do you think I could borrow some?'

'Of course,' Jim replied, chuckling. 'Have a good sleep and I'll see you in the morning. You must have some breakfast with us before you go.'

He went out and shut the door, leaving a candle on the chest of drawers next to the bed.

'Come on,' Beth said. 'I'm going to teach you how to use soap and water.'

It felt strange washing in a basin instead of a stream or a pond; turning on taps for water and getting the strange foamy lather from the white block of soap. For Nab it was a series of new and exciting experiences and for Beth a poignant reminder of all that she had left behind; the smell of the soap, the feel of the towel on her face, the gurgle of the water as she pulled the plug out of the basin and the scent of the talcum powder. When she had finished washing, she went over to Ivy's dressing table and, bracing herself, sat down on the little stool and looked in the mirror. What she saw surprised her. She had expected to be shocked and a little dismayed but instead she was strangely fascinated. Her hair hung in a great shock of curls down to her shoulders and looked fairer than she remembered it because it had been bleached by all the sun that summer, and her face was brown and weatherbeaten. But it was her eyes that really surprised her. They seemed much bigger and rounder than before and she saw in them what she had seen in Nab's that very first time they had met, so long ago, down by the stream. They were indescribably clear and deep and she had the uncanny feeling that when she looked at them in the mirror, she was looking straight down into her own soul. But she saw more than that. Her eyes were those of a wild animal; full of energy, constantly alert, and with an innocence and purity that made them shine back at her from the mirror with such intensity that she sat riveted for so long that eventually Nab came over to her and put his face next to hers so that, to his delight, it too was reflected. They looked at their reflections in the mirror and smiled at them and then Nab pulled a funny face and Beth stuck out her tongue and they began to laugh.

There was a wooden-handled hairbrush on the dressing table top and Beth began brushing out all the tangles and curls and tousles in her hair while Nab watched entranced. It felt lovely to be using a brush again and she spent a long time running it slowly down her head from the top of the crown right down to the very ends of her hair. When she had finished she got up from the little stool and told Nab to sit on it.

'It's about time you had a brush through yours,' she said, laughing. 'You look as if you've been dragged through a hedge backwards.'

Nab marvelled at the confident way she handled all these hundreds of different human instruments and at all their many uses, taps, knives, forks, plates, towels, brushes: the list went on for ever and he tried to go through them all in his head while Beth brushed his hair but he soon became muddled and confused. It was all very complicated, he thought with amusement.

Finally she finished and, going over to the bed, Beth pulled back the sheets. Ivy had put them clean on that day and they were white and crisp and smelt of lavender. Slowly she got between them until, at last, she lay full length on the big soft bed and savoured to the full that delicious first moment of utter relaxation when the whole weight of her body was supported by the bed and she was able to let go of it completely. She closed her eyes and sighed; a long blissful sigh of happiness and contentment. Nab stood looking down at her. It had been a long time since they were able to relax together and he was enjoying the sight of her golden hair spread out on the white pillow and the look of perfect peace on her face.

When she opened her eyes and saw him still standing, she patted the bed beside her. 'Come on,' she said, 'get in; it's lovely.'

Carefully he copied what Beth had done and pulling back the sheets, gingerly climbed into the bed. At first as he sank into it he felt terribly unsafe and insecure as if he were lying on a bed of air and he lay tense and stiff, but after a minute or two he began to relax and by the time Beth leant over to blow the candle out he was fast asleep. She smiled to herself and gently kissed him on both his closed eyelids.

'Goodnight, Nab,' she said softly. 'Sleep well,' and, snuggling up with her arms around him, was soon lost in a deep and peaceful sleep.

CHAPTER XX

In the kitchen, Warrigal had woken up to see the dying embers of the fire casting red shadows on the inert sleeping bodies of Brock and Perryfoot and, in the middle of the room, he saw the old couple lying fast asleep on some cushions on the floor. Everything was quiet except for the sound of the wind outside and the gentle snores and heavy breathing of Brock and Jim inside. He felt refreshed and invigorated after his long sleep and decided that he would go outside to explore for a while. Luckily a window had been left open and soon the owl was out in the night, winging his way under the stars over the gorse and heather of the silent, sleeping moorland. The rain had stopped now and the smell of the damp earth filled the air, but the storm had broken the hot weather and the wind that blew down off the mountains was cool; an autumn wind, Warrigal thought, that signals the ending of summer. The sky was clear, black and infinitely deep and although there was only a tiny arc of the new moon, the stars twinkled and danced brightly.

The cool fresh night air felt wonderful to Warrigal as he glided silently, like a dark shadow, through the night. He felt happier and more contented than he had for a long, long time. Nab, Beth and the others were safely resting inside the house; tomorrow they would leave and, if luck was with them, they would very soon arrive at the home of the mountain elves and their journey would have come to its conclusion. 'What then?' he thought. 'Where would it all end?' and for a few moments he allowed his mind to wander back to Silver

Wood and to the early days. They seemed a long way off now, almost a dream, and when a picture of the wood as they had left it at the end flashed in front of his eyes he felt a wave of bitter grief and anger well up inside so that he wrenched his mind away from those painful memories and gave himself up to the sheer joy of flying.

He dipped and dived and swooped and glided, feeling the wind rush through his feathers and clear them of all the dust and grit that they had gathered during the long dry arid days when they had been making their way across the lowlands. He was flying back along the Roosdyche they had been following the previous day when they were being pursued by the Urkku when gradually he became aware of sounds in the air. It was nothing very much at first and he dismissed it but the further he flew back down the hill the more persistent and loud did the noise become. It seemed to be coming up the hill towards him; a steady regular noise, constant with no breaks and yet punctuated by a steady relentless rhythm in the background. Warrigal felt his brief moment of optimistic confidence evaporate until it was entirely gone and he was left with the empty sick feeling of fear with which he was becoming more and more familiar.

There was a large bushy hawthorn tree on his left and he decided to perch there in the cover of the branches until he could see what was causing the noise. He made his way silently into the thickest part of the foliage and found a good spot where he could see out quite clearly through gaps in the leaves but experience told him he could not be seen. He settled down nervously to wait and then, suddenly, way down in the valley below and just beginning the long climb up on to the moors, he saw it. At first he was not quite sure what it was; it looked like an enormous caterpillar, the body of which was black but which had a bright red streak stretching all the way along its back. It wound its slow and ponderous way through the twists and turns of the foothills, weaving like a snake alongside the meanders of the stream in the valley up which it was coming.

The owl watched mesmerized as the thing came nearer and then as it left the foothills and started out on to the edge of the moors, he realized with a shudder what it was. Its body was made up of hundreds of Urkku wearing dark clothing and walking in twos and threes as if they were in a procession. Most of them were carrying flaming

266

torches raised above their heads and it was these that had looked at a distance like the flickering red gash along the caterpillar's back.

He shook himself free of the nausea that had gripped him and forced himself to think. They were coming up the same path that the animals had followed yesterday, and so they would probably be at the cottage in a very short while. They must leave now. Quietly he flew out of the hawthorn and, keeping low so that he was flying just above the tops of the heather and bracken, he sped back up the hill, keeping the path in sight but flying some distance away from it so that he would be less likely to be spotted. In fact he was soon out of sight of the Urkku although he could still hear the constant low murmur of their voices and the steady drum of marching feet along the ground.

Fortunately the wind was behind him and it seemed no time at all before the little cottage loomed up out of the darkness. The immense peacefulness of the scene with its quietly slumbering croft and the gentle waving of the tall grasses in the wind contrasted jarringly with the turmoil in Warrigal's mind and he had to stop on the wall outside and gather his thoughts. It was almost as if he had dreamt the whole thing. He flew back in through the open window and inside every-thing was exactly as he had left it with Brock and the old man still snoring contentedly. His first task was to wake everyone, so he flew up to the top of the Welsh dresser and called loudly. There were grunts and mumbles from the sleepers and Brock turned over but no one woke up so he called again, a piercing cry so loud that the plates rattled and the window-panes vibrated. This time Brock sat bolt upright as did Perryfoot; their eyes blinking and the hackles raised on their backs. They had heard Warrigal's first Toowitt-Toowoo through a mist of sleepy dreams about Silver Wood but the second had been full of such intensity that it had shattered the dream and left them awake and frightened. Warrigal flew down.

'We've got to leave now,' he said. 'I've just been outside and seen a whole mob of Urkku coming up the hill. I'm certain they're coming here. Come on, rouse yourselves. Ah, good, the Eldron are awake,' he added, looking over to the cushions where Jim and Ivy were yawning and rubbing their eyes.

'What's to do?' said Jim. He looked at the clock on the wall. 'Half past three,' he said. 'Oh dear, what a time. Do you want to go out? I left the window open for you,' he said, looking at Warrigal, 'but we couldn't leave the door open for you, Brock.'

Warrigal had flown over the windowsill and kept looking at Jim and then outside in an attempt to explain to the old man the danger that was coming up the hill.

'Let's have a light on,' said Ivy, and she found the box of matches which she had left by the bed on the floor and lit a candle.

'I think he's trying to tell us something,' she said, seeing the owl on the sill. 'We'll have to wake up Nab and Beth.'

There was no need, for just then the bedroom door opened and they came in.

'Warrigal,' said Beth. 'Was that you? What is it?'

Quickly the owl described what he had seen. When he had finished Beth repeated it to the old couple.

'You must go now,' said Jim. 'It seems they know you're here. I think perhaps they knew all along; I thought my story was accepted a bit too easily. They just wanted time to organize themselves.'

'You must come with us then,' said Beth. 'If they know you've hidden us you'll be in some danger, won't you?'

Jim laughed. 'Don't worry about us,' he said, 'but thank you. Now listen; there are things you ought to know about what's been going on since you left home, Beth. You'll have to tell Nab in his language, when you've both gone. There's a lot that's been happening that folk like Ivy and me don't really understand so I can only tell you what we know and what we've heard in the village and so on. Anyway, it seems that our world, the human world, Beth, is about to collapse. The countries are all at war with one another and no one trusts anyone else. Everything is in short supply so they're all fighting for what little is left. The rivers are dirty and stagnant, fish are dying in the sea and the crops won't grow. It's every man for himself, Beth. Even the police have long since stopped being able to control things;

in fact they hardly even exist any more and the ones there are, are worse than useless. We're quite lucky up here because we can grow most of what we need and we keep out of the way but it's been terrible in the towns. And then, to make everything worse, about six months ago a terrible disease began to spread throughout the world. It started here, so they say, and was carried overseas so that now it's everywhere. Thousands have died and those that are left scrabble over what little there is. How it started no one really knows but the rumour, and the story which the authorities put out, is that it came from you, the five of you, and that it is you who are spreading it around the country. That's why they're after you. There've been patrols out everywhere looking, spurred on by fanatical leaders who have been killing all the animals like you that they've seen in the hope that in the end they'll get you. They've burnt great areas of the countryside in the hope of containing the disease, and the bodies of those who've died along with those of the animals they've killed, are burnt to try and stop it spreading. Fire, they think, kills the germs, and in any case nobody will dig the graves. So you see there's not only war between countries; this disease has meant that there is virtual civil war in each country as well.'

Jim stopped talking and listened. Carried on the wind they could hear, outside in the distance, the tramping of the column coming up across the moors. Beth sat silent on one of the chairs by the dining table; unable to take in or even begin to comprehend all that she had just heard. She shook with fear; suddenly the night seemed very cold and she began to shiver.

'But you,' she said. 'Why did you let us in and help us if we are the carriers of this plague?' She began to cry and she buried her face in her hands. Jim put his arm round her gently.

'Come on, don't cry. There are many who don't believe it; even in these parts, that we know of, and over the whole world there must be many more. Before the disease started, they were messing around a lot, experimenting with different kinds of weapons; germ warfare and so on. We've always thought that something went wrong at one of the places where this research was being done but of course no one will admit it and they've blamed it on you. You are the scapegoats. They may not even know anything has gone wrong themselves and so they really believe you are the cause. I don't know.' He paused again. 'Listen, Beth, you must all go now. While there's still time. The place that you want, I think, is what we call Rengoll's Tor. There's an old legend that I heard from my grandfather that the mountain elves live there. Follow the path straight up; it cuts through a cleft between two large hills at the top and then straight ahead you'll see, some way ahead but still easily spotted, a strange collection of large rocks leaning against one another and sticking out of the earth at odd angles. It's on top of a large mound and to get to it, it's about half a day's walk through rough moorland country, but it's quite flat so you've not got much more climbing to do. Come on; you must go out the back way. There's less chance of being seen.'

'Here,' said Ivy, 'take this; and think of us when you look at it.' She took off a beautiful little gold ring with a deep green stone set in the top, which Beth had noticed and admired when they had been cooking last night's meal. 'And here is something for the journey,' she added, passing Nab a bag full of sandwiches and fruit. 'I packed it last night, ready for this morning.'

They were at the back door now. Jim opened it and they felt the cold night air on their faces.

'Are you sure you won't come with us?' Beth said, but they both shook their heads.

'Don't you worry about us,' said Jim. 'We'll be all right. Now, off you go. Take care and good luck.'

Beth kissed them both goodbye sadly. Ivy gave Nab a quick hug and Jim grasped both his hands in his, in what Nab realized was a gesture of affection.

'Goodbye. Thank you,' said the boy and then resolutely they turned their backs on the little house where they had been so happy and started to run steadily and slowly up the path through the heather following Warrigal, Brock and Perryfoot. Beth did not dare look back, for if she had, she knew she would have burst into tears and it would have been impossible to leave. Jim and Ivy watched them go, their eyes misty and damp with emotion, and then when the darkness had swallowed them up they turned and went back in the house.

270

'You know what to do?' said Jim, for they had discussed this last night.

'Yes,' Ivy replied, and she started barricading all the doors and windows with furniture while Jim nailed battens of wood across them on the outside, both for extra strength and, more important, to make it appear obvious that the cottage had been barricaded.

At just about the same moment that Nab, Beth and the animals arrived at the top of the path and began making their way through the little valley between the hills that Jim had described, the Urkku reached the cottage. Because of what they saw, they assumed, as Jim and Ivy had intended, that the travellers were inside so they immediately surrounded it and began trying to bargain with Jim and Ivy to make them hand them over. It must have been at least half an hour before Jeff and the other leaders lost their patience and began more direct methods of persuasion. Hearing the bleats from the goat shed they first of all dragged Amy out and killed her and then, when Jim still refused to release his guests, they killed Jessie, only more slowly so that every whimper and cry of pain shot through Jim and Ivy like a red hot poker in their stomachs and tortured them with doubt and anguish.

When that proved no more successful, and another half-hour had been wasted, they began to break in through the doors and windows until finally, after yet more precious time, the Urkku, having smashed their way in and searched in every corner and cupboard in the house, realized that they had been tricked. Their anger was horrible, and cruel were the deaths they inflicted on the old couple and yet, even as they died, their faces were fixed with such an expression of confidence and contentment that those who killed them, and all those who witnessed their deaths, were frightened deep within at the force that could inspire such strength.

The hounds by now had picked up the scent at the back of the house and were straining at their leashes to get away up the path, barking and yelping in a bedlam of noise. Many of the Urkku, having looted the house for anything of value, were now packing hay from one of the outbuildings around the outside walls and inside in the kitchen. Then coals from the fire, still red-hot from last night, were gathered in a bucket and scattered over the hay, which flared up

271

immediately into high crackling flames that danced and flickered against the walls in the early dawn. Soon the flames were leaping over the roof and, by the time the column of Urkku, led by the hounds, was halfway up the back slope, the little house had been almost completely consumed by the fire.

CHAPTER XXI

By dusk that day the animals found themselves standing at the foot of the mound on top of which the strange rocks of Rengoll's Tor loomed large and mysterious; casting strange shadows on the ground around them as the sun, yellow, weak and watery in a cold autumn sky, started to go down behind the mountains. The earth and the heather all around them smelt damp and mist hung in the air so that the sounds of barking which had been behind them all day now seemed muffled and remote. Nab and Beth had thought of the old couple as they jogged steadily along the track towards the Tor which Jim had described, and a terrible sense of foreboding had come upon them once or twice as they travelled but it had quickly been pushed aside; the thought of anything happening to them had been too awful to contemplate. Once, as the path took them on to the top of a small ridge, Beth had even believed that she could smell smoke on the wind but she immediately put it down to imagination or the fires in the distant lowlands.

They had no idea how far behind them the Urkku were. Soon after dawn they had seen them coming through the little valley between the two hills at the top of the slope but they had not seen them since; nor had they been seen for the cover was good and the path had run for much of the way alongside a little mountain brook which cut its way deep into the earth leaving banks of rich dark peat on either side through which the tangled roots of the heather stuck out and in which cotton grass grew.

They had stopped for a very short break around Sun-High and eaten Ivy's packed lunch, which had tasted delicious and made them feel as if they could go on running for ever. Now, however, Beth felt tired again; she had not really recovered fully from her exhausted state, and the fact that she was soaked to the skin again because of the damp mist made her feel worse. At her side Brock suddenly gave a frantic shake in an attempt to get rid of the large droplets of water which the mist had deposited all over his coat. They were staring at the huge rocks and wondering, now they were here, how they would go about finding the mountain-elves when suddenly they heard a sound from way above them. It was a high plaintive tune, the notes of which floated down to them on the wind almost as if it was being played by the breeze itself.

'Look,' said Perryfoot, and they all saw on top of one of the rocks a little elven figure sitting cross-legged and playing a reed pipe.

'Jim was right,' said Beth. When the elf saw that they had seen him he stopped playing, stood up and waved at them, beckoning them towards him up the mound. Quickly they clambered up the slope and met the elf at the base of one of the rocks which towered over them, completely blotting out the sun.

'I am Morar,' said the elf. 'There is no time to lose; follow me,' and he began to climb back up over the rocks, leaping nimbly from boulder to boulder, while the others did their best to follow, groping for footholds and grabbing on to pieces of lichen and moss as they made their way up these enormous pieces of granite which leant against one another as if they had been thrown down by some giant and so precariously that the animals felt they were liable to collapse at any moment and did not dare to look down.

Suddenly they were at the top, bathed in a pale yellow light as the sun tried to shine through the mist, and Morar was urging them to descend down into a dark gaping opening in the rocks. Beth climbed in first and helped Brock and Perryfoot down. Warrigal and Nab were about to follow when the mist suddenly cleared for an instant and to

their horror they heard a chorus of shouts from behind them which rose swiftly in a crescendo of triumph. Looking round they saw the column of Urkku not far from the base of the mound, pointing at them and yelling excitedly at one another.

'There they are. We've got them. They'll not get away this time.'

Nab felt his stomach turn to ice. He had a vision of a sea of howling faces, mean, pinched and dirty with empty narrow eyes and slavering mouths which dripped hatred like blood, and then he felt Morar push him and he half-slid and half-clambered down into the dark space under the rocks where the others were waiting. It was blessedly quiet in here and he felt his heart thumping.

'They're here,' he said breathlessly. 'Just outside.'

The others looked at him, their eyes wide with fear until Morar spoke.

'Come on,' he said. 'Follow me. They don't know exactly where we are and they'll never find us where we're going.'

Their eyes were now growing accustomed to the gloom and they could dimly make out ahead of them a small rectangular entrance formed by two columns of stone at either side with a stone lintel on the top. In the centre of the lintel a large rune had been expertly carved by the hand of some elven stonemason. The mountain elves were renowned for their stonecraft and as they passed under it the animals marvelled at the delicacy of the work and Warrigal whispered that it was their symbol; a new crescent moon, a single blade of grass and a craggy mountain peak. In those few simple lines the artist had captured the very essence of the mountains and the moors so that all who saw it felt their hearts stir.

They found themselves now in a large low-ceilinged chamber, roughly square in shape but completely empty except for rows of swords and shields which hung on the walls. Each was different; the handles had all been carved to represent a different mountain creature and the blades were all embossed with a different runic symbol.

'We each have our own hereditary sword,' said Morar. 'Rarely used, but cleaned and sharpened every day.' The points gleamed silver in the dark and the colours on the shields seemed to flicker and move as what little light there was caught them.

They crossed the chamber and went through another smaller doorway at the far end and now they began to descend some stone steps which ran down a narrow tunnel. They were small and there was a dip in the centre of each one where it had been worn away by endless centuries of use. A type of bannister had been carved into the stone on either side of the passageway but this was not much help to Perryfoot and Brock, who kept slipping and had to be guided by Nab and Beth. As they went further and further down it grew very cold and damp and their teeth began to chatter loudly in the intense quiet. It felt to the animals as if they were descending into the very heart of the mountains; their footsteps echoed loudly in the stillness and they could hear the steady dripping of water all around them.

They seemed to have been going down for ages when the tunnel gradually began to grow much wider and lighter. The walls were now streaked with different coloured minerals; bright blues and golds and crimsons and even at times an intense snowy white which bathed the tunnel in silver. The path was almost level now and frequently they would come across little caverns and grottoes at the side which were filled with stalagmites and stalactites of strange shapes and sizes; either very tall and thin or else rounded like a thick mushroom; some hanging down while others grew out of the dazzling multicoloured rock gardens. They kept stopping to wonder at these magical sights and Morar explained about each one; its name and history and the legends surrounding it. Many of them were believed to contain the spirits of ancient, long-dead, elven heroes so that there was the Peak of Eynort, the Sword of Braewire or the Spike of Ardvasar. The elves each had their own special one which looked after and guided them and which they in turn repaid by caring for and guarding and making sure, above all, that they were not touched for they were so delicate that they were easily broken and the dead elves' spirits would then be released to wander, homeless for ever.

So involved were the animals in these fantastic surroundings that they forgot all about the danger that lurked behind them up on the surface and even where they were and what they were doing, so that it came as quite a shock when Morar called them to a halt and they found themselves standing in front of a large stone door on which were many carvings portraying the old histories and sagas. Morar pulled his reed pipe out of his belt and began to play a strange lilting air. When he had finished he waited a short while and then played the same tune again. This time, when he stopped, the great door very slowly started to swing inwards. They walked through the doorway, whereupon Morar played a different tune, again twice, and the door silently closed behind them.

Now they were standing in a high vaulted cavern roughly oval in shape with huge stone pillars round the walls that formed archways through which were many different anterooms and chambers. Some of these had doors while others were open, and in them the animals could see the elves going about their work. It reminded Beth of a medieval cathedral, particularly as the stone floor had been inlaid with hundreds of different coloured minerals to form patterns. It was from these that most of the light came and, as they followed Morar along a central aisle in the cavern with gold and blue and silver light shining up under their chins lighting their faces from below, they had the eerie feeling that they were walking upside down. High above them, an occasional streak of silver showed up massive natural rock columns which supported the roof.

Soon they were at the far end of the cavern, standing in front of a door set into the rock face. Morar lifted the stone latch and the door swung open easily at his touch to reveal a small room with a figure sitting on a seat at the far end which had been hewn out of the rock. Morar bowed.

'My Lord Malcoff,' he said. 'I present the travellers from Silver Wood.'

The animals all followed Morar's example and inclined their heads. When they looked up again Malcoff was smiling. Nab's first impression of him was of immense age; his skin was of a deep dark brown and it was covered with hundreds of little lines and wrinkles like a piece of old bark. The hands which clutched the carved armrests in the rock were very long and thin and bony. Long grey hair the colour of granite hung down his back and there was a band around his forehead with a shimmering blood-red stone in the centre. The single ring on the index finger of his left hand was carved with the same rune as that on the lintel outside the cavern and around his neck he wore a great oval-shaped amulet made of the precious blue stone from the mines of Thurgo in the far west. His deep-set grey eyes peered out from under two thick bushy eyebrows and his thin gently hooked nose gave his face an expression of sternness and gravity. Perched on one of the arms of the seat was a large golden eagle which stared at the newcomers with curiosity. When Malcoff spoke, it was with all the craggy dignity of the mountains themselves.

'I bid you welcome,' he said slowly and gravely. 'You will forgive me, I hope, if I do not stand to greet you. My legs will not permit it. They have grown old before their master and will no longer obey him. But I have Curbar,' he looked up fondly at the eagle, 'and I have my chairs.' He pointed to what looked to Beth like a sedan chair which lay on the floor at his side.

'Come closer, so that I may see you,' he went on. 'We have heard a lot about you; you would perhaps be surprised at your fame. You have done well to get here, there have been occasions when we have thought you lost. But I fear there is little space for pleasantries; our time runs short and the Urkku know you are here. You will be aware of course, of the rumours that pursue you?' he asked, and Beth replied that the old couple down the hill who had protected and sheltered them for the night had told them. At the mention of Jim and Ivy the Elflord's eyes grew cloudy.

'It was indeed fortunate that you passed their way; perhaps Ashgaroth guided you. We have always known them as of the Eldron; they would come often to Rengoll's Tor and we would try to speak with them. Yet I have grave news for you.' He looked down at the floor and the friends' hearts turned over with the grim certainty of what they knew he was about to say.

'No!' Beth cried. 'Oh no.'

Malcoff continued. 'They did not die in vain. They gave you time and without that you would not be here now. So do not weep or grieve for them; they would not wish it. They loved you and they died for you and they died contented. They are with Ashgaroth, watching you. Come and sit.'

He gestured towards a stone bench in the wall and Nab, with his

279

arm round Beth's sobbing shoulders, led her across to it. They both felt sick with grief and remorse. If only Jim and Ivy had come with them or, better still, if they had never met, then the old couple would still be alive. Malcoff's assurance that they died for the travellers only made their gnawing feelings of guilt worse. Yet Nab somehow found a strength and put his heart into trying to comfort Beth who was weeping uncontrollably.

Malcoff spoke again. 'You must be tired and in need of rest. Nab, do your best to soothe her. I will see you later. Morar; show them their chamber.'

They went back through the door and into the great cavern, where Morar led them off into a little square stone room with a huge blazing fire at one end. Food and drink had been laid out for them on the floor.

'I will come for you later,' said Morar, and he went out.

They walked over to the fire which was warm and welcoming and Nab sat Beth down next to him on a stone bench which he pulled across from one of the walls and put in front of it. None of them had much appetite and they picked disconsolately at the food and ate in silence.

'Come on, Beth. Try and drink this. It'll make you feel better,' said Nab gently and he handed her a stone goblet full of a dark golden liquid which he'd picked up from the floor. She took a sip and felt stronger and thought of Malcoff's words. Now that the initial shock had worn off, they did seem to bring some comfort. With a supreme effort she forced herself to take hold of her emotions and, looking up at Nab, she forced a smile. She was rewarded by the look of relief that came into Nab's eyes.

'I'll be all right,' she said. 'Why did they do it, Nab?'

'That's what we're fighting,' he replied. 'That's why we're here and why we've come through everything.'

'I wonder what's going to happen now,' said Perryfoot, moving a bit further back from the fire where he was getting too hot.

'The Lord Malcoff will tell us soon,' Warrigal muttered to himself. 'We shall know soon enough.'

Brock looked up at his old friend where he was perched on the stone bench next to Beth.

280

'You look tired,' he said with some surprise. He and Perryfoot had been in an exhausted daze ever since they had arrived at the cottage of the Eldron but Warrigal had always seemed to be on top of himself, always clear-thinking and in control. Now he also seemed worn out. His feathers looked dull and scruffy and his eyes had lost their usual fire and sparkle.

'I am,' said the owl. 'We all are. We could go no further. I want to go home; back to Silver Wood to sit on the Great Beech and look out over the fields towards the pond. I want to roost in the rhododendrons and go to the quarterly Council Meetings to gossip and chat about small unimportant things. I want to stay in one place and watch the seasons as they come and go. Yes; I'm tired of travelling.'

They looked at Warrigal and were grateful to him for expressing what they all felt. No one spoke for they became lost in thoughts of home; for Beth a home that she was now certain she would never see again and for the other animals a home that was no more. The elves had laid out some dry brown bracken in one corner of the room and Brock suggested that they lie down and try and get some sleep. It crackled as they settled down in it and a little cloud of dust rose into the room and made Perryfoot and Beth sneeze. The familiar, fragrant, almost scented smell of the bracken was comforting but, despite the fact that they were all very tired, it took them all a long time to get to sleep, and when finally they did, it was a restless, fitful sleep full of strange confused dreams in which pictures of the past mingled with those of the present. In all their minds was the thought that tomorrow would see the end of their mission, the culmination of everything, and the blood was racing through their veins far too quickly to leave them in peace.

It was Moon-High outside when Nab suddenly woke up to see Morar standing by the door.

'The Lord Malcoff sent me to ask you to come to him again. There is much to discuss before the sun rises.'

Nab looked at Beth tossing beside him and gently laid a hand on her shoulder. She woke immediately and seeing Morar guessed that it was time for their talk with Malcoff. The others had woken up at the sound of the elf's voice and now they followed him out into the main cavern and back to the Elflord's room, pleased to have escaped from the dark unsettling world of their dreams. There was a lot of activity in all the various chambers and anterooms round the walls; elves were bustling to and fro, there was much hammering and banging, and music was everywhere; an intensely rhythmical music with a heavy beat and many pipes playing together to form a stirring wave of sound.

Malcoff welcomed them as they entered.

'I trust the noise of our preparations did not disturb you,' he said, 'but there is a lot to be done. Please sit while we talk. Now,' he continued, leaning forward and with an urgency in his voice, 'our scouts have been up to the surface to see what the situation is and they report that the Urkku have completely surrounded the Tor and have erected huts and tents with an obvious intention of remaining for a long time. They know you are here somewhere and will stay until you come out. They have plenty of supplies and will bring in replacements if needed during the winter. Many of their leaders are goblins who have assumed the appearance of Urkku and their powers are such that they can persuade the rest to do their bidding. They could of course bombard the Tor with their weapons; they have them here, in the hope of destroying you, but they will not for they want you alive and in any case you would be safe under here and Dréagg knows that. This is his last chance of finding you and he wants you alive so that he may discover the intentions of Ashgaroth.'

Here Nab interrupted, for there was something that was puzzling him. 'But I do not know what I am to do next,' he said.

'Have patience,' replied Malcoff. 'Morar. Play your pipes; play us an air that is gentle and soothing.' He turned back to Nab and went on. 'We must all have patience.' He smiled. 'What you are to do is not known to any except Ashgaroth. The ending of the legend is unknown. All that I know, for he has spoken to me, is that you must travel from here to the sacred high peak known as Ivett which is but a half-day's journey from here and it is there that he will speak with you.'

'But we are surrounded by the Urkku,' said Nab, who was depressed and angry at the realization that his travelling was not yet over.

The peaceful sound of Morar's pipes floated around Malcoff's chamber and contrasted strangely with the muffled sounds of activity outside. Curbar, the Eagle, looked intently at each of the animals in turn as if he were able to see through their eyes and right inside their minds. Beth felt a nervous twinge of apprehension in the bottom of her stomach as Curbar stared at her with his sharp, hooded eyes.

'We have a plan,' said Malcoff. 'The battle-chiefs and myself have talked it over and it seemed to us the best, if not the only way. Our army is far too small to hope to defeat them in battle. The scouts have reported that they have a numerous host; their tents resemble a field of mushrooms stretching as far as the eye can see. But the plan involves your separation for a time and it would mean great danger for you, Beth and the animals. The strategy we have devised is as follows. Our small army of elven warriors would engage the Urkku in battle so that the whole of their attention is taken up with fighting. Then, when the time is judged right, Perryfoot, Brock, Warrigal and Beth, who would have changed into your clothing, Nab, so as to appear as much like you as possible, will come out of the entrance on the Tor and then, making sure that they are seen, will escape west through a gap in the battle-lines that the elves will have organized. The Urkku, believing that you have all got out, will attempt to give pursuit. The elves will hold them back until Beth and the others are almost out of sight and then their fighting will deliberately weaken so as to allow the Urkku to chase after them. It is then, Nab, that you, who have been hiding in the entrance, will make your exit heading north towards the Peak of Ivett, I hope unnoticed, while the Urkku are in hot pursuit of the others. Then, when and if they can evade their pursuers, Beth and the animals will make their way towards Ivett to rejoin you.' He paused, then, seeing the reluctance in their eyes, he added, 'I know that separation is a lot to ask of you, particularly after all you have been through together, but there is no other, better way. And I trust it will not be for long.'

'Could Beth not come with me?' said Nab. 'She is tired. The others are faster but she is not used to living as we do. I am worried for her safety if she has to go with them.'

'We have thought of all that you have just said but unfortunately she plays the most important part of the plan. The Urkku must believe that she is you. As it is, they will only see one where there

283

should be two but we will have to hope that in the heat of battle they will not notice.'

Beth interrupted. 'Don't argue about me,' she said. 'I will go. I can see that it is the best way and I know that we shall all meet again. I have come this far; it is not much further that you are asking me to go.'

Nab looked at her and took her hand. Malcoff smiled.

'You are very brave,' he said. 'Ashgaroth indeed chose well.'

'When do we go?' asked Brock.

'In the last dark hour before the sun rises. You will have heard the sounds of preparation outside; the sharpening of arrows, spears and swords and the final treatment of shields. I understand from Morbann and Mendokk, the two battle-chiefs, that they are almost ready and Morar tells me that his players have rehearsed their battle songs until they would bring the very rocks themselves to life. In the meantime we shall talk. You will tell me of the early days and of your journey here, and give me news of Wychnor and Saurélon for it is quite some seasons since I saw them. And I will tell you of my home in the far west where the mountains scrape the sky, and from the top of which one can see the whole world; where it is so cold that breath forms icicles as it comes from your mouth and your eyelids would freeze together if you did not wear a helmet. Come then; Morar will play for us and we will talk and drink of the golden elven-brew made from the heather and the gorse and we will be happy until the time arrives, for these hours before a battle are the dangerous hours. It is then that the battle is won or lost and we must not let ourselves brood on the uncertainties of what tomorrow may bring.'

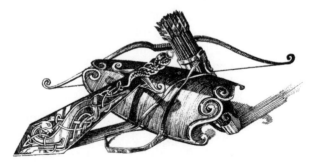

CHAPTER XXII

The walk back up the steps in that long, cold, damp tunnel seemed endless. Ahead of Nab walked the small band of elven warriors, their bodies glowing silver in the gloomy light. First had gone the archers, then those who would be using swords or spears and, ahead of them all, leading the column, went Malcoff, his gaily coloured chair carried expertly up the steps by four large elves. Behind the travellers, and bringing up the rearguard, came Morar's players with their pipes and drums. Only their leader played now and the haunting strains of his pipe echoed all the way up the tunnel. It was the only sound apart from the soft padding of elven footsteps as they met the hard stone and an occasional metallic clink as a quiver banged against the wall.

The first sign that they were nearing the end of the long climb came when Nab felt the unmistakable fragrance of the cool night air on his face. He closed his eyes and breathed it in deeply but at the same time his heart sank for it meant that they were nearly at the surface and the moment of separation was approaching. The column moved more slowly now for, as they passed through the large square chamber at the head of the tunnel, all except the archers had to collect their swords and shields and spears. The bows were kept in the main cavern underground to protect them from the damp and the constant changes in temperature which they would have been subjected to near the surface but all the other weapons were kept here to save carrying them up and down the steps.

When the animals finally reached the chamber they found the

walls bare and only Malcoff, Curbar and the chair carriers inside. Morar and the players filed past them in silence and followed the rest of the warriors out on to the Tor to take up their positions. The Elflord spoke quietly.

'Here, Nab; take this casket. It contains the Faradawn of the Mountains and the High Places.' Nab took the small silver-grey stone casket and, carefully opening the last of the three lockets on the Belt of Ammdar, he placed it inside and snapped the top shut. It felt wonderfully satisfying that the Belt was now full and he thought back to the time when he had first seen it in the Forest of Ellmondrill when Wychnor gave it to him and showed him how to work the lockets. It seemed a long time ago now. Then Malcoff continued, 'We will watch the battle from a high vantage point behind one of the rocks and you will remain close by my side, ready to run when the time is right. I need not tell you how important it is that you are not seen. Come then; follow me.'

A strange and eerie sight met their anxious gaze when they emerged from the tunnel entrance and scrambled out on to the rocks of the Tor. The moon shone fitfully as it came out for short spells from behind the large black clouds that raced across the night sky and in these occasional flashes of silver light they could see the elven army drawn up in battle ranks in a circle all around the summit; those with swords in front followed by the spearthrowers and, lastly, the archers, who stood with their bows ready while the front ranks knelt. The pipers stood right on the summit on the rock where the animals had first seen Morar. At the very front of the army, one on each side of the Tor, stood the two battle-chiefs Morbann and Mendokk with their huge swords raised high above their heads ready to give the signal for battle to commence. The overwhelming impression was of a mass of shimmering, twinkling lights; silver from the elves' bodies and reflected from their swords and spears, golds and reds and crimsons and greens from their helmets and shields.

Just down the summit, in another circle, stood the tents of the

Urkku. Outside many of them the smouldering remains of last night's camp fires flickered red in the darkness while inside their occupants slept. It was very still and quiet and the air was cold. A light breeze from the mountains made the heather rustle and wave gently. Behind the shelter of a large rock that seemed to have pushed itself straight up through the earth, the animals all stood in silence, hardly daring to breathe, with the sound of their hearts pounding furiously in their ears. From where they stood they could see all around them. Malcoff pointed out the great high peak of Mount Ivett where it stood in the middle distance just beyond the near range of hills, its jagged spire silhouetted by the moon. Morbann, Mendokk and Morar were all looking intently at the Lord Malcoff to give the signal for battle to commence. Their throats were dry with nervous anxiety; not since the days of Ammdar had the elves fought in open battle and, although they had constantly kept in readiness preparing for a moment such as this, they could not help being a little afraid.

Slowly, Malcoff raised his right hand and then suddenly brought it down. Immediately there was a massive skirl of pipes and the heavy beat of the drums began to reverberate over the hillside. Nab felt the blood start to race through his veins. He turned to Beth and took her hand tightly in his; it was shaking and as he looked in her eyes he saw that they were wide and glazed with fear. The pipes and drums rose in a great wall of sound and the Urkku were emerging from their tents, bleary-eyed and drugged with sleep, to see what the noise was. They stood looking out into the night, puzzled and bemused by the commotion, until Nab saw Malcoff raise his hand again in a signal at which the archers pulled back their bows and loosed their arrows. For a second or two the air was full of a whistling, rushing noise as they sped through the air, and then, as they found their targets, pandemonium broke loose. Amidst the groans and cries of those who had been hit came the guttural shouts of the leaders as they tried to organize the rest and the frantic yells of others as they stumbled about in the dark attempting to get back in their tents to find their weapons. Only the goblin leaders, in their guise as Urkku, knew what was happening, and they rushed around the camp shouting, cursing, cajoling and threatening the panicking mob in an attempt to get some kind of order into the fearful, bewildered Urkku who had no notion who could be firing arrows at them. No sooner had they been gathered into line than another hail of arrows would be released and once again chaos would take over. Finally, however, the goblins managed to assemble the remaining Urkku into a number of ranks and they began firing uphill at an enemy they could not see and whose identity they did not know. It was then that Malcoff gave the signal to charge and the sword and spear carriers raced off over the heather to the sound of a different, more urgent, rhythm from the pipes and drums which mingled with the sound of the elves as they each shouted their own individual battle cry. At the sight and sound of these ferocious, yelling creatures leaping and running towards them, the Urkku froze with astonishment and then fear. They were blinded by a whirling kaleidoscope of blood-curdling noise and flashing colour and many of them turned and tried to run, only to find, standing in their way, the squat fat ugly shape of a goblin – for many of the leaders had changed back into their natural state – slavering and twitching and bawling at them to turn round and fight if they did not want to be buried amidst the powers of hell. Then, abandoning themselves to the nightmare, the Urkku would face back up hill towards the elves and fire blindly.

The animals watched, their fears for the moment forgotten in the tension of the battle, as the elves ran through the shower of bullets, many of them being knocked down by the force of the blast but then, because the Urkku bullets could not kill them, picking themselves up and charging on until with a huge clash they met the enemy who, realizing that bullets were useless, had begun in desperation to use their guns as clubs and shields in an attempt to prevent the elves from cutting them to pieces with their swords. At first the battle seemed all one way as the elves swarmed over the Urkku forcing them back down the hill but then the goblins drew out their swords from under the ill-fitting Urkku garments now stretched tight over their natural bodies. In each of these had been welded a fragment of the Sword of Degg which Dréagg had forged from Arnemeze, an evil metal mined from the Halls of Drāgorn which he obtained while he was banished there. The Sword had been so cast by Dréagg that it could halt the flow of time, destroying the elves' immortality, and so each of these swords which the goblins now wielded was also imbued with that terrible power. Now the goblins swept forward to bolster up the tattered ranks of Urkku and the roar of battle swelled until the hills echoed. The elves were halted and their line began to waver as the magic of their weapons, woven with the light of Ashgaroth, met the evil force of Dréagg. The sun rose and streaked the sky with gashes of crimson and red and orange and the tumult of the fight rose in the chill morning air, shattering the stillness of the mountains with the clash of sword on shield and the dreadful cries of the wounded. When the elves fell, a cloud of silver lifted from their bodies as their remains vanished like a puff of smoke. Malcoff watched and his old eyes grew blurred with tears at the departure of those whom he had known and loved and their passing was like the dying of a flower.

The battle raged on as the pale sun climbed in the cold grey sky. First one way, then the other did it ebb and flow until by mid-morning the elves finally claimed the ascendancy and the air grew foul with the smell from the dead goblins whose black blood stained the heather. Slowly they pushed the hordes of Dréagg back until there was a clear gap in the fighting, and Beth, Perryfoot, Brock and Warrigal knew that their time had come. Malcoff turned to them.

'You must go now,' he said. 'May Ashgaroth shelter you and guide you.'

Nab's heart felt as if it would break under the torment of the thought of their leaving and his throat ached with the effort of holding back his tears. Quickly he embraced them all, the soft feathered body of Warrigal, the deep fur of Perryfoot and the familiar warm shape of Brock. Brock who had first found him and brought him up and shared everything with him and who was as much a part of him as his own eyes. Finally he held Beth tight as if he would never let her go and the din of battle matched the tumult in his brain so that when she gently pushed him away he was dazed with grief.

'We must go,' she said. 'We'll meet again soon; I know it,' and she turned abruptly away and ran out from behind the shelter of the boulder after the dark brown shape of Warrigal as he flew across the heather towards the gap. Perryfoot followed and then Brock and as they ran a cry went up from the goblins and the Urkku. Slowly as the news that they had been spotted spread, the cry grew louder and the Urkku pressed against the line of elves, fighting to break through and follow but the line held firm.

Soon the animals were through the gap and racing away over the moors, yet still the elves held back the frantic yelling mass until finally, when they were just a speck in the distance, the line broke and the goblins and Urkku, with a massive triumphant shout, plunged through and thundered in pursuit of their quarry. Nab watched painfully as he saw his friends finally disappear around a small hill on the far horizon and then, some time after, their pursuers were lost to sight around the same hill. Now the last link with them was gone. He turned back to the battlefield where the remnants of the elven army were wearily walking back up the hillside. Many had fallen, but they had achieved what they had set out to achieve against that vast army and they were satisfied. Now they would rest, and in the evening they would begin the distasteful job of burying the dead goblins and Urkku. Of their own kind who had gone, nothing remained except a scattering of silver dust which would soon be blown away.

Then Malcoff spoke, and there was a tremor in his voice.

'They have done well,' he said, 'though I am deeply sad to have lost so many. And now you must go, Nab. Take care; you now have the three Faradawn and are at your most vulnerable. Dearly would Dréagg like to take you at this time. You should be on Mount Ivett by nightfall. Farewell; perhaps we shall all meet again some day.'

Sadly Nab turned north and began to make his way towards the distant peak on the skyline, pausing before he was out of sight to turn round and take a last look at the Tor. There was only Malcoff sitting where Nab had left him with the great golden eagle perched on a rock to his right. The Elflord was looking towards him and, when he saw Nab turn, he raised his hand and waved slowly. The boy waved back before he rounded a hill and the Tor was lost from sight.

By the middle of the afternoon Nab was on the lower slopes of the great peak which towered high above. He was tired; his legs ached and his breath rasped as it came from his weary lungs. The sun had long been lost behind great dark banks of clouds that came rolling in from the north, and an icy wind blew down from the mountain. He sat down on a rock to have a rest and wondered again, as he had constantly since he left the Tor, how the others were getting on. He missed them terribly, hardly believing that they were not with him and feeling as though a part of him was gone. He had begun to imagine, a while back, that they actually were walking at his side and he had started to talk to them, making up conversations as he crossed the rough stony ground.

As he sat looking out over the bleak mountain side he slowly became aware of a thick damp mist descending from the slopes above. He watched it come down, fascinated by the steady pace at which it moved, covering everything in its path. One minute everything was clear and the next it had vanished behind this thick dark grey wall. He saw it rolling towards him and felt it envelop him with its wet clammy tentacles as it moved on down the hill. A cold chill went through his body, partly from the mist but also because he suddenly realized that he could see nothing in any direction except the few paces of ground in front of him; the peak was completely lost from view. He looked around desperately but there was no way in which he could tell the right direction to travel. 'Still, if we make sure we're always walking uphill, we can't go far wrong,' he said out loud, to an imaginary Brock. 'Come on then,' and he got up from the rock and began to move very slowly in what he hoped was an upwards path. He had thought that keeping his feet pointing uphill would be easy but he was surprised to find that after only a few steps it became extremely hard. The difficulty was caused by the little dips and hollows which kept occurring in the general upward slope. When he came to these and felt his feet going down he would turn around and go up a few paces only to find that he was going down again.

After this happened a number of times a growing sense of panic began to swell up in his stomach and he had to fight hard to control it. Terrible memories of the walk through the Marshes of Blore came back to him. At least then he had been with the others, now he was utterly on his own.

He tried again, putting one foot carefully in front of the other on the stones and scrub on the ground. This time he walked for a while and was just beginning to gain confidence again when he started to go downhill. 'It'll only be a small dip,' he said to himself. 'In a few steps we'll start to go up again.' But the slope went down and down so, thinking that he had been walking up the side of a hollow at first, he turned and re-traced his steps back up only to find that when he went down the side he had originally walked up it went on for ever. Now he was really frightened and suddenly, as if for the first time, the enormous weight of the responsibility he was under came to him. Before, there had always been the others to share it with, but now it was his and his alone. He could not let them down, all those who had given their lives to protect him and and those who were now playing their part so that he might succeed. He stopped, his heart beating violently at the crushing thought of failure. Failure! Pictures of Bruin and Rufus and Sam flashed into his mind so clearly they could almost have been there with him and an overwhelming shadow of misery closed around his mind with a grip like an iron vice. The mist seemed to be growing thicker all the time and his body was so damp and cold that he began to shiver uncontrollably. He sat down on the ground and, burying his face in his hands, allowed despair to take him over.

He stayed like that for a long time until he felt something indefinable penetrate his numbness and make him look up. Then he saw, through the mist, a warm welcoming golden glow. His heart leapt with joy – Ashgaroth! It could only be he. He got up and began to make his way towards the faint flicker of light which seemed to beckon him on. As he walked he became mesmerized by it and could see nothing else and feel nothing else except the warmth of that light. It drew him on so that his feet felt as if they were walking on the mist and his body floated through the moist atmosphere. He was no longer tired or miserable or afraid; he was suddenly invincible. He could have gone on for ever, such was the power and strength that surged through his body even to his fingertips. He seemed to grow so that when he looked down, the ground below him was very far away. He strode effortlessly over valleys and gorges, deep ravines and raging rivers and high mountains; they were all his playthings far below. Dimly, through this haze of euphoria, he could sense that the source of his energy was centred around his middle, where the Belt of Ammdar was securely buckled, and had he looked he would have seen the hasp glowing with that same golden light that beckoned to him in the distance and that now shone also in his mind. On, on he walked until there was nothing else but the joy of this effortless travel in his brain. Everything was forgotten; the Urkku, the Eldron, Ashgaroth, Dréagg, the Elves; even Beth and Brock, Warrigal and Perryfoot seemed dim remote figures from a faint shadowy past that had nothing to do with him now.

Suddenly he began to fall; down, down through a long narrow tunnel in the ground he tumbled, and as he fell the sides closed in over him, folding across his head as if the walls were made of soft mud that collapsed in. Once or twice as he fell he tried to catch on to the sides but when he did so and began to haul himself up they gave way and he felt himself sliding backwards again into the dark gaping vortex beneath. Further and further he dropped and around him all he could see was an inky swirling blackness which flashed in front of his eyes, and his mind whirled around so that he was unable to think or feel anything except an icy chill of fear. As he fell it seemed to get hotter so that now sweat was dripping off him and his whole body burned and tingled with a prickly fire that came from just under the skin. He felt himself shrinking as well and vaguely remembered that whereas when he began to fall he could almost touch the sides, now he could not even see them, so vast did the shaft seem.

Down and down he fell into the abyss, as if he would go on for ever, when he felt a sudden thump. He sat for a moment dazed and shocked, unable to control his thoughts and struggling to find something ordinary to tell him where he was. He looked down at the ground and saw a tuft of heather growing from amongst some stones. Gingerly he reached out and touched it to make sure it was real and his fingers closed around the soft feathery purple flowers. Slowly his mind stopped spinning and he looked up. He was still on the mountain where he remembered being before although it seemed a long time since he was there. And still all around was that thick damp mist, but now just ahead of him was the mouth of a huge cave at the base of a sheer rock cliff the top of which was lost in the mist. He looked inside the cave and saw, deep within, the familiar golden glow which once again started to draw him towards it. He got up and half-walked, half-stumbled across the few paces to the entrance, and

293

then further in, deeper and deeper towards the light until it was just ahead of him. He stopped and stared at it, mesmerized by the little tongues of golden fire that leapt and danced against the cave wall. Then a voice came to him out of the light; a warm seductive voice, gentle and soothing, making him feel warm and safe. It called him by name and thanked him for all he had done; he had been chosen wisely it said, and he had justified all the faith and trust that had been placed in him. All manner of trials and hardships he had been through but now finally all that was over. This was the end; the journey was finished. Now he would always feel as he had felt when he strode like a giant over the mountains and the valleys; all-powerful and surging with strength. Look at the wall, the voice went on, and as Nab turned, the great high wall of the cave seemed to shiver with silver light until slowly it melted away and a picture took its place. So real was it that he felt a part of it; he could almost have walked in and touched what he saw. A great white coach was travelling slowly and steadily along a straight paved highway. Nab looked closely at the coach and saw that it was made of whalebone and ivory which shimmered in the silver light. On either side of the highway stood neatly clipped hedges and bushes and on the verge stood thousands of cheering Urkku, waving giant flags and shouting, 'Hail, hail to the leader. Hail to the ruler.' As far as the eye could see they stretched, and the coach moved through the middle of them with its two occupants staring straight ahead hardly noticing the crowds. Nab could only see them from the back and he watched as the coach carried them finally to a great palace with huge pillars and arches and a wide flight of steps leading up to a palisade on which courtiers and attendants waited in file. As the coach stopped and the couple alighted a band began to play and the music blended with the cheers to form a tumult of celebration. Up the steps they walked, and when they reached the top, two servants pulled open the mighty doors which opened into a massive hall. The floor was covered in rugs made from the skins of animals. Nab recognized some; sheepskin, deerskin, goat and badger but there were others he did not know from strange exotic animals who resided in the far north or west – reds and golds, blacks, oranges and whites, all mingled together to form a kaleidoscope of colour. Nab looked up to the walls. Arranged in rows on either side were the heads of numerous different animals, mounted on shields of wood. There hung the fox, the badger, the otter and deer and again a thousand others which he did not recognize, all with their mouths twisted in a half-snarl, half-sneer and their false eyes staring lifelessly at the scene below. Nab had still not seen the couple from the front but now he stared at their backs as they walked slowly over the rugs. They wore long cloaks of white fur which hung down to the floor and as they moved Nab could see their long leather boots trimmed with tufts of a different coloured fur. There was a familiar yet disturbing look about them as they made their way towards the two great thrones set on a raised dais at the end of the hall, and then, as they reached them and turned round, his heart stopped and his blood froze, for there, staring back at him from the picture was the exact double of himself. He looked fearfully at the other figure and saw that, as he had half-expected, it was Beth. On their heads they wore crowns of ivory and around their necks dangled necklaces of teeth and bone. Badger-hair bracelets adorned their wrists and two tortoiseshell combs held back the long flowing tresses of Beth's golden hair. An awful doubt now began to nag at Nab's befuddled mind. Was it really Ashgaroth who was showing him all this? He watched as the couple in the hall smiled at him and held up their arms as if beckoning. Then his double started to speak.

'Yes,' it said, but Nab did not recognize the voice. 'Don't look so in disbelief. I am you and you are me. All this could be yours, and more. You have seen the power of Dréagg and his glory. Follow him for this is what he offers you.'

The dreadful truth now began to penetrate. Dréagg was speaking to him; he was face to face with the Lord of Evil. Yet his brain was so numb that he was unable to move or even to think clearly. He stood rooted to the spot and, from a long way off, heard himself say,

'What do you want of me? What must I do to follow?'

His double smiled again and put his arm around Beth, who also looked pleased and relieved. Never had Nab seen her looking so beautiful with her golden hair falling down over the sparkling white fur.

'It is good,' the double said. 'You have chosen well for as Dréagg has shown you his glory so also has he given you a taste of his anger; an anger which had you rejected him would have followed you for ever.'

There was silence for a short spell; not a sound could be heard. Then a voice came once again from the golden glow in the corner of the cave.

'You have the three Faradawn,' it said, 'locked in the Belt of Ammdar. Only you can unlock the Belt. Come then, take off the Belt and give it to me.'

The voice was gentle and seductive and much as Nab struggled with himself he found his hands going, almost of their own accord or as if someone else was guiding them, to the buckle on the Belt. He grasped one side in each hand and pulled quickly. The Belt came off and hung from his right hand.

'Now come over to the corner and hand it to me.'

Nab started to walk mechanically across the floor of the cave, the Belt hanging limply from his grip. Deep inside himself a great clear voice was crying out 'Stop' but the force of Dréagg had so completely gripped his mind that he was powerless to resist. Then suddenly, as Nab was almost at the corner, something, some animal rushed into the cave and with an almighty leap fell upon the boy who stumbled and toppled over to the floor. Then Nab felt his face being licked and slowly as his mind began to clear he saw a wonderfully familiar sight.

'Sam,' he whispered to himself and then as the truth of the miracle made itself felt in his mind he shouted out joyously 'Oh, Sam' and flung his arms around the dog's neck. A dreadful shriek pierced the air and they both looked in the corner. Gone was the golden glow and gone was the picture on the cave wall. All that was left was a great black shadow, twisting and writhing its sinewy way through a narrow crevice in the rock. For an instant they saw it and then it was gone, but the horror of that fleeting image remained with them for ever. As it went it cried out in a voice so full of venom and hatred that even the mountain shook and the boy and the dog huddled together in fear. In it was the threat of revenge and terror and a return so dreadful that it was beyond understanding.

'Come on,' said Sam, 'we must get out of here quickly.'

Nab's legs felt shaky but he forced himself to stand. He picked up the Belt from where it had fallen on the floor and then they scrambled out of the cave which suddenly felt icy cold and damp and had begun to fill with foul yellow vapour that burned their throats and eyes. Nab could remember nothing about coming into the cave but Sam knew the way and he led the boy through narrow gaps where the walls came together and over heaps of fallen rock. The walls were running with water and mosses and lichens grew out of the cracks and ledges in the stone. Their eyes were now stinging terribly from the fumes and tears fell down their cheeks when finally, to their immense relief, the air became sweeter and they saw daylight. Faster they ran now and in his delight at being free Nab forgot about his bruised and battered legs and feet. Then they were out and into a golden autumn afternoon, running through the heather and gorse to get as far away from the cave as possible. As they ran they laughed and played with the joy of being together again and Nab kept looking at the fawn shape bounding along at his side, afraid it was all a dream and the dog would go away again as suddenly as he had come back. 'Sam's alive; Sam's alive,' he kept saying to himself, and every time he said it a new flood of pleasure swept through him washing his mind clean of all the black horrors he had been through.

Finally when they could run no more they flopped down on a thick clump of heather and lay there, out of breath and panting, looking up at the clear blue-grey sky and watching the little white puffs of cloud scudding across it. Then they talked. First Nab told Sam all that happened since they had seen him clubbed by the Urkku on Elgol and thrown into the boat. They had all thought he was dead, the boy said, and Sam replied that he had been unconscious for a long time. Then Nab told him about Jim and Ivy and the mountain elves and finally the plan for his escape which meant that he was now separated from the others and did not know where they were.

Sam then related how he had woken up in a shed and chewed his way out of it and then followed their trail, partly by intuition and partly by eavesdropping on Urkku conversations from which he had learnt not only their supposed whereabouts but also all about the plague and the state of the Urkku world. He had come across the burnt-out dwelling of the old couple back down the hills and guessed that they had given the animals shelter.

'Did you know that one of the leaders of the Urkku is your old master?' asked Nab and Sam replied that he had smelt his scent from the lowlands and that following it had helped him to find the trail of the animals up to Rengoll's Tor.

'The Lord of the Mountain Elves met me there and told me where you had gone. He was concerned that you were on your own and worried that Dréagg would try again to capture you.'

'I can't remember much of that,' said Nab, forcing his mind back. 'I remember getting lost in a thick mist that swept down from the top of the mountain, and I can remember following some kind of light and entering the cave. Then everything seemed to go hazy and blurred until I felt my face all wet when you were licking me. I must have been under some kind of spell which you broke when you found me and I recognized you. I don't know how the Belt of Ammdar came to be on the floor though.'

He paused and let his mind wander through many thoughts. Then he and Sam got up and started to make their way up the last stretch of mountainside to the top of the Peak of Ivett.

CHAPTER XXIII

It was early evening by the time they clambered up over the last little stony ridge and found themselves looking out across a small plateau dotted with clumps of cotton grass and tussocks of heather. The ground was black with peat and the air was heavy with the damp smells of autumn. Not a sound could be heard except the whistle of the wind through the grasses and they seemed so high that they felt more a part of the sky than the land. This was a different world, an ageless timeless world which the Urkku had never touched, and Nab stood rooted to the spot, awestruck by the power of the place and feeling its strength surge up through his body. He looked back and saw, stretching away as far as the eye could see, a great mosaic of colour as heather, gorse, trees and boulders fell away down the mountainside to merge eventually into a patchwork pattern of fields, woods, rivers and valleys, while the evening sun bathed everything in a misty golden haze.

He looked back to the plateau and saw, in the middle, a large pool of water, around which grew reeds and rushes. On one side of it there stood an ancient wizened oak tree whose twisted branches stretched out over the pool like the protective arms of an old, old man. Nab felt himself drawn to the pool. He walked over to it slowly and looked down into its black depths. He could not see the bottom and so black was it that the still water shone like a jewel. Then as he was standing on the side, he looked up into the sky and saw that the clouds were all coming together to form one huge billowy cathedral of white, tinged at the edges with pink and gold. Majestically it floated towards the peak and then stopped overhead. At the same time the wind suddenly got up, a warm caressing wind that blew the hair back from his face and bathed his eyes gently. He looked back at the pool and saw it shimmering with a strange light almost as if it were glowing like a fire and then he saw the oak tree give a great shudder and its branches moved up and out to stretch towards the sky. Every part of the tree, from the largest bough to the smallest twig, seemed to be moving. And now the Voice of Ashgaroth came to Nab on the wind.

'Remove the shawl,' it told him.

Nab had worn the beautiful multi-coloured shawl in which Brock had found him wrapped as a baby for so long that he had almost forgotten he had it. Next to his skin it lay as it always had. He took off all his outer garments until he reached the Belt of Ammdar and then, gripping the two clasps firmly, he unbuckled it and placed it on the earth. Now the shawl flapped loosely about his shoulders in the wind, its colours flashing in the sun. He took it off and laid it out on the ground. Seeing it again filled Nab with memories of Silver Wood and especially of Tara; Tara who had looked after him for so long and with whom he had had so many happy times in those early days, laughing and playing on long winter nights or on warm balmy summer evenings outside the sett.

'Now unlock the caskets on the Belt of Ammdar. Remove the Three Faradawn and scatter them over the shawl. First the Faradawn of the Woods, then the Faradawn of the Sea and finally the Faradawn of the Mountains.'

Nab did as he was asked and as the contents of the caskets fell over the shawl the wind seemed to hold them firmly down so that none blew away.

Then the Voice of Ashgaroth spoke again, high, clear and pure in the wind.

'Now is the end. And we are only just in time, for the world of the Urkku is coming to its conclusion. They are destroying themselves. Yet as I pledged, the animals and the Eldron will be saved. You have achieved what I asked of you; you and the chosen ones from Silver Wood, and I am well pleased. Take the caskets from the Belt and fill them with water from the pool. Then sprinkle the water over the shawl and the way will be clear.'

The three metal caskets unclipped easily. Nab bent down and scooped each one in the pool till it was full and then carefully carried them back to where the shawl lay flat on the dark peaty earth. Sam sat patiently watching a few paces away at the edge of the plateau. Nab could feel his heart thumping under his chest in excitement and apprehension but there was no fear, simply a sense of satisfaction. Then very gently, his hand shaking a little, he lifted the first casket and began to sprinkle the brackish water over the brilliant colours of the shawl. Nothing happened. He picked up the second casket and sprinkled the water from that over it but again nothing happened. Now it was the last of the caskets. The water fell evenly in little droplets and then, when the last drop had fallen the shawl burst into brilliant life and gave forth a glow so bright that Nab and Sam turned away and covered their eyes to shield them from the light. In a second it had died away and cautiously Nab looked back. All the colours and patterns had come together to form a picture of the world. On it they could see all the mountains and the woods and the seas, and over all the picture were lines which shone with a pure white light; a network of lines each leading to a point on the map. Nab looked at the picture of his own country and recognized the points as the Scyttels and the lines as the Roosdyche along which they had journeyed. Unknown to Nab, at the same moment that he was staring at the picture on the summits of the Peak of Ivett, so did the lines appear over all the lands and seas of the earth yet they could be seen only by the animals and by the Eldron and they wondered at them and felt themselves drawn along the lines so that throughout the world all the animals and the Eldron began to journey together along the ancient pathways and tracks of the Roosdyche.

It was then that the world was shaken by the first blast. Beneath his feet Nab felt the mountain shudder violently and he fell over. Before he could get up another, louder, blast filled the sky and he felt himself thrown backwards by a searing blast of heat which scorched his flesh and singed his hair. Sam crawled across to him whimpering and terrified and they raised their eyes and looked out on a gigantic mushroom which billowed and grew up from the earth. Nab watched, transfixed by its awesome beauty as the brilliance of its colours burned themselves into his brain and the evening grew light again. Higher and higher it rose, growing all the time until the sun was blotted out and the sky was merely a frame around its edges. All the time Nab watched he could feel the earth quivering and shaking under him and then, out of the corner of his eye, he saw the oak tree moving its branches gracefully over the pool and, tearing his eyes away from the hypnotic beauty of the great cloud, he saw the pool suddenly drain of water so that there was simply a gaping hole in the earth where it had been. But then he saw that there was a roughly hewn flight of steps down the side of the hole; steps which appeared to lead down for ever for he could see no end to them.

Then screams and cries rose in a gigantic wail all over the world as explosion after explosion rent the air and the sky became filled with clouds of flashing colour. Terrible was the sound of pain as waves of heat rolled out over the land and the buildings of the Urkku collapsed like thistledown in the wind. And as the world destroyed itself the animals and the Eldron ran frantically along the silver paths and many were lost as they were caught in the blasts. Those that came to the end of their paths found the earth opened up for them and they escaped down these tunnels and caves, thankful for their deliverance out of the holocaust of horror which had come upon them. Men, women and children ran blindly down these unknown ways, without thinking or doubting, as the animals raced alongside them, badgers, foxes, lions and tigers, bear and bison, elephant and elk, every type of animal that lived on the face of the land. Under the seas, great caverns opened and through them swam the mighty whale and the gentle seal, the majestic shark and the playful dolphin and all the other fishes and mammals of the ocean.

By now Nab had begun to get very worried about Beth and the others. Suddenly a large mountain hare appeared over the edge of the plateau and scampered towards the steps. He stopped abruptly when he saw Nab and Sam and stared at them hard for a few seconds with surprise and pleasure for he knew who they were.

'Aren't you coming down into the tunnel?' he said. 'There cannot be much time left for this world. The heat was terrible further down the mountain. Look!' He pointed to where a big patch of his fur had been scorched leaving the skin showing through.

Nab's heart leapt into his mouth and a terrible fear pounded in his brain so that his head felt as if it was being beaten against a rock. 'They should be here,' he said to himself.

'Have you seen the others?' he asked. 'The girl, the hare, the badger and the owl.'

'I saw them a while back,' the hare replied, 'before the explosions started. Being chased, they were, by a great pack of goblins and Urkku. They weren't far behind and the girl looked tired. I wouldn't wait if I were you. If they've escaped, they'll come anyway. If not, well, there's no point in sacrificing yourself, is there?'

Nab said nothing.

'Come on,' said the hare gently. 'It's only sense, isn't it?'

The boy turned to him, and his dark eyes, which had seen so much, were brimming with tears.

'I am not leaving here until they come,' he said. 'You go, Sam, but I must stay.'

The dog turned to him with a reproachful look.

'Very well, then. Since you're both determined to stay, I must go on my own. I wish you the best of luck. Goodbye.' And the hare started to hop down the steps and was soon lost from sight in the gaping black hole.

It was then that a further explosion shook the air, this time nearer the mountain. When the initial deafening blast had died away, Nab lifted his head from where he had buried it in his arms and shouted to Sam above the noise.

'I'm going to look for them. You stay here,' and he got up from the damp ground.

'I'm not leaving you again,' Sam yelled back. 'I'll come with you.'

Cautiously they walked over to the edge and looked over. A great blast of heat met them and they gasped for breath. Nab smelt his hair burning and covered his face with his hands. Sam put his head down and they took a few steps down the side of the mountain. Then, above the din, they heard a shout. They stopped and looked at each other for reassurance that it had not been a figment of their imagination. Then it came again, louder this time and seemingly from behind them. Warily they turned around and looked back up the mountain. Over the edge of the plateau they saw Beth waving down to them with Warrigal perched on her shoulder and Brock and Perryfoot on either side. They were as surprised and overjoyed to see Sam as he and Nab were relieved to see them. The boy and the dog ran back up to the top where the six of them, all together again, greeted each other with joy and tears of thankfulness.

'We were so worried. We were just coming down to look for you,' Nab said when he was able to speak again without laughing for joy.

'We nearly got caught,' said Beth. 'They were almost on us when the explosions started and then they panicked and most of them ran off. Then we seemed to be drawn towards a track that shone with a bright silver light which I don't think they were able to see and the few that were left seemed to fall back so that we were on our own.'

They all walked slowly over to the dark hole where the pool had been and Sam told them how he had escaped from the Urkku. Then they sat under the old oak tree and Nab related all that had happened since they had parted on Rengoll's Tor. They listened intently; Warrigal perched on one of the great roots that were exposed above the peat, his deep round eyes fixed unblinkingly on Nab. He had heard of the legend of the Map of Lines from Wythen on one of the long talks they used to have together sitting on summer evenings up in the Great Beech in Silver Wood, but the legend had been almost lost in the mists of time and even that wise old owl had known very little about it. How fascinated he would have been to have learnt about the part it was to play in their lives. Warrigal wondered whether or not the old owl had managed to escape the final destruction of the wood and, if he had, whether he had followed one of the lines to a tunnel such as they were sitting beside. Perhaps even now he was about to escape down one of the Scyttels and was thinking about them and of the ending of the story that he, Warrigal, had brought to him that first night when Brock had told him of his strange little discovery.

Perryfoot sat by Nab's side, his ears flat along his back, contented and happy that all their struggles seemed to be at an end. Where they were going none of them knew but as long as they were together then he would have a home, and what a mighty collection of stories he had built up during their travels. Beth sat at his side stroking his back gently. He thought of the first time he had seen her down by the stream on that wonderful spring afternoon and how he had danced and played in front of her to catch her attention while Nab crawled close to see her more clearly.

Beth was also thinking about that afternoon, so long ago. She wondered whether or not it had been fate that they had met or whether Ashgaroth had somehow arranged it. How strangely her life had turned out! She thought of her parents and her brothers. As Eldron she knew they would have seen the lines and somehow she had faith that they had escaped down one of the Scyttels. She remembered the night when she had seen Nab's face through the window on Christmas Eve and the turmoil in her mind when she had gone with him. How little she knew then of the world she was entering, the world of animals and elves and goblins, and little did she guess what horrors and wonders she would see. Now, perhaps, they had arrived at the end of their journey and all the things she had yearned for in her life with Nab would be possible.

Sam sat at her feet thinking back to his old life with the Urkku and to the early Council Meetings when he used to sneak out of the house to run across the fields and tell the wood of the Urkku plans. He remembered the cold wet evening when he had been shocked out of his peaceful doze by the fire to see Nab standing, wild and frightened, by the foot of the stairs and how he had raced to the wood to organize the escape.

Nab had finished his tale now and they sat without speaking while the earth juddered and shook beneath them. He felt a strange sense of calm and tranquillity as he looked around at the others, all of them lost in their private thoughts. He turned to Brock and saw that the badger, who was sitting at his side, was looking at him. Their memories were the same for their lives had been so intertwined, since that faraway snowy night when Brock had watched the strange couple come walking over the frozen fields carrying their little bundle, that they had shared everything together. They thought of Rufus who had been so suspicious of Nab at first but who had been killed trying to protect him, and of the others, Sterndale, Pictor,

Thirkelow, all of them dead. They thought of Zinndy and Sinkka, Brock's cubs who had left the sett and whom he had never seen again, and they thought of Bruin. Brock could still see the old badger charging at the Urkku with all the strength his tired body could muster and then, as he raced to escape and catch the others up, the way he had been flung in the air by the shot which took his life. And they remembered Tara. How they both wished she could have been here with them now. They thought of her without the sharp pangs of pain that they had felt at first but rather with a numb sense of loss as if a part of them was missing. They remembered all her little ways clearly and could see her vividly in their imagination. Their minds wandered through all the happenings of the past like a series of little pictures appearing in front of their eyes. Nab buried his face in the thick fur around Brock's neck the way he used to and put his arms around the badger's shoulders. Then suddenly a gigantic explosion sounded in his ears and looking up he saw the evening sky disappear behind an enormous black mushroom cloud and the world went dark.

'Come on, old friend,' he said. 'I think it's time we went,' and he stood up. Then he took Beth's hand and with Warrigal, Perryfoot, Sam and Brock following, he walked slowly over to the gaping hole in the earth and, without a backward glance, began to lead them down the rough stone steps into the dark void beneath.

AUTHOR'S NOTE

This book is the result of an encounter I had some years ago with a strange old man whilst walking in the deep forests near my home. At the time I believed the meeting to be purely accidental but now I am not sure and it may well have been intentional on his part. Why he chose me to tell the story to I do not know. Perhaps it was because I spent many hours walking through the forests and moorland and he had grown accustomed to my face and perhaps also because he could detect my strong sympathies with the animal kingdom and the natural world.

Whatever the reason, the fact remains that, after our first meeting, we met on a number of occasions and he related to me each time a part of the story you have just read. We always met by chance, at least on my part, and there seemed to be no particular area he favoured for our meetings so that we met sometimes in the forest and at other times by a mountain river or somewhere on the moors. Also our meetings were sporadic; sometimes we would meet twice in a week and then two or three months might go by before I would see, quite unexpectedly, his familiar shambling figure coming towards me and we would select a suitably comfortable spot for our conversation. I call it a 'conversation' but in reality it was more a one-sided monologue with myself doing little more than listen and interpose the odd question to clarify some matter or other over which I was not clear. However, all my inquiries as to his family, background and

307

home were pushed to one side and remained unanswered; he literally seemed to have 'come from nowhere'.

After each conversation I returned home and recorded, as faithfully as I could, every detail of what he had told me. I determined early on that I would attempt to put my notes together in the form of a book and to this end it has been necessary to make certain changes in the way the story was told to me. These relate however only to style and format and I trust that I have remained true to the spirit in which it was related. Any errors there may be are of course entirely mine.

From the first I challenged the truth of his story but he simply smiled and told me that whether I believed his tale or not was of no consequence though he would be grateful if I would at least listen. This I did and as the story progressed I grew more and more fascinated and began to look forward to our meetings so that I could hear the next part of the tale. I also became less convinced that it was untrue until towards the end I became almost certain that it was, at the very least, based on fact. This, of course, must be left to the reader to decide for himself; it is not my intention to attempt to prove either way.

Our meetings lasted approximately two years; the first one taking place on a cold January day when I was making my way, in the late afternoon, up a steep path through the forest, and the last two years later in December when the snow was thick on the ground and I was sitting on the moors by a little brook that raced its way along through high banks of snow-covered heather. Since that day when he finished his story, I have not seen him, although I have spent as much, if not more time walking through my old haunts as before. Sometimes, however, I have felt aware of a 'presence' as if he was watching me and have been grateful for that knowledge. I am certain that someday I shall meet him again.

When he came to the end of the tale there were a number of very important questions which I wanted to ask him. Firstly I was anxious to learn what had happened to the animals and the Eldron after they had entered the tunnels and caves where the Scyttel had opened up for them.

'They had not gone down many steps,' he said, 'when they seemed

308

to be walking in space as if they were floating through the darkness. Then, without realizing it, they drifted off into a deep, dreamless sleep and they slept for many, many moons in the arms of Ashgaroth. They did not grow old for Ashgaroth had frozen the passage of time for them and when, eventually, they awoke they found the sun streaming down upon them where they lay in their resting places in the Scyttel. When they walked out on to the face of the land it was to a new world; a world free of the Urkku, a world of infinite colour and magic.'

I remained intensely curious as to the fate of Nab and Beth and the other animals and still not wholly satisfied by his explanation of this 'new world' to which they had gone. 'Were they happy there?' I wanted to know. 'Was it what they had dreamt of and suffered for so much?'

The icy wind blew little flurries of snow through the air which settled on our hair. The sun shone pale and watery in the steel grey winter sky. He looked up at me and smiled and as I gazed deep into his eyes I suddenly realized with a huge shock of amazement that the old man was Nab. My head spun for a second or two and I was unable to think straight but when I collected my wits again a further revelation came to me. If this old man was Nab then the world to which they had come was the same as that from which they had escaped – our world. A great wave of disappointment spread through me.

'Then it was all for nothing,' I blurted out. 'Ashgaroth failed you.'

Nab looked down at the ground and was silent for a long time. When he spoke again there was sadness in his voice but there was also hope.

'The Urkku,' he said, 'were created out of hatred, for revenge. They had no choice in the way they acted. But they are no more and because of what we did there is now a world peopled only by the Eldron. They have a choice; that is what separated them from the Urkku. The story then is not yet ended, for whether or not we have failed is for you and yours to decide. You are all the children of the Eldron.'

'What of Beth and Brock, Warrigal, Perryfoot and Sam?' I asked him. 'And what of the elves; did they perish with the old world?'

'When the old world destroyed itself,' he said, 'the elves remained. They cured the wounds and healed the scars left by the Urkku and gradually they, with the help of Ashgaroth, brought the world back to its natural state. All this time we slept and it was only when the task had been completed that Ashgaroth released us from sleep. The elves are always here. As for the rest of us, Ashgaroth granted us the immortality of the elves. We live together still in the forests and the hills. They have seen you and sometimes you may have seen them though they, like all the other animals, have become wary now even of the Eldron for many of them have denied their true nature and grown similar in their ways to the old Urkku.' He paused and then as the sun began to sink in the evening sky he got up. 'I must go now,' he said. 'Beth will be waiting for me,' and he walked off over the snow towards the edge of the trees. I sat, still shaken by all that he had told me, and watched him go. He was about to enter the darkness of the forest when I thought I saw, coming out to meet him, a little group of animals. With my heart thumping wildly in my chest I stared hard through the gloom of the evening and was almost certain that I could make out the shapes of a badger, a dog, a hare and, flying low over their heads, a large brown owl. Then just behind them another figure; the figure of an old lady with her arms outstretched to greet him. I watched them for a second or two and they seemed in turn to be looking at me. Then suddenly they were gone, swallowed up by the forest.